JUST BREAKING THE RULES

HOCKEY EVER AFTER

LAUREN BLAKELY

COPYRIGHT

exclusive rights under copyright, any use of this publication to "train" generative artificial intelligence (AI) technologies to generate text is expressly prohibited. The author reserves all rights to license uses of this work for generative AI training and development of machine learning language models.

ABOUT THE BOOK

Hockey superstar Corbin Knight is a recipe for trouble... and I'm ready to take a bite.

The sexy single dad is not only a world-class hockey player, but my brother's best friend. Strictly off-limits, and always has been.

But when I inherit an old firehouse to transform into my dream bakery? The bossy, protective athlete also becomes my hero, buying in when the financing falls through.

I have to keep reminding myself – no more flirting with my new business partner... no matter how tempting he looks helping me paint.

It's a good rule to remember when he starts making surprise shirtless appearances after each win.

Insists I wear his jersey to games.

Stands up for me when a celebrity chef is rude.

Soon, his heated glances make me feel like I'm the answer to his dreams.

Falling for the hockey player I work with could cost us everything: the bakery, his friendship with my brother, and my family who already thinks I'm a hot mess.

But when Corbin shows up after a rough game one night and tells me he can't stop thinking about me and hasn't been able to for years?

I'm ready to break all the rules.

This is Corbin and Mabel's romance. Tropes include: Brother's best friend, single dad, workplace romance, hockey, the one who got away, love letters

DID YOU KNOW?

To be the first to find out when all of my upcoming books go live click here!

PRO TIP: Add lauren@laurenblakely.com to your contacts before signing up to make sure the emails go to your inbox!

Did you know this book is also available in audio and paperback on all major retailers? Go to my website for links!

For content warnings for this title, go to my site.

JUST BREAKING THE RULES

BY LAUREN BLAKELY

A Hockey Ever After Romance

1

———

THE LLAMA-KISSING EX

MABEL

What's more nerve-racking than decorating a delicate heart-shaped cake in front of a few hundred strangers and the world's most scathing food judge, who's scrutinizing every swoop of your frosting?

Doing it thirty feet from the big-screen TV where a promo plays of your douchey ex hitting on a fellow reality-show contestant.

I'm not saying the universe has it out for me. But I'm not *not* saying that either.

I force myself to stop sneaking peeks at the expo's nearest high-def monitor. I've got exactly five minutes to finish my "Hearts and Flutter" cake. The gigantic kitchen timer ticks ominously on the long table, where the final five contestants vie for the cake-decorating prize at Webflix's Love Is in the Air romance fair. The local expo, right next to the Ferry Building, is to promote their fall slate of new rom-coms and—thanks, universe!—their hit reality dating show starring none other than my annoying ex.

As I position the last baby-pink fondant heart in the cascade of hearts spiraling around the vanilla cake, I'm hoping

—no, make that *begging* the universe—that the publicity of a win here today will help me finally nab the financing I need to open a bakery in San Francisco. The cash prize would help too.

Not a pop-up shop. Not a ghost kitchen. But a real, honest-to-goodness storefront after years of trying and failing.

To take the top prize, I need to impress guest judge Ronnie Legend—the intimidating British celebrity chef whose own baking show can make or break bakers. He's been stalking my station the whole time, making me sweat.

All that's left to do is mount a half dozen dainty rice-paper butterflies onto white chocolate sticks, then insert them on top of the cake. The heart-shaped wings are so light they'll flutter in the breeze for the ultimate *aww* effect.

With quick, efficient moves, I line up the first butterfly on the edge of the pretty pink cake. Ronnie prowls in front of me, his bald head shining like a cue ball as he emcees the action on the center stage of the expo's big tent. He speaks into the mic as if he's narrating a nature documentary: "And now here we have a local pop-up baker attempting the very risky rice-paper butterflies. They take several hours to make at home. One single misstep in front of the crowd could spell disaster for her."

Gee, thanks. I'm totally not picturing all my painstakingly prepared butterflies wilting in the San Francisco heat now.

I offer the crowd a small smile, and thankfully, Ronnie moves down the table to unnerve the rest of the bakers. I keep my head down and try to concentrate.

The huge screens in the aisles run promos of Webflix romance-themed shows. *Romance Beach,* among others. The sound is turned down, thank god. My ex—or Dax Strong, as he calls himself on TV—dumped me for that show. I don't want to even accidentally catch a word of it.

Out of the corner of my eye, I spot a man in a dark suit at the edge of the crowd. Big shoulders, broad chest, messy brown hair—something familiar about him catches my attention. Before I can place him, Ronnie's back, telling the enrapt audience, "This is the do-or-die moment for the butterfly baker. Hold your breath with her."

A hush falls over the tent, leaving the conversation on the closest monitor the *only* sound, just as a woman asks Dax why his last relationship ended.

Ignore them, Mabel. Just ignore them.

I do my best as the man I used to live with lounges beachside in a cabana, a garish blue drink in his hand, holding a very intense conversation with the woman on-screen. "The thing about my ex is she's kind of a hot mess," he confides.

What the hell? I whip my gaze to the screen as he blathers on *about me.* "She's been chasing her own tail for years now, and we're just not in the same league. It's sad, but the breakup was a long time coming. I mean, this is a girl who dreams of making cakes with two llamas kissing on them but doesn't do a damn thing to make it happen!"

Lies! I don't put llamas on my cakes. I put llamas on my logo.

Seething, I reach for the final butterfly oh-so casually—too casually for someone who's just been cruelly mocked on TV.

But the universe unleashes Ronnie on me. The host's steely blue gaze locks onto the illustrated llamas on my apron, twined together in a heart-shaped hug, and he pounces. "It's you! The kissing llama ex!"

"Nah," I say breezily. "You must have me confused with someone else." I dismiss the comment with a careless wave.

Too careless. The last butterfly slips in my fingers, knocked loose from the chocolate stick, and it flutters away into the October breeze.

Frantic, I lunge for the breakaway butterfly. Stretching

across my station, I balance on one sneakered foot. I grasp for the wing and I wobble—once, twice, three times—and *kersplat*. I plant my arm in the middle of all those pink hearts.

"Oof." My elbow sinks through cake, filling and fondant, all the way to the ceramic cake stand.

The audience gasps. Ronnie clucks his tongue. Phones lift. In seconds, everyone's recording me.

Well, if this frosting fiasco doesn't tie into the hot mess narrative Dax just wove about me, I don't know what does. I'm up to my elbow in demolished dessert, and I kiss the prize money and publicity goodbye. I catalogue the crowd's wide eyes and unhinged jaws.

I could slink off, saying nothing, and disappear down the shame spiral staircase.

Or, I could try to make this cake still rise.

Yanking my elbow from the once-beautiful creation, I slap on a smile. "Surprise! It's the birth of a new cake era. May I present the I Meant to Do That smashed heart cake." I commit to the improvisation one hundred and ten percent. I spread my arms, *ta-da* style, toward the pile of crumbs and frosting. "Smash cakes aren't just for a baby's first birthday. Nope, adults can have fun with their cake, too, and it still tastes delicious!"

I lick a big dollop off my finger to make my point.

There's nervous laughter and curious looks. And one what-the-hell-are-you-up-to host shooting a dagger stare at me. Then his gaze drops to his shoes, where a chunk of pink frosting has dripped off my arm and onto his motorcycle boots, which scream *cool chef*. He simmers a moment longer, then sighs heavily before he turns to the crowd. "Smash cakes. What a fascinating idea. A sobering reminder that anything can go wrong in the kitchen. Like this"—he points to the ruined cake—"*disaster*."

His grin carries sympathy but a clear message: *I'll handle the audience, thank you very much.*

He lowers the mic and shoos me away from the station. "I'll see if my assistant can grab you a towel," he whispers, guiding me from the dais and toward the edge of the noisy tent. "You can clean up before the photo shoot with the winner and the runners-up then be on your way."

I'm about to utter a quiet and embarrassed *thanks* when someone cuts in.

"A towel? Is that the best you can do?" The voice is rough, commanding, stern.

Ronnie whips his gaze to the stranger. Who's...not a stranger at all.

That vaguely familiar face earlier? All becomes clear when I get a proper look at the man who'd been at the edge of the crowd. Clean-shaven, chiseled jaw? Check. Clever, gold-flecked green eyes? Check. Soft lips and a take-charge vibe that makes you want to listen to him? Checkmate.

Because of course Corbin Knight, the guy I crushed so hard on when I met him seven years ago, would show up today when I'm a mess and a half.

And the unfair universe makes my brother's best friend hotter and more together every time I see him.

Every time I'm *not*.

Corbin stands in front of me in charcoal gray slacks that hug his thighs, a crisp white shirt that shows off his strong chest, and a matching jacket slung over his arm. He looks like a guy who doesn't ever break a sweat, though, of course, he does. He plays a pro sport for a living.

Judging from the suit, it must be a game day. But how did he happen to pop in here just now?

Ronnie gives him a tight nod, spins around and points to the tiniest trailer I've ever seen. It's maybe ten feet outside of the tent. "That's mine. You can freshen up in there. I don't want to see any cake on you in the photo. Is that clear?"

"Crystal," I say.

"I'll have her back for the photo shoot," Corbin confirms.

"In fifteen minutes. Don't be late."

"I never am." Corbin's voice brooks no argument. He's so capable that it's a little tingly. Ronnie returns to the contest while my unexpected knight in shining tailored suit pins his gaze on me and says, "Let me help you."

As we walk, the words echo. *Let me help you.*

He said that seven years ago when I met him at the scene of another public disaster. Maybe that's what I should name the future bakery that I'll clearly never get financing for.

Dessert Disaster.

2

———

IT'S A THING

CORBIN

Sometimes you just need to pivot. Like when you're skating backwards, but you need to open up to receive a shot.

Or, say, when you're at a Webflix event with your buddies before a game, and one minute you're checking out cookies, and the next, you spot your best friend's little sister landing in the middle of the cake she'd been making.

Sure, Mabel was ad-libbing like a pro, but a good teammate has your back. That was all I'd wanted to do back there.

Now, I shut the door to the closet-sized trailer and place the towel Ronnie's assistant gave Mabel on the few square inches of counter. There's a tiny couch, a dollhouse-sized table, and a bathroom smaller than one on an airplane. The sink there is too small to be useful, but there's a bigger one between a microwave and a coffee machine. That'll do to get her ready for the pic.

Tossing my suit jacket on the couch, I turn to Mabel and finally ask, "Smash cake, huh?"

"It's a thing," Mabel says with a little jut of her pretty chin.

"That save you attempted was worthy of a top goalie."

"Thanks," she says dryly. "But I'm pretty sure I'll need a

new career after that." Her shoulders drop, and she shudders out a heavy breath, slumping against the trailer door and groaning like a wounded creature. "What have I done? I'll never get my—" Mabel's voice catches, and she doesn't finish the thought.

"Never get what?"

She blows out a breath, then shakes her head. "It's nothing. I'm fine. It's one contest."

She waves toward her hair, the swoopy tendrils tumbling out of her clip. "I'll move on if I can ever get this frosting out of my hair, that is."

Mabel gazes at her arm, coated in frosting, which is... hmm. Sort of gray, maybe white? "Goodbye, cake," she says to the remains of her creation. "You would have served me well."

Ah, hell. I can't let her wallow.

I swipe a finger through the sugary mess coating her arm. "You're right. It did go out in a blaze of glory." I bring the frosting to my lips for a taste. "It's fantastic."

"Thanks," she says. "The universe giveth and taketh away. Good baker, but a terrible competitor."

She squeezes her eyes shut for a few seconds, dragging her hand through her hair, and oh shit...Before I can stop her, the damage is done. She's combed frosting all over her pretty locks.

I wince but then school my expression when she opens her eyes.

She tosses the towel over her shoulder and scrubs her arms over the sink. Once they're clean, she dries them off, then wipes most of the frosting from her apron too. She peers around, like she's looking for a mirror before she asks, "I think there was some in my hair?"

I stifle a laugh. "*Some* being the operative word."

"Seriously?"

I point at her hair. "Remember when you got so annoyed with yourself you shoved your hands in your hair, oh, about three minutes ago?"

She lets out a low moan, like a tire leaking air. "How bad is it?"

I should resist touching her again, but my hands seem to have a mind of their own around her today. Maybe I have a thing for cute women in aprons with llamas kissing on them.

Maybe you have a thing for the woman you wanted to ask out the day you met her.

Setting a palm on her shoulder, I spin her around and... wow...it's a fucking nest of frosting and cake. "On a scale of one to desperately-in-need-of-a-wash, I'd say it's one hundred."

She beelines for the locker-sized bathroom and squeezes in to deal with the problem. She attempts to wipe off bits of frosting from her hair with her towel, but her elbows bump against the wall. The bathroom's so small she can't quite get the right angle.

She turns back to me with a look of surrender. "Fine. Go ahead. Be nice if you insist. *Help.*"

I give her an *I told you so* look as she emerges. "I insist," I say.

When she's standing in front of me a second later, I pace around her, reviewing the damage. Once I've done a full loop, she meets my eyes and says: "Level with me. Is it time for a buzz cut?"

"Hmm," I say as I take the towel from her. "Have you got clippers in that apron pocket?"

Her brown eyes pop. "It's that bad?"

I don't mince words. "Mabel, you *are* the smash cake. It's everywhere." But I'm fast on my feet and quick with a solution. Years of taking care of my mom, of raising my little girl, and of executing plays on the ice mean I don't fuck around when it comes to taking care of people or problems. "I have an idea."

She holds up her hands, but she's not defeated. Her words crackle with a spark that hasn't been snuffed out from a rough day. "Let's see what you've got."

"Game on," I say and reach for the clip in her hair, letting her waves fall in a dark mess, a contrast to her fair complexion. I wet the end of the towel under the faucet and dab the frosting off the strands near her face.

As I touch her hair, she shudders in a breath, then goes quiet, and I work steadily.

I wet the towel once more, then clean the sugar and cake bits from the back of her hair. I check the time. She's due out in eight minutes for the picture. "Done."

"Is it all gone?"

"Yes. But your hair's damp now."

"Does it really matter? No one's going to be looking at the llama-kissing ex," she says with a snort.

I spin her around, shaking my head. "You're wrong. They will."

Her look says she doesn't buy what I'm selling. "To stare at the five-car pileup on the side of the road?"

The question hangs in the air, taking up the very small space between us.

The mere inches between us.

It's the first time I've been *this* close to Mabel. I've seen her a few times over the years. At hockey games. At barbecues. In the diner, when she stops by Cozy Valley to see her family.

With her shiny hair, her expressive eyes, and her bow-shaped lips, Mabel Llewelyn's always been pretty. I've thought so ever since the day I met her at a fundraising event for the local fire department in Cozy Valley—her hometown, and now mine too.

But I knew it in an empirical sense.

Now I take a beat to drink her in, and the answers to her question are clear and bright.

Why? Because freckles dance across the bridge of your cute nose. Because your lips are so lush. Because your eyes shine with fire and humor. And because you're so fucking brave.

"Because...you're you," I say at last.

There. That's safe enough. Just because I'm thinking things about her for the first time—or, really, the first time since I learned who she was—doesn't mean I'm going to say them out loud. Let alone act on them. Our lives are too... connected. It'd be messy, and I hate messes.

But helping her right now? That's easy, so I keep going. "Which means you're going to have the best French braid ever. Now, turn around."

"Yes, sir." Mabel spins around once more. I take the clip and run the teeth of it through her hair, combing out the wet strands, then separating them into three chunks.

Checking the time on my watch, I put the clip on the counter, then grasp the right chunk in my hand. Her breath hitches.

I weave that handful over the middle section, then loop in the left chunk. I gather more locks on the right, add it to that strand, and weave it into the braid. I do the same on the left side, then slowly, steadily work my way down her hair, crafting a tight French braid.

As I go, I sneak a whiff of her sugary scent. No surprise—Mabel smells like the treats she makes. It's the best kind of smell, like candy and butter, with a hint of vanilla.

When I reach the nape of her neck, my thumb slides

across her pale, creamy skin. I don't want to stop touching her, and this is a problem.

A problem I like far too much. My chest heats as I steal another touch, grazing her neck once more.

She stifles a gasp, and I pause, absorbing the realization that she likes the way I'm touching her hair, maybe even the way I have to pull on it to braid it. When I near the end, she goes still, as if she's holding her breath. I fight the urge to tug on the end of her braid. But I focus on finishing, neatly looping one strand over the other until I'm down to the middle of her back with little hair left.

I grab the clip once more and use it to secure the end of the braid. "Done. And with four minutes to spare."

She turns around, and there's something in her brown eyes that wasn't there before—curiosity with a touch of heat.

"Thank you, Corbin." She lets out a laugh, then adds, "I should bake you a cake to show my appreciation."

"That's not necessary. I'm just glad I was here."

"You don't like cake?" From her tone, indifference to cake would be blasphemy.

"I ate some off your arm a few minutes ago."

"But did you like it?"

I'd have thought that was proof. "Of course I like cake."

"Why of course?"

"Because I like things that taste..." I pause, trying not to look at her mouth, but failing, "really fucking good."

Maybe that came out a bit naughtier than it sounded in my head. Maybe I'm flirting with my best friend's little sister.

"Like what?" she counters.

This woman doesn't back down. And there are so many reasons I shouldn't answer that question. Her brother's the acting general manager for my hockey team, filling the role after the longtime GM retired last season. As if that's not enough, with the season barely underway, a rough end to last year's playoff hopes, and my daughter extremely busy with middle school in the city, my life is complicated enough.

But there's something about the space in this trailer, or the lack thereof. There's something about the flirty way Mabel asked, *Like what?* And there's definitely something about the way she's waiting for my answer like she *needs* it.

My gaze drops to a tiny bit of frosting still left on her forearm, then returns to her eyes. "Things like frosting."

3

I'VE BEEN RADICALIZED
MABEL

I really shouldn't do this. But I probably shouldn't have done that whole smash-cake routine either. Let's just call it the day for impetuous decisions, since I swipe off the cherry-pink frosting, step closer, then flick it at Corbin's cheek, where it lands in a glop on his fair skin, right below his strong cheekbone.

He blinks, clearly taken aback.

I laugh, but not for long.

He darts out a hand, grabs my wrist and holds it tight. "Did you just fling frosting at me?"

It's that stern, bossy tone he used with Ronnie, and I shiver. I like the tone as much as I like the possessive way he grips my wrist.

I bob a shoulder and answer, "You said you liked cake."

"Did you think that meant on my face?"

"Better than on your pretty suit. I know how important the pre-game photos are."

"So I should be glad you didn't throw cake on my shirt?"

"I mean, it's a good test of your devotion to it."

He stares sharply at me. "Are you testing me, Mabel?"

I stand my ground. "Yes."

With a look that says, *You're on*, he lifts his free hand, swipes the sugary goodness from his cheek, then licks some off slowly.

Oh.

Oh my.

I believe I've just been radicalized by the unexpected hotness of a man eating something sweet. Why has it taken me so long to witness this thirst trap? But damn, the way his tongue flicks past his lips, the way he catches the last bit of frosting with the tip, the way he doesn't break my gaze...His green eyes are locked on me the whole time as he licks. My chest feels fizzy. My heart is beating so fast.

He lets out a low, satisfied murmur as he finishes. "Believe me now?"

I swallow down my hormones, then nod toward the smidgeon left on his finger. "I would believe you, but I don't think you got it all."

He tsks. "You're right. I didn't." In slow-motion, he brings the last bit of frosting to his lips, but with a quickness I don't see coming, he smears it on my cheek instead.

I gasp. "I was already covered in cake!"

"I'm so sorry," he says dryly.

"You don't sound it."

"Let me show you, then."

"You'd better," I say.

Corbin steps closer. When he's inches away, he whispers a very unapologetic, "Sorry."

It's soft and sounds like a promise, then it turns into...a kiss on my cheek.

"Oh," I say. Or maybe I squeak it as he kisses the frosting off my face, gently, slowly, like he's savoring the taste. I catch another hint of his aftershave. I caught the scent earlier, but now that he's even closer, he smells like campfire and the lake. I've never been outdoorsy—I despise camping, and I think hiking is worse than CrossFit—and yet, I want to roll around in a tent right now.

I fantasized about a moment like this for months after I first met him. But I was finishing college, and not only was Corbin Theo's friend, but he had a young daughter. I didn't want to date or even sleep with a guy who had a kid, let alone someone my brother knew, so those dirty dreams stayed just that. Now, though, I'm relishing this kiss, this gentle press against my cheek that somehow feels far dirtier than it should.

When he inches away from me after several druggy seconds, he rasps out, "I told you I like cake."

"Me too," I say, keenly aware I'm not in college anymore. I don't feel *so much younger than him* like I did then.

A loud knock echoes through the trailer and straight into my very bones.

We jerk apart, Corbin ripping away from me, backing up to the sink. I blink, then brush my hands down my stained apron. I reorient myself to the present, not the filthy future of my dirty dreams.

"Yes?" I croak out as Corbin smooths his shirt and adjusts himself from a safer distance.

"It's Poppy, and it's photo time," says the cool, feminine voice of Ronnie's assistant.

"Okay," I say, sounding breathless and, I suppose, horny.

I try to clear the fog of lust by thinking about a recipe for something challenging to make...like a chocolate éclair.

Choux pastry is the lava pit of bakers, just waiting for you to misstep.

I review the first round of cooking the dough. She knocks again.

I clear my head as best I can, then call out: "I'm on my way."

"Lovely. Since it's photo time now," she says, sounding completely unamused by how long this is taking.

I whirl back to face Corbin.

And...oh shit. My gaze lands on his expensive shirt. It's white...and a little pink now. "Corbin," I whisper. "I think some frosting from my apron got on your shirt. I'm sorry. I'll get you a new one."

He glances down at it, curses under his breath, then looks up quickly. "I can wash it. It's fine."

"But you have to go to the arena."

Then again, what am I going to do? Go rush out and buy him a new one now, when he's due there any minute?

"Go, Mabel. I'm all good," he says, in that same *I've got this* tone he used when he ushered me to this trailer fifteen minutes ago.

I burst out the door, leaving that unexpected frosting kiss behind.

4

THE TEETH OF A SHARK
MABEL

I arrive at the baking stations in a flurry, breathless because I raced over from the trailer. The crowd's even bigger now. Great.

"How good of you to join us," Ronnie remarks coolly.

I stay strong, though, my smile never wavering.

After five more seconds of trying and failing to make me wither, he huffs and shifts his attention to the four bakers who didn't fall into their cakes. Lucky fuckers. "You all did so well," he says. To them. Rare praise from the tough-as-nails chef. But it also feels a little pointed against me.

I try to ignore it, taking this opportunity for publicity.

Poppy assembles the five of us before the audience, making sure I'm farthest away from the photographer. When I look behind me, I see my cake has magically disappeared, and my station is spic and span. All the other cakes are still in place, including the one with a red, heart-shaped trophy perched in front of it. Reality smacks into me—Ronnie handed out the trophy while I was in the trailer. He really doesn't want me around.

But most of the crowd is still here, and even as his assistant lines us up for the group pic, I'm pretty sure the folks in the front row are snapping pics of me. The people behind them too. Come to think of it, most of the phones are angled my way. Should I ham it up? Lean into my fifteen minutes of viral fame? I might as well smile. There's no such thing as bad publicity, right? Before I know it, I'll be *The Inventive Baker*. Or *The Fast on Her Feet Baker*.

Ronnie steps in front of me for the official pic, so I have to kind of peek around him to be seen. I smile for the camera without looking like I'm photobombing. At least, not too much.

When the photographer lowers her Nikon, Poppy materializes at my side, thrusting a canvas bag my way. It's full of… my things. My measuring cups and spoons, some of the special tools for my frosting, and so on.

"Thank you so much," she says, then snags a piece of paper from her back pocket. "A voucher to validate your parking." She points toward the tent's exit.

In case I was thinking of lingering, the message is clear— *don't.*

"Thanks for everything, Poppy. Sorry again about the—"

"It's all done," she says tightly.

That's clear. Time to go.

Chastened, I adjust the bag on my shoulder and head through the romance fair toward the exit, which is full of late afternoon sunlight. I check the time—it's just past four. The contest started this morning, and it's been…a day.

As I walk past a long row of food stalls, my phone trills.

When I grab my phone from my back pocket, I see it's the banker guy I'm meeting with tomorrow before my volunteer shift at the animal rescue.

"Hello?" I'm wary since I wasn't expecting a call.

"Hey, Mabel, it's Jonas over at Neighborhood Capital Trust and Loan. How the heck are you?"

I've never spoken to Jonas before. We've only emailed. I didn't realize he was so laid-back. "I'm fine," I say, careful but hopeful. "Everything set for tomorrow?"

I plan to make my pitch in person, even though I've already emailed him my business plan.

"Actually, the committee meets today to finalize our small business loan portfolio for this quarter. Any chance I could convince you to drop by in the next half hour or so? Just need you to sign this proof of income. Cross the t's and dot the i's, and all."

Sunshine floods my chest. That's good news. Maybe that means I got the last spot for the quarter. I cross my fingers. "Of course. I can be there by four-thirty."

"Sweet. Perfect timing."

"It is," I say and hang up. This is wild. My grandmother always said timing is everything. She always encouraged me to chase my dreams, whatever they were. She always said, *You'll know when things are right*. This feels right.

I hustle down the aisle toward the exit of the romance fair, and I spot Corbin up ahead, headed the same way. He's walking with two guys who *also* look like they juggle couches for fun. One's in a sapphire blue suit with a plaid print, the other's in dark purple. They're doing that athlete swagger, taking their sweet-ass time as they stroll, knowing they don't have to rush unless they're on the ice.

Meanwhile, I'm trying out for the Olympic race-walking event.

Head down, I push ahead aiming to put that trailer incident behind me, because an in-person meeting with a banker has to be a good sign. Maybe my frosting fiasco has appeared online but people are admiring how I saved it with the smash-cake comment. Perhaps the bank's excited about my ability to improvise.

I race to the parking garage then hop in my car, ready to scurry across town. I zip through surprisingly light traffic and rush inside the bank, asking the greeter where Jonas Gideon's office is. "Right this way," she tells me, then guides me past the tellers, back to the banker's office, where I expect to be greeted by a pasty man in a navy-blue suit crunching numbers.

Instead, the guy strums an acoustic guitar, and a shark's tooth hangs on a rope necklace against his tanned throat. He wears a bright white Henley and mauve pants, and I can seriously appreciate the way he's paired the two shades, as well as the rocking-it vibe.

"Mabel, how the heck are you?" he asks, still plucking out some notes. It's a Hozier tune, I think.

"Good song. And I'm well." I glance down, and...okaaaay. I'm still in my apron. I untie it and fold it hastily. "Sorry about the apron."

"No worries. Authenticity matters to us." He sets down the guitar, leaning it against the desk, and shoots me a gleaming white smile. He must own stock in Crest Whitestrips. "Thanks again for meeting me today. I had to move up the meeting because it's gonna dump in Tahoe tonight."

Wait. What? "You mean snow?"

"Yep," he says, eyes sparkling. "Climate change sucks, but you have to grab the chances when you can to hit the slopes."

Did I get the chillest banker ever or what? "Then let's get down to business so you can hit the road," I say.

"Aww, thanks," he says, then nods to a stack of papers on the corner of his desk. The proof of income, I presume. He blows out a long breath and strokes his chin. "And listen, trust me when I say I love your bakery concept. The idea of being open in the afternoon and early evening is brill. I mean, who isn't jonesing for a cookie or a cinnamon bun after work, right?"

"Exactly," I say, relieved he understands and appreciates that not all bakeries need to keep early-bird hours.

"I'm sure I don't need to tell you how important social media marketing is."

"So important. But all marketing is good marketing, right?"

He hums thoughtfully. "A strong online presence is vital. We need our businesses to talk up their offerings and so on. We need good press. Social media marketing is part of what we evaluate when we consider the financing."

"Terrific! Even as a pop-up bakery, I've tripled my following in two years. My engagement is up fifty-five percent year over year. I've done collabs with a local animal rescue for cakes with dog designs, with a romance bookstore for a Sweets and Spice night—even with Elodie's Chocolates for a Tempting Treats evening. And I'll work on growing my social media presence even more. Would that help?"

He's quiet for a long beat, then reaches for the papers on the corner of his desk, pulling them toward him with one long finger. "Mabel, I don't need you to sign these."

My brow knits. "You don't?"

"Like I said, social media is super important. And right after I called you, one of my colleagues sent along some viral footage. Of you smashing into a cake."

News of my bake fail traveled even faster than I'd thought possible, but the local station was streaming the contest. Still, "That was less than an hour ago," I say.

"Yes, and that ship has sailed. We can't back a woman known as a hot-mess baker girl. Or the girl who got dumped so her ex could go on *Romance Beach*. And we definitely can't back smashed cakes."

I roll my lips together, sealing in my dismay. This was one of my last chances. I've applied for loans left and right in order to launch a retail storefront for You Deserve a Treat. I've even looked at several spaces over the years. But like the loans, they haven't happened. Either my credit score isn't high enough, or the cash flow is too inconsistent, and do I even realize the failure rate of small businesses?

Yes, I *am* the failure rate.

"You're not giving me a loan," I say heavily, processing the obvious.

Jonas shoots me a sympathetic look. "No, but look on the bright side. Keto's so popular these days, maybe I'm doing you a favor!"

He shows me out so he can go snowboarding.

5

STEALTH MODE
CORBIN

I open the door of the players' entrance, stride down the corridor of the Golden State Foxes arena, and hope so damn hard no one will notice the frosting remnants on my shirt.

My teammates walking next to me, for instance.

Or the social media manager, Hassan, up ahead. The new photographer, Leighton, too, who's there snapping pics as we head to the locker room.

As I near Hassan and Leighton, I don't smile for the camera. Don't want fans, the media, or other teams to think I'm soft, or that *we* are. I've told Riggs and Miller as much too —it's best if we look like stone. We've got enough to deal with, given how our team collapsed at the end of last season. The last thing we need is to look like we're having too much fun at work.

With my poker face on, I turn the corner to the locker room, ready to get out of this shirt ASAP. It's not like I have lipstick marks on my collar, but my teammates saw me slip into the tent. They knew Mabel was there for a contest, and for all I know, they might have seen me go into the trailer with her.

I don't need them sniffing around, wondering what went down in those fifteen minutes. Especially if Theo's here. It's a game night, so he'll be in the arena, but he usually watches from the executive suite. Good, because I'd like to avoid him while his sister's lodged front and center in my mind. While I can still taste her frosting kiss on my lips.

On the walk to the arena with Riggs and Miller, I kept the conversation about collecting on the bet—that's why we went to the romance fair, so Riggs could meet his crush, but he did not get a second with Sapphire, the *Romance Beach* hostess. I near my stall, feeling like I escaped scrutiny when Miller slaps me on the arm.

"Dude, do you need a bib?"

I groan privately.

Snorting, Riggs shoots me a sideways glance. "Seriously, Knight. Eating is hard. We can give you some tips."

Lake, the right winger, looks up from his stall, where he's lined up his equipment in the order he'll put it on. It's a new arrangement from last season. If anyone ever tells you goalies are the most superstitious, I have a winger to show you.

He nods at my shirt. "That looks good. Did you bring any cupcakes for the rest of us?"

So much for stealth mode.

"Could be your new pre-game ritual, Axman," Miller tells him. We like Lake's nickname better than his last name, Axelrod. "A cupcake before every game."

"Hmm. Not a bad idea. But would that work on my meal plan?" Lake tosses back, which starts a debate about pre-game snacks.

I'm grateful for the distraction. I just hope Miller's legendary goalie focus stays squarely on Lake while I chuck the evidence in my stall. As I shed my suit, my mind drifts back to the trailer.

And I can*not* get lost in the tempting memory. I shove away the thoughts, imagining—I don't know—the dirty laundry bin as I pull on my compression shorts.

That's better.

I grab my shin guards next. It's earlyish, so it's just the four of us getting ready for now. Miller glances around the mostly empty locker room, then clears his throat, locking eyes with me as he hangs up his dress shirt neatly. "Seriously. Did you roll around in some cupcakes when you disappeared?"

"Speaking of, where the hell *did* you go?" Riggs seconds, like they're discussing missing minutes of video footage from a robbery.

"Wait. Did you assholes do something fun and not invite me?" Lake asks with a frown. "You always fucking do that with your *single dads club*."

I roll my eyes at the glowering winger, who's never stopped giving us shit since he learned a bunch of the guys—some dads, some not—from both the Foxes and the Sea Dogs play bocce ball and cornhole together in Cozy Valley whenever we can. "One, we don't have a club. And two, you don't want to be invited. To *anything*. That's literally your thing—*not going*."

Lake mimes slamming his hand on a buzzer. "Wrong. I want to be invited so I can turn it down."

"Congratulations. You've truly perfected the art of avoiding socialization," I say, sitting down in the chair in front of my stall and tugging on my shin guards.

"So Clem always says," Lake grumbles, referencing his sister.

Miller chuckles as he grabs some gear from his stall. "You make Axman sound as antisocial as a cat."

"Actually, did you know one of the least social animals is the snow leopard?" Riggs tells us. "They live and hunt alone. Tigers too. They only socialize to mate." Riggs is intensely serious as he tapes up his stick. He's never met a trivia game he didn't want to win.

Lake wiggles an eyebrow. "Sounds about right. I'm like a tiger."

"Sure," I put in. "If you're counting your hand as a mate."

"And we're not counting it, so you're very, *very* wrong," Lake says, lasering a stare my way. "And you should invite me to your club. I'm a cat dad."

"It's not a club," Riggs points out, because...facts matter.

"So you can turn us down and spend the night at your ranch?" I ask Lake as I pull on my socks.

"It's a nice ranch," Lake adds, then lifts his stick and pokes my thigh with it. "Shirt. Frosting. What's the fucking story, Knight? Asking because I care."

And we're back to this. I decide to throw them a bone and hope they give up the scent. "Mabel was at the Webflix launch. Theo's sister. She needed some help with a cake that fell, so I gave her a hand and—"

"Looks like you were a lot of help, man. Getting it on your fucking shirt." Riggs cackles.

Miller snorts. "Can you help pick up my stick? Try not to trip on it as you grab it."

"I need help tying my skates," Riggs goads. "Don't tie them around your wrist though."

"Pretty sure you needed help at the event earlier today," I say. "Next time, ask your teammates to open a path for you."

"Fuck off," Riggs replies.

"Now, this I want to hear," Lake says.

As Riggs details his failed efforts to meet Sapphire, I turn around and put on the rest of my equipment, grateful the guys have moved on, but I'm hung up on something else.

The spark I felt once again with Mabel, along with the

annoyingly persistent thought that maybe I should...ask Mabel out on a date.

It's like a buzzing fly I can't swat away. The idea feels a little crazy. No, *a lot*. But I can't shake it, not during stretches, not during warm-ups, and not during our pre-game meeting. Not even when I hit the ice as the announcer booms: "And now, it's time for your Golden State Foxes."

The crowd cheers.

And...jeers.

But that's when I finally put her out of my mind. We've got loyal fans, but also angry fans who aren't afraid to let us know we need to do better than we did last year.

And they're right—we do.

The last thing I need this season is a distraction. And definitely not one as big as trying to figure out how the hell to date my longtime friend's frustratingly beautiful and endearingly chaotic little sister.

Five minutes later, I'm racing down the ice. I flick the puck over to Lake when a Las Vegas Saber defender barrels toward me. Lake snags it, flies toward the net, then feeds it to one of our D-men, who ferries it around the net, and back to me.

I've got a clean shot on goal, and the Saber goalie's been protecting the left side of the net more, so I shoot it to the right.

But he lunges for it, saving it with just enough time.

"Fuck me," I mutter.

A perfect shot, and it's still not enough.

The game goes on like that, with too many shots on goal and not enough to show for it.

At the end, the Sabers beat us in our barn, and I trudge off the ice, annoyed that we're playing like we were at the end of last season.

In the locker room, I try to put it behind me. "It's one game," I say to the guys. "We'll get the next one."

"We fucking will," Miller seconds as he lumbers across the room in his leg pads.

Lake glowers as he starts taking off his gear in the exact same order he put it on. "Maybe we do need lucky cupcakes."

"No, we just need to capitalize on scoring opportunities," I say, stating the painfully obvious.

As I toss my jersey into the laundry bin, I noodle on that word—opportunity. Is that what today was with Mabel? An opportunity to do something different than I did when I met her seven years ago? It was the wrong time then, for a lot of reasons. Should I go for it now?

As I shower, I weigh that word more, and the costs that come with it. While I don't *need* Theo's permission to ask out his sister—she's a grown woman with agency and all—maybe I'll give him a courtesy heads-up.

As I get dressed, I avoid the frosting-covered shirt, stuffing it into a duffel and instead grabbing a T-shirt with my alma mater's name on it from my stall, then putting on my suit jacket.

"Dude, my eyes hurt, and it's not from the color, man," Miller says, shielding his face from my mismatched outfit.

"Not sure I can be seen with you. It'd hurt my rep as a stylish motherfucker." Riggs scowls as he runs a hand down the plaid pattern of his suit jacket. Maybe it *is* fashionable. Who even knows? "But seriously, you can't pair suit pants and a T-shirt *with words*."

I lift my chin. "Ask me if I care." I do care a little, but not enough to do anything about it.

Shouldering the duffel with the evidence, I leave the locker room. I'm headed down the hall to the players' lot when a sharply dressed Theo rounds the corner toward me, head bent over his phone. "Asshole," he grumbles at the screen.

He spots me when he looks up from his phone and stops, his dark eyes full of fire. "Knight, my man. Have I told you how much I hate Dax Strong?"

Why does that name sound so familiar? "Don't think you have."

"I hate my sister's ex more than I hate losing."

Oh right. That's who Dax is. Mister Romance Beach. I swallow roughly but keep my poker face as Theo keeps going.

"I swear if I ever see him, I will slice him to pieces with my rhetoric."

"And your rhetoric has claws," I say, grateful it's not aimed at me.

"Damn straight." His phone rings, and he glances at it. "Gotta take this," he says, continuing down the hall.

I make for the exit and push open the door, the night air like a smack of reality.

What was I thinking? Theo's the most protective guy I know, and he's made a sport of hating his sister's exes. I do *not* need to get on the bad side of the acting GM.

I can't afford something messy like dating my best friend's sister right now, or even entertaining thoughts of it.

Sometimes a kiss is just a kiss.

6

BLACK AND WHITE
AND BRIGHT PINK

MABEL

In the morning, I'm up at an ungodly hour. Is it actually eight-thirty? I'm not sure when I was last awake and working at this time. But early birds and all. I'll turn over a new leaf and get a head start on making and then freezing next week's wedding cookie order.

As I walk to the ghost kitchen, I click on my email to confirm the flavors, only to spot a new one from the bridezilla. She's upped her order from two hundred cookies to six hundred.

Is she inviting Cookie Monster to her wedding? It's going to be a real stretch to do these in the ghost kitchen. But I'm determined. Maybe I'll just be a ghost-kitchen baker for the rest of my life, until I die in a ghost kitchen and every kitchen becomes a ghost kitchen to me.

When I arrive at the space, a woman in a tailored navy-blue suit is click-clacking down the hallway, talking on her Bluetooth. "Yes, we had an all-cash buyer. It's great." She stops when she sees me and holds up a wait-a-second finger. "Call you right back."

After she ends the call, she looks down her straight nose at me. "You must be Mabel. You're on my call list for today."

The hair on the back of my neck stands on end. "Why?"

"I'm a real estate attorney. We just sold this space to a baker who wants to capitalize on the keto craze," she says.

I roll my eyes. Is Jonas an oracle? "You're kidding me."

"I assure you. I don't joke. But we'll consider letting you use the kitchen for one day a week, if you're willing to pay for the deep-cleaning afterward so you don't contaminate the keto products."

Could this day get worse than yesterday? And the answer —as I'm cleaning out my supplies while searching for a new kitchen to rent at the last minute—is yes.

My phone rings, and it's another lawyer, the one who's been overseeing my grandmother's estate for the last year. He's twenty-three going on fifty, and he belongs on a TV show—the small-town whippersnapper attorney who wears suits three sizes too big and everyone underestimates.

As for me, I'm the heroine in a horror movie who enters the house when the whole theater knows she shouldn't. Because I answer the call.

"You just found a long-lost Van Gogh in my grandmother's storage unit?"

I mean, why not manifest something good? Grandma loved art. It's not such a stretch to think she might have accidentally acquired one.

"Betty always said you were the funny one," he says, his voice squeaky.

"And a Rembrandt too? Excellent. I'll be right there to pick them up."

"Perfect. Why don't you swing by my office later today?"

I freeze, a whisk in one hand on its way to a box. "Wait. You really need me there? Last we spoke, you were nearly done with the estate." And I've managed the whole thing, doling out the antique mirrors, the jewelry, a few artsy photos for me, some books and a boat for Theo, and the proceeds from the sale of her small house to my mother, who in turn used it to pay off her mortgage.

"We were going through the final boxes—your grandma really did keep everything—and we found a wrinkle in Betty's estate."

I shake my head. "Of course you did."

We set a time, and I walk back to my apartment, grab my car, and return to the ghost kitchen—that name feels awfully apropos now—to pack up all my supplies before they lock me out. I load up my car and leave from there, headed to a town I avoid if I can help it. Because that was where my seven-year streak of bad luck began.

* * *

Grandma's personal mantra must have been, *If it can fit in a box, I'll save it.*

It's made the management of her estate a long, complicated affair after she died twelve months ago, a few years after her husband. When Garth tells me there's one more box to go through, I can only assume it's newspaper clippings about Betty's mother, who was one of the town's first female firefighters, or old macaroni artwork that Garth really should just feel empowered to throw out.

After I stop by the lawyer's, I'll dash out of Cozy Valley as fast as I arrived—ideally avoiding my parents, who'll be busy penning world-class research papers for the university, anyway—and spend some time with Google, hunting down a new place with an oven.

On the forty-minute drive to Cozy Valley, I call my brother

to see if he knows anyone, like some of the private chefs who work with the players, who might have access to a kitchen. But Theo doesn't answer. As the miles tick off and the pastel yellow sign for Cozy Valley looms over the hill, a knot of tension wedges into my chest. When, at age twenty, you're single-handedly responsible for the Cozy Valley Sanctuary llamas knocking over the pancake breakfast fundraiser at the town's fire station because they were jacked up on the sugar cookies you left in the back of the fire truck...well, you can become a bit of a local laughingstock.

Small towns have long memories.

I flick the turn signal for the exit and swallow my dread. Too bad the lawyer's office isn't on the outskirts of Cozy Valley. He's smack dab on Main Street in a white clapboard building marked with one of those old-fashioned signs hanging on the porch, saying, *Funkle and Son, Esquire.*

I park on a side street to be safe and pop on my sunglasses.

I fly past Whiskers and Kisses, where the store's tuxedo lounges in a cat tower. After turning the corner, I trot up the steps to the law offices, a bell tinkling as I push open the door.

"Come on back," calls a squeaky voice. I follow it and find Garth hunched over his desk, a wad of tissue stuck to his pale jawline—a shaving cut, presumably. He's sorting through old banker's boxes and...is that one of Grandma's jewelry boxes?

A pang of nostalgia hits me square in the heart. But I've cried enough around Garth. "Fine, if you can't locate a Van Gogh," I say, trying to make light of the situation, "I'll take a diamond ring. I could sell it and use it as a down payment for a bakery."

Looking up, all baby-faced and nicked, he smiles. "The number of rings my clients have sold...the stories I could tell you." He shakes his head, and I arch a skeptical brow. He's barely out of high school. How many stories could he have? But it's not my place to judge.

He pats a well-worn box. "Listen, Mabel, I thought we were all set, but the new owners of Betty's house called about a couple of boxes we must have overlooked in the attic, including this one." The jewelry box is covered in minty green fabric with illustrations of flowers all over it. Grandma loved her girly stuff. We always had that in common. "I was about to put all this jewelry in the estate sale when I found something in the jewelry box."

Garth pats a manila folder on his desk, then takes out a sheet of paper with a neon pink Post-it note on top. I can't read the handwriting.

"I'm thinking she meant to give this to you, but since her stroke was sudden, she didn't have the chance," he says.

The room goes quiet. My heart beats louder. A sense of foreboding cloaks me. But maybe also, strangely, hope? It's almost embarrassing how much I'm craving a hug from beyond from the one person who always believed in me.

I swallow down those emotions, though, as Garth hands me a crisp sheet of paper. There's a four-letter word across the top.

Deed.

I blink. I wasn't expecting *that*. I take the paper, but the words feel like they're levitating off the page. It feels like someone else holds the paper, like someone else reads it, like someone else is wondering why my grandmother left me a deed for...a small firehouse in the town of Cozy Valley.

"She bought the abandoned firehouse?" I ask, taking my time with every word. "The...one?"

As in, the one where not only the llamas knocked over the pancakes, but a goat ate all the money raised, and a pig flipped the bacon table. (Well, that was understandable, and more power to his protest.)

"Yes, that one. She bought it about a week before she died. Bid on it at a property auction."

"Why?" I ask, my voice trembling.

The answer is in black and white and bright pink. Now I can see the Post-it note, and it reads in her loopy, pretty handwriting: "For Mabel, as you see fit."

My heart stutters. It's a message. Short and sweet, but crystal clear. And it does feel like a hug from her. Especially those four words—*As you see fit.*

They're full of a faith in me that I didn't feel from Jonas, or Ronnie, or my ex. A faith I don't feel from my parents. Maybe a faith I need.

I meet Garth's eyes, grappling with this life-changing news. "Is this for real? My grandmother left me a...fire station?"

Not just any station. This is *the* station. The place where Grandma took the photos for the calendar. The station where my great-grandmother pioneered a place for women in the fire service.

"I didn't think it was for sale," I say, dumbstruck.

"It had been closed for a while, then some company bought it and began renovations, but when they went into foreclosure, it was put up for auction. Your grandmother won it. The deed was issued a few days later, after the payment was received." He taps the paper with a well-manicured finger. "Looks like she meant to give it to you before she died. It's yours. *As is.*"

I can't move. I can't breathe. I'm so shell-shocked I can barely process this gift from the afterlife. Except for one little detail.

Or really, one big one.

"Does it...have a kitchen?"

7

I'M NOT THINKING ABOUT MY BEST FRIEND'S SISTER

CORBIN

I race down the ice, flicking the puck back and forth under a stick attached to a cone. Then the one next to it. And the one next to that too. Quick, efficient moves in a stickhandling drill I've done my whole life.

I fly past the half dozen cones with sticks I've set up at the Cozy Valley indoor rink, then call my shot. Right corner. I snap my wrist, smack the puck and shoot.

It lodges in the net because of course it does.

I'm alone, trying to redo last night.

Focused only on this practice, and nothing else, I move the cones and the sticks, setting them up around the rink in a new obstacle course. Then I ferry the puck around each one, down the ice, again and again.

Lather, rinse, repeat.

Crossover, aim, shoot.

Like I'm a determined kid again, practicing solo on a frozen pond, doing whatever it takes to improve my game.

That's what I need to do now too.

To win the next game, and the next one and the next.

No distractions.

When my legs are screaming obscenities at me, and my lungs are burning, I finish, putting away the cones and sticks, thank the rink manager, then head home.

And would you look at that? I haven't even thought about Mabel. A secret romance with my friend's little sister is definitely not part of my plan for the season. It won't help me stay healthy, guide my team deep into the playoffs instead of getting humiliatingly swept in round one, or take care of my little family.

That's what I focus on instead. My daughter and I are going to bake brown butter chocolate chip pumpkin blondies with nuts when she comes home this afternoon.

I'm not someone who's into pumpkin spice *anything*.

But she is, so I prep the ingredients.

I text my kiddo, keeping my focus right where it should be.

Corbin: Here's the blondie report. I've got everything lined up and ready. I repeat—all baking systems are a go.

World's Best Daughter: Copy that! I'll be reporting for baking duty in three hours! Also, good job with the mise en place.

Corbin: Nice job with the culinary words.

World's Best Daughter: I have a good teacher. Also, can we save some blondies for Benny? I want to train him to like pumpkin from an early age.

I shudder. Pumpkin should really be abolished, but I reply with a resounding yes, since I'm damn grateful Charlotte has a three-year-old half brother and I had nothing to do with it. I know firsthand how tough it is to be an only child, and I seriously appreciate that I didn't have to produce another kid for her to have a sibling. In fact, her mom deserves some treats for doing that for our daughter.

I tap out another message.

Corbin: Why don't we give some to your mom and Travis too?

World's Best Daughter: Mom says she loves pumpkin anything!

I laugh. Yup, Sarah does, though that's not the reason Charlotte's mom and I didn't work out after a two-night stand. When she learned she was pregnant, we toyed with the idea of trying to be together, but after a few more trial dates, it was clear we didn't have that forever kind of spark, and we were both okay with it. We agreed, too, that we wanted to raise Charlotte together here in Cozy Valley, where Sarah lives and works.

I set the phone down, and I swear this time I don't ask myself if I should call Mabel. What was I even going to say if she'd wanted to talk? "Life is complicated, with my schedule and your brother working for my team, but, hey, I want you to know if I were in a different place, I'd want to take you out. But I can't right now. Sucks because I can't stop thinking about you."

I shake my head.

Pointless.

What's not pointless, though, is an extra workout. I have the time before Charlotte returns, so I head to my bedroom, change into a pair of basketball shorts from the stack in my drawer labeled *navy blue* and a T-shirt from the stack labeled *gray and white*. I return to the kitchen, grabbing a water bottle from next to the mugs on the drying rack. As I fill the bottle, the rustle of leaves from the quaking aspen drifts through the open window.

I turn off the tap, then an unholy clatter rends the air. Mugs clatter and an infernal *meow* pierces my eardrums as a big, striped tabby cat skids past the mugs he knocked over, then leaps right onto my back.

"Seven," I howl. The neighborhood cat might as well have dug his claws into my very soul and not just my skin. He jumps down, then immediately administers emergency bathing on his paws.

"So that's how it's going to be?" I ask.

He doesn't even look up—just licks himself clean like I've contaminated him. "And to think, I feed you," I add, as I check out the scratch on my arm. It hurts, but I'll live.

Seven stops, looks up, and emits a plaintive mewl, looking like he's about to hold out his bowl and ask, *Please, sir, may I have some more.*

"You need to go home to Annabelle."

I grab a chunk of the monkey bread, pre-sliced and wrapped in tinfoil, and a few minutes later, I pop the cat and the bread into the tote bag on the front of my bike, where he's used to riding shotgun every time he comes to my home for one of the seven or so daily meals he attempts to convince the entire neighborhood he needs.

After I've secured my helmet, I cruise the rest of the mile or so to Annabelle's bungalow at the end of the street, wind chimes in her trees greeting me with a tinkle as I pull up on the sidewalk.

A few seconds after I ring the bell, Annabelle swings the door open, bracelets jangling on the warm brown skin of her arms, long black braids piled high on her head, and a reprimand in her crinkled eyes for the cat.

"Seven. You were supposed to help me garden, not wander off," she chides, then reaches for the naughty feline. Once the critter is in her arms, she scrutinizes my face, then whispers, "I'm picking something up from you right now, honey. Your energy. It's vibrating.

It's like lightning is crackling all around your head. As if a storm is brewing in your mind."

Well, shit. Is it that obvious I'm thinking too much about Mabel? "Nah," I say, with a *no big deal* smile, then I hand her the monkey bread. "Here's something for you. And I assure you, the only thing on my mind is our next game."

She takes the bread. "Come inside. That way, I can give you a proper energy reading."

I believe in things I can see and things I can do. I believe in exercise. I believe in showing up. But Annabelle's an old friend of my mother's, and my mom tried to visit her more in the end, to learn whether energy *could* heal you. That was a futile effort—you can't cure Parkinson's.

My throat tightens uncomfortably. "Another time. I really should go."

Her eyes go glassy for a beat, like she's focusing on a point way off in the distance. "Don't let the storm in your head distract you from making a good decision."

"Thanks, Annabelle. Enjoy the bread," I grunt, then hop back on my bike and take the hell off.

Don't let the storm distract me? I make decisions all the

time—split-second ones on the ice. Pass here, shoot there, pick off the puck from the other team, skate the other way.

I've made plenty of decisions off the ice, too, like finding the best doctors for my mom, visiting the top physical therapists, moving her in with Charlotte and me at the end.

All I've done for the last few years is make lots of quick decisions. Lots of big ones too.

As I bike to the gym, getting some distance from that conversation, my phone rings. It's Theo, telling me to meet him at the old firehouse where he's with his sister. Tension slams into me. Does my best bud from college know I flirted with his sister yesterday and kissed frosting off her cheek?

It wouldn't hurt to show up at the firehouse with some apology bread, just in case he has heard about my cake clean-up kiss. I hang a U-turn and pedal at rocket pace back to my house. Then it's back to the bike and a race down Main Street.

I sprint past the new, state-of-the-art firehouse, then swing a sharp right onto Holly Springs and pull up in front of the old firehouse.

Jumping off my bike, I let it clatter against a streetlamp. I unhook my helmet, grab the bread, then beeline for Theo and Mabel, who are checking out the garage door of the single-bay fire station. Mabel, arms spread wide, says something about a *sign*. Her hair falls in waves down her back. I can tell she has streaks in it, lighter than the rest, but I don't really know what shade of brown her hair is. I know how her hair felt, though— thick, shiny, and soft, even when a little sticky with frosting.

I shouldn't get sidetracked remembering how my pulse spiked when I touched her. As I come closer, sneakers slapping against the pavement, Theo spins around. Mabel does too.

Theo grins my way, then his gaze drifts down to my hand. "And what do we have here?"

"Just made some monkey bread last night. Here you go."

He'd be insulted if I handed it to him, so I lob the chunk his way. He catches it, then holds it up high, like it's a treasure found deep in the jungle. "And this, my man—this is why I knew you'd be perfect for this hookup."

My brain snags on the last part of the sentence. "Hookup?" I choke out.

"Consider me a matchmaker," Theo says, squeezing Mabel's shoulder, and my chest tightens. "A business matchmaker, because my sister has always wanted to open a bakery."

"Right," I say, since I've known she's been looking for a place in the city for a while.

As he unwraps the chunk of monkey bread, Theo turns to her. "And Mabel, did you know my man Corbin *also* wants to open a bakery?"

She whips her gaze to me. "You do?"

It was Mom's dream to open a bakery. We even planned it together, plotting which of her recipes we'd use. Dreaming up the desserts we'd make together and offer each day of the week, from lemon shortbread to chocolate cupcakes, from seven-layer bars to mini key-lime pies. She went so far as to take me around to visit spaces to lease. But then, one weekend, she held out her shaking hand and said quietly, "I think it's too late."

The tremors won. Soon, she stopped baking entirely.

I bat away the tough memories, focusing on Theo. "When I retire," I correct him. "It's my retirement plan."

Shrugging like that detail's unimportant, Theo plucks off a chunk of the sticky-sweet treat. "Plans change. Mabel found out today that she was left this firehouse by our grandma."

"That's...huge," I say. That is an understatement. Bits of the conversation start to line up. "And you're going to turn it into a bakery?"

She grins, the kind of smile that acknowledges the idea's a little out there. "I didn't ever plan on opening a bakery *here*. I don't know if you recall, but after *the incident*"—she stops to sketch air quotes—"the town's online gossip column titled their article *Old McMabel and the Four Animals of the Firehouse Apocalypse*. Their most popular piece ever. Which was ridiculous since the math was wrong. There were six animals that day."

That day I met the gorgeous, spunky spitfire in this firehouse and offered to help her clean up the mess of syrup, pancakes, and bacon caused by the farm animals she'd been overseeing as a sanctuary volunteer. While we corralled and cleaned, I plotted how to ask her out. Then I learned she was Theo's sister, home from college, and I shelved the plans for a date. Just like I did again last night.

"For what it's worth, I didn't know about the headline," I say, in case that eases the sting.

"Thanks. But everyone else did. I haven't really wanted to set up roots here, or a business. I still don't, but this is my best shot at a shopfront. But the space needs some pretty serious work."

"Well, it *is* a firehouse, not a bakery."

"I know, but the prior owners did some work on it, so it's not like it needs a complete reno," she says, then offers a small smile. "Desperate times call for desperate measures."

"And they involve brilliant brothers," Theo adds, as he finishes another bite of the bread. "When she got the deed, she asked me if I had any ideas for how she could cover the cash for the extensive updates. Since I am the king of dealmakers, I told her to meet me here. Then I called you."

"I've been trying to get a loan to open a bakery, but I've had no luck. And the kitchen I rented is going keto. Now I finally have a space, and that solves one problem, but the upgrades are a whole other issue. I need an investor if I'm ever going to be able to do this. I need..." She stops and takes a big breath. "Capital."

Theo's shit-eating grin grows as he turns my way, and I'm no longer a bystander. I'm the main party. I figure what is coming next, right before he says, "That's you, man. That is fucking *you*. You love to bake too, and you want to open a bakery."

But that is the someday plan. "I can't open a bakery now, Theo. I'm busy. I have a kid. A J-O-B. You might recall it's with the Golden State Foxes, the team you manage. I don't have time to run a bakery now."

Theo's entirely unfazed by my argument. "Which is why Mabel's offer is perfect for you." He turns to his sister. "She has experience running a bakery. She has the time to run it. She even has, of all things, a firehouse with a kitchen." He swings his gaze to me. "And you, man? You have the desire and the cash."

This is all happening real fast, and I'm not so sure *I'm* the logical conclusion to Theo's arguments. After all, Mabel is a property owner now. I point to the structure she just inherited. "But if she has an asset, won't that make getting a loan easier?"

Theo lifts a finger as if to say, *Good point.* "Sure, that's an option."

"And I can definitely do that," Mabel says with a wince. "But if I wait around for bank financing, which can take forever, I'll be losing potential money."

Ah, so she needs a friend with cash sitting around. "So I'm the money?"

"Yeah," Theo says evenly, making it clear being *the money* isn't a bad thing. "But you also have a dream. A similar one." He makes some good arguments. But still...now? Today? I blow out a breath, shoving my hand through my messy hair. "This is *a lot*."

"I get it. You're worried Mabel won't think you're as good as she is in the kitchen," Theo says, stirring the fucking pot.

I pull a face. "Not my worry."

"But just to assuage those concerns," he says, closing the distance to Mabel and holding the tinfoil with a small bite left in it, "here you go."

She plucks it out with polished nails, gives it an inquisitive look, then brings it to her nose and sniffs. I go both tense and hopeful all at once. Sure, we've baked together before, but there's always that held-breath moment when someone tries your cooking for the first time.

She pops the piece between her lips and chews thoughtfully. I watch her like I'm a plaintiff waiting for a verdict to be read in court. She hums, then says, "Ten out of ten."

I scoff. She's just buttering me up. "Right."

"Seriously. It's really good, Corbin." She holds my gaze, making it clear she means it. "So good, I'm a little annoyed all I got was one tiny little bite."

Theo holds his hands out wide like he's saying, *Problem solved*. He turns to me. "There. You passed the taste test."

He strides over to me, claps my back. "I know you're busy with hockey and raising a kid. But you can pitch in when you're free. And listen, I get it, man. This feels like I sprang it on you, but sometimes life happens that way. If it's not you, it'll be someone else, and then when you're ready to open a bakery here in a few years, you'll be facing stiff competition."

Are you kidding? He played the competition card? But of course he did. He negotiates like he breathes.

"Heard," I acknowledge, but that's all. I've been pivoting a lot in the last few years, in big ways and small ones. I'm not sure I'm ready to pivot again.

Mabel offers a warm smile. "I didn't know I had inherited a firehouse with a kitchen until thirty minutes ago. I'm not even sure they have pickleball courts here."

I huff out a laugh. "We have pickleball courts here. And Wi-Fi."

Theo glances at his Rolex. "I've got a meeting with an agent. I'll leave you two to work out the details, and I look forward to hearing about the new Cozy Valley bakery later."

He takes a few steps toward his shiny electric sports car, then stops and turns, lasering me with his sharp stare. "And listen, this is a great opportunity. You should take it. You really should. But whatever you do—do not hurt my sister."

I jerk my head back. "Dude," I say, meaning, *Of course I won't hurt her.*

But I'm pretty sure he also means, *Do not touch her.*

And I won't. In my head, I add, *Ever again.* Out loud, I say, "I would never do that."

"Good," he says.

Mabel sighs, but it's full of affection for her older sibling. "Theo, I can take care of myself."

"True, but I will take care of anyone who hurts you."

He strides off with the confidence of a man who got what he wanted, leaving me to stare stupidly at his sister as I try to figure out if I should seriously go into business with a woman who, seven years ago, I wanted to date. And in the years between, I never really fell hard for anyone else.

Only, her smile vanishes, and she stares at me now with worry in her eyes.

"Corbin, your arm is bleeding."

8

UNDER ONE CONDITION
CORBIN

My gaze snaps to my arm, where a small stream of blood appears to have traveled down my biceps and dried there. "What the—oh, it's from the cat."

"Let me get you a Band-Aid."

I jerk my attention to Mabel, who's empty-handed. "You carry Band-Aids with you? Also, no. I don't need a Band-Aid. I'm a hockey player."

"Right. You just free bleed. Cool." She drops the mockery and stares at me like I've lost my mind. "Also, gross."

"Mabel, it's a cat scratch. I've gotten back on the ice after being cut with a blade."

"You're not on the ice right now." She circles me and gasps when she gets to my back. "I hate to break it to you, but there's a streak of blood down the back of your shirt. How did you not feel this?"

"Like I said, I've been cut before."

"Yes, by blades and by men. But cats are like gods. They are stronger, and also, this could lead to infection. We're cleaning this up now."

"Cats are not stronger than—"

But there's no point in arguing since she's already gone, marching down the street to her car where she yanks open the door and grabs a backpack. When she returns, she eyes me in full triage mode. "Let's go inside the firehouse. I don't want anyone to know you're human."

"If you think you can handle my bionic self, go ahead."

"I definitely can." There's a little bit of flirt in her voice. But, with a mischievous grin, she moves on, nodding to her new property. "Want to see it?"

I really do, but I don't want to sound too eager. "Sure."

Mabel nods to the door, and I follow her. "Theo and I only took a quick look around. Not enough to kick the tires. Apparently, some company bought it a while ago and started to work on it, so it's...half-converted." After she slides in the key and turns it, the door opens with a loud and aggrieved groan, like it's been ages since it moved its rusty hinges.

Once inside, Mabel stares wide-eyed at the open, empty space, a smile shifting her lips. Light streams in from the doorway. The floor is concrete, and the ceilings are high with exposed beams, giving an industrial but surprisingly cozy feel. A vintage fire department sign hangs on one wall, next to an antique helmet. But there's also a new set of turnouts hanging next to it. The sliding brass pole looks like it was polished recently.

A freshly framed wall divides the space. It's been drywalled, but not finished, so it definitely needs work. But right away, I can see how this could house a bakery—after a bunch of upgrades. The half-done reno has left a clear front and back of the house.

"I was pretty skeptical when I first opened the door with my brother, but then I looked around and I thought...*this could really work*," she whispers, as if speaking too loudly would ruin the dream. She points to the ceiling. "There are even still bunks upstairs from when the crews slept here. Maybe that space could work for storage."

I can hear now how much she wants this. I don't want to rain on her parade, but I'm not sure the time is right for me. Still, I'm intrigued by that newish fireman's outfit. I stride over to it, reaching out a hand, and discovering...

"Mabel. I think these are tearaway pants."

She gasps, then her gaze whips from the gear to the pole and back. "I bet they were going to convert it into a strip club. Please say they were going to convert it into a strip club."

"I believe the evidence speaks for itself," I say.

"I'm almost sad that didn't happen. I so would have gone to a fireman-centric strip club in Cozy Valley," she says.

"Maybe you can open a combo. Bakery by day, strip club by night."

She spins around, eyes flickering. "You'll be my star dancer?"

I scoff-laugh. "Yes, moonlighting on a pole won't pose any risk of injury whatsoever."

"Excellent," she says, then heads over to the brass pole and runs a hand down it reverently. She turns quiet, looks thoughtful. I don't think she's picturing the strip club anymore. "My grandmother was so...bold. I still can't believe she pulled this off. *For me.*"

"It is an amazing gift," I say.

"It sure is. It feels unreal." As if testing the integrity of it, she walks toward the wall and raps on it. "Looks like the expensive structural work is done. It's far enough along to be functional quickly but not too finished yet."

"It's got good bones," I acknowledge. "But there's probably not even running water, so no need to play nurse with the cat wound. I'm all good."

She snaps out of her decorating haze. "C'mon, tough

hockey player. Good news is there's a bathroom. Which is great because one of my life's mottos is *Yay for indoor plumbing.*"

"What do you know? That's one of mine too."

"See? Good team," she says.

I'm not ready to agree to that. Instead, I tip my chin toward her. "So, pickleball?"

She juts out a hip. "What? I don't look athletic?"

I shake my head. "That's not what I meant. I didn't know you liked...playing sports."

"Oh please," she says with a scoff. "I don't."

"But you play pickleball?"

"For the fashion. The outfits are so cute."

Does not compute. "You took it up for the clothes?"

"Of course. I have a whole collection of thrifted dresses. Some with ruffles, some in gingham, one has a super-cute preppy collared top. They're all ridiculously adorable."

I don't get it. How do you play a sport for the fashion? "Do you just...model on the courts?"

"I play. *Badly.* Like most people," she says, then motions to the doorway.

I leave that perplexing conversation behind as we push through an open doorway leading toward the back of the house. And yup. Strip club for sure. This room has been half outfitted as a dressing room, with makeup tables in front of mirrors framed by lightbulbs. The kitchen is on the other side, where the afternoon light streams in through a window above a big farm sink. "Not sure what the plan was—maybe they were going to serve wings and mozzarella sticks in the club?"

"Sticks and dicks," she offers.

I groan, dragging a hand down my face. "That's a terrible name for a strip club. I'm not sure I want to know what you'll name a bakery."

"Just you wait. I've been letting some ideas percolate." She waves to the kitchen. "I know you've been waiting for me too. But I'll check you out soon," she says affectionately...to the stove.

It's distractingly adorable that she's talking to an appliance.

And I cannot get distracted, so I move past her, turning the corner into the bathroom. When I switch on the tap, nothing happens. It just spurts air. "See. I was right. No water."

She pats the backpack. "I have hydrogen peroxide. And listen, tough guy, your back is covered in blood, and you're not on the rink. Let me help." Echoing my words from yesterday, she adds, "That work for you?"

I heave a sigh but relent. "Fine."

I close the lid on the toilet and sit down, grumbling for good measure.

She squeezes my shoulder, and it feels better than a shoulder squeeze should. But I stay stoic as she says, "I know, I know. You're so tough. Still, let's clean you up. I get that you're in love with your gray shirts but make like a Sticks and Dicks dancer and strip."

Cracking up, I drag a hand down my face. "Mabel, you missed your calling. You really should open that strip club. Are you trying to tell me something? Is that what you really want us to do?" I reach for the hem of my shirt and peel it off, getting a good look at it. Shit. It *is* streaked in blood. That cat did a number on my back.

When I glance up, though, Mabel's frozen. She hasn't responded. She hasn't fired back. Instead, her eyes are locked on me—my chest? No, it's the abs she's gawking at. Or could it be the biceps? Wait. Seems it's the forearms now.

Well, how about that? Might as well help her out, give her a better look. Blowing a lazy breath, I sit a little taller, stretch my arms over my head, and give her a full view of whatever she wants.

Several seconds later, she seems to blink the fog out of her eyes, her voice a little gravelly as she says, "I'll...um... so..."

This just got real interesting. Even though nothing can happen between us, my ego and I sure like knowing she *wants* something to. "Cat got your tongue?"

She lifts her chin, then scrunches her brow as if she's trying to activate her brain cells. "Of course not. Just...turn around."

I smother a smile as I shift so she's got a full view of my back.

Her breath hitches again. I stop fighting my smile. What can I say? I have back muscles for days.

And a bit of a troublemaker streak. "Feel free to enjoy the view."

"Oh, shut up."

"You were the one who wanted me to be your star dancer. If you think about it, Sticks and Dicks isn't a bad name if you have hockey players here," I muse as she roots in her bag for supplies, then opens a bottle of peroxide and dabs some on a cotton ball. She presses it to my back. It's cool to the touch. Gently, she swipes it down. I fight off a wince. It's just a sting from the peroxide. That's all.

"That's going to leave a scar," she says.

"It'll have good company," I remark.

She pauses, then says, "Yeah, I see another one here." She taps my other shoulder.

"Yup. And here." I point to my abs, but she's behind me.

As she leans over me to get a look, her hair tickles my shoulder. That feels too good.

"Where?" she asks.

I clear my throat, then point to my lower stomach, on the right side.

"Did you take a blade to your stomach?" she asks with avid curiosity, like she's trying to figure out how that'd work. That's not an easy injury to pull off.

"Nope. This one's courtesy of fate. Ruptured appendix when I was ten."

She laughs, then smacks my shoulder. "And I thought you were showing me your hockey war wounds."

I lift my right arm, showing her the underside, home to a long, jagged scratch. "Now that one's from a blade."

She reaches for it, slides her thumb down the scar like she's tracing it, memorizing it maybe. Now it's my turn to suck in a breath. I don't really know how we went from her brother asking me to finance a bakery to exploring wounds and touching scars. But I also don't entirely want it to stop.

She might though. A few seconds later, she straightens and says, "Let me finish up your back."

Focusing on her nursing mission, she grabs supplies from the sink where she set them down, cleans my arm, then returns to my back. She rubs more peroxide onto the cat scratch there before reaching into her first-aid kit and pulling out a large bandage.

When she puts it on my back, I groan in protest. "You're really doing that?"

"Did you want to mess up another shirt with your blood?"

"I don't have another shirt with me. This seems to be a recurring theme in my life—the ruination of shirts when we're together."

She seems to give that some thought. "Hmm. That's true. Maybe I need to keep some extra shirts around for you."

"Yeah, you do that, Mabel." I rise and toss the bloody one over my shoulder rather than pulling it back on. Why wear it when she seems to enjoy the shirtless view so much? I'm a nice guy after all. This is a nice thing to do.

She drops the supplies into her backpack, picks it up from the tiled floor, and heads to the door.

"All right. Are we doing this?" I ask as we leave the bathroom.

"You're saying yes?" It comes out as a squeak.

"I mean, talking about the bakery."

"Yes. Of course. Let's talk about the bakery and check out the rest of the firehouse. Like the kitchen." She sounds as if she's about to explore a quaint alleyway in Paris with possible treasures around every corner.

"Lead the way through your inheritance," I say, as we head past the mirrored dressing room toward the kitchen. Cabinets loom high above the appliances, so that's a plus—lots of work-space and storage.

Mabel stops in front of one of the two industrial-sized ovens, running a hand across the top with a happy sigh. "I could see this as my bakery." Then she quickly corrects herself. "Ours."

But that's the thing I don't get. "Mabel, why do you want to start a bakery with me?"

She opens the oven and inspects it. "Why not?"

I laugh, but the sound is quickly snuffed out by...reality. "That hardly seems like a reason."

"Your monkey bread was good," she says with a mischievous grin, but it fades too quickly.

"And you tried it *after* you and Theo asked me," I press.

"I know, but I've had your baking before."

"Right, but that doesn't answer the question."

She's quiet for several thoughtful seconds. When she speaks, her voice is pensive and vulnerable. "I think some things just happen at the right time. My grandmother always said *If not now, when*?"

Those are powerful words, and I understand why they'd drive *her* to act. But even so, she's talking about huge changes. "So that's why you decided to turn a firehouse into a bakery when you hadn't even planned on returning to Cozy Valley?"

"Yes. I don't want to move here. I love the city, and I still want to open a bakery there, but I have *this* now, and it's a place to start. I've been wanting to open a bakery since I went to college. It was always my dream."

"You think that adage applies to us going into business too?"

"Sure. I think that's the point of the saying. Take a chance and all."

But it's not that simple. I gesture from her to me. "It's a big deal going into business. Sure, some of the work is done. But there's so much more to do." I leave the kitchen, motioning for her to join me as we return to the garage area. "We'd need a glass garage door for natural light and street visibility. The cool kind you see in trendy restaurants in Brooklyn." I gesture to where the counter would have to be. "We'd need to buy display cases, and of course, we'd have to paint the exterior bricks some pretty, frothy, bakery color. Something...you know, floofy. We'd need to paint the inside too."

I pace toward the garage door, sweeping my hand across the space. "We'd need tables and chairs and merch. We'd need to plan the offerings. Are we a cupcake bakery, Mabel? Are we doing cake and cookies and brownies? What about bread? That's a whole other area, and one I'm just not that into. And will there be muffins? That's a deal breaker for me. I hate muffins. Then there's the issue of nuts. Some people hate nuts, though I'm not sure I could ever get along with such a monster. Pecans are proof of life."

And I shut up because she's smiling at me. A pleased, wide, closed-mouth grin.

"What's that for?"

"You can see it," she says, delighted with her *gotcha*. "The bakery."

Maybe, but I'm not ready to admit that out loud. "I'm just saying it needs a lot of work."

"But you can see it turning into a bakery. You can picture it. You just listed off *nearly everything*. You've clearly mapped this all out. I know you wanted to wait till you retired, but Corbin..." She pauses, twisting her fingers together. "I need the help. I can't afford it all, but this place is amazing, and it landed in my lap. I can use it to keep my existing business going, and I can run everything from here. I'll handle things, and you don't have to do much. Just benefit from it and, like my grandmother used to say, you won't know unless you try."

She presses her hands together in a plea.

Dammit, she's pulling on my heartstrings. But I can't make this choice just because I want to help. So, I'm not sure why the next thing out of my mouth is: "I don't like pumpkin stuff."

Tossing back her head, Mabel laughs. "But I do. I can make the pumpkin things, and I won't make you taste-test them. And I hate peanut butter. Most nuts actually."

I sneer. "How is that possible?"

"Peanut butter tastes like cardboard."

"That makes no sense."

"But see, this makes perfect sense. I can be the pumpkin taste-tester, and you can be the nut taste-tester." Again, she has a solution to every problem I fling at her. "Also, I can't stand muffins either, so they will never be on the menu. I just want it to be full of really great sweet treats that satisfy cravings. So it sounds like we're kind of on the same page." She flashes me another flirty, dirty, hopeful grin that's working its magic on me. "Are you in?"

Am I? This is a huge leap. "Mabel, we might screw this whole thing up. Then what?"

"We act like adults," she says, giving a simple and real answer. "We handle it like grown-ups. And we give ourselves a time limit."

"I gave myself a year to make a success of this or I'll go corporate."

I can hear the clear desperation in her tone.

She steps closer; she's a foot away now.

"And look," she continues, "I have a lot of experience making and selling baked goods. I've studied the bakery business too. I can tell you the best bakeries in any city. Plus, I take amazing pictures of what I make. My grandmother taught me some of the basics of photography, but I taught myself food photography. I know what's pretty, what looks good, and what looks mouth-watering in a photo. I can hustle like nobody's business. I can market my ass off on social media."

"I can't do any of that stuff. Nor do I want to," I admit.

That seems to drive her on, the simpatico-ness of this all. "I can help you learn what it takes, for when you want to run your own bakery someday. And I can keep growing my brand and then hopefully open a bakery in the city." She takes a beat, then offers a hopeful smile. "I think we'd make a good team."

I can't believe I'm seriously weighing this wild, crazy, outrageous idea of going into business with her.

I have plans. I have a timeline. I've even devised names for my one-day bakery. But I'm also shit at designing the way bakeries have to look these days. And I know, I fucking know, how important the whole pink, pretty décor thing is to these kinds of businesses.

But that's just not something a color-blind guy can pull off without a lot of help.

My mind keeps spinning as I think of how Mom never pulled the trigger when she could. How she regretted that. How she wished she'd taken the chance. My chest tightens at the memory of her hands, of the tremors, of the way she couldn't work a mixer in the end. I turn away from Mabel, taking in this space one more time, the way it'll look with natural light streaming in through the garage windows, the kitschiness of the polished fire pole, the roominess of it all. I try to see it through my mom's eyes.

She would have loved this place.

There's just one little issue. Or, maybe one big issue.

Here goes nothing.

I turn to Mabel. "I have one condition."

"What is it?"

"My dream isn't simply to finance a bakery. If that was my dream, I would have done that already. I want to help run one. I can't be around every day, of course, with travel, games, and parenting. But when I can, I'd like to try my hand at the mixer. The counter. The oven."

I'm practically holding my breath, but Mabel beams, like I've made her entire year. "Let's open it in a month and a half."

"Why the hell not? Deal."

"Deal." She pauses. "I have one condition too." She points at my bare chest. "Can you wear a shirt on the regular? That's awfully distracting."

I smirk. "We'll see, Mabel. We'll see."

9

DEATH BY UNDERWIRE

Mabel's Accidental Texts to Corbin

Mabel: Hey Alexa, set a reminder to text Corbin.

Mabel: No, set a reminder to text Corbin about the bakery's name.

Mabel: He's going to die when he hears the name I have.

Mabel: And my plan.

Mabel: Set a reminder to tell him it's a little naughty. The name, that is.

Mabel: And funny.

Mabel: And brilliant.

Mabel: Hey Alexa, what's the ideal color scheme for a bakery?

Alexa: Pink and white.

Mabel: Yep, I knew that.

Mabel: Tell Corbin the bakery must be pink.

Mabel: I don't care if he wants to fight me on it. I will die on a pink hill. He can peel my pink ass off the pink hill.

Mabel: Hey Alexa, is pink the greatest color ever?

Alexa: Pink is a popular color associated with sweetness, romance and—

Mabel: Stop Alexa. Pink is the greatest.

Mabel: Hey Alexa, make a note to suggest to Corbin that we don't want to tell everyone in town about the bakery just yet. Let's wait until we have a more concrete opening date. Also, make a to-do item to discuss more menu items with Corbin. And my ideas for cookies. With vegan marshmallows.

Mabel: Wait, does he know that marshmallows are made from beef gelatin? Gross. We are not serving anything with marshmallows unless they're vegan.

Mabel: Also, make a note to discuss my brilliant idea with him to make dog cookies and all proceeds from them go to the local rescue. And make a to-do item to email the garage door company. The windows are going to be so pretty with our pink-and-white sign.

Mabel: Also remind me to buy new bras tomorrow. These underwires are stabbing me to death.

Corbin: Mabel, I think your phone just picked up you talking to yourself.

Mabel: Oh shit! Oh fuck. Noooooo…it didn't.

Corbin: Yes. It did. Also, pink works for me. All in with the dog cookies and the donation. And I will peel you off a pink hill, but don't die from the underwire.

Mabel: This is so embarrassing.

Corbin: It's not. I like seeing how your brain works. Also, what's this naughty bakery name?

10

—

KNIGHTY NIGHT

CORBIN

I should feel bad that my daughter sees herself as my manager. But I don't. She took it upon herself, just like she's taking it upon herself right now to review our calendars as we walk from her middle school toward The Embarcadero.

"Let's see," she says, studying her phone as we wait at a light. The bay glitters on the other side of the waterfront, with shadows from the Bay Bridge shimmering across the calm waters. "There's an afternoon practice today. I'll work on my homework with Jessica and Violet at the arena. But I also took the liberty of making a punch list for everything you need to accomplish over the next five weeks."

I stifle a smile as I reach for her hand when the crosswalk light changes. The Cozy Valley Middle School was an option, but the STEM program at this school in the city is unbeatable, and Charlotte's already decided she wants to be a veterinarian. She's eager to take as many science classes as possible. Since she's a few blocks from the arena, that also means it's "bring your daughter to work day" pretty often, and you won't see me complaining.

"Okay, what's on this list?" I ask, hoisting her backpack

higher on my shoulder as we walk along the waterfront, the salty air floating past us as we near the Ferry Building.

She sticks her tongue out in concentration, scrolling through some app on her phone that I don't even recognize. She stops at a color-coded schedule labeled *Timeline*. Bars stretch across the screen, but they blur together, mostly looking like blue and mustard to me.

"Oh, wait, let me switch." She changes the bars to patterns instead of colors, like diagonal stripes and cross-hatches. It's thoughtful, the way she's figured out tips so that I can see things better, but I don't want her to feel like she has to take care of me. It's my job to look out for her.

"You don't have to do that," I say. "I can read the words on each bar. See? Painting, display cases, menus—"

"You can read, Dad. Well done." Charlotte shoots me a look. "But I can change them to make it easier for you. So why wouldn't I?"

A kernel of guilt wiggles through me that she's done this on her own. Sure, I'm organized, so on the one hand, it's like father, like daughter. But is she growing up too fast? It's one thing for her to use her chip-off-the-old-block organizational skills to manage her homework; it's another to use them to manage me. And evidently, the bakery.

"You made a timeline for the bakery?" I ask as I get a good look at her screen.

She gives me a stare that I translate as *Obviously*. "How else would you know what you need to do and when you need to do it? I keep our calendar. It's good training for me. Organization is important for any scientist."

She's not wrong, and I suppose I don't need to feel guilty. Independence is a good thing, right? Right.

"Okay, hit me," I say as my kid reviews the schedule as we walk past the statue of a giant, fearsome fox outside our arena.

"And then the garage doors will be installed," she says.

The sound of sneakers slapping against stone grows louder. Miller jogs up beside us, barreling right into the conversation like he belongs there—that's the goalie's style. He's a Golden Retriever off the ice, a Pit Bull on it. "You getting a new garage? Please tell me we're gonna put a home theater in it, with a big screen and a popcorn machine."

She scrunches her brow, no doubt picturing the suggestion. "That's not a bad idea. Maybe we should do our garage too, Dad? A movie theater would be fun for my documentaries."

Miller chuckles. "Of course that's what you want to watch."

I ruffle Charlotte's hair. "And we like that."

"I know. Trust me, I wish Hayden wanted to watch, I dunno, science docs," Miller adds, a note of longing in his voice as he talks about the teenage brother he's been raising.

As we near the main doors to the arena, Charlotte turns to my teammate, waggling her phone. "You can tell Hayden to text me if he needs any help organizing sessions with his band."

Miller gives her a *don't go there* look. "You are *not* gonna encourage my little brother to spend even more time *shredding* his guitar."

He turns to Charlotte and rubs his hands. "So, is it a movie theater? I might come over and catch up on some thrillers."

"By all means, make yourself at home," I say dryly, though of course Miller needs no encouragement on that front. He's like Seven. Sometimes he appears on my doorstep at mealtime. Or snack time. Or movie time.

Charlotte laughs, shaking her head. "No, the garage is for the bakery my dad is opening."

Miller jerks his gaze to me, eyes wide and full of questions. "Well, this just got real interesting."

I wince, scratching my jaw. Yeah, I haven't told my friends. Not sure why. Maybe because it still feels personal? Because there's a part of me that wonders if they can detect that I have a thing for Mabel? Or because I worry they'll say I'm sucking up to the acting GM by helping his sister? It could be all of the above.

Charlotte purses her lips. "Oops. You haven't told your teammates yet? You're going to have to let me know about these things for my task management list, Dad. I have them down to help us with the display case set-up and moving furniture and tables in."

Miller's stare sharpens. "Spill."

* * *

Thankfully, Coach Ahmed is working us hard on skating drills. Explosive starts, quick turns, and never-ending sprints. You can't talk during drills this intense or, honestly, think about much either. That's good, since I don't want to do a damn thing but play at the top of my game while I still can, and that means I need to do better this year than I ever have before. I race past the blue line, stick in hand, legs burning, blades scraping across the ice.

The clatter of sticks on the slick surface rebounds from the boards as we fly again and again till Coach blows the whistle. Everyone snaps their gazes to the commanding man leaning against the glass, who's been our coach for the last several years. Coach Ahmed played in the pros too, all the more impressive since he was born in Egypt, which isn't exactly a hotbed for hockey. But his family moved to Canada when he was six or seven, so he took up the Canadian national pastime, and the rest is history.

"All right, men. Anyone in the mood to score some goals?"

Not sure if he's being ironic, since we've been struggling in that area, or just trying to keep things light. Either way, Miller grunts from the net, "Like I'd let them."

"It's shooting practice, Lockwood," Coach calls out to Miller. No one ever uses first names on the ice.

Miller just shrugs as he guards the net, helmet covering his face, that smile long gone. He's stone now as he shifts back and forth in front of the net—he'd consider it rude to ever let a goal in. But we set up in two lines, taking turns passing and then shooting. Miller's good, one of the top goalies in the game, and I'd really like to make his job easier by putting more points on the board when we play against opponents, but right now I'd like to score on him.

I try to fake him out, feinting to the left, but he tracks me with those unflinching eyes, and when I flick a wrist shot toward an opening, he lunges and sends it right back out.

He does it again and again and fucking yet again.

But the next time I'm ferrying the puck down the ice, I move to the left like I'm going to snap in another wrist shot, only I switch it up at the last second...with a backhand.

And, yes!

It slides past him, lodging in the twine. I can actually hear him growl, then curse himself.

It's just a goal in practice.

It's meaningless, ultimately.

But it's a fucking ray of hope compared to how the last few games have gone.

Maybe it's a reminder, too, that sometimes I need to do things a little differently.

We head down the tunnel when practice ends. Charlotte will still be working diligently in the kids' lounge, which is what she and some of the other players' kids have dubbed the players' lounge. That means I guess I'd better tell the guys about my...gulp...bakery.

Why the fuck am I so nervous about this? Miller already knows, since I had to tell him the details after Charlotte spilled the beans. And my friends know I kick ass in the baking department. Hell, I've gone to their homes and saved them when they needed to make pies for Thanksgiving, cakes for Mother's Day, or Valentine's Day goodies for their spouses or partners.

But maybe that's how to approach this—I've helped others with my whisk-and-apron skills. Now I'm actually doing this for myself. Marketing myself.

The rest of the team filters down the tunnel, and I hang back with my closest friends. We make our way along the cavernous corridor, skates clunking against the floor, and I draw a big breath, bracing myself to share personal shit. But then Miller claps my shoulder and flashes his signature grin. "Guess what, boys? Knighty Night has some big news for us."

I can't stand that nickname, which is why he uses it now and then. To poke the bear. His favorite pastime.

"You finally learned how to use social media, Dad?" Lake asks, with an overly earnest tilt of his head, his shoulder-length hair falling in a sweaty mess around his face.

"Yes, and I figured out how to dial on a rotary phone too."

"Sweet. I always had faith in you," he retorts.

Miller's practically bouncing on his skates, a kid at Christmas, eyes glinting. "Guys, this news is good."

Riggs furrows his brow, studying me intently with nearly black eyes. Then he nods, like he's figured it out. "We're letting Lake into the club?"

I groan, scrubbing a hand down the back of my neck, then give Riggs a look. "It's not a club. You know it's not a club, Decker," I say, using Riggs's last name.

Riggs whirls around. "And if it's big news, my money is on you finally dating someone."

I scoff.

The irony. His guess hits uncomfortably close to something I almost did. Which means it's time to get the truth out. No more joking and no more delays. I stop outside the locker room and dive off the cliff.

"I'm opening a bakery. Well, I'm investing in it, and I'm also helping out. With Mabel Llewelyn, Theo's sister." Fuck, those words sound weird coming out of my throat, like someone else is saying them. But it's not just how this new project might look that's tripping me up. It's how it might go down. It could bomb, and I don't like failing.

There's no guarantee that this bakery will succeed. In fact, the odds are probably against us. That's why I feel like I'm standing here, peeling off a layer of skin.

But Riggs shoots me a *proud of you* smile, tugs off a glove, and offers me a fist for knocking. "Right on. It's about fucking time."

And I did not expect that—support.

"Right?" Miller says, enthused, coming up behind me and patting my shoulders. "I'm stoked."

"I'm hungry. And I really want cupcakes now," Lake adds. Then he shifts gears and gives me a serious nod. "But also... good on you, man."

Holy shit. They're not mocking me. They're not giving me a hard time about working with Mabel either. "Thanks, guys. Appreciate it."

"Anytime," Miller says, then steers me into the locker room, where some of our D-men are already changing out of their practice gear. "And don't worry. When no one wants to see your ugly face on the marketing materials, you can always use me."

He gives some sort of over-the-top smoldering look.

I have no choice but to pretend to gag. "No one will want to eat there, then."

"Wait...we eat for free, right?" Miller asks, always looking for an angle.

"You make millions. You don't need to eat for free," I say.

"And yet, restaurants are always wanting to give athletes free meals. Especially me since I'm so pretty."

"Pretty full of yourself," Ivan mutters from his stall as he unlaces his skates. Like a good D-man, he sails in and out of conversations like they're plays on the ice, never missing a beat.

"Got that right," Riggs says, peeling off his practice jersey, pausing in front of his stall. "But I'm with Pretty Boy here. You'll do us a solid and not charge, right?"

"No. I'll charge you all double."

"That's fair," Ivan says with a wry wink as he snaps on his Gucci watch. The dude loves his designer duds.

I turn around and change out of my gear, grateful that's done.

When I'm showered and back in jeans and, of course, a gray T-shirt, I head out. Riggs and Miller catch up with me in the corridor. Riggs gives me a chin nod, then scrubs a hand across his dark beard. "Seriously though. If you need help lifting heavy shit or whatever, hit me up. Since we all know I can bench more than anyone."

"Keep telling yourself that," I say, since I'm seriously strong.

"So that's a no," Riggs says dryly.

I heave a sigh. "I'd love the help."

"Besides, Charlotte already booked us," Miller says to Riggs. But then, like something just occurred to him, Miller turns his gaze to me. "Dude. This is a sneaky-ass way to make sure Theo doesn't trade you in your final years. Going into business with his sister."

"Oh shit. You're an evil genius," Riggs says.

"Exactly. I'm sucking up to the acting GM," I say, mostly to steer the conversation away from the acting GM's sister.

But to no avail. Riggs wiggles a brow. "Or maybe he's trying to get closer to the woman he wanted to see in the baking contest. Haven't seen you this into someone in...a long-ass time."

Fuck me. This is the problem when you work with people who are good at reading other people. They can see through you. And in this case, they can see there's something different about Mabel.

"It's just a good investment. That's all," I say, then head toward the kids' lounge, leaving that conversation behind me.

I don't need either of them getting wind of these feelings I have for Mabel. It would only be a matter of time before word circulated around the organization and right back to Theo. I shudder at the thought of how he'd react. He hates everyone who's ever dated his sister, and the depth of his disdain has only ramped up since his longtime girlfriend split and moved to Tokyo a couple years ago.

He'd probably hate me even more now that I'm also Mabel's brand-new business partner. Especially since I'm very much looking forward to seeing her tomorrow.

And I'm wondering if she'll be wearing a new bra.

* * *

That night, as I do a light stretch in my home gym once Charlotte's in bed, my thoughts are entirely too tangled up. There's so much to do to open a business. I knew that. Of course, I knew that. But still, one thing smashes into another like bumper cars in my head.

What to make.

How many items to offer.

What people want the most.

What will surprise them.

I'm not sure I have any answers after I finish my hamstring stretches on the foam roller. I leave the gym and head to the kitchen on autopilot, the faint counter lights guiding me there while the fridge emits a welcoming hum.

I breathe a little easier when I reach the kitchen island. This room feels like it has a heartbeat and has been a safe space ever since my mom taught me to bake and cook. I never knew my father; he was a no-name, one-time kind of guy, and that's fine with me. Growing up, it was just Mom and me baking until she met Ray, my stepdad, when I was ten or eleven. After that, it was often the three of us in the kitchen, the one place where I stopped thinking only about hockey, stopped running plays, stopped picturing wrist shots, stopped imagining how to make them better.

It was relaxing.

Tonight, I don't need to relax. I do need to work through some of these ideas though. I lean on the counter and click on the tablet I keep there. I swipe open my recipe app, jotting down some notes.

Maybe something with pretzels? The salty snack is a secret weapon when it comes to baked goods. Mix it with chocolate, and it's heaven on a plate. I note a few more ideas, then close the tablet, ready to hit the hay.

Except...

I check the time. It's earlyish.

Ah, hell. Why not?

I open the pantry and grab the ingredients, then find a

playlist on my phone that's usually better suited for a gym. But the workout music keeps my rhythm as I mix and measure, whisk and bake.

Finally, my mind settles as I finish making a sweet and salty bar with a graham cracker crust and salty pretzels, topped with bittersweet chocolate chips and a sprinkle of sea salt.

I take a bite, and damn. This is fucking good. So good, it'd be a sin to keep them to myself.

I find a delivery service and place an order for pick-up in the morning. Can't hurt for my business partner to taste these too.

11

SWEET EDGING
MABEL

I read the note again. It's one sentence, but the fact that it's a
letter makes my heart beat faster than I want it to.

Dear Mabel,

You seem like a salty and a sweet.

Corbin

I run my finger over the sentence, even though it's typed out
on a sheet of white paper. But it's signed by him in ink. I
don't know why this delights me so much. Maybe because no
man has ever sent me gifts of food. Dax certainly never did.
Nor did other guys I dated. *Maybe* I got flowers once in a
while, and hey, flowers are nice, so I'm not dissing them. But
what's even nicer than flowers? A personalized, homemade
gift.

Not that Corbin and I are dating. Of course we're not dating. But even so, his words feel true, and I feel understood.

I *am* both salty and sweet.

I reach into the Tupperware container that a delivery service dropped off five minutes ago, with the note on top.

I take a bite of the bar, and I know two things instantly.

That we must serve it, and how we'll present it—with a heart-shaped piece of paper that says *You're My Salty and My Sweet.*

I open the design software on my phone and whip up a simple graphic, which I send to him.

Mabel: What do you think?

Corbin: And here I was just hoping you'd like the taste.

Mabel: I do. I really do. What do you think of the description? It's like a story for the item!

Corbin: I didn't realize baked goods needed a name or a story.

Mabel: Every baked good needs both, but especially a story.

Corbin: Speaking of names, are you ever going to tell me the name of the bakery?

Mabel: Soon.

This is presumptuous. This is so presumptuous. But *I'm* presuming he'll like my potential name. Still, I'm having too much fun teasing the reveal. So as I finish getting ready to

meet him, twisting my hair into my lucky clip in the bathroom, I dictate another text.

Mabel: I know I left you hanging with the name.

Corbin: Yes. You did. I was…hung.

Mabel: I see what you just did.

Corbin: What did I do, Mabel?

Mabel: You know what you did. And all I'm going to say is you'll love this name. It suits you.

Corbin: Oh, it's The Hung Bakery? Cool.

Mabel: I don't think I would go to The Hung Bakery.

Corbin: You prefer…Rise to the Occasion?

Mabel: You're getting closer.

Corbin: Creamed and Frosted? The Hot Box? The Nibbler?

Mabel: Confirming you like all these names?

Corbin: I have an open mind, Mabel.

Mabel: I'll see you in an hour.

Corbin: I'll be there with a project schedule and a breakdown.

Mabel: A schedule?

Corbin: Yes, it's that thing where you keep track of your days and activities.

Mabel: You made one?

Corbin: My daughter did. Ergo, it's mine now. Also, at the risk of being serious, I suppose I just assumed you'd call it by the name you've been using: You Deserve a Treat?

Mabel: Maybe that can be its tagline?

Corbin: Bakeries have taglines now? Good to know.

Corbin: Also, you really like teasing, don't you?

As I'm grabbing my bag, my makeshift sign, and my computer —because I have a schedule too, thank you very much, even though it's in the form of a list, which, of course, is a second cousin to his much fancier schedule—I stop at the door, juggling keys and a phone as well.

I swing my gaze to the text exchange. Does *he* like teasing me? Seems like it. I'm a little desperate to confirm it.

Don't do it, Mabel. Really, don't do it.

I shouldn't answer the last text. I should leave him hanging like I've done before. I should edge him. Truly, I should.

But I don't like stopping.

Mabel: Do you though?

My pulse skitters. Something bubbles up inside me—the frothy sensation of flirting and all the goodness it brings with it.

Which leads me to the next thing I probably shouldn't do. Setting my stuff down, I race to the closet—not far away, since I live in a studio—yank it open and flick through my pickle-ball outfits. It's late October, but since it's San Francisco, that just means it's in the high sixties. I grab the black dress with the polo collar, strip off my jeans and top, and tug on the new outfit with its built-in sports bra.

And...suddenly everything's better.

After I pop on cute sneakers, I grab the matching jacket I picked up when Skylar and I went on one of our clothing trea-sure hunts. On my way back to the door, I snag my paddle.

Well, I *might* feel inspired to play. You never know. Then I tap one of Grandma's postcards that's tucked into the corner of the mirror by the door. This one has a line drawing of a sleeping cat and, under it, the caption: **I do what I want.**

On the back are Grandma's words. *Do what you want! Life is better that way, Mabel. Today, I'm floating down the river on an inner tube! What about you?*

I scan my reflection. "Well, Grams, I'm wearing what I want. This counts, right?"

I listen for her voice. Imagine her smile. Pretend I can hear her say, *Of course, doll.*

Then I add, for me, "Maybe it'll drive Corbin a little crazy."

As I hustle to my car, I keep checking the chat. But it's quiet. Dreadfully quiet. The whole drive up to Cozy Valley, he doesn't answer me.

* * *

I'm a little thrown off that Corbin hasn't responded to my question, but I tell myself it's no big deal as I pop into Rise and Grind. Nothing like a little caffeine to boost my morale. I head to the counter with my to-go cup and ask the bored-looking barista with a nose ring for a pour-over.

Her expression is blank. "What's that?"

She works in a coffee shop. Shouldn't she know? I'm about to answer her when the owner, a pale blonde with frizzy, eighties style hair, hustles to the counter and says to her employee, "Cassie, that's a slow-drip coffee method where you pour hot water over the grounds in a circular motion. I taught you that last week, hun." The owner—her name is Joni—snaps her gaze to me. "Well, Mabel! How the hell are you? I haven't seen you since..."

Since I made a complete ass of myself. "Yeah, it's been a while."

"Just saw your mom the other day. She didn't mention that you were coming up here."

I guess that's because I didn't mention it to her, even though I was in Cozy Valley yesterday, finally finishing that big wedding cookie order. Right under the wire. So I haven't had much time to see my parents or talk to them. "Oh well, you know, it's just been crazy busy."

"Of course. Animals to corral," she says with a wink, like it's an inside joke. "Cookies to make for them. I get it."

That's when I realize this is what I'm up against with my business here in Cozy Valley. People know me as the daughter of two prominent university professors. The ditzy daughter who publicly screwed up.

What was I thinking? That I could suddenly change the way they perceive me?

"That was a mistake," I say. Maybe it's best to own it.

"Of course, sweetheart," Joni says. "You were just doing

your thing. Like that time you tried to parallel park and ended up on Mrs. Henderson's lawn."

I wince at the reminder but don't bother to point out that I was learning to drive then, and who doesn't knock over a mailbox or two along the way?

Still, best I change the subject before this trip down Memory Lane drags up more of my past. "Anyway, how's everything going here? Shop looks great."

"It is great, but you know, I wanted to tell you your ex is a real wiener, and he can just kiss off."

And if I'd thought I was going to escape the *Romance Beach* incident, I just learned I was wrong about that too. "Thanks?"

"I mean, really. Some things you should keep to yourself. That man needs to learn to shut his trap. So what if you like to do things how you like to do things? And I swear I'll never use that meme," she says, and I wince again, knowing that somewhere out there, I'm a meme.

"Appreciate that," I say, wishing we could just move along.

"Honestly, I say we should name a sugar cookie after you. We can call it...*the Llama Lover*."

Oh shit. She sells cookies here, too, of course. Is she going to think we're competing with her? I'm not serving coffee though. I don't even want to learn how to make coffee. I want to send people here.

"What do you think about that?" Joni asks with wide eyes.

"That's something to think about," I say, avoiding a real answer.

Behind me, someone says, "I don't think we need to name cookies after Mabel."

I blink and turn around at the strong, confident voice of the man I've gone into business with.

"Hi," I say, and it's a little embarrassing that I'm kind of breathless as I roam my gaze up and down Corbin. He's wearing jeans and a dark blue shirt. He seems to like gray and dark blue. That's all I ever see him wear. He's not clean-shaven today. There's a few days' worth of stubble lining his jaw, and it's unfairly hot. Like him.

"But, Joni, if you need a new cookie supplier, I might have someone for you in a few weeks," he adds, and holy shit, I could kiss him.

Her eyes sparkle. "I've been looking for one! I've had to get these at the local supermarket," she whispers, pointing to the cabinet.

"I'll be back. We'll talk. For now, I'll take a drip coffee. And whatever Mabel wants." He taps his phone at the register and pays for our drinks before I can even grab my device from my back pocket.

"Of course," she says brightly to him, while I mouth a *thank you*. Joni keeps talking as she takes Corbin's to-go cup. "And how is your sweet little girl doing?"

"She's great. I'll pick her up from school later."

"Such a smarty-pants. And did I hear that there's something happening down at the old firehouse?"

Yep, small towns have long memories and a lot of interest in everything.

"Did you now? Whatever did you hear?" Corbin asks evenly.

I keep a straight face, enjoying how he's pretending he doesn't know a thing about it.

"Just that there's something happening there. Maybe a new fire station? I do love me a firefighter." She wiggles her brows.

He sighs heavily. "A hockey player just can't compete."

Joni laughs. "Well, hun, there's something about a man who can save both you and your cat." Then she turns to me. "Am I right?"

"Yes," I reply, but only because I'm not sure what I'm supposed to say. I'm on the outside here. They're insiders.

A few minutes later, we leave the coffee shop with our drinks. "Thanks for the coffee and the save," I say to Corbin, but it comes out a little listless because that interaction reminded me that people here see me a certain way. It's not like the townspeople hate me. It's not like I have a *bad* reputation. But I definitely have a reputation for being...scatterbrained. I hate that.

"Anytime," he says, then looks me over with avid curiosity, gesturing to my outfit. "Is this for the fashion, or is there a game later?"

I'd nearly forgotten my intention when I put on this dress. To tease him. To amuse him. To *entertain* him. But now that I'm wearing this very short dress—even though yes, cute athletic dresses with under shorts and sports bras can and should be worn everywhere—I feel even more like the tra-la-la girl that people think I am. "Yeah, I think I am going to play later," I say with more gravitas than usual. "With some of my friends."

"Cool."

"Do you play?"

He takes a drink of his coffee, then meets my gaze. "I have, yes. Worked on it with my strength and conditioning coach. It's good for hand-eye coordination, agility, and so on."

Well, now I feel even fluffier, like I'm not playing pickleball for the right reasons. I just mutter *cool* right back to him.

We're quiet for a beat as we walk past a bookstore called The Meet Cute, where a blonde Chihuahua mix with a frosty face lounges on a neon pink chair in the window. Because it's easier to talk about the bakery than the way I feel, I point to the chair. "That shade is perfect."

He swings his gaze to the window, squinting at it, then gives a one-shouldered shrug.

"We could use it in the signage, maybe? Or somewhere inside? What do you think?"

"Sure," he says, but it sounds entirely noncommittal.

Maybe I embarrass him too? I hope not. If so, why would he have gone into business with me? I chew on that and on the inside of my lip as we pass a yarn shop and then a small gallery displaying local art.

But it turns out this woe-is-me space is no fun, so I focus on him instead. "That was a good idea you had in the coffee shop. Becoming her cookie supplier. I love how you teased her a little bit too."

"Thanks. Hopefully, the teasing will pay off."

He exhales thoughtfully, like something's on his mind. "Did that bother you? Back there? What she said?"

"Did it bother *you*?" I ask, bracing myself for the answer.

He jerks his head back, furrowing his brow. "Yes, but only because it looked like you'd rather be anyplace else when she said it."

Oh. Wow. He's so protective. "You really like saving the day."

"It's not that. It's that you told me you didn't want to open a bakery here because of the incident. I figured you didn't need to keep revisiting it."

My heart squeezes from his kindness, but the question I didn't want to ask remains on the tip of my tongue. Better now than never. Even though my gut twists, I ask, "You don't think I'm a joke, do you?"

"God, no. I wouldn't go into business with you if I did."

"Oh, good."

"But it bothered you. What she said."

I can hear his unasked question. *Why?*

I could blow it off. I could shrug and make that moment seem like no big deal. But I've already opened this topic, and he's answered me in such a caring tone that I find myself wanting to share the truth.

"It's just that hardly anyone takes me seriously," I say, and I keep the rest to myself—*which is kind of how my family has treated me my whole life.*

He sips his coffee, as if he's considering my comment. "I take you seriously."

I blink, surprised, and I'm not sure why. "Yeah?"

"I do," he says. "I mean, I did deposit a big sum of money in our joint checking account."

"That was really nice to see. All those zeroes."

"Those zeroes were very serious," he says.

"They were. And I like serious zeroes."

He smiles, but not for long. His thoughtful green-eyed gaze holds mine. "I believe in you."

My heart squeezes. "Thank you." That means more to me than I can express right now. "I appreciate that."

"You're welcome. But I'm sorry you feel that others don't. Is that why you don't come here a lot?"

"That's probably it. But I suppose it's silly," I say, waving a hand, like I can dismiss my strange relationship with Cozy Valley. "So what if I amuse the town."

"Exactly, Mabel. Let them laugh."

I stop at the street corner outside a boutique called Reprise that sells secondhand clothes and consider what he just said—giving myself permission not to care. "Maybe you're right."

He wiggles an eyebrow. "I usually am." Then he licks his lips and says, like he has all the time in the world, "And to answer your earlier question...*yes.*"

As we turn onto Holly Springs, his answer to my last text

hangs in the air. Yes, he likes teasing me too. "Thanks again for wearing a shirt." I pause, lift an eyebrow. "*I think.*"

He tugs at the fabric. "You're welcome. *I think.*"

Then he gives me a long once-over. "You don't really have a game later, do you?"

My lips twitch. "I might."

"Hopefully you got that new bra you wanted. I wouldn't want you to have to play pickleball with an underwire stabbing you to death."

I square my shoulders, which has the effect of lifting my boobs just so. "No underwire today. It has a built-in bra."

His lips part. His eyes turn a little glassy. "So...no bra?" It sounds like he's swallowed gravel.

"Correct," I say.

If this is flirting with your business partner, I'm going to need to be real careful around Corbin. Because I like the way bubbles are flowing through me right now. I like them the way I like cookies.

I almost always want more.

* * *

"Close your eyes," I tell him.

"Really?"

"Yes, really."

Corbin sighs but relents, shutting his eyes outside the firehouse garage door. I unzip my backpack and grab a white poster board where I've mocked up the name, and I slap it against the door.

For a few seconds, doubts bombard my brain. Am I just barreling forward, my way or bust? Is this even how you partner with someone? Shoot. It's not. You don't say, *I came up with the name, take it or leave it.*

"You can say no," I say earnestly. "I swear, I won't be upset. We can do a whole brainstorming session."

"Mabel, can I open my eyes now?"

"Since you asked nicely."

He opens them, cocks his head, and reads the sign. "You were right. It's naughty."

I twist my fingers together. "And?"

He steps closer, inspects the name again, and looks me over. "So I can say no?"

"Of course," I say, trying not to let on how much I hope he'll say yes.

"I can veto this or anything else? Like, say you wanted to serve oatmeal raisin cookies."

"Corbin," I press him.

"Oh, sorry, I thought you liked edging," he says, but it's more like he drawls it. He's taking his time with his words, like he's taking his time with me. He gives me a sexy, lazy smile. My stomach flips, and my thighs ache, and I'm jumping ten steps ahead to what would have happened in the trailer if he'd pressed me against the door and satisfied all my cravings.

"I do," I say, my voice huskier than it should be.

"Good," he says, then steps right next to me, so close I can smell his aftershave. The scent of campfire and a summer lake teases my nose. I try not to inhale it, but I'm a sneaky little thief, and I lift my face just enough to catch a second hint of it.

My chest warms.

And my gaze stays locked on this man as he traces the words I'd written in bright pink script. Slowly, teasingly, he says each letter like he's tasting it the way he tasted frosting on my cheek last week.

When he's done, he turns his face to me. "I like...Afternoon Delight."

And I'm so hot and bothered it takes me a second or ten

before I process the fact that he likes my naughty bakery name.

"Really?"

"I really do," he says, then adds more soberly, "I'd tell you if I disagreed with you. Would you tell me?"

I snap out of my haze. "I would," I say, trying to clear the lust from my voice. "And we have a lot to talk about." I let go of the sign, grab my backpack, and pat it. "Like all the things we need to do."

"And where we'll donate proceeds from the dog cookies to," he says.

I smile. "Definitely the dog cookies. I have a list of everything else, and you have a project schedule. We should start with the interior. Finish priming the drywall, then paint it. And order the garage door. Well, after we pick one. I think we should do all that before we move in tables and any furniture and, of course, display cases."

I'm babbling, but it's working, reversing that spate of lust.

When I pause for breath, Corbin adds, "And we need to plan a menu."

"Right. Yes, duh." Maybe I can try to be okay with letting the town laugh at me, but right now it feels deserved. How could I forget that mission-critical detail?

"It sounds like we agree on one important thing," he says.

"The name?" I confirm.

"No. Mornings. Fuck mornings," he says.

"That should be our tagline."

He arches a brow. "Deal."

I offer a hand to shake, and I'd be lying if I said I didn't imagine him yanking me against him and running those strong hands down my dress, fiddling with the undershorts, and figuring out expertly how to maneuver everything off.

But at least I'm satisfied that we both contributed to the

store's identity—I supplied the name, and he devised a cheeky tagline.

We go inside, sit down on the floor, and take a stab at the menu. The *You're My Salty and My Sweet* is a must, of course. So is lemon shortbread, one of his favorites. Orange habanero cookies, a trademark of mine, along with the pistachio ones too. Seven-layer bars, with and without nuts, Corbin adds.

I stare at the ceiling for a minute, falling into the memory of baking a cake for my grandma's seventieth birthday. Fresh strawberries and whipped cream, her favorite. "In the summer, we should make a strawberry cake."

He holds my gaze for a few seconds, head tilted, a flicker in his eyes that seems to say he likes that image of us being open in the summer, serving cake.

We finish the rough draft of the menu, then plot our next steps in getting this dream off the ground. I'd like to say I'm being all adult and businessy as we work. That I don't think once about rubbing up against him, but that'd be a lie.

12

THE DAY I LOVED SWEAT

MABEL

Divide and conquer.

That's the plan. As Corbin tackles the garage door ordering—fine by me, since he has lots of opinions on that—I tackle paint picking.

I enlist my interior designer friend, Skylar, to help me out, along with Remy, my glass-all-full friend, who's surprisingly opinionated when it comes to paint chips. She works for the hockey team, handling community relations, but not full-time, so she's been able to join us in checking out furniture and baking equipment.

And right now, we're at the paint shop she likes in the Dogpatch District in the city, and Remy holds up a sample the color of Pepto-Bismol, mincing no words. "This makes me want to hurl."

"Next," I agree, and grab a soft mauve shade.

"Nope." Skylar shakes her head, her red hair swishing. "That color can't decide where it wants to go for dinner."

I tuck it back into its paint-chip home, then grab another. "This?"

"It looks like bubble gum," Remy says, as if that disappoints her.

"It's called Bubble Gum," I point out, reading the name on the card.

She taps her chin. "I don't like bubble gum."

"You are so picky," I say.

"Which is exactly how I found Jameson," Remy says proudly, adjusting the messy bun that holds her lush, chestnut hair. "By being picky."

"I thought you found him because he works at the arena too?" I have to give her a hard time, of course.

"Among other factors. And I was picky when he said he'd seen me several times walking past his craft cocktail bar and did I want to finally go out with him," she says.

"You *should* be picky when it comes to craft cocktails and dating," Skylar says, "and also to the colors you're going to paint your new business." She leans closer to the shelf and studies the paint chips, then hums in concern. "Actually, these are all a nope." I don't have time to ask why before she whips out her phone and quickly looks something up. "The brand's not cruelty-free. I just checked."

"Oh, thank you," I say, genuinely grateful she thought of that. She's an eco-friendly designer and tries to source secondhand, recycled, and ethically made items. "I hadn't thought of that with paint. But I'm glad you did."

"Happy to help." She peruses the information on her phone, then nods. "Let's try this brand." She points to a nearby sign, and we head that way, debating paint colors for another thirty minutes before we settle on a handful of finalists. Even though I'm ready to move full speed ahead with my favorite, I have to slow down. I'm not the only one making the decisions. It's a weird feeling for someone who's used to being utterly independent.

"I should show these to Corbin," I say, adjusting to my new reality of having a partner. "Along with pics of the furniture and stuff. I don't want him to feel like I've been making all the decisions."

"By all means," Remy says, and I fire off a text.

Mabel: I have fun things to show you! I can text you gobs of photos, or we can try to find time to meet? I'm in the city.

Corbin: Same here. Just arrived early at the arena. Charlotte's doing homework, and I have a game tonight.

Mabel: So, later, then?

Corbin: Come by now. I'm just working out.

Oh. That means I'll be talking to him while he's...lifting weights. I'm both thrilled and worried.

But mostly thrilled since having a hot business partner has its perks.

* * *

I walk past the fox statue outside the arena, heading to one of the main doors.

I've been here plenty of times. Having a big brother who was obsessed with sports law, sports management, and sports deals meant I was in and out of rinks and stadiums a lot growing up. Worked for me, because while Theo shouted at refs and umpires, I watched videos about food styling, detailing how to present food in the most visually appealing way and how to take photos of it too. I taught myself all about the color wheel and complementary hues, and what looks good together.

The arena, though, is the opposite of my cozy, pretty, sugary world. It's the opposite of the paint chips too. It's all dark purples and soft whites. It's mammoth ceilings and massive banners of men holding sticks and looking mean.

They're supposed to intimidate opponents and rally the fans.

When I open the door and stop at the security turnstile, I'm greeted by a thirty-foot-tall Corbin. There he is, hanging from the top of the arena, scowling, his helmet on, his gaze fixed on the puck as he flies down the ice with it. A captured moment in time—the hockey player dead-set on scoring. His jaw tight. His eyes dark. His attitude ferocious.

It's a little scary.

It's even scarier how turned on I am.

I tear my gaze from the banner and focus on the security guard, who's asking, "What can I do for you?"

"I'm Mabel Llewelyn. I'm here to see Corbin Knight." I wonder if I sound like a groupie, and I'm tempted to add, *I'm his new business partner.* But that sounds even more like an excuse made up to creep on him.

The man with the mustache scans his tablet, and a little frisson of excitement runs through me at the idea that I'm on some list. I feel a little like a star. Like a VIP.

Then my fantasies come crashing down when he says, "Nope, you're not on here."

"I'll just give him a quick call," I say, grabbing my phone. I ignore the sound of approaching footsteps on the polished floor until I hear my brother's voice.

"She's with me."

I turn, and of course, it's Theo right here, with his polished wingtips gleaming and a smile that says whatever he says goes.

The security guard nods deferentially. "Of course, Mr. Llewelyn," he says, then scans my bag and lets me through the turnstile.

I thank him, then look at my brother with a furrowed brow. "How did you know I was going to be here?"

His eyes darken. "Don't you know, Mabel? I know everything."

His tone is ominous, with zero mirth. For a few terrifying seconds, I believe this is his way of telling me he knows that I'm fantasizing about Corbin coming up behind me as I mix batter, wrapping his arms around me, then kissing the sugar off my neck and stripping me to nothing but an apron.

Holy shit, my fantasies are getting weirdly specific.

I perform an immediate mind-wipe. "If you know everything, then what's the temperature for baking an upside-down pineapple cake?"

But Theo laughs and says, "Actually, Corbin sent me up. I was walking past the weight room, and he told me he was going to meet you here. I said I'd get you since I don't want him to break his workout routine. But now that I've got you, how's everything going? Do I need to fuck him up for any reason?"

"Have you always been pugilistic?" I ask as we head down the escalator to the food concourse, where workers prep snacks for tonight's game.

He stops at a plant wall and gives me a serious look. "Yes."

I roll my eyes and motion for him to resume walking. "You don't need to fuck him up for any reason."

"Noted. But the offer stands. Also, I put in a call to the lawyers at *Romance Beach* and made it clear they shouldn't talk about you again."

"Seriously?"

"Yes," he says, pulling no punches. "Look, your ex is a prick. What the hell is his problem—talking shit about you on TV?"

"I've mostly tried to ignore it," I say, though it's not always easy to put my head in the sand about the fallout—losing a shot at a loan. Plus, I'm a meme.

"Good," he says. "You should. But that's why you've got me —so I can handle this for you, and they'll know better."

"What did they say? The lawyers?"

"They said...*Heard*."

I stand up straighter. "Oh. Really?" That's code for understood.

"Yep." He drapes an arm around me and pulls me in for a brotherly hug. "And next time, when you decide to date again, let me meet the guy first. Vet him. Make sure he's not an asshat. Or better yet, how about you take a timeout from dating and focus on this bakery, and let's launch the fuck out of it?"

Oooh, did my brother just expressly tell me not to date? Normally, nothing would make me want to date more, because I don't need or want his permission to see *anyone*. But...that's some solid advice. I wasn't even on the apps—I deleted them all after Dax dumped me—but this is a good reminder that it's best I focus on my love for sugar and butter, rather than on hearts and flutters.

I hold out a hand to shake. "It's a deal."

Theo blinks.

I might have fallen into a parallel universe because my brother never blinks. Metaphorically, of course.

"For real?" he asks.

I glance around like I'm checking for spies. "For real. And look, don't tell anyone that I agree with you. I need to give this business my all. I want Afternoon Delight to be a big, raging, ridiculous success. Romance is a distraction."

"Damn straight it is."

When we resume our pace, he tilts his head. "Afternoon Delight, huh? That's a little naughty."

"So's Sweet Cheeks. So's Hot Buns. So's Tease and Taste." I rattle off the names of some of the top bakeries in Los Angeles, Seattle, and Portland. "Know what all those bakeries have in common?"

"No, but I bet you're going to tell me."

"They're successful." We arrive at the double doors that lead to the personnel-only entrance. Theo slides his key card against a lock and swings the doors open. The corridor's mostly quiet, but up ahead, a man in a purple polo pushes a laundry bin down the hall.

As we pass a series of framed photos of the lineups over the years, my brother takes me to the weight room. Corbin's alone on a bench, doing preacher curls. Have his biceps always been so...big? So strong? So mouthwatering?

"Have fun," Theo says, then takes off.

Easier said than done. Corbin lowers the big barbell to the gym floor, lifts the hem of his T-shirt, and wipes the sweat off his brow.

Is this a test of my newfound resolve? If so, I'm failing.

I swallow and stare, my eyes darting across the expanse of fair skin, glistening and firm, but not in a picture-perfect, polished way. A bruise lives right under his pecs, that appendix scar dips in his abs, and a dark trail of hair travels down and disappears into his shorts.

And his muscles are just so...hard. And so muscly. And so—

"That work for you?"

Shit. I jerk my gaze up, meeting his eyes and rolling my

lips together. "Mm-hmm," I say, without opening my mouth. I have no idea what I'm agreeing to, but hey, I only told my brother I wouldn't date. I never said I wouldn't ogle his hot hockey-playing best friend.

"Great," he says, then grabs a towel and slings it over his shoulder.

I snap back to reality. "If you have a towel, why did you wipe your forehead on your T-shirt?"

His smile is wicked. "I did it for you, Mabel. I did it for you."

I let out a big breath. Corbin crosses the room and sets his water bottle right next to an exercise bike.

"We're going to talk while you're on the bike?" I ask as I follow.

"Are you worried I can't bike and talk?"

I shake my head. "No...I...I'm not." I'm just still stupidly flustered by that shirt-brow-move, and I kind of want to see it again.

He steps closer to me and sets a finger under my chin. "Are you sure? I did ask if you minded if we talked while I did cardio. I need to get my twenty minutes in."

Ahhhh. "Riiiiight," I say, dragging out the word as I nod. "You did. Of course you did. And I heard you perfectly. I knew exactly what you were saying. Twenty minutes. Who doesn't need to get twenty minutes of cardio in before an NHL game?"

He laughs, shaking his head as if he doesn't believe my lies. "You get me," he says, then hops up on the bike. At least he's still wearing his shirt.

The second he starts pedaling, he nods to me. "What do you want to show me?"

I am a woman on a mission. I will not be distracted by miles of glistening skin or how his thigh muscles show off with every pump of the pedals.

I hold up a finger, then reach into my bag to grab my tablet. "I took pictures, but I also have paint chips," I say, but when I raise my face, he's...shirtless again. "Corbin!"

"What?" he asks so innocently.

"I asked you not to—" I wave a hand, dismissing my prior request for him to keep his shirt on. "Never mind."

Taking a soldiering breath, I show him the pics on the tablet, and if I thought he smelled good before, that's nothing compared to how his lake-and-campfire scent mingles with the sweat of his workout.

I really should have talked to my friends before I agreed to this partnership. They'd have sat me down and made me face the reality of the fact that I want to bang my business partner. They'd have made me confront my newfound attraction to... sweat so I could be aware of the perils of this situation.

But right now, it's just me, and the photos. As Corbin pedals like the wind, I start with the furniture, showing him pics of the chairs and tables I've been scoping out, along with some baking equipment, including a few items we can snag used. He looks closely, checking each one, offering some suggestions, asking questions, then picking favorites from among mine.

"That was easy enough," I say with a smile.

"It was."

After I tuck the tablet away, I take out the paint chips, carefully setting them on the bike console, then I lean over, pointing to each one. "This is Morning Mist, but they should just call it salmon pink. This is I'm A Showgirl, but it's really neon, like the couch in the bookstore. Here is Cherry Blossom, like the cake I made at the romance fair. We've also got a pastel pink called Blush. Then this peachy one is Sunrise Mist."

The only sound in the room as he studies them is the

mechanical *whoosh* of the bike until he finally looks up. "The names don't really matter," he observes.

"Right, right. That's just marketing. I know I kind of bulldozed you with the name of the shop, but I want this to be collaborative." I speak with all the enthusiasm I feel for the process and for working with him. Which is...gobs.

"Sure," he says, with a nod, squinting at the squares of color as his breath comes faster. I steal a glance at the console. He's logged seventeen minutes already.

I'm glad he's studying the paint chips so carefully. It even feels as if he's spending as long staring at the colors here as Remy, Skylar, and I did at the paint store.

"Which one do you like best?" I ask.

He's pedaling hard as he looks back at me. "Honestly?"

"Yeah, of course."

"They all look gray to me. You pick," he says.

His tone is warm, friendly. But I'm a little lost. "Gray? Does that mean—"

He lets go of the bike handle to place a warm palm on my arm, as if he's reassuring me. "I'm color-blind. You should pick."

I part my lips to speak, then hesitate. I don't know what to say. I had no idea. Have I been railroading him about color too? Or teasing him unfairly? I replay our interactions, like last week in Cozy Valley when I asked about the couch and he seemed uninterested, then to the day I tended to his scratch and joked about the color. I feel a little queasy about that one. "Was that rude when I said *You're in love with your gray shirt*?"

"No," he says. "Gray matches everything. It's easier."

"True, and that's part of the beauty of gray. But I don't want to be a dick. When I asked about the neon pink couch, and when I said pink was the best color—have I been excluding you?" I really hope not, but I worry I might have been.

He laughs, shaking his head, his forehead shiny from sweat. "You would have had no way of knowing, except you noticed I wear a lot of gray."

"But you *can* see gray?"

He seesaws his hand. "Definitely. But some pinks often look gray, and some blues do too. I have red-green color-blindness, which means red and green look sort of brownish or dull and pale-ish. And a lot of blues kind of blend together."

"So a lot of colors are basically muted?"

He seems to give that a second or two of thought, then nods. "That's a fair way to put it."

My mind is a little blown. Of course, I'm aware of color-blindness, but I don't think I've known anyone who is color-blind, or thought hard about how it must be for them to navigate life, and traffic lights, and fashion, and sports.

"Does it affect how you play?"

Obviously, it doesn't. He's an elite athlete and has been for more than a decade. But still, I'm so curious how he works around it.

"When I was younger, yes, but only for practice when you're in different colors and you need to figure out who's on your team. But not now. The team knows, and I've asked the coaches to always put my line in white practice jerseys, so I never have to wonder who's on my line.

"White is easy for you to see?"

"Yes. It's a high contrast color."

"That's good then," I say.

He just shrugs, as if to say, *It is what it is.* And I suppose, it is for him.

"And with home and away jerseys always being light and dark, it's not an issue on the ice. Plus I know who to pass to and so on."

He explains it with the confidence he carries around with

him every day. I'm kind of amazed, especially since this is second nature to him. I want to understand him better.

"I'm sorry if I was barreling on about colors that didn't mean much to you." My mind races several steps ahead. "Is there something I should do differently when it comes to... design?"

He slows the pedaling, his chest rising and falling with the exercise as he slides into the cool-down. "Yeah. Take the lead, Mabel."

I blink, processing that. "Really? You just want me to be in charge of design stuff?"

"You said I could be the nut taste-tester, right? Because you, for some unholy reason, dislike nuts?"

"Do you dislike color?"

"It doesn't...inspire me. It doesn't excite me. But it excites you, right?"

Is it weird that I feel incredibly seen right now? "It does," I say, with a light, nervous laugh. "I love color combos, looks, and design. I'm pretty sure Pinterest was made for me. And there's nothing as enjoyable as picking a design for a cupcake box. Except maybe doing a paint-by-numbers mural."

He tilts his head, perhaps considering me or my remarks. Looking at me with a scrunched brow like he's really taking that all in. "What's your favorite color? Is it pink?"

"You might think so, and I do think the bakery should be pink and white, but actually, I've been having a love affair with lilac for a long time. It's pretty much perfect."

He smiles in a way I've never seen before on him—it's amused meets fascinated. As he stops and steps off the bike, he says, "I'm not into any of that stuff since I'm no good at it. You should pick the colors. And pick the mural—we should have one on the wall in the shop. But I'll show up and help you paint, especially since it'll be paint-by-numbers. I'd be baller at that. And then you'll help make the things with nuts." He pauses then adds, "You trust me when I say people like brownies with nuts, right?"

That's an unusual way of putting it, yet it makes perfect sense. "I suppose I do."

"Then I trust you when it comes to how things look. Just let me know what colors you pick for the sign and the store and all. So I can act like I know what they're talking about if a customer mentions it," he says, and I file that detail away—he's learned how to manage his color-blindness.

The least I can do is make the picking easy for him. "I'll tell you right now. It's pastel pink," I say, then show him my favorite one. "We can use it for boxes, for the sign, for our cards with QR codes and so on."

He looks at the paint chip, and at first it seems like he's studying it, committing the color to memory. But then he looks up at me, locking eyes for a beat before he says, "Very pretty."

My breath catches. My chest squeezes. "I'm glad you like it," I say, sounding breathy. "The color, that is. It's called Blush."

As if to demonstrate, my cheeks flame. Heat rushes up my neck, too, as Corbin's gaze holds mine for even longer.

"Blush," he repeats, with a crooked smile forming on his lips, like he's having fun with the name of it, or perhaps the manifestation of it. "It sounds perfect," he adds, wiping the back of his neck with a towel. "And this is one of the reasons I said yes to this venture. With you, I don't have to think about how anything looks. Or stress about the design. Or worry it'd be ugly. It's a relief."

A smile teases my lips. I feel a lot less foolish and a lot more useful. "Yeah?"

"Yeah. Because I know you have great taste," he says.

"How do you know?"

He steps closer, tilts his head, and lets his gaze roam up and down me. "Because you're hot for me."

Then he walks to the door, leaving me with my pink paint chips and his unfiltered assessment of my lust.

He looks like he's about to turn down the hall on that mic drop. But instead, he turns around, shooting me a thoughtful look. "You want to come to the game tonight? I can leave a couple VIP tickets for you."

I furrow my brow, thinking through my schedule. But really, my schedule for tonight is picking a mural for the wall of our bakery. Something fun, frothy, and playful. "Would it bother you if I was researching murals on my tablet while you're chasing a little black disc?"

"Only if you don't cheer when I score a goal."

I tilt my head. "You already know you're going to score tonight?"

He points to the exercise bike. "I just did eight and a half miles in twenty-two minutes. That's an average speed of over twenty-three miles per hour. Better than my average." He pauses, exhales. "Maybe you're my good luck charm. Guess we'll find out tonight."

I guess we will.

As I leave, I congratulate myself for sticking to the deal I just made with my brother. Well, it's not like I was going to date Corbin in the weight room.

But still, I'll count that exchange as a victory.

13

___

A LITTLE BIT SECRET

CORBIN

I don't believe in Lady Luck. But I figure, like Mother Nature, it's good policy to respect the principle.

So tonight I do what any self-respecting athlete with more than a decade of experience would do: stack the house with people who support the home team.

The Foxes need every advantage, even where chance is concerned.

On my way to the locker room to change, I detour to the arena's lobby gift shop. It gleams with polished glass windows and clear shelves stacked with stuffed foxes, and more foxes, and even more foxes. And, of course, every variety of sweatshirt, hoodie, and jersey that fans could want. I hate shopping for anything but food or gifts for my kid. But clothes shopping is a special brand of torture. I loathe it to the depths of my soul.

I stare at the endless sea of options, and my chest tightens.

When I had this idea after leaving the weight room, it seemed...right. Fun. Playful. Something Mabel would enjoy. But I'm lost in this place.

I break for the open doors leading toward the place I

belong—on the player's side of the arena. On the way, I linger at a display, so it doesn't feel like I'm making my escape. A woman with light brown skin and a bouncy, dark brown ponytail intercepts me. Her name tag says Jacinta. "Can I help you with anything, Mr. Knight?"

Right. Of course, I'm not incognito here. Not with my thirty-foot image on a banner overhead.

I draw a breath. "I need something for…a friend."

Her eyes sparkle. "Got it. And what does this friend like?"

I think of Mabel and her penchant for cute athletic clothes. "Um, tennis dresses? Pickleball outfits?" The words feel terribly awkward.

She gives me a *so sorry* frown. "We don't have any. But those are good ideas."

I picture what Mabel's worn at other times when I've seen her, but the way that short dress hugged her curves and boosted her breasts is the *only* image in my head right now. I blow out a breath and look around at the T-shirts, pullovers, sweatshirts, hoodies, and jerseys.

Everyone likes sweatshirts, right? "It's for a friend who likes lilac. Can you tell me if any of these sweatshirts are lilac?"

"Of course!" She guides me to a shelf of feminine-looking sweatshirts and hoodies. "We just launched a new line of jerseys geared toward fans who like softer colors."

Jerseys.

Holy shit.

But when Jacinta hands me a jersey with my number—15—on it and my name, it feels a lot like luck.

"So this is lilac?" I confirm.

"It is," she says.

I hold it up, unsure if this will work for Mabel. If she'll like it. I hate asking for help. I prefer giving it, but I can't finagle my way out of this with swagger or a slapshot. "Can you give me your honest opinion? Would it look good on a woman with..." I don't know how to describe Mabel's hair either. Shopping is hell.

"Do you want to know if it's an attractive cut and style?" Jacinta asks helpfully.

I guess this isn't her first retail rodeo. "Yes," I say, relieved.

"It's super cute," she says, "but there's another one I like better. It's kind of a V-cut."

I perk up as she guides me back to another shelf in the same section and shows me my jersey in a V-neck style.

"I don't know your...friend, of course, but I'd like this."

"Thank you, Jacinta," I say, grateful and then some.

I buy it, then ask her to hold it for a woman named Mabel. "I'll text her and tell her to come here before the game starts?"

"Of course," she assures me.

"Perfect."

A smile teases at Jacinta's lips as I say that. "Mabel," she says quietly as she writes it on a Post-it note, like she's been entrusted with a secret. She sets it on top of the jersey and pats it when she looks up. "It's safe and sound."

And a little bit secret.

Especially considering I kind of can't wait for Mabel's reaction. Even though I'm pretty sure I shouldn't be buying clothes for my business partner. But I probably shouldn't be thinking about all the dirty things I want to do to her either.

I thank Jacinta, then leave, texting Mabel as I return to the personnel area.

Corbin: There's something waiting for you at
the gift shop. You should go before the game.

* * *

It's not over till it's over, but we're up by three when we return to the ice before the third period. None of those points are courtesy of me, but who cares? They belong to the Foxes, and that's all that matters.

Actually, that's a lie. I'd really like at least one to be mine.

I'm centering the line for the face-off. The ref drops the puck, and I tie up their center's stick, kicking the puck back to Ivan. He snags it, then passes it back to me two seconds later. The ice opens up ahead, and I hit the blue line with the same —no, more speed—than I used when I raced myself on the bike earlier. It's just the goalie and me now. He's sliding out ahead of the posts, playing the angles.

So am I. I fake the shot high, and he bites, going for it, then I hit it low and precise. The puck screams right past him.

The lamp lights.

I thrust my stick in the air, and the tension I've been carrying for weeks starts to unknot. Riggs and Lake crash into me along the boards as the crowd goes wild. It's louder than a concert in here. The cheers reverberate in my bones.

This is what I love—when it comes together. For the team, the fans, and me.

Through the noise, I scan for Mabel, and there she is with a friend in the seats at center ice, jumping up and down and wearing my jersey.

She's not working on her tablet. She's just looking good in lilac and being my good luck charm.

The Foxes close it out with a 5-2 W that feels really fucking good.

So do the texts she sends—or accidentally sends, since they arrive in multiples. In the locker room, I look away from my teammates as I read the exchange while stripping off my jersey. Don't want anyone to see my face.

> **Mabel:** You didn't have to.

> **Mabel:** You seriously didn't have to.

> **Mabel:** Even though this jersey does make me look kind of sexy, doesn't it?

> **Mabel:** Maybe I should ask Alexa? Alexa, does this lilac low-cut jersey make me look sexy?

> **Alexa:** I can't see it, but sexy is in the eye of the beholder.

> **Mabel:** Alexa, even you can't get me down.

> **Alexa:** Get down often refers to—

> **Mabel:** Alexa, stop. You didn't have to, Corbin. But also, you should know I look really good in lilac :)

> **Corbin:** I know, Mabel. I absolutely know.

I don't turn around and look back at my teammates for a good, long time. Once I'm showered and changed, I slide into dad mode. Time to shut the door on this inappropriate flirtation and focus on Charlotte.

I head to the kids' lounge to pick her up. It's after nine, but I should be able to get her home by ten. A bunch of the guys got together and arranged for a sitter during home games, following the example of Rowan Bishop, who set up a family suite over at the Sea Dogs, our cross-town rivals. It's a huge help to the dads on the team.

When I push open the door, Charlotte pops up, grabbing her backpack and trotting over to me. "Good job tonight, Dad. That broke your three-game point-less streak."

"Thanks," I say, though I frown at the reminder.

"It's a good thing," she assures me, then pats her backpack. "I finished my homework super early, so I did some analysis on your stats. Want to go over them?"

I stretch my neck from side to side. Tonight, I need to spend a little time with an ice pack rather than a spreadsheet. "How about tomorrow?"

"Fair enough." She shifts gears as we head into the hall. "Theo stopped by during the second period. He offered to help me with math, so I gave him an extra problem to do, even though it wasn't on my homework."

"That was...tricky of you," I say, impressed with her brain.

"Thanks. It amused me."

"Glad something does."

"A dog would amuse me more," she says, lifting her eyes hopefully.

I wish I could say yes, but there's no way. "Charlotte, we hardly have time."

"I could come up with a schedule for the dog and for us. We could make it work. I know I could figure it out."

"If anyone could, it's you. But you're only at my house half the time. Plus, my schedule is complicated. I'm gone a lot."

She sighs. "I know. I wish there were an algebra equation for adopting a dog."

"Me too, kid. Me too." I squeeze her shoulder, then grab her backpack from her and sling it over my shoulder. Least I can do is carry it. "Did you let Theo think he was helpful? With the math?"

She shakes her head. "No. It's not my job to make a man feel useful."

I toss my head back and laugh, then I pick her up and give her a big hug. "That's my girl."

She smiles impishly, clearly pleased with herself. "I told him when he solved it that he did a good job, but that I'd already finished my math."

"Keeping him on his toes," I say. I set her down as we pass the media room, where the last of the press are filtering out.

"And then he was so excited when he saw his sister on TV. He kept saying, 'Brilliant marketing,' and 'Next time, put her in an Afternoon Delight jersey.'"

A kernel of guilt crawls up me. "He said that?"

"I heard my name." Theo catches up to us and claps me on the back. He must have been in the media room. "Brilliant marketing tonight, man. Like I was telling my goddaughter," he says, ruffling Charlotte's hair.

"So I heard."

"Mabel in your jersey was perfect. The cameras loved it. The bakery is going to blow up when you open. You two are marketing geniuses."

"My dad is very smart," Charlotte says, patting my elbow with pride.

I hardly feel smart right now, with the post-game high curdling in my stomach. My brain repeats *marketing genius* and *business partnership*. If only I had been that calculating when I bought Mabel the jersey.

But that's what our partnership needs to be.

I pivot, asking Theo, "How are things looking with the search for a GM?"

I expect a smirk from my friend. Something full of his normal cocksure attitude—an attitude that benefits him as he wheels and deals for players.

Instead, there's something like vulnerability in his eyes as I mention the very real possibility that he could move from *acting* GM to *official* GM with the job hunt. "I think I have a real good shot at the opening," he says, holding up crossed fingers. "Let's catch up over dinner soon?"

"Sounds like a plan," I say.

He points to Charlotte. "You in, math genius and future best vet in America?"

"I'll be there," she says.

Theo's already my closest friend.

He looks out for my daughter.

He's also the man who's playing a key role in running the team. If he nabs the opening for good, he'll officially be...my boss.

I don't want to lie to my boss any more than I want to lie to my friend.

* * *

Later that night, after Charlotte's tucked into bed, I wander into the kitchen, yank open the fridge, and stare at the options for a late-night sandwich. But I barely notice the ingredients. I'm wishing I could ask my mom for her advice.

How do I balance *this*...what even is it that I feel for Mabel? Lust, sure. But sometimes it feels like longing.

I grab some slices of fresh chicken, an avocado, and a block of Gouda delivered from the gourmet cheese shop in the heart of downtown Cozy Valley. But before I snag the loaf of bread on the counter, I reach for my phone.

I click on my email, then search for Penny. My mom's name pops up right away. She lived with me the last few years of her life. Well, here on my property, in a cottage across the yard that she shared with my stepdad, who took care of her most of the time. I helped as much as I could when I was home—cooking for her, even though she'd lost her appetite, doing balance exercises with her, even though that was hard. And, maybe most importantly, just hanging out and watching sports and TV shows together.

But while she was often close to me, she still sent me emails every day when I was on the road.

I click on a random one.

Today I walked to the cheese shop with Ray. Well, okay, I didn't walk there. We drove there, but then I walked several blocks downtown to pick up the cheese. I'll make a grilled cheese sandwich for Charlotte when Sarah drops her off. She loves it with the fake bacon. I think I even like fake bacon now! My hands were shaking as I carried the cheddar, but I think I did okay otherwise.

I walked back to the car at the edge of downtown with Ray by my side. Doesn't sound like much, but I did it. No falls, yay! Didn't have to call the fire department, so it was a good day. The doctors say the more you exercise, the more you can perform daily activities. So I'll keep walking as long as I can. I watched your game last night. Nice goal, kiddo!

Love,
Mom

My throat tightens horribly, thinking of all the daily activities that felt like mountains to her at the end. Walking to the kitchen. Mixing flour and butter. Opening the oven.

Eating, even.

Mountains that meant there were no more good days.

I close the email and remind myself to focus on my goals for good days—the game I play, my kid, the team.

I look at my hands—steady, sure, confident. I'm not worried about Parkinson's for me. That's not my concern. But I have to remember *this* is a gift—the things I can do. The way I can play. The fact that I can score goals in the NHL.

I can't take that for granted just because I *long* for my best friend's sister.

14

THE BEST LAID KIDNAPPING PLANS
CORBIN

The next day, I drop Charlotte off at school, then head to the arena for a workout and morning skate. When I return home, there's a small box left on the front porch, and I stop to pick it up. It's familiar, the color. I squint at it, like that'll make the difference. Maybe I should try those color-blind glasses again so I can see it better.

But I don't want to walk around wearing tinted glasses all the time. And really, what's the point?

It's a bakery box from our bakery—still feels so strange to think of it like that. But that means I don't need glasses. It's blush.

And it's tied with a white polka-dot ribbon. A stupid smile takes me hostage. Dammit. I shouldn't feel this way over a ribbon-wrapped box, but it's from Mabel.

Drawing a breath, I will myself to calm down. It's just a little thing—this gift. A little thing with a tiny card tucked under the ribbon. I grab that first and flick it open.

Dear Corbin,

All that lilac made me think of lavender, which made me think of Earl Grey and lavender, which made me think that those are one of the most delicious combos ever, which made me turn them into a London Fog cake. And then I thought of the perfect "story" for this treat too. What do you think?

Mabel

P.S. The color of the box is Blush.

"I know," I whisper to myself.

There's a paper heart inside the card, like the one Mabel first mocked up.

When it rains, I gaze out the window and eat cake...

It's a little poignant, the short story of the cake. The gesture's thoughtful too, not just because she's showing me the color of the boxes we'll use but she's baking for me. Mabel doesn't take anything for granted. She wants to prove herself to me too.

I go inside, shut the door, and absently run my thumb and forefinger along the satiny ribbon. What did she wear when she baked this? Did her T-shirt slope down her shoulder, exposing her collarbone for stolen kisses? Would her neck have tasted like lavender, sugar, and warm kitchen calling me home?

For fuck's sake, she's your business partner, not your damn girlfriend.

Thank god that voice in my head is also rolling its eyes as it laughs at me. Yup. The voice is right. I can't get caught up in these feelings, in these ridiculous daydreams. That's all they are.

I take the note and the box to the kitchen and focus on business. *Just business.* I dip a fork into the cake. It's moist, sweet, and silky. I shouldn't eat all this cake, or I won't be able to make the plays I need to make on the ice.

I slice off the section I took the bite from and set it on a plate next to the note and the heart. The rest of the slice is neat and clean now. I place it back in the box and hop on my bike, then head up the street to Annabelle's. She answers the door with a knowing tilt of her head, her braids swishing. Seven is at her feet, rubbing up against her calf. "I brought you something."

I hand her the box, then make a move to go. I'm itching to take off. I don't know why. I like Annabelle. She's only ever been good to me and to my mom. But this intense impulse to jet is pulling at me uncomfortably.

She smirks, eyes the box then me. "You do know that giving me this won't stop you from thinking of the woman who made it for you."

I flinch. "How did you know a woman made it for me?"

My god, is she that psychic?

Her smile widens, shifting into a laugh. "I took a good guess. But I was right, I see."

"I'm not thinking of anyone," I lie. Maybe this is why I want to leave. She's too astute, and I'm not sure I'm in the mood to be read, energy or otherwise.

"Corbin," she chides, then her eyes soften. "It's been a long while, hasn't it?"

Not just a while. But a long while. "Since what?" I ask.

To her credit, she doesn't roll her eyes. She does, however, push on. "Is she someone special?"

That's a loaded question. I could tell her Mabel's the woman I can't stop thinking about. That she's someone I wanted to ask out seven years ago. Or I could say she's my new business partner.

Maybe she's even my good luck charm.

All of those may be true, but none matter as much as this: "Yes, she's the woman who's finally helping me make my mom's dreams come true."

Annabelle's smile turns sad. "I'm so glad to hear that, honey."

I give her a tight nod, then turn to go. But halfway down the steps, I stop and turn around. That same uncomfortable feeling from the Foxes gift shop returns, but I push past it once again. "Annabelle, the cake?"

She tilts her head. "Yes?"

I grit my teeth, then blow out a breath, trying to release the tension. "What color is the frosting?"

Humming thoughtfully, she looks down at the cake, studies it, then raises her face. "It's the soft blue of the early morning before the sun rises. It's calm, restful, but a little wistful."

I thank Annabelle and say goodbye to her and to Seven, I hop on the bike and head home. Once I'm in my house, I text Mabel. It's the right thing to do.

> Corbin: The cake tastes as good as it looks. It's the color of the pre-dawn sky, right?

> Mabel: Yes!!!! How did you know?

Corbin: I asked someone.

Mabel: I'm so touched. Also, I have to tell you something.

Ah, fuck. Nothing good ever starts with those words. I can't even imagine what's coming. But I brace myself as I reply.

Corbin: What do you want to tell me?

Mabel: I wasn't sure if I'd be any good at working with someone else. I'm a little…

Corbin: Lone wolf? Free spirit? Intensely, incredibly, unequivocally independent?

Mabel: Tell me what you really think.

But I can't do that, so I write back with something else.

Corbin: You were saying?

Mabel: You make it easy to work with someone else.

Easy is not how I'd describe this desire for her. There's nothing easy about it.

Corbin: Same for you.

As much as I want to text more, I stop there. I have to.

* * *

Fine, fine. Mabel's clearly not my good luck charm, and I'm not complaining. We win the next game on the road, and since she's not here in Phoenix, it was foolish of me to think she'd been the thing that broke my point-less streak.

It's just hockey, plain and simple. And it's best I keep my eye on the game.

In the visitors' locker room, as we get dressed to travel to Los Angeles this evening for tomorrow night's game, Miller is riding that post-game high. "I'm feeling like some bocce ball, boys."

Lake rolls his eyes from his stall. "You're such a weirdo."

Miller cups his ear. "What did you say? Miller is such a friendly, outgoing, interesting guy? Why, yes, I am."

"Yeah, that's what I said," Lake mutters, then gives us a chin nod and says, "See you on the plane."

Once he's gone, Miller spins around, looking at me, then Riggs, then Ivan. "I say we kidnap him and make him play once we land."

"Team bonding now involves kidnapping?" I ask as I grab my suit jacket and put it back on.

"I'm in," Ivan says, since he's always game.

The thing is, so am I. I can't resist a little trouble. Fucking with my teammates is too fun. "It's on."

"You got a plan?" Riggs asks.

I tap my temple. "Course I do."

The plan that's forming requires input from Mabel. She did say she knew the best bakeries in any city. That's absolutely the only reason I text her once we board the team plane.

Corbin: Got a favorite cupcake shop in Santa Monica?

Mabel: Are you ready for us to make our first acquisition? We haven't even opened yet. Sheesh.

Corbin: Think big, Mabel, think big.

Mabel: How big, Corbin?

She ends her message with emojis of eyeballs, and I'm pretty sure she's not talking about the size of dreams or ambitions.

Don't engage, don't engage, don't you dare engage.

I settle into my cushy seat in the second row next to Riggs. He seems pretty engrossed in his own text exchange, so I write back to Mabel.

Corbin: Very.

Fine, I engaged a little. But I quickly add another text.

> Corbin: Now, do I need to rely on Google, or are you the best market researcher in the bakery world? Like you said you were.

> Mabel: Obviously, I am the best. I would go to Sweet Cheeks.

I snort-laugh.

> Corbin: Is that name for real?

> Mabel: Google it.

I do, then I place the order as the plane takes off, leaving the desert behind and hurtling toward the coast. After I set my phone down, I grab my tablet, so I can work on recipes, when I catch a stupid grin on Riggs's face.

I know what kind of grin that is. I'd bet good money he's texting a woman.

And since he's not bothering to hide his phone, I do what I must—ignore my tablet and check out his screen. The message says *I'm so excited to meet you in person too!!!* with triple exclamation points courtesy of the sender. This is like a wide-open net and nothing but ice.

I clear my throat. "How much did you bribe the *Romance Beach* hostess for that meeting?"

He flips the phone over, smirks, then makes an O with his thumb and forefinger. "Zero. I used my brain," he says, tapping his temple. "I sent a gift to her—well, to her PR team

—along with a card. She has a thing for otters, and I found an otter necklace."

I stand corrected. "Holy shit. I was messing with you. But you're really talking to her?"

The smirk widens. "Yep. We have a date when we're back in town."

Talk about persistence. "Good on you," I say, offering him a fist for knocking.

"Thanks. I'm a little excited," he says. "Her work is awesome. She's not just a hostess. She's an actress. And she's done some streaming rom-coms."

As he goes on about Sapphire's talent and emotional range, I'm ready to make Fanboy his new nickname. But I'll wait till he actually goes out with her.

* * *

Once we're checked into The Resort hotel on the beach, I gather Riggs, Miller, and Ivan in my room and tell them the plan as they lounge on the couch.

Ivan rubs his big palms together. "Henrik would seriously kill to be a part of this. Sucks to be him."

"If your husband ever gets traded from Seattle to San Francisco, he can join us," I say.

"Sure, that's what we'll be doing if he gets traded. Team pranks," Ivan says dryly.

"This is no prank, men," Riggs says, popping up from the couch.

"That's right," Miller seconds. "This is serious business."

Like a heist crew, we gather the materials and enlist some extra help. We snag a room service tray, and on it we set the box of cupcakes we picked up from the bakery. Then, we convince a hotel bartender named Kara to place the call from the bar, since we need it to come from a hotel phone.

It's possible that a big tip helps convince her.

When she's ready, we're ready.

Riggs waits in the bar with Kara, texting us that she's making the call, while Ivan, Miller, and I wait outside Lake's hotel room. When she lobs the call, saying there's a special delivery heading his way of a dozen cupcakes from Sweet Cheeks, courtesy of his agent, Miller slides the tray quietly in front of the door.

He knocks and says, octaves higher than his own register, "Sweet Cheeks for my favorite client."

Like a dog lured out of his den, Lake swings open the door, pokes his head out, and—*bam*.

Target acquired.

"Winger-napping," I declare, slipping the pillowcase over his head.

"Are you kidding me?"

"Not one bit," I reply then hoist him up by the shoulders while Ivan grabs his legs, and we carry him down to a waiting Lyft.

* * *

Lake thrusts both arms in the air and struts like a peacock across the lawn where he's vanquished us in mere minutes. "And that's how you do it."

I shake my head. "Are you kidding me? Have you been secretly playing?"

Lake scoffs. "Nope. I'm just that good, boys."

"I bet you played *us*," Miller says, slumping into a lawn chair at our table at the Back Porch Pub, a mile from the hotel.

"All that time claiming you didn't want to go while you were secretly practicing so you could show us up."

Rolling his eyes, Lake runs a hand through his longish hair. "First time, baby. First fucking time. The sooner you accept my supremacy in all things, the happier you'll be."

"No. I challenge you to a rematch," Ivan says, cracking his knuckles and looking fearsome. He's a defender, and that's part of the job.

Lake just shrugs. "Fine, if you want to be dragged again, feel free."

"Next time, can we teammate-nap someone who doesn't, I dunno, school us all," Riggs suggests.

"I second that," I say.

"Be careful what you wish for," Lake says, then smirks and grabs the ball, ready for another round. "Now, as I hand you your asses, what's on the agenda next week for the club?"

"Oh, are you a regular member now?" Miller asks.

"Maybe," Lake says with a wiggle of his brow. "Now that I know how much fun it is to beat you all in games."

Riggs claps me on the shoulder. "We have to help Knighty Night with his bakery soon."

"Yeah, how is that going?" Ivan asks casually, his deep, gravelly voice filled with some innuendo as he adds, "You're doing that with the GM's very pretty sister, right?"

I snap my face to him and lift an eyebrow. "What did you say?"

He laughs. "What? Do you think because I'm married, I didn't notice she's pretty?"

"No," I say, scowling.

Riggs lifts his beer, laughing. "Jelly that Ivan noticed your business partner is hot?"

I drag a hand down my jaw, still a little rattled. Honestly, I don't know what threw me off, but maybe it's that we're all talking about her when I was hoping *not* to talk about her. To use this trip to reset my mind. To stop thinking about Mabel so much.

I grab a bocce ball, then knock back some beer before I give an answer that focuses on the business. "Yeah, it's going well, we have a name, and we're getting it ready. Going to open it soon."

"And she's pretty?" Miller goads.

"She's also smart and funny and interesting," I point out quickly. Maybe too quickly.

Ivan whistles. "Well, well, well."

"I'm just saying."

"Oh, you're definitely just saying," Miller adds.

"More like you're just saying you think she's a whole lot more," Riggs points out.

"I thought Henrik was pretty and smart and funny and interesting, and look—I married him," Ivan says with a cocky grin.

Lake cracks up as he strides to the front of the court, a ball in hand, ready to toss. "I had no idea how much fun it would be to watch you all knock Corbin down several pegs. This is almost better than cupcakes."

Why did I think going out with these guys would get my mind off her?

Especially since when we return, Lake doles out the cupcakes. As I eat the frosting, I'm definitely thinking of Mabel, and I really, *really* shouldn't be.

15

SWEET DISPUTES

MABEL

"Admit it. In the history of market research, has there ever been better market research than *this* market research?" I ask Corbin on the phone as I fluff out my hair, making sure the honey blonde streaks are peeking out through my chestnut locks. What's the point of streaks if you can't show them off?

But wait—can Corbin even see my streaks?

Doesn't matter. You're not going to date him. You're not even going to flirt with him. You made a promise to yourself.

"There is no better research than eating," Corbin agrees on the other end of the line. He's just returned from his road trip, and we've planned a bakery crawl for today.

"Actually, can I bring along my daughter?" he asks. "Her after-school science lab was canceled, so I just picked her up when I landed. She's informed me her sweet tooth is top-notch and should be used for legitimate business research."

I pause, but only because I remember my reservations when I was younger. When I was twenty and didn't want to date a man with a kid. But since we're not dating now, what does it matter?

"Hell yeah," I answer.

I can hear Corbin's smile even before he says, "Great."

Thirty minutes later we meet at The Sweet Spot, a newly opened bakery in Hayes Valley. The sister shop has been up and running in nearby Darling Springs for some time, but it's just expanded with a store here.

I register the handsome man waiting for me in front of the shop, but my attention, and my exploding nerves, are all for the girl with the high ponytail, who stands beside Corbin. She wears faded jeans, a peach-colored shirt, and a backpack.

I've met his daughter before, but we've never *hung out*. What if his kid hates me? What if I don't know what to say to her? Will he think I'm a terrible business partner if I have zero kid skills?

Just be yourself, girl.

Pep talk engaged, I march up to them and say to Charlotte, "Top-notch sweet tooth, I hear?"

Charlotte nods. "I've had years of practice."

"Then, you've got a job to do. Are you ready to be our taste-tester?"

She stands taller. "I am."

"You'll also need to be our arbiter."

Her brow furrows for a few seconds before she says, "Someone who helps settle disputes?"

My smile widens. "You know that word?"

"I do vocabulary quizzes for fun."

I blink, processing the detail about this smarty-pants. "You'll need to arbitrate any sweets disputes between your dad and me. Can you handle that?"

"Definitely," she says. "I like to give my opinion."

I offer a hand for high-fiving. "Opinions rule."

* * *

"Dad, technically we've been doing market research every time we've baked together," Charlotte says as we settle into a table in the corner of the white bakery with pink polka dot walls.

"Of course we have," he says, gesturing to the treats we selected—a seven-layer bar, a dark chocolate brownie, and a blondie. "I want to record our input." Charlotte whips out her phone and shows me a color and pattern-coded task management program. "This way we can make sure we have data-driven menu decisions."

I set a hand on my heart. "Those are some seriously beautiful words."

Corbin nods to his daughter, then says to me, "Someone's a little organized."

Charlotte breaks off a bite of a brownie, finishes it quickly, then says to her dad: "Would that someone be you?"

With avid eyes, I look to my business partner like I've caught him. And, really, I have. "The apple doesn't fall far from the tree, does it, Corbin?"

He sighs as he looks at his kid. "Charlotte, you're killing all my cool cred."

"That's assuming you had any to start with," I say, then turn back to the little chatterbox. Wind her up and watch her go. I tap the table. "Tell me about Organized Daddy."

Charlotte finishes a bite of her seven-layer bar slice and jumps back into the conversational fray. "He labels all his food. On the day he buys it, he marks down the date it entered the house. Then he marks it off on an inventory app."

As I break off a bite of a blondie, I make a beckoning gesture with my other hand. "More. Tell me more. Don't leave a single detail out. Did he make the app himself?"

Charlotte chuckles, shaking her head. "No! He's not a techie."

Corbin clears his throat. "I feel like we've discussed enough about the app."

I meet his gaze head-on. "We will never discuss enough about your inventory ordering app. This is like a whole new level of Corbin intel." I return all my focus to the precocious girl in front of me. "Do you have to update items on the app when you use them?"

"Of course. How else would we know when something is low?"

By checking. But I don't say that since different strokes and all. "Are his pantry shelves labeled?"

"You're creating a monster, you know that, Charlotte?" Corbin asks.

But Charlotte seems to like feeding me. "He keeps ingredients on particular shelves. And don't even try to put anything away on the wrong shelf. I'm pretty sure my dad has a camera in the pantry."

"I do not," Corbin says with a huff.

"Dad! If I put something in the wrong place, you'll come in and move it back where it belongs."

"Like, the next day," he retorts.

She shakes her head. "Within hours, Dad. You hate mess."

Mess.

For a few seconds, that word rolls down my spine uncomfortably.

Messes...like me?

I mean, it's a fact I'm a bit of a hot mess.

But hot messes like to have fun, so I keep feeding quarters into Charlotte as we sample the treats. "Can you get video of him reorganizing his shelves for me? I feel like that would be something I could watch over and over while eating popcorn."

Her grin is the stuff of legend. "I can do that. It's like a homework assignment."

I smile smugly before I look at Corbin, who's heaving a sigh as if he can't quite believe Charlotte is rolling over on him so quickly.

I can't quite believe I ever worried we might not get along. Turns out teasing this man is a shared passion.

* * *

Next stop is a bakery on Fillmore Street. Charlotte's got the hang of it already, assessing the decor, the display case, the vibes, and then the pastries.

We order a selection—chocolate chip cookies, a snickerdoodle, and a lemon poppyseed cake—then find a small table by the window.

I break a chocolate chip cookie in half and offer her a piece. "When did your dad teach you how to bake?"

"Actually, my grandma did," she says, taking the piece and chewing. "She was amazing in the kitchen. Baking is like a science—that's what she always told me. That might be why I like it so much."

"My mom," Corbin confirms, but there's something heavy in his voice.

I file that away as I turn back to Charlotte. "Were you close with her?"

"She lived with us for a while. Well, right next to us. Like in a little house across the yard. It was nice to have her so near. She died a couple years ago."

"I'm so sorry," I say to her, then I turn to Corbin, my throat tightening. "I'm so sorry about your mom."

He gives a solemn but grateful nod. "Thanks," he says, then takes a beat. "She...left me her recipes."

"Oh, Corbin," I say, clasping my hand to my heart. That just does something to me. Tugs on all my heartstrings.

"That's lovely. You'll be using some of them in our bakery, right?"

"Count on it," he says with a note of emotion in his voice I haven't heard before. And a promise too. "She loved baking so much. It was her passion. But it was hard for her in the end."

I wait for him to supply more info. He doesn't though. Instead, he takes a bite of another cookie, and maybe that's all he wants to say now.

I pause for a few seconds, then ask the next thing on my mind. "Is she why you wanted to do this?"

"She is," he says, full of vulnerability but also restraint. There's more to the story, but it's clear he's not ready to share it, so I focus on our market research, taking notes with his daughter, and then moving along to our final stop—a cupcake shop in the Marina District that's become all the rage.

While we're there, we take bites of their *top picks* and then make a list of our favorite flavors.

"My grandma always said cupcakes should focus on flavor, not flash," Charlotte offers.

Corbin turns to the window, a faraway look in his eyes and, I imagine, a feeling of loss in his heart. I can tell because I feel the same way myself when I think about my grandmother. Some days, the missing is an ache that won't go away.

Soon, he turns back and meets my gaze, a resolute look in his eyes as he says, "Should we keep going?"

"Yes," I say, and we move on, since that's what you have to do, too, even when you miss someone.

We review our rough draft of the menu against the notes, and we settle on our favorites for potential inclusion at Afternoon Delight.

But Charlotte stops at one item, arching a very curious brow. "Dog cookies? Is this dog-shaped or for dogs?"

"Both. And they'll all be made of peanut butter, since, for some unholy reason, dogs like peanut butter just like your dad does," I say, turning Corbin's words back on him.

Charlotte turns her gaze to her father, clasping her hands together. "I would like to take a treat home to a dog."

I tilt my head. "You have a dog?"

With a frown, she shakes her head. "No. My dad's too busy."

"We're *both* too busy. And I travel a lot," Corbin corrects, and it sounds like it's not the first time he's explained his reasoning to Charlotte.

It's solid reasoning, I have to admit. But where there's a will, there's wiggle room. "Maybe you could volunteer then? I volunteer with Little Friends, and you could apply on their website. Except you usually need to have an adult with you." I tap my chin. "Corbin, do you qualify as an adult?"

The eye roll he gives me is magnificent, but the sigh he heaves is even more indignant. "I do, Mabel. I do."

I brush one palm against the other. "Problem solved. Charlotte, you have a qualified adult at your service."

She pats her dad's shoulder. "I'll sign us up tonight, Dad."

Charlotte excuses herself for the restroom, and once she's gone, he arches a brow and leans closer. "Is that a new sport for you?"

"Is what?"

"Mocking me?"

"New? Please. I've been playing it for a while."

"I think you took it to a new level today," he counters.

I blow on my fingernails. "What can I say? I'm good at baking *and* teasing you."

"Yes, Mabel, you really are," he says.

Something shifts in his expression as his gaze lingers on

me. The wistful emotions vanish. The businesslike intensity disappears too. His eyes are darker, more intense than usual, and they send heat right through me.

I think about that look in his eyes after I return home.

16

———

WET PAINT

MABEL

Repeat after me—*painting is not sexy. Painting is not sexy. Painting is not sexy.*

And yet here I am, practically melting as I watch Corbin perfect the llama's eyelashes with the tiniest brush known to mankind.

I ordered this paint-by-numbers mural from Maeve Hartley, an artist whose online store is full of adorable stencil-like animal designs she can customize in days. When I went to Corbin's game, I requested a fox and a llama sharing a cupcake under a tree—sweet, innocent, and perfect for a bakery. Then I placed the order.

What I didn't account for was how Corbin would look painting it.

He's wearing a worn gray T-shirt that clings to his pecs and jeans that do absolutely sinful things to his hockey ass. But it's not just how he looks—it's how he moves. The way he concentrates, brow slightly furrowed as he drags that tiny brush with surgical precision. The careful dip into the paint, the gentle stroke, the way he steps back to assess his work like he's creating a Georges Seurat instead of decorating a bakery wall.

"What do you think?" He steps back, paintbrush still poised in his strong fingers.

"It looks so wet," I breathe out before I can stop myself.

His gaze snaps to mine, curious. "It *is* wet. I just applied it."

"Oh, it's very wet," I say, then immediately want to crawl into a hole. I flash him my brightest, most innocent smile and focus intently on the llama's chest. "And so is the teal you did before." I stop my work and meet his green-eyed gaze. "I read that someone who had red-green color-blindness might see teal as a...flatter shade of blue? Is that what it looks like to you?"

His lips quirk up. "You researched it?"

My chest flutters a little from his response. "I did. It was really helpful. And I wanted to understand more about you."

He stops painting. "That's...cool." He sounds taken aback, in a good way. "And that teal looks sort of like a murky blue to me. What does it look like to you?"

I think about the question, wanting to give it the answer it deserves. "It's like..." I search for something vivid, something alluring. "The color of a tropical lagoon."

His smile is soft, genuine. "Hmm. Okay, I can see that better now. Like an island escape. You're on the beach, relaxing, drinking a piña colada, and the waves are so calm, they barely move."

"Yes," I say, laughing.

He points to the shade of red at the top of the pink—what else?—cupcake. "What color is this one?"

"Candy apple for the cherry. It needs one more coat."

"So I should want to bite it? The cherry?" The question is innocent, but the way his voice drops is not.

Now I'm thinking about him biting things. Specifically, me. "Yes," I say, then I roll my lips together to seal in the murmur.

"The color works, then," he says.

I turn away so I don't, I don't know, throw myself at him. I have a sky to paint. As I dip my brush in the paint can, a drop of robin's-egg blue splashes onto the top of my foot.

I bend to grab a rag from the drop cloth and swipe off the color. I'm painting barefoot—it's just more comfortable this way.

We work alone, with music filling the space between us. A Frank Ocean tune, which isn't helpful since that man's voice is sex. But I focus on the bakery instead of just how good Corbin's being with his hands.

"Tomorrow the garage door gets installed," I say, sticking to practical details. I'll oversee that since Corbin has a game. "I know it makes you sad that you won't be here to discuss 'manly garage things' with the contractor."

"Yes, that's exactly what I want to do," Corbin says. Then he stops his strokes of blue, shooting me a curious look. "You're not wearing one of your pickleball dresses?"

It's said like a question. I can hear the *why not*.

I glance down at my painting ensemble. "It's a skort," I say, then pluck the ruffly hem of the combo skirt-shorts. I've paired them with a white crop top that's a few years old, something that won't bother me if it gets paint on it. I also chose it since he said he can see white easily. "This skort is from a few seasons and a few thrift shop trips ago, so I don't wear it when I play."

"They're not *premium* clothes?" he asks dryly.

I laugh at his description. This is safer than talking about shades of color. "Exactly. I have my cute little athletic numbers for when I play, and I have the fun pickleball dresses for errands, and I have last year's skorts and stuff for painting and working."

"Got it," he says, grabbing a fresh brush and dipping it into the red again, probably for the second coat on the cherry. "You have the first line and the second and the third."

"That's one way to put it," I say.

"Will you wear pickleball dresses when you're working at the bakery?"

I toss him a playful look, unable to resist saying, "I don't know. Do you want me to?"

He steals another glance at me. "They're cute, I guess. Even though skort is a weird word."

"But they don't look weird?"

A smirk comes my way this time. "Not in the mother-fucking least, Mabel."

I hide a smile. I should stop flirting with him. I really should. "And yes, I'll sometimes wear them when I work here."

He paints some more, scrunching his brow like he's noodling on something. "But I'm still not sure I believe you *actually* play pickleball, Mabel."

I step closer, lock eyes with him, and drag the paintbrush down his shirt, leaving behind a stripe of robin's-egg blue.

His green eyes pop. "You just painted my shirt."

I slow-clap. "You're right."

He shakes his head, sighs heavily. "Good thing you're wearing the third line."

In a flash, he dips his brush into the red paint, then darts out a strong arm, wraps it around my waist, and grips me in place. He lifts the brush and brandishes it.

Inches from my face.

My breath catches.

Everything goes silent between us. The Frank Ocean tune finishes. The air crackles. He's holding me and staring at me, all while threatening me with red paint in a way I want to be threatened, judging from the heat climbing up my legs.

"I have no choice," he murmurs at last, then he drags the brush along the hollow of my throat.

It's cool and soft, the paintbrush slick and surprisingly sensuous as he runs it slowly down to my chest, bristles turning a swath of my pale skin red. He stops at the neckline of my shirt.

All thought flees my head. I'm nothing but atoms and vibrating molecules. I can't even speak. I'm just breathing—and breathing him in.

The scent of paint, delightfully non-toxic, mixes with his aftershave. Or maybe it's bodywash. I don't know, but that campfire-by-the-lake scent is not only going to my head, it's going to my thighs. I squeeze them together, lick my lips, and try to find a word, a phrase—something to tease him with.

But when his brow furrows again, like he's at war with himself, I stay quiet. His silent debate stretches a few seconds, then he gives in with a raspy, "You have red paint on your chest."

"Like a candy apple," I say.

His gaze strays to the canvas of me, his eyes turning darker, glimmering like emeralds. When he raises his face, he drops the brush to the floor. It clatters against the drop cloth, a spray of red splattering on the ground. But I don't care where, since the sound of the brush falling feels like a before and after. Mine falls from my hand and splatters too.

Slowly, teasingly, Corbin runs his calloused finger across the paint on my body. I pant ludicrously loud. It feels too good.

"Good enough to bite," he muses as he traces a circle near my breastbone.

"I don't think the paint would taste good," I say.

"Probably not, but this would."

His lips come crashing down on mine, and I grab him, my

fingers roping through his messy hair, tugging him close. He kisses me hard, a little ruthlessly, all teeth and heat and need.

My brain is buzzing, my body humming, but somewhere in the back of my mind, I'm keenly aware there's a pretty mural inches from us, and I just don't want to mess it up.

"The mural," I whisper with concern.

He backs up, away from our work, scanning it to make sure we didn't smear it. It's safe. He spins me around and pushes me against the brass pole.

Is that a sign? "Do you want me to strip?" I ask in between hot, wet, deep kisses.

"Don't tempt me," he mutters, then returns to my mouth like a sniper.

He kisses ferociously, like he wants to consume me. And I think I want to be consumed. There's been something restrained in the Corbin I've come to know in the last few weeks. He's confident and cocky, sarcastic and witty, but he's also controlled and precise.

This is another side to him.

Wild.

Untamed.

Ravenous.

He grabs my waist and moves me around the space, pushing me up against a wall—the one where the tearaway pants once hung. There's no risk to the llama and the fox here.

He stares hotly at me, his chest rising and falling. "I told myself not to do this. Not to give in. I made myself a promise."

I blink. I wasn't expecting that. "You did?"

He nods, rough and jagged. "Last week. After the game."

This confession makes my stomach swoop. "Why?"

He breathes out hard, then drops his face to the side of my neck, dusting open-mouthed caresses there—the slow, lingering kind. I feel like I'm swimming in desire. I'm hot and achy, and it's all too much.

"Because I can't stop thinking about the way you taste. I can't stop wanting you, and it's messing with my head. With my focus. With everything," he says, pulling back, looking at me with confessions written in his eyes.

No one has ever talked to me like this.

No one has ever said anything that's made me feel like I'm something forbidden. Something dangerous.

Something irresistible.

It's heady.

I slide a hand up his body, traveling across his firm abs and strong pecs so I can grip the neck of his shirt. "What else?"

His eyes are hazy. It takes him a beat. "What do you mean?"

"What else do you tell yourself?"

He breathes out hard and rough. "Mabel," he warns. But he started this conversation, and I want to finish it. I inch closer, so I'm rubbing myself against his firm, muscular thigh.

The moment it hits him is delicious. The realization of what I'm doing flashes in his eyes as I press myself to him.

"I tell myself to resist you," he admits.

"I should resist you too," I say.

Corbin's *my* business partner, and I made a promise to myself to keep my focus on *our* business. No romance till I get my act together. But still, I ache for him.

The ache is winning.

Maybe for both of us, since he pushes me back against the wall and slides his thigh between mine, spreading them apart. He stares down at me, shaking his head. "You're trouble," he says as he cups my cheeks, holding my face hard.

"How much trouble?" I ask, grinding down on his thigh.

His jaw tightens. He blows out a breath, then adjusts his

stance so he's rubbing his thigh against my hot, wet center, riling me up. "So much that I think about the things I want to do to you. I think about *you* all the time. The way you smell and taste and look...and *fuck*."

He sounds angry with himself.

"There's too much at stake," he adds, but he's kissing my cheek, offering me his thigh, letting me use him.

And I'm using the fuck out of him. I'm grinding and rubbing, and I'm fucking his leg in our unfinished bakery.

"I thought about you when I was gone too," he mutters.

"On your road trip?"

"Yes. Tried not to. Fucking thought about you anyway."

His confessions kick me to another level. Pleasure pools low in my belly, tight and sharp. My body is a coil. "I'm close," I whisper.

His eyes squeeze shut for a second. For a fight. For the last ounce of resistance he's letting slip away. He opens them. "Do it. Want to watch you come undone."

My lips part as I fuck his thigh until I'm gasping, then crying out, an orgasm seizing me, bright and sharp.

And over far too soon.

But he never takes his eyes off me. Not till I relax against the wall while the pleasure floats away.

Then he looks down. "Oh fuck."

I follow his gaze to the trail of candy apple red footprints all across the drop cloth and the concrete floor. I guess I stepped in paint.

What a mess I've made. I tense, flashing back to the bakery crawl with his daughter, when she teased him about how much he hates messes. Will this piss him off?

No, that's the wrong word. Corbin doesn't get mad. He's not an angry man. But he's an observant one, an organized one, a man who likes things the way he likes things. And I thrive in chaos. "I'd better go find a rag to clean that up," I say, mobilizing quickly for his sake.

He shoves a hand through his hair, holding the other up as a stop sign. "I will. You'll leave more footprints."

"Right, of course," I say, feeling a little foolish for not realizing that.

He walks off in a cloud of determination, his footsteps echoing till he reaches the kitchen. The sound of running water filters through the space. I picture him washing his hands before he grabs the rags. So very Corbin. He's neat and orderly. I should be the same.

I force myself to focus on cataloguing the work we need to do to finish the mural, clean up the paint, and put everything away when I register the sound of the cupboards opening, then something scraping against a shelf.

Corbin's voice comes from the back of the station, loud and clear. "Mabel, did you know there's a cookie jar in here?"

17

ONE A DAY
CORBIN

After I set the rags on the kitchen counter, I study the cookie jar as if it's an ancient artifact. Maybe it is. It's ceramic, a little chipped, and the shape of a strawberry, with a cap that looks like leaves. I don't think the strip club owners left it behind. But then, *who* left this?

Gently, I shake it, and something moves inside, but the sound is muted. It's not full of marbles, then, or petrified cookies. But it holds *something.*

My heart beats a little faster. Grabbing the towels and holding the jar tight, I return to the front of the bakery. "There's something other than cookies in it," I tell Mabel, brandishing the jar while handing Mabel the rags. "I don't know what."

She takes the ripped-up cloth but doesn't move, just stares at the strawberry, curiosity lighting her eyes. "You found *that*?"

I figured that was obvious, but she sounds transfixed, maybe even freaked out, so I stick to the facts. "Yes. Do you want to clean up the paint first before you open it?"

She shakes her head—not a no, but like she's shaking off

cobwebs. She quickly swipes the paint off her feet, then the floor, saying, "I know you hate messes."

Huh? That's what she's worried about now? "It's fine. I swear it's fine. I didn't want the jar to get paint on it, or for us to slip in the mess and break it," I explain, as she sets the rags on the drop cloth neatly, more neatly than I'd expected.

But her focus snaps back to the jar. She points at it, shifting away from the mess altogether. "You really found *that*?"

"I did," I say, sensing she knows what *this* is. It's something precious, judging from the look in Mabel's eyes. They're so wide her pupils look blown.

"My grandmother loved strawberries," she whispers.

The meaning of those words echoes loudly, full of a dangerous hope. The kind you don't really want to let yourself feel because it's so easy to be let down. The kind of hope that believes in cures. That believes in a gift from the other side.

Could an old, chipped cookie jar really be so much more? No. No way. Everything rational and logical in me screams to make sure Mabel doesn't get her hopes up. Even though I think they already are. "Mabel, this is probably nothing," I say, calm and measured. "It could be receipts. Or flour. Or just—"

"I don't care. I want it," she says, her voice desperate. She's frozen as if she's afraid to take another step toward it. A hush falls between us. A new tune plays—something sultry, moody—and I swear I can hear her heartbeat.

So much for tempering expectations. "Do you want me to open it?"

She swallows, nibbles on the corner of her lips, then nods several times. "Please."

There's a tremble in her voice. She's already ten steps down this road. But I just can't let myself believe this contains some kind of treasure. Someone needs to be the realist.

Still, I'm careful as I wiggle off the top, though what would I disturb? Junk maybe? Rubber bands? Piping nozzles? "It's probably just...recipes." But wouldn't that be something?

"I love recipes," Mabel says breathlessly.

And yeah, that was a bad example.

"It's likely some paperwork on the firehouse," I say, lifting the top the rest of the way.

I peer inside. I'm holding my breath now, like an intrepid explorer in a treasure hunt flick when he steps into a cave and discovers more than dust. My pulse spikes as I reach inside, wrapping my hand carefully around a stack of paper that's not paperwork at all.

"Mabel, I think there are letters in here."

She clasps her hand over her mouth, gasping, then whispering so quietly I can barely hear her. "Are you sure?"

Sure, this stack could be someone's handwritten poetry or a novel. But I'm staring at a stack of letters, postcards, and maybe greeting cards, tied with a ribbon. "I think so."

The proof is in the looking though, so I take out the stack. They smell like old paper and time, with maybe a hint of something floral. I close the distance between us and offer her the bundle, tied with a shiny ribbon around the middle.

She swallows again and looks at the ribbon, then up at me. "It's lilac. The ribbon color."

Since that's her favorite color, this discovery has to be from someone who knew her. Someone who loved her. "Is it from your grandmother?"

She runs a finger along the bow, then slips it aside, revealing a Post-it note. "Oh my god, Corbin! It's my grandma's handwriting. The same writing that was on the Post-it on the deed. Holy shit, holy shit, holy shit."

With shaking fingers, she peels off the note and holds it out to me. "Read it. I need to know I'm not hallucinating."

I push my own longing aside. This moment belongs to her. I take the Post-it note and draw a steadying breath so I can give this moment the weight it deserves.

Then I read out loud the message left in curvy hand-writing.

Dear Mabel,

I always said you came from a long line of women who follow their hearts. I thought you would enjoy knowing more about one of them. These letters are for you, just like this firehouse is for you. You'll know what to do with them. Oh, but be a dear and remember my number one rule: letters are like cookies—don't eat them all at once!

Love,
Your biggest fan

Mabel stands with her hand over her mouth, tears streaking down her pretty face. She rolls her lips together as if sealing in all her emotions. I know that holding-back feeling too well.

I step closer and swipe a finger across her cheek, wiping away one of her tears. "Mabel, your grandmother orchestrated this entire thing. The firehouse, the letters, the timing...This is incredible. Way more than a ten out of ten."

She smiles through her tears. "It's a hundred."

She sinks to the floor, the weight of the discovery seeming to hit her all at once. I kneel next to her, unsure what to do. I just kissed her senseless, offered her my leg to ride, and then we found a treasure.

Where's the guidebook for what to do next?

Out of the blue, Mabel throws her arms around me, holding me tight. I didn't expect that, or her next words: "Do you want to read one with me?"

Whatever jealousy nipped at me before vanishes. Because suddenly, I want that more than just about anything.

18
—————

FOUND RECIPE
MABEL

I'm really not a crier. Scratch that. I try not to be a public crier. But in the last few weeks, I've rained down tears in front of Jonas the snowboarder-slash-banker and now my sexy hockey-playing business partner, whose leg I also just humped.

No wonder my mother is always trying to give me life advice.

Clearly, I need it.

I can hear her stern, commanding tone: *Don't cry at work because people see it as a sign of weakness.*

Oops.

I take five, head to the restroom, clean up my face, and wash my hands. I don't want to touch the letters with paint-streaked fingers.

Once I'm done, I take some calming breaths, will my heart to stop racing, then attempt not to run back into the bakery. It's not every day you stumble across a stash of decades-old letters.

Even though I want to gobble them up, I also know how to follow orders. Grandma's rules to slow down exist for a reason.

When I was seven, I once ate a dozen or so cookies at her house, and I had the worst stomachache.

Best not to rush headfirst into anything. And besides, this gift of letters from the past—I haven't even begun reading but I already know I won't want it to end. If I savor each one, I can enjoy them more.

When I return to the bakery area, I sit cross-legged on the floor with the stack of letters and do what I should—I take my time. I pick up the stack. I flip through it. I imagine what this stack of letters and cards might become if I follow a recipe.

Because that's really what this is. It's my grandmother's recipe for...something. I don't know what, I don't know how, but it's clear she had a plan.

I doubt Corbin was in her plan though. How could she have known he'd be my business partner? But somehow, it feels right having him here for whatever comes next.

Because he just made you come.

I silence that very naughty voice in my head. I mean, sure, the man has a way with his thigh. But he also has a steady presence and an air of patience as he joins me on the cool, concrete floor, stretching his legs out in front of him. Maybe she knew somehow that I'd need that.

As I undo the satiny lilac ribbon, I focus on opening the stack carefully, on figuring out what ingredients Grandma left me in this surprise recipe, on taking time to consider each one.

"I have no idea if these are her letters or someone else's," I say, feeling like I'm opening the door to an escape room, unsure of what the puzzle is, but eager to solve it.

"Did she ever mention anything about letters? From a friend? A lover? A relative?"

I shake my head as I fiddle with the corner of the first

sheet of paper. "No. She sent me postcards. I sent some back to her. It was our thing."

"Maybe this is your thing now," he offers.

"Or our thing," I suggest. I don't want to be a greedy little pig. The letters might have been saved for me, but he discovered them. Only, I don't want to imply I think *we* are a thing, so I backpedal. "Our thing at Afternoon Delight."

His gaze strays to the garage windows, covered by brown paper as we work, but a section's peeled back, a sliver of a pane letting the sun filter through. "It is afternoon."

It is.

And it's time.

I look down at the first letter, searching for clues. There's no envelope, no postmark. Just a fragile sheet of paper from the past, folded in thirds. "What if it's...?"

I trail off, afraid to say what I truly want—my grandmother's guidance. Her support. Her words, directing me through whatever happens next in my life. I don't get that from my own parents. It's not really my brother's place to do it. Grandma was always the one with the gentle hand and the willing ear.

"What if it's...what?" Corbin prompts.

I shake my head. I'm not ready to let on how much I need someone to lean on, because that someone I leaned on is gone.

"What if it's nothing?" I say instead. That feels safer.

"It's not nothing," he says with the certainty I wish I felt.

I run my finger over the paper once more.

My chest tightens with the wish for something magical in here. For the transformation of flour and sugar and butter into something that melts on your tongue. With that delicious possibility dancing in front of me, I unfold the first page and scan the handwritten note and the date.

"Corbin," I whisper, "it's from seventy years ago."

His smile is full of wonder. "Yeah?"

"Yes. And it says..."

Dear friend,

Can I call you that? I'm pretty sure I can. Because that's what you were to me today. A friend when I needed it most. I walked into the firehouse, nervous and excited and stoic, determined not to show my nerves. A woman in a man's workplace. I expected cold shoulders and stony faces.

There were fewer than I'd anticipated.

And then there was...you.

You walked straight up to me, shook my hand, and said, "It's nice to meet you. I'll show you around."

For that, I thank you. You did show me around. You did make me feel comfortable. You did make me feel like this could be my place too.

I'm really looking forward to working with you.

Thank you for being a friend.

My best,
Your new friend,
Harriet

My heart slams uncomfortably hard against my chest. This *is* a window into another time. A movie where the heroine wanders up the creaky steps to the attic and discovers a long-lost photograph.

"This is the start of a love story," I say, then catch myself. I don't want him to think I mean anything but what's on this ink and paper. "I mean, historically speaking. For them. Seventy years ago."

Corbin's brow furrows. "How do you know? It says *friend.*"

"Harriet's my great-grandmother. She worked here. She met her husband here. But that's all I ever knew about them."

"Wow," he says, drawing a big breath as if he's taking this all in, trying to figure out what to do with this information. "She was brave. A woman firefighter back then? That took guts."

"It did. And he was so kind to her. He made the new person feel welcome," I say, proud of the man I didn't even know.

"That's what you have to do when you get a new team-mate," he says, then holds up a hand, like he's making a correction. "But we don't send letters to the new guy in the locker room. Or discover love letters at rinks."

A laugh bursts from me. "I don't write letters to other bakers. Well, I usually work alone." Except, I don't any longer. "Until now."

He looks around at the bakery we're building with something like pride in his eyes. Maybe wonder too. This is a man who can fly down the ice, shoot a black disc past fearsome goalies, get slammed against the boards, and do it better than most other elite athletes. But he seems proud of this little bakery, which we haven't even finished yet. "Pretty wild that we're building a business in the same spot where your great-grandparents met in another century."

But I'm also painfully, awkwardly aware that we're sitting in a space where someone in my family fell in love. That isn't happening here. One leg hump does not a romance make. "At least we know this place has a history of people getting along," I say, making light of it. Otherwise, he might think I want more, and that's too risky.

"Good thing for business partners," he says with a tight nod.

It says we're resetting again. It's a relief that he feels the same way. I barely know how to manage my own desire for him, let alone his for me.

"I told you it had good bones. I guess it has good vibes too." Even if I like magic, I won't let myself get carried away in magical thoughts. This is just family history I'm reading. It doesn't mean anything about this place, or Corbin and me. Besides, it's not like my grandmother's playing matchmaker from the great beyond.

But when it comes to these letters, I'm not sure I want to go it alone. I want to talk about them with someone. To figure them out. To enjoy them. And that's when I can see the recipe come together.

Take one letter for each milestone. Make a cup of tea. Have a treat. And read them as a team.

"Corbin, what if we take our time with these? Treat them like rewards? For each thing we accomplish at the bakery— getting through opening day, landing our first wedding cake order, getting a great review—we get to read one. What do you think? Do you want to? Read these all with me?"

"As if I'd let you read them alone," he says with a smirk.

"Really? I don't want to pressure you," I say. "I mean, they're love letters. Or they will be."

He scowls. "You think because I'm a hockey player I can't handle a love letter?"

No, I think it's because you said you can't stop thinking about me, can't stop wanting me, and that's messing with your head.

Or maybe that was just the heat of the moment talking. "I didn't want to presume," I say, a little coolly.

He stares at me like I've lost my mind. "Look, if you're asking if it was on my bucket list to find your great-grandmother's love letters and read them with you, then of course it wasn't. But you found them—"

"*You* found them."

He stares at me sternly. "This isn't a hockey game. This isn't a finders-keepers situation. And I'm not some douchebag twentysomething who thinks romance can be found on a reality dating show where everyone is acting."

"I'm not entirely sure what that has to do with love letters, but keep going," I say, both amused by the insult to Dax—since I love insults to my ex—but also intrigued by this train of thought.

Looking away, he rubs his jaw, something he does when he's weighing something. When he returns his gaze to me, and the letter in my hand, he says, "Look, maybe I see a little of myself in this guy."

"The firefighter? Because you like to help?" I ask, thinking of how he rescued me at the romance fair, then rescued me again when I needed an investor.

"Maybe," he says with a shrug. That's as close as I'll get to an admission for now. "But if I found something like this, whether it was recipes, or letters, or a journal from my mom, I'd want someone to read them with me."

My throat tightens, but then that annoying doubt creeps up again. He said *someone.* He didn't say me.

"It's been two years since she died," he continues. "Of Parkinson's complications. It was...rough. Really rough. Some nights, I look up her old emails to me where she'd tell me about her day." He exhales as if this admission costs him something. "And I don't think I'm finding anything she left behind. There are no letters. So, I think what I'm trying to say is"—he stops, holds my gaze with such vulnerability in his emerald eyes—"I'd really like to do this too."

My throat catches. It's happening again. Stupid tears. Annoying emotions. Doing my best to swallow them, I offer a smile, and I say, "Let's do this then."

"Let's do it," he confirms. Then he lifts his brow and glances around the space. "But we also need to do *that*." He points at the mural. "Open a bakery. And incidentally, we need to put a smash cake on the menu."

Those words echo in a whole new way. He was supportive of me that day at the romance fair. He was helpful. He stood up for me.

That's what I needed then. And I hope that whatever he needs, I can give to him. Or maybe the letters can.

"And monkey bread too, Mister Ten Out of Ten," I say, and we're returning to friends, to business partners, to two people trying to realize their dreams together.

With a plan in place, we tuck the letters away in the jar, put the jar on the shelf, then return to the mural.

When it's done, it feels like he painted my chest and I rode his leg in another lifetime. But we need to talk about it.

"Corbin, are we just forgetting about earlier?" I wave a hand breezily toward the wall. The scene of the leg hump.

His eyes darken, perhaps from the memory. But quickly, he nods. A decisive gesture. "We have to. *I* have to. It's the only way. I want this to be a success. You get that, right?"

I do. More than before. I understand the things he's been sharing in bits and pieces about his family, his mother, and her dreams. And the things Charlotte has shared. *This*—our bakery—matters.

"I do," I say.

He steps closer to me, like he's going to cup my shoulders. Like he did that day in the trailer. But instead, he tucks a loose strand of my hair behind my ear, and that's even better than a shoulder squeeze since he lingers, his finger brushing the shell.

I shiver.

"I meant everything I said earlier. How much I think about you. It's ridiculous. But I've got to do a better job resisting you." He lets go of me, stands, and smooths his hands down his shirt. "You have my word that I will."

I wasn't looking for promises, but I know—I really know—I should take his offer.

Because this isn't a love story like in the letters.

This is my messy, real life, and I don't have the good fortune to look back at it with rose-colored glasses while I'm living it.

19

A LITTLE STRESS RELIEF
CORBIN

I remember it with stark clarity.

The way the puck slipped by me when Riggs passed it to me last year in our final playoff game. It was one of countless mistakes we made in the first round of the playoffs—the round we never left. From missed shots to slow skating, we were never in sync. But we also didn't do enough. As a team or as individuals.

It haunts me, but it also fuels me.

A few nights later in Vancouver, it mostly fuels the fuck out of me. Don't want a game like that again. Don't want a season like that again. Don't want a chance like that slipping past me one more time.

Especially since my mind is never far away from Mabel. I have to work even harder than usual to make sure my focus stays squarely on the ice when I'm on it.

I'm fast and aggressive in the first period and the second, nabbing an assist to Riggs, collecting rebounds in the slot, and blocking shots.

See? I can do both.

And I have to.

I know what the pundits are saying. That I'm heading into the sunset of my career or that I'm already there. But they don't know that I can handle *a lot*. When I started playing, I managed having an infant and a key role on the ice. Then, I handled raising a kid while helping to take care of my mom when she needed it most alongside my job. Now, I manage a middle-schooler, a demanding career, a new business, and an intense fucking obsession with my best friend's sister.

As I'm skating toward the Vancouver net, their defenders swarm me. I catch sight of Riggs, several feet away. He's not quite open, but he might be any second. But any second will be too late.

I drop my shoulder like I'm about to pass to him. But instead, I flick the blade of my stick around and I shoot the puck right back through my own legs and in front of me again, where none of their defenders are looking, where the goalie isn't looking, where not even the refs are. One wrist shot later, and it flies past the goalie.

Yes!

Riggs skates over to me, jaw agape. "Did you just shoot between your fucking legs?"

"I fucking did."

Lake smiles as he joins in. "What the fuck was that?"

It was me controlling my career. Setting the pace. Defining my legacy.

Because that's what I need to do—play well—and sometimes that means surpassing expectations, showing everyone who I am. And that's a guy who's driven to win even when he's thinking of a woman all the time, even though he can't have her.

He really, really can't.

* * *

Later on the plane, Riggs drops down into the seat next to me, unknotting his tie. "Hello, highlights reel," he says.

I give a not-at-all humble shrug. "It's good to be me tonight."

"Sure is. But it's good to be me too." He waggles his phone. "Second date coming right up this weekend."

I arch a brow. "And she knows it's *you* she's dating? The crass, cocky, trivia-obsessed, hockey player who has fewer goals than me? Or do you wear a mask to your dates?"

He rubs his middle finger against his cheek.

"So, a mask then. Makes sense."

With an eye roll, he answers, "You only have more goals since you're older. I'll pass you soon, Dad."

"Ouch."

"Yeah, maybe stand down."

I smile, letting go of the ribbing. "Glad the first date worked out," I say, shedding my suit jacket and my envy too. He has no roadblocks to dating Sapphire. Must be nice.

"Yeah, me too," Riggs says. "I kinda crushed on her for a while."

"Kind of? You called her your future girlfriend before you met her."

He claps me on the shoulder. "Guess you'll have to add prescient to your list."

I'll give him that. "True," I say, then mutter, "Fanboy. That's your new nickname."

He shrugs happily. "Works for me."

He fiddles with his phone for a few minutes, texting Sapphire, judging by his dopey smile, while I answer a couple of emails from Charlotte's school about an upcoming science fair.

When Riggs is done, he blows out a breath, then furrows his brow, his thoughts clearly shifting to something else as he turns to me again. "Do you ever, I don't know, feel the pressure?"

"From the game?" I ask, wanting to make sure I'm understanding his question. Now and then, we're thoughtful with each other, rather than dickheads.

"Yeah, but also just from having had such a good career," he says earnestly.

Ah. The pressure of time. He's a little younger than I am, so it's understandable he'd ask me that. "I do," I admit.

"How do you handle it?"

I'm not sure my answer will help him. "I bake."

He laughs, then drags a hand through his hair. "I should have known better."

I sigh, giving his question more thought. "But I also use positive self-talk, you know?"

He nods, clearly listening, since we've all been to the group meetings with team psychologists where they talk about this topic. "I tell myself I'm an excellent hockey player. And then I act like it. I tell myself I can handle the game, the promotion, my family, and then I fucking do it."

He leans back against the cushy, vegan leather seat like he's absorbing that. "Makes sense."

He's quiet for a beat, blowing out a heavy breath.

"Are you stressed?" I ask.

He shakes his head. "Nah, I'm like a Dane."

I furrow my brow. "What?"

"The Danish people. They're one of the least stressed people in the world. After Monaco, Lichtenstein, Switzerland, and a few other countries."

"Okay, but you're not like a Dane, you are a Dane. Isn't your family from Denmark?"

"My mom is. But I guess that explains my chill," he says with a grin, then grabs his headphones.

He shoves them on, then toggles through playlists on his phone till his screen shows an image of rain gently falling on a glass pane.

Huh, maybe that's his stress relief. I suppose we all have to have something.

Me?

I look up recipes on my tablet. I plan out new things I want to bake. I make a schedule to buy ingredients.

And I imagine Mabel biting into a pretty pink cupcake, frosting catching on the corner of her lips.

I picture her taking a bite of a lemon shortcake and making a sinful sound.

I see her dipping her finger into cake batter and sucking it off.

And I have to smother a groan.

I do not need to get turned on while we're flying home.

I close my eyes and try not to think of her, but she's there, in the bakery, wearing only an apron. She's in my kitchen, sitting on the counter, asking me what my favorite thing to bake is.

She's letting her hair down at the end of a long day, shaking it out, then asking me to rub her neck. And I do, while I kiss the back of it, then down her body till she's—

Stop.

Just stop.

But when I open my eyes, Theo's standing by our row. "Nice game tonight."

I blink off the filthy thoughts.

"Thanks, man," I say, then shift gears, stat. "How's it going with the GM job?"

He raps on the back of the seat in front of Riggs even though it's made of plastic. "Good. Knock on wood."

"Glad to hear," I say as the plane hums quietly while hurtling through the night sky.

"What about you and Afternoon Delight? It's clearly not distracting you from the game," he says.

"It's not," I say, but then I drop the subject because I don't want to let on that the bakery's not the distraction.

His sister is, and she plays on a loop in my mind—a loop that is driving me mad since I don't do loops. I don't have obsessions. I don't lose my head over a woman. I never thought this much about Sarah, not about the women I dated after her.

This? There's nothing easy about the way I can't stop thinking about Mabel.

But I made a promise not to go there again, and I'm going to keep that promise the second time around.

Not for Theo. Not because he's her brother. But for me, and for her, and the dream we're both chasing together.

I invite her brother to grab the empty seat next to me, and we shoot the breeze the rest of the flight, playing cards, talking shit, and having a good time. That helps, too, with my promise.

* * *

The next day, I pick up Charlotte from school, and my mind is fixed firmly on being a dad. When she slides into the car, she says, "I just got an email that our volunteer application for the animal shelter was accepted. The one Mabel told us about. We could do that together soon. Isn't it going to be great?"

"It sure is," I say, half wishing she hadn't brought up Mabel, but half grateful, too, that it's not my fault this time when my mind wanders to the woman I work with.

Besides, I'm good at what I do. I can handle it all. I can definitely handle it.

20

THAT LITTLE BAKERY
MABEL

I'd rather be baking, *but* I also know I need to, how shall we say, mend some fences? To some, I'm still the girl who took off from Cozy Valley and hardly ever came back, and if I want these townspeople to come to my bakery, I need to say hi and let them know I'm sticking around.

Well, for a year at least, but that counts.

I'm running some errands in town today, and that gives me the perfect chance to spread the word about Afternoon Delight. The business—not what Corbin did to me a week ago *in* our business. I definitely need to put that incident out of my head. And I'm doing my best to quit daydreaming about it.

I swear I'm trying not to think about Corbin's magical thigh.

After I stop by Reprise to pick up another set of adorably mismatched plates, I invite the owner to check us out when we open in around two weeks, handing her a fresh new card with a QR code on it for Afternoon Delight. "Would love to see you there, Zakiya," I tell her.

I've gotten to know her a bit from my trips here to forage for dishes. Originally from Bahrain, she's newish to Cozy

Valley too, her makeup game is on point, and she has a wicked sweet tooth. In short, I adore her.

"You know I'll be there. I like to see my goods represented," she says, then wraps up some of the white plates with the yellow flowers on them. An image of Mrs. Henderson's mailbox flashes before my eyes. She had a flowered mailbox that I ran over years ago, didn't she? Guilt creeps into me, but I shoo it away and focus on the moment, rather than another mishap.

"You will definitely be represented at Afternoon Delight. I'd be happy to put some of your business cards on the counter at the bakery or a card with a QR code," I say, grateful to have hit it off with someone from the town.

"Yes. Let's do a trade," she says, grabbing a postcard for her shop with a scannable code on it. I take it as she adds, "And be sure to stop by the gym with some of those cards. I bet you can get some of the gym crowd right after they work out and feel virtuous enough to afford a cookie."

I laugh. "Good plan."

I pop into the gym next, where a young woman with shiny blonde hair stands at the counter, her head bent over her phone as she scrolls and scrolls.

She even scrolls as I wait for her to notice me.

Something must draw her attention away from the screen since she snaps her head up, then blinks twice. "Whoa. You're, like, Dax's ex."

I cringe. Everywhere.

"That's me," I say, a little bitter.

And shit. That won't sell my bakery to a town that's tepid on me. I pour on the sweet. "I'm Mabel, and it's good to meet you. I'd love to invite you to come to my bakery that's opening in early December," I say, then give her the name and date.

"Oh, I don't eat sugar," she says, then waves a dismissive

hand. "But I love *Romance Beach*. I even sent that meme to a friend last week. I have got to get my act together too. Selfie? Because...you? Me? Same."

Oh, wow. Oh, shit. This is not the notoriety I wanted. But it's too late, since she's already flown around the desk, wedged herself next to me, and is making a duck face at her phone.

"Thanks, babe," she says, then returns to the desk to scroll again.

Yeah, I don't think I'm going to have any luck here.

I leave in a funk, that familiar feeling of not being enough hitting me square in the solar plexus. But as I sink into the front seat of my car, vaguely tempted to return to Afternoon Delight and hunker down with my good friends flour and sugar, I hear my grandmother's voice asking *If not now, when?*

Dammit. She's right. I can't quit this mission. That would be like leaving town all over again. I soldier on, doing my damnedest to see myself as something other than the girl who's too impulsive, too loud, too bold. I can be the woman who gets things done. The woman who follows recipes when she bakes. Well, most of the time.

I hit a few more shops before it's time to return to the bakery, sit down with my laptop and market in other ways. I draft some social posts, schedule some mouth-watering pics of cupcakes and cookies, and organize more photos for next week. Then, I install some shelves.

As I work alone, I let myself daydream about the other day here, from the painting to the kissing to the reading, and all of that carries me into the night too.

* * *

"No, girl, no. You serve underhand," Trevyn calls out from next to me on the pickleball court the next day.

I roll my eyes at my doubles partner and friend. "I know. I was just seeing if you were paying attention."

That's a lie.

I'm daydreaming. Totally daydreaming about the mural Corbin and I finished, the garage door that's now installed, the windows inviting in streaming sunshine throughout the day as we get the little bakery ready. I'm thinking about the sign that now hangs above the garage door, pretty in pink, with a cheeky little winking dot above the *i* in Delight. I'm picturing the display cases fully installed and ready, right next to the shining fire pole, and the appliances, checked, polished, and tested.

And I'm daydreaming, too, of the way Corbin held my face when he kissed me, the tension in his jaw as he fought to resist, the desperate rasp in his voice as he gave in, and the words that play on repeat in my head.

I think about you all the time.

Trevyn clears his throat, pulling me from my wandering thoughts once more.

He steps closer to me on the court. He's every bit as committed to pickleball fashion as I am in his tight white shorts and equally tight white shirt, which contrasts elegantly with his rich brown skin. He points at me, drawing a circle in the air at my outfit, a patterned little white-and-pink number. "We all know you look good, friend. But some of us like to look hot and win. Now, either focus on the game or tell us all in delicious detail why you're zoning out."

"Because we've been betting that you got some D," Skylar chimes in from the other side of the net, flicking her auburn hair for emphasis.

Remy—her pickleball partner—just nods sagely in agreement.

My jaw drops. "You all bet on that?"

"Of course we did," Skylar says with a nonchalant shrug. "You just have that look about you."

"My money's on you wanting more," Remy adds, giving me a thoughtful once-over as she heads toward center court with Skylar.

So much for the game. It's gossip-over-the-net time.

We're playing in Cozy Valley today. That will endear me to the town, right? People will see me embracing all the activities this town offers.

But for now, I focus on the immediate issue—their dick radar. "So, why do you think I got some D?" I ask, hungry for every detail of their assessments.

"Because you aren't denying it," Skylar says, tapping her racquet against the net.

"Spill," Remy demands, adjusting her visor. Her bouncy chestnut hair is cinched tight in a ponytail above the strap.

I blow out a breath like I'm *so annoyed* they've wheedled it out of me, even though I've been dying to tell them. But this is the first time the four of us have been able to get together since that fateful afternoon. Fateful in more ways than one.

I stretch my arms above my head as if limbering up my muscles after the incident, even though it was days ago. "Well, let's see. If memory serves, I'm pretty sure I spent the other day climbing my business partner's leg until I came."

Remy's eyes pop. "Wait, did you do a full-on leg rub, a bump and grind, or a straddle and ride him into the sunset?"

Skylar whips her gaze to Remy. "That's very specific. Do you cover styles of grinds on How We Met?"

That's her podcast, which she started for fun, inviting viewers to share stories of how they met their love.

"No," she says, faux offended. "But I'm still an expert in all these things."

"Of course you are, hun," Trevyn says.

"And there are many varieties of dry humping. It's important to know which one it was." Remy counts on her fingers. "First, there's the straddle and grind down. I like to call it The High School Lap Dance. Number two is when he lifts you up against the wall and you simulate wall sex. That's The Wallbanger. The third is when you rub up against him like a dog, AKA The Dirty Dog. And number four, he sticks his leg out and offers it to you like a fucking filthy gentleman and you ride it." With a pop of her lipsticked mouth, she adds, "I like to call that The Filthy Gentleman."

We all bow down to the expert among us.

"All hail the queen," Skylar says.

Remy waves off the adulation. "Thank you, thank you. But your supplication is unnecessary. The *truth* is necessary." She turns to me and, with a pointed look, asks, "Which one was it, our little horndog?"

A tingle rushes down my spine as I recall every stomach-swooping detail. Primly, I lift my chin. "He was a very filthy gentleman."

Trevyn emits a low, appreciative whistle while Skylar squeals. Remy gives me an approving look.

"No wonder you can't focus on pickleball," Skylar says.

"Your head is replaying that whole move, isn't it?" Remy asks with an arch of a brow.

"You'd all do the same," I counter saucily before I remember to tamp down my enthusiasm. As I grab a ball from a bucket on the side of the court, I put on a serious face. "But the thing is, it's not going to happen again. It just can't."

The mood shifts instantly.

"Because you're business partners," Skylar says with a sad smile.

"But *not* because your brother's a protective caveman," Remy clarifies. "Though he is."

"A hot caveman," Trevyn points out.

"Gross," I say. "But Theo's not the issue. Sure, I appreciate that they're friends, and I wouldn't want to cause friction between them, but it's also not my brother's call who I do or don't date."

"Preach," Skylar puts in.

Trevyn voices his take on the problem. "It can't happen because you're chasing the same dream and you need to keep your focus on it."

Bingo. "Yes. That. But also, I'm taking a break from dating. That last breakup really sucked. I felt so stupid." The familiar self-loathing swims up inside me, as it does whenever I think of Dax, the way he left, and the things he said about me. Things that clearly resonated, judging from Gym Girl's weird excitement over meeting me. "I feel stupid half the time in this town too. When I go up and down Main Street introducing myself to the other business owners, sometimes I feel like people are waiting for me to fail just like Dax was waiting for me to fail. Like this woman at the gym," I say, then tell them about the selfie sneak attack.

"I hope you took her phone and smashed it," Trevyn says.

I laugh. "Why didn't I think of that?"

"But it doesn't sound like she was waiting for you to fail. More like she thinks she's kind of floundering and saw some sort of kinship," Remy says.

I chew on that for a beat, then concede, "Maybe."

"The people here aren't that bad," she reassures me.

"I know." It's true there's been some real kindness. Like from Zakiya, of course, as well as the woman who owns the Green Pantry, and the bookshop owner. But I can't shake the mailbox incident, the llama drama, the meme. "But really, why do I want to get into a relationship that might not work out? I've got to focus on the bakery. I don't want to fail at that."

"You're not going to," Remy says, firm and supportive.

"I have faith in you," Trevyn seconds.

"And we're all going to show up at your opening day and gorge ourselves to make sure you sell out," Skylar adds.

And at the end of that day, Corbin and I will read another love letter from years ago.

I can't wait for our opening for many reasons.

I toss the ball in the air once and catch it easily. "Now, stop distracting me with your names for dry-humping styles. I have to serve underhand this time."

And I do.

* * *

When the game ends, my friends take off, and even though a part of me is dying to walk the long way downtown by going around all the shops via side streets, I force myself to go along Main Street, saying hello.

I say hi to Luis, who runs a cute little clothing boutique with a rainbow flag in the window. I avoid the town square, where the retired guys who play chess outside like to eat grocery store Danishes and drink gas station coffee and disparage hipster bakeries (they told me as much when I handed out a flyer earlier in the week for the upcoming opening day). But I stop for a minute to chat with the woman who runs the sandwich shop that makes excellent vegetarian fare. She's been particularly supportive, one vegetarian to another.

I pass The Meet Cute, where the frosty-faced little dog lounges in his chair sleepily. I wave to Clementine, who owns the store, and she waves back from behind the counter. She's a friend of mine, and it's comforting to know that she'll definitely be coming to the opening since not only do we get along, but her brother, Lake, plays on the Foxes with Corbin.

A Good Yarn is a couple of shops up ahead, and then I'll turn onto Holly Springs.

A trio of older women pours out of the shop. The knitting club, I think, judging by the craft bags slung over their shoulders, some with needles sticking out, another with the tail of a knitted scarf flapping in the breeze.

One of them says, "I give it a month."

I wonder what they're talking about.

"Three," the woman in the middle says. "The hockey player will keep it open."

My gut twists as I have the answer. *Me.* They're talking about me.

"She's a good baker," the third one admits. "I've ordered stuff from her place in the city. But she doesn't belong here. She's a city girl."

The first one nods. "She didn't stick around the last time."

I've stopped outside the bookstore, my feet glued to the sidewalk, refusing to move. They're betting on me to fail.

My skin crawls. My stomach aches. I suck in a breath, only it feels like I can't breathe. I try again, but inhaling is hard all of a sudden.

Is this a panic attack? I've never had one before, but I think it might feel like this.

Why did I think it would be okay for me to come back to Cozy Valley just because I inherited an abandoned fire station? Did I think I could welcome-wagon myself into their hearts with a cheery, *Hi, I'm Mabel, and I want to sell you cookies from my firehouse-turned-bakery!*

I spin around, searching for the quickest route out of sight. I still can't catch my breath, and I don't want anyone to see me freaking out like this.

Think fast.

Ah, there's a slim alley next to the bookshop. I dart down it, into the shadows, and lean against the wall. It's a mural of spines for some of the most popular romance books of the last few years. I breathe in. I breathe out. I try to slow my jackhammering pulse.

What if no one shows up on opening day? What if not enough people do? What if I'm too chaotic? Too crazed? Too obsessed with my baked goods? What if I put too much salt in a recipe? What if I pick the wrong merch, or not enough merch? What if the chairs are uncomfortable, or the decor is too pink, or it's not pink enough?

My mind swims with too many possibilities.

I breathe again, trying to calm my wild thoughts, my racing heart.

Another breath.

It's fine. I'm fine.

Another slow breath.

I'll prove them wrong. That's what I'll do.

After a minute or two, I've gotten myself together enough to slip out of the alley, where I run smack into...my mother.

She's all tweed and polish, her stick-straight brown hair cut in a bob, her horn-rimmed reading glasses perched atop her head. The strap of her leather satchel full of books rests on her shoulder.

"Oh, what a lovely surprise," she says. "How are you?"

"What are you doing here?" I blurt out. I haven't seen her in a few months. We've talked. We've texted. I had to tell her I was opening a bakery here. I couldn't hide that. But I've been too busy to meet up. At least, that's what I told her.

She gives me a confused look at the question. "I live here."

"Right." Of course, I knew that. I'm just so flustered. I jam my hands through my hair. It's still a little sweaty from the game. "I didn't expect to see you. I'm sorry. Was I supposed to meet you?"

"No, I'm just picking up lunch at the Green Pantry. Do you want something? We could get a bite and chat about some ideas I have for you in case things don't work out with the bakery."

Gritting my teeth, I heave a sigh. "You too?" Is there anyone in this town who doesn't think I'm a loser?

"What do you mean you *too*?"

But I'm not about to let her know that the knitting club is placing bets on how fast I sink into business quicksand. "Nothing. I just meant...I'm sorry. I'm a little—"

She sets a cool, moisturized hand on my arm. "You're scattered, dear. I get it. It happens. And if you don't have time for lunch, just put this little nugget in the back of your mind. I could help you get a job at the university in the food services. They have some openings. The benefits are great. There's a wonderful retirement plan. I know you're determined to make this little bakery work, but sweetheart, you really need to be in a job that has benefits. It's so important. You have to think about the future."

The sidewalk tilts. The world is upside down. I feel small all over again for daring to think my *little bakery* could work.

I drag a hand down my face and say, "I'll think about it, okay? I need to go."

"Let's do lunch soon," she says.

"Right. Soon," I say robotically, then escape down the street toward the firehouse.

I need to bake.

I need to prove I can do this.

I need to show them all I'm not a hot mess.

But when I spot a pack of strong, sturdy men carting in tables and chairs, I remember. Today, the guys from Corbin's team are setting up the furniture we ordered from a consign-ment shop.

It looks like Riggs is hauling a pink chair from a pickup truck that belongs to Lake's ranch.

I'm not sure I can face all of them. I'm not sure I can face anybody. I'm about to double back to...do what? Retreat? Like everyone expects me to?

I stop maybe a hundred feet away and try to think.

Corbin strides out, says something to the guys, then laughs, but the sound cuts off when he turns my way.

"Just set it up in the corner," he tells someone. "Back in a minute."

He jogs to me, concern etched in his thoughtful eyes, like he already knows everything that's happening in my head, like he can read all my feelings on my face.

"What's wrong, Firecracker?" he asks when he reaches me.

The new nickname settles some of my spiraling thoughts. "Did you just call me firecracker?"

"Seems about right for you." His eyes narrow as he assesses me, then he reaches for my shoulders, squeezing them. His gaze burns, intense, like he'd destroy anybody who hurt me. "Mabel? What happened?"

The question is urgent, insistent.

"It's stupid," I say quietly.

"It's not stupid."

"It is. I'll be fine," I say, trying to swallow the hurt—a hurt I brought on myself.

"Mabel," he says, his voice a warning.

"I swear."

He glances over his shoulder then back to me, his eyes alight with a plan. "Stay here. I'll be right back."

21

HE HAD IT BAD

MABEL

He jogs to the firehouse, ducks his head in, and then returns to me in less than a minute. "There's something I want to show you."

"What is it?"

"Something I think you'll enjoy. Seems like you need it right now."

My chest warms. "I do. Thank you."

He rubs my arm. "I had a feeling."

I push the knitting club and my mother out of my head as we get in his car.

He drives to a little flower and plant store on the outskirts of town. Its face is made of white bricks, and the name, Enchanted Blooms, is written in a wistful script on the gleaming window.

When we reach the door, Corbin pauses, then swallows like what he's about to say is uncomfortable for him. "It's... wisteria. The color of the door."

I stare at the color...and he's dead on. The door is painted a soft, delicate shade of purple. "How did you know?" I ask, my voice pitching up with wonder.

"The owner is a friend of my mom's. I went in here the other day to pick up a plant."

That doesn't explain *how* he knows, but I keep listening.

"And I could tell that everything in here was some kind of..." He pauses, waves like he's casting about for what to say next. "Pretty color. But I didn't know what. I just knew you'd probably want to see it. Do you want me to show you?"

My breath catches. "Yes." I'm more eager than I've ever been to bake, to read, to spend time with friends.

I want this color tour badly.

He takes me inside the little shop, where a big orange tabby sleeps lazily in a sunbeam on the floor. An elegant, older woman with Black braids gives a warm nod from the counter.

I smile back, then look around. There are kelly green, emerald green, and forest green plants hanging from shelves or sitting on little tables with mosaiced tiles on them. Corbin guides me to one in the corner. Like foreign words he's practicing for the first time, he says, "That's robin's-egg blue."

"It is," I say, breathless.

With a pleased nod, he gestures to another plant table. "And this is sunshine yellow."

I'm stunned. "Yes. It's bright and happy."

He gives a faint smile. "I'll trust you on that."

He sets a hand on the small of my back, sending a hot shiver up my spine as he leads me a few feet to a shelf full of terracotta pots.

"I had a feeling you'd love this place, so I asked Annabelle," he says, tipping his forehead to the woman at the counter, "the color of everything in the store. I wrote them all down to remember them, and where they were. I wanted to give you the tour myself so I needed to learn the colors to show them to you." His smile is warm and kind. "I was going to do it soon, but it seemed like maybe you needed to see it today."

My heart stutters, then speeds up to double time. He did this for me. Learned and memorized so he could share it with me. Just because I love places like this, colors like these. Emotions rise in my chest, climb up my throat. "I really do. Thank you."

He shows me a pot at the end of the shelf. "This is teal blue." The one next to it. "Baby pink." Another one. "Cherry red." He lowers his voice to a deadly whisper. "Like the paint."

The memory slams back into me, hot and sharp. "Just like the paint."

He takes me around the shop, showing me a sign for a wall that says *All My Friends Are Plants*. "Sage green."

"Yes," I say, and my smile takes over my face. No, it steals my entire afternoon.

He bypasses the cooler holding bouquets of flowers. Those are probably tougher to memorize, since they must change more regularly.

But he finishes at a high white wooden table teeming with bouquets of irises. "Lilacs aren't in bloom now in California. But irises are."

My heart is too big for my chest. "This is incredible, and I needed this so much," I tell him, and he deserves to know why. "You asked what's wrong. The women in the knitting club are placing bets on how fast I fail."

I tell him everything. His eyes burn with fire.

"They're not betting on how fast you fail. They're betting on how quickly *we* fail," he says, his voice as protective as it was that day at the romance fair.

My heart softens, but the reality is I know it's me they're betting against. "No, Corbin, they think you're a success. They think I'm a joke."

Stepping closer, he slides a thumb across my jaw. My chest flips. "But you're not a joke, and we are going to prove them all wrong. *Together*." Then he says, "Do you like flowers?"

"Of course I do."

"I had a feeling. That's why I wanted to show you the irises. They're close to your favorite color. Let's put them in the bakery. I think we should have some flowers there every day, and they should be in your favorite color."

All at once, he's turned my day completely around.

When he buys a bouquet of irises, the woman at the register—Annabelle—smiles at him like she knows something. "Told you," she says to Corbin, her dark eyes twinkling.

"Annabelle," he warns.

I don't know what she knows, but I like her already, especially when she says to me, "That was one hell of a London Fog cake you made."

"Thank you." Then it hits me—she's the someone he asked about the color of the London Fog cake I left on his doorstep as we were getting started. She must matter to him if he put himself out there in that way. A fond feeling digs into my breastbone.

Corbin nods to the back of the shop. "There's a garden out back. Want to see it?"

"How can you even ask?"

He sets a hand on my back and guides me along a skinny hallway, past boxes of plant food. "I also took the liberty to bring a little something along."

My brow knits. "What do you mean?"

"Maybe we don't want to wait for opening day to read another letter. I hope you don't mind. But I think you popping into other businesses and saying hello is a milestone and deserves—"

"A cookie?" I ask, anticipation bouncing inside of me.

He pats his back pocket as we reach the door and stop. "I took one."

"Did you read it already?" I'm only a little worried. It doesn't seem like his style, but I need to ask.

"What do you take me for? A guy who has no patience?"

Considering I'm ahead in the O department, he clearly has plenty of self-control. "Nope."

He opens the door into a tiny garden, teeming with winter jasmine and white lilies stretching toward the sun. A small Japanese maple stands proudly in a corner, and a green slatted bench commands the center of this emerald enclave.

"This is incredible," I say, soaking in this refuge in the middle of this small town.

"Glad you like it," he says, pride and something else in his voice.

Something that makes me feel warm and shimmery. It's a feeling I could get lost in though. A feeling that could distract me from my business, my plans, my dreams.

"All right. What have you got?" I ask, heading to the bench and patting the seat next to me.

He joins me, takes the letter from his back pocket, and carefully unfolds it. My fingers are tingling to touch it, this lovely artifact from a romance decades ago. "It was already folded," he explains. "Don't want you to think I put a crease in it."

"I would never think such a thing," I say, eager to learn what happened next for the young lovers.

Corbin hands it to me. "It's yours."

But it feels like ours, especially when I read the first two words.

Dear Harriet.

"It's to her," I say breathlessly. "He wrote it to her." I feel like I'm holding a piece of history—someone's personal history. It's a privilege, this sneak peek into another century, another love affair.

I offer it to Corbin. "You read it out loud."

He takes the paper, clears his throat, and reads.

Dear Harriet,

Today was a tough day. Calls like that are always hard. The things we have to do in our line of work are never easy. But you're brave, and you made a difference in our community.

I sensed it was hard for you, though, the way the other guys didn't seem to want to let you do things—even things rookie firefighters do, like pulling hose lines.

But you trained for this. You can do it. And I just want to say—don't let them get you down.

They'll come around.

They'll see who you are. Gutsy, determined, focused.

And, you're funny.

Well, maybe don't let them see that.

Save that part just for me.

Your friend,
Russ

I'm quiet, as if speaking might pierce a magic spell cast by the past and those words. I want to live in this bubble for a few more shimmery seconds.

After a moment, he breaks the silence. "Seems like he had it bad for your great-grandmother. He had it bad from the start."

A warm, hazy smile keeps tugging at my mouth. I didn't know Harriet and Russ, but thanks to my grandma's last gift, I get to experience their love story. "He sure did," I say, kind of amazed.

And we sit on the bench, neither one of us wanting to move, just soaking in the next chapter in a love story I didn't expect.

22

―――

SHIRT SWAP

MABEL

On the eve of opening day, with a digital sign in the window boasting "Grand opening tomorrow!" I bake alone. This is normal for me, and Corbin's at the rink for morning skate anyway. We've spent the last two weeks on the final details: painting the exterior brick, printing menus, finalizing recipes, and creating hype on our new socials accounts, and now we're ready. On time, as planned, in early December.

Right now, though, I'm not baking goodies to sell at Afternoon Delight. I'm baking dozens upon dozens to give away to townspeople. I don't know why I didn't think of this sooner, but maybe I can win them over with food. Studies show that sharing food releases oxytocin. And firefighters who cooked and ate meals together had better team performance and cooperative behavior. I might have gone down a rabbit hole. But it was a useful one, since I'd like to have the town on my side—especially if I'm going to make this place work. The last thing I need is the locals thinking I'm the scatterbrained, careless girl who left Cozy Valley after the original firehouse fiasco and then swooped in and ruined their beloved firehouse.

I make my signature orange habanero cookies, but not

everybody likes spice, so I whip up some pistachio chocolate chip ones, along with normal chocolate chip, because the classics are the classics for a reason. I make mini cupcakes—chocolate with caramel buttercream and sea salt, vanilla with raspberry, and coconut cake, too—and I include the sweet and salty bars that Corbin made for me, baking both a regular and a gluten-free version. Finally, I whip up some cinnamon rolls, just because the icing is divine. By mid-afternoon, I'm sweating and half-exhausted as I swipe pieces of hair from my face and back into my bun. With the scent of warm treats in the air, I fill box after blush-pink box and put stickers on each one: "A little Afternoon Delight for you."

When I'm done baking and ready to deliver them to the shop owners around town, I stop, catching a glimpse of myself in one of the dressing room mirrors—because of course we kept them.

But mirrors don't lie, and this one is a billboard telling me I'm a little too hot and sweaty to be my own welcome wagon. "Dammit," I mutter. Why didn't I think of that?

Wait. Wait a hot second. This place has a shower on the second floor. The perks of converted firehouses.

On the flip side, I don't have any shower supplies. I hustle out to a home decor gift shop on Main Street and grab some soap, then a towel for good measure, even though it's barely bigger than a kitchen towel. Actually, I think it *is* a kitchen towel.

I thank the proprietor, a folksy woman with gray hair and a name tag that says Mariah.

"Thanks, sweetie. You come back if you need anything else," she says.

"Do you like cookies?"

"Am I alive?"

"I hear you," I say. Back at the bakery, I shut the door

behind me and lock it, then grab one of our T-shirts—that's a good thing about offering merch; I've always got a change of shirt when I need it—and head upstairs. The pipes groan from disuse, and the water takes more than a hot minute to heat up, but once it does, I jump in and wash off the major stink zones with the soap that smells like sweet pea. After a satisfying inhale, I turn off the shower. Stepping out of the steam, I wrap the towel around myself.

Well, mostly.

It reaches the edge of my boobs and leaves a long strip of skin exposed down my side.

I leave the shower, turn into the former sleeping quarters, and step smack-bang right into Corbin.

My towel pulls a Houdini.

For a few seconds, I stand there naked in front of my business partner.

He doesn't move either. He just swallows, Adam's apple bobbing, eyes locked on me. All of me. Every inch of me. Just...me. Flames flicker in his green eyes, turning them molten. His lips part. His fists clench.

I should grab the towel and be all demure. But when he stares like I'm a dessert he wants to devour, it's hard not to bask in the eye-fucking. And this man gives good eye-fuck. My skin tingles everywhere his gaze lands. I ache between my thighs from the evidence of how much he likes what he sees— the outline of his hard-on.

I've never felt so...deliciously ogled. So sexy. So wanted. It's more addictive than awkward. But I'm also pretty sure he's not about to toss me over his shoulder, drop me on the firefighter's bunk, and fuck me to pieces.

"I was...showering," I say, recovering from the hot stare-off as I bend to grab the fallen towel. When I rise, Corbin's already stripped off his T-shirt and thrusts it at me while looking away. Like he had to jerk his head so as not to look.

"Here. Just in case," he says, his voice strained.

I tug it on, laughing. "I mean, what exactly is this in case of?"

"Um," he says, still staring at the concrete wall. "In case you don't have...clothes. Yeah. Clothes."

"I could have worn just an apron," I tease.

"Mabel," he says, a gravelly warning. Does Corbin have apron fantasies of me?

"Do you like aprons?"

He breathes out hard through his nostrils. If I peeked, I'd bet his eyes would be closed.

"Yes," he bites out.

I'm tempted to say *You, me, same page.* I'm so tempted to shed this T-shirt and put my apron back on. But I don't. I'm a good girl.

For now.

With his shirt falling to mid-thigh, it's probably safe for him to turn around. "I'm decent," I say, and when he pivots around, shirtless now, I notice he's holding a gift-wrapped box and offering it to me.

"You got me a present?"

"For opening day," he says, and every word still sounds rough.

I take it, but the tables are turned, and I'm distracted by his shirtlessness and, it turns out, by his scent. I dip my nose so I can inhale the lake-and-campfire aroma of his shirt.

"Corbin," I say, "I think...I should get dressed, and you should put this back on. We seem to have traded one problem for another."

He breathes out hard, his gaze swinging down to my bare thighs, then back up my frame, like he's taking in the full impact of me in his T-shirt and nothing else. "Yeah," he says. "I guess the shirt swap didn't help."

He exits, and I quickly strip off his shirt, then get dressed again in my skort and the T-shirt from the shop with the bakery's name across the front. I call out, "It's safe now. I promise."

Footsteps echo across the concrete floor, and Corbin strides back into the dorm area, still, of course, shirtless.

"Not safe for *me* yet," I joke, as breezy as I can be to try to douse the heat shimmering between us. I toss him his shirt. He catches it with one hand and tugs it on.

Shame about the loss of the view. But it's for the best.

"Let's try this again," he says, then picks up the gift box from where I left it on one of the bunks. He hands it to me.

"What is this?" I ask, a little wonder in my voice.

"It's a gift. Also called a present. You open it and you pretend to like it."

I roll my eyes, but even so, my heart feels squishy. "I don't have to pretend to like it."

Something flashes in his eyes. Fondness maybe? I'm not sure, but it seems heartfelt. Dangerously so. He clenches his fists as if fighting the impulse to stride over and take me in his arms.

I run a finger along the pretty purple ribbon with white polka dots. "It's almost too pretty to open. I don't even care what's in here. I just love the way it looks," I say.

"Open it, Mabel," he says, a clear command that sends a shiver down my spine.

"Yes, sir."

"Troublemaker," he mutters.

I bat my eyes. "But I thought I was 'Firecracker'?"

"Troublemaker, firecracker, sweet and salty. It's all you," he says, then nods again to the gift, urging me on. The air between us is all kinds of crackly as I undo the ribbon, then unwrap the paper and open the box.

My jaw falls open. "You didn't."

He gives a casual shrug. "You said you needed a new one for opening day."

"It's perfect." I take out the gift, set down the box on the floor, then hold up the pretty pink-and-white pickleball dress with the pleated skirt and the polo collar. "It's preppy and sporty, and I love it."

I squeeze the dress against me, hugging it in thanks, even though I want to be tossing my arms around him. But I'm not sure I wouldn't wrap my legs around him too, then suggest he perform The Wallbanger on me.

Corbin's smile is pleased, but a little boyish at the same time. "Will you wear it tomorrow?"

It's asked like it would mean the world to him.

I give the easiest answer ever. "I will." I finger the soft material of the pink skirt. "It's—"

"Blush," he finishes, then adds, "The color of our bakery."

"Corbin," I whisper. "How did you do this?"

But of course, there are so many ways he could have matched this color without really seeing it. He could have brought a bakery box along to the store. Except he doesn't like to ask for help.

Rubbing a hand across his jawline, he blows out a breath. "I memorized the shade."

His eyes are etched with raw vulnerability.

"For me?" But the second the question comes out, I walk it back. "I mean, *for us*. For the bakery, of course."

"Sure. For the bakery," he says, shoving his hands into his pockets.

As I'm folding the dress carefully and putting it back in the box, he adds, "It's the color of your cheeks when you're a little...hot."

I'm on fire right now. As I close the box, I look over at him. "And my chest," I say, and then lift my hand to drag my fingers along the neckline of my shirt.

His eyes darken. "Yes."

I roam my fingertips along my throat. "And here?"

He gives a rough staggered breath as he stands in the doorway, gripping the frame. He nods again.

I set a hand on my cheek, softly running my fingers to my jawline.

His grip intensifies as he nods. "Yes," he grunts, then rasps out, "I happen to think blush is very, very pretty."

The fire engulfs me.

And I'm the one clenching my fists now. It takes everything in me not to throw myself at him.

Must stop flirting.

Well, you paraded naked in front of him moments ago.

Rude, I tell the voice in my head.

I force myself to focus on manners with Corbin. "Thank you. I feel bad I didn't get you anything."

"Don't worry. You can owe me," he says with a wink. "Now, what's up with all the boxes I saw downstairs? Do we have a huge pre-order?"

Bakery business. This is perfect. "Actually, I planned to give them out to all the townspeople in the shops today."

His lips quirk up in question. "Can I go with you? We are business partners after all."

And I'd do well to remember that.

23

____

A LITTLE HELP, PLEASE

MABEL

Together, we load up canvas bags full of baked goods, then head out to go door-to-door.

We say hi to Clementine at The Meet Cute. Even though she's already on our side, she deserves cookies too. We pop into the Green Pantry, and then I bound up the steps of the cheese shop. But Corbin lags behind, gesturing to a bench right outside it.

"I need to deal with some emails," he says, waving his phone. Weird. He's not a _deal with emails_ kind of guy. But there's something sad in his eyes, so I give him the space and go in alone.

I haven't been in here yet. A bearded man behind the counter shoots me a skeptical look as I stride toward him, a pink-and-white box in my hands. His name tag says Abe. After I say hello, he asks brusquely, "Your parents work over at the university?"

"Yes, they do," I say. "I'm Mabel Llewelyn, and I'm opening up Afternoon Delight with Corbin—"

He waves a hand. "I know him. He's lived in this town for a long time."

Implication—*and you haven't.*

"Okay. Anyway, I—"

"And you haven't been around town since the pigs knocked over the syrup and the llamas got into the sugar cookies?"

I wince at the reminder. "Yes."

He blows out a long whistle. "So you roll back into town wanting to open a bakery?"

"Yes," I say, owning it.

"That takes some serious guts," he says, shaking his head. I can't tell if he thinks I'm crazy or if he admires me. Maybe a little of both.

"Well, I'm not really a sweets person myself," he goes on. "But at least you're not competing with me."

Small victories. I waggle a box. "I made some treats for the other local business owners," I say, then rattle off what's in the box. "Just as a little welcome gift." But before he cuts me off again, I quickly add, "If you don't like sweets, do you have someone you can give these to?"

He seems to consider that, then nods. "Yeah, my husband has a sweet tooth."

"Well, I hope he visits us sometime. He'd be more than welcome."

The man gives me a once-over, blows out a breath, and says, "Good luck."

It doesn't feel like I've won him over, but it doesn't feel like I've lost him either.

When I leave, Corbin's on the bench, staring off into the distance, his phone out of sight.

I drop down next to him with some concern. "You okay?"

There's a long beat. "It was my mom's favorite place," he says, his voice flat, like he's had to strip the emotion from it to speak.

I set a hand on his strong, firm bicep, and I squeeze it. "Are you thinking of her right now?"

Another steadying breath. "She used to send me these emails, Mabel. She called them Monday Agenda, Tuesday Report, Wednesday News. That sort of thing. At the end of each day that I was on the road." He still doesn't look my way, just gazes at the sky as if that's easier. "She liked to walk to this store. It was...a benchmark for her, I think. They have really good cheese, so I get it." He laughs, but it feels forced.

I rub his arm, letting him know to keep going.

"Anyway, it just got harder at the end. She'd freeze up. It happens," he explains. "And sometimes, she'd fall. Eventually, she had to stop walking here."

My heart cracks in two. "I'm sorry. That must have been so hard for her."

He gives a tight nod and a tighter, "Yeah." Then he squeezes his eyes shut and opens them again, like he's resetting. "I should be over it."

"Corbin," I say, gently chiding him. "You don't have to be over it. Ever. I don't know if we can get over grief. You can only go through it, and sometimes you realize it repeats in new ways. With new memories."

"It does."

I think for several seconds. "Do you want me to get something there for you? I can go back in and get your favorite. What's your favorite cheese?"

His confident smile returns. "Gouda."

"That makes sense. It's a little nutty," I say.

He laughs. "But I'm all good. I have plenty."

"Are you sure?"

"I'm positive."

But I'm pushy sometimes. I hold up my thumb and forefinger. "What if I just got you a slice?"

"Fine," he says, relenting, but like it wasn't hard to give in.

I pop back in. "Abe, I'd like one slice of Gouda."

He arches a bushy brow. "One slice?"

"Fine, make it five," I say.

"That's more like it."

After he slices the cheese, he hands me five pieces wrapped in paper, and I give them to Corbin when I leave. "See? Now you got a gift."

He takes a slice of cheese, rolls it up, and takes a bite. "I did."

I smile to myself. This man does so much for me. It's nice to do something for him.

We pop into other stores, and when we pass the town square, I'm vaguely tempted to give some treats to the guys playing chess, but the looks they give me are withering. Another time. I stop in the home decor shop and give a box to Mariah.

"I feel so alive now," she says brightly.

"You made my day," I say.

Corbin nods to the box. "When you try her pistachio cookies, you'll really be saying that," he says, selling me, and selling us.

Mariah grabs one, takes a bite, and smiles wickedly when she's done chewing. "I'll take one a day."

Next is Rise and Grind, and I steel myself for some kind of laugh at my expense as I march straight up to Joni behind the counter. "Just a little gift for my neighbors," I say, handing her a box.

She takes it with a smile as big as her frizzy hair. "Sweetheart, this is really lovely. And it's good to see you too, Corbin. But did you two hear about—"

Before she can finish, an espresso machine hisses, and it doesn't sound good.

Joni swivels around and then groans in despair. "No, no, no, no, no. You turned it the wrong way," she says to an employee, then rushes over to fix the espresso mishap. As she's working on the machine, she waves us off. "Thanks for stopping by. That was really kind of you."

When we exit, I replay her words as worry wiggles through me. "What do you think she heard?"

He shrugs. "No idea. Probably nothing."

"I hope so."

We pop into a few more shops, saving the toughest one for the end.

It's knitting club day again at the yarn shop, according to the poster promoting their meeting times in the window. My stomach flips upside down like a pirate ship ride as I open the door. The ladies in the knitting club are perched on comfy sofas in the back of the shop, needles clicking. One works on a sparkly white beanie, the other a red-and-green sweater, and another a pair of mittens. One of them says something about needing some magenta chenille yarn for a Christmas scarf she wants to make, which is impossible to find, while another says she plans to wear her Christmas sweater to an upcoming punk rock show. Okaaaaay.

But the conversation stops when my shoes creak on the floorboards. Their eyes are filled with question marks as they stare at me as I stride past rows of yarn. A woman behind the counter gives me a curious stare.

I square my shoulders. "Hi, I'm Mabel, and this is Corbin," I say, motioning to the man next to me. He gives a quick hello.

"We know him," one of the ladies says coolly as she finishes a row in the mittens. I think she's the one who said it would only be successful for a few months because of him.

"We're opening a bakery tomorrow," I continue.

"We just wanted to stop by and say hi and offer you a little gift," he puts in.

Another woman arches her brow, her tone full of skepticism. "So you're giving out free things? To the people of Cozy Valley?"

"We are, just to say hi. And if you want to stop by the bakery when it opens, we'd love to see you," I add.

The lady making the beanie snorts. "What a great way to run a business. Giving everything away for free," she says derisively.

Ouch. Why did I think this would be a good idea?

The woman behind the counter taps her needle against it. "Now, Dottie, take the cookies. It's a gift, you old bird."

Dottie, the woman working on the white fluffy hat, huffs, sets down her knitting and motions to me with a wrinkled finger. Corbin says nothing—just shoots me a look that says he's got my back if I need him.

But I can do this. Even with nerves chasing me, I stride across their knitting circle and hand Dottie the box. "I hope you enjoy them," I say.

"So you can trick us into coming in and buying more things," she mutters.

I try to untangle her response, but then decide to say, "I'm just trying to be a good neighbor."

Dottie stares at the box quizzically.

The lady making the sweater taps the box with her needles and admonishes her friend, saying, "Just open it. Maybe it's good."

Dottie hums doubtfully but takes a bite of a classic chocolate chip cookie. The corner of her lips quirks up. Her eyes dance. And she fights off a food moan.

I smother a grin and steal a glance at Corbin, who's watching the scene with admiration.

Dottie mumbles around the crumbs. "It's okay," she says, begrudgingly.

"I'll take that," I say with a smile.

"It wasn't a compliment," she snaps.

"I know, but it wasn't an insult either," I say, with a happy shrug.

Corbin waves. "Goodbye, ladies. See you all tomorrow, maybe."

"Maybe," Dottie says.

"Oh, hush," the owner tells her.

We leave, and when we're on the street, I turn to Corbin, a burst of gratitude filling my chest. Gratitude for him, and, well, for me. "Thank you for not rushing in to save me. I needed to do that on my own."

"I had a feeling. Plus, it was clearly important to you."

The way he says that, with pride, makes my stomach flutter once again. I like that he knows when to save the day and when to let me try to save it myself.

Back at the bakery, that flutter kicks up several notches when he sets down the now-empty bags and gives me a once-over. Stopping at my hair, he lifts a hand and ever so tenderly runs a finger down a strand, like he's never felt anything softer or silkier. "Your hair would look really nice with that ribbon tomorrow."

My heart thunders. "I'll wear it."

If he stays a second longer, I'll want to try out Remy's Dirty Dog too. "And you need to go. You have a game tonight."

"I know," he says with some reluctance, then glances toward the street that'll take him back to the city to play the sport he loves. "I should head out."

"I'll be rooting for you."

"Just need to grab something," he says, trotting upstairs.

I need to clean the kitchen anyway, so while he's up there, I head for the sink where I left some bowls and the basting brush from the cinnamon rolls. I start with washing the brush, and I'm drying it with a dish towel when Corbin returns.

I turn off the water, and he stops a foot away, his gaze straying to the brush. He picks it up from the rack, considers it, then dries it off one more time with the dish towel.

"Just helping," he says, his voice edged with a playful roughness.

"Are you now?"

"I like to help," he says, leveling a hot and flirty gaze my way, one that sends a wave of heat rolling down my spine.

"I've noticed."

"You have?"

"Yes," I say, curious what he's up to. He seems to have an agenda.

His eyes never stray from me. They're molten, full of dirty ideas. Ideas that have been flickering since he walked in on me. Ideas I'm very curious about.

"Do you need help with anything else?" he asks, holding the basting brush, flicking the bristles against his long fingers.

Only with this ache between my thighs.

But I bite my lip so I don't say that out loud.

He tilts his head, the corner of his lips quirking up in a tease. "What did you just *not* say, Mabel?"

He noticed I edited myself. But I keep my mouth shut and shake my head.

"Not going to tell me?" He runs the pad of his finger over the bristles now, then roams his eyes over me.

"I guess not," I say, clenching my thighs as if that will ease the ache between them.

"Then I can't help," he says with a frown, flicking the bristles like he's testing the texture, the softness, the possibilities.

I whimper at the sight of him assessing the kitchen implement. Somewhere inside of me, I know what he's planning to do with it. Everywhere inside me wants him to.

"Are you sure you don't want to tell me what it was? Maybe I *could* help?" There's a husky edge to his voice as he dips his free hand into his back pocket and produces the towel I wore earlier. He brings it to his nose and inhales it. He closes his eyes, growling, like he's savoring the scent of me. "When I grabbed this upstairs, it was all I could think about."

So that's what broke him. The scent of me on the towel. Knowing that, I say "fuck it" too.

"You could help with the ache between my thighs," I offer.

His eyes fly open. Smiling salaciously, he tucks the towel back into his pocket, then lowers the basting brush between my thighs, running it along the fabric of my skort. He rubs me there, right there, where I want him. It's such a relief.

"That helps," I whisper breathily.

"Does it help enough?"

I shake my head. "I need a little more."

"Yeah, you really do," he says, then drags the bristles with more pressure down my center, then up, sliding against the fabric covering my swollen clit. With each stroke, I ache more and more.

I haul in a breath. "Don't stop."

"You need more help?" he asks teasingly.

"I do."

He coasts the bristles over the fabric of my skort that's getting wetter and wetter. My legs are already shaking.

"More," I whisper. I can't believe he's doing this to me again. Practically getting me off without his hands, without his tongue, without his cock.

Before, it was his thigh. Now it's a goddamn basting brush.

I'm close, but I'm not quite there. He pushes one leg of my skort to the side, exposing me in my panties to him. I'm dying for him to tear off my clothes, but I also know this is a game we're playing. He rubs the bristles against the cotton of my panties, faster, a little harder, just right.

I gasp. I shudder. I grab his shoulders.

"This helps?" he asks innocently.

"So much," I say.

"Would this help too?" He lifts the brush and slaps my ass with it. I yelp, because it hurts so good.

"Again?"

"Please."

He smacks my other cheek as pleasure ripples through me. He smacks me one more time, and I tremble. "Helps so much," I pant.

"Good," he says, then returns to my pussy, where I'm aching for him. "Use this basting brush. Get it all wet with your juices. I want you to soak your panties so badly that I can taste you on this when you're done."

Pleasure zips through me. I rock against the brush as he strokes me with it until an orgasm seizes me. I moan. I cry out. I whimper. And I come so goddamn hard.

"So, so pretty," he praises as he lifts the brush and sucks off the bristles. It didn't even touch me. He used it through my panties, but he's tasting it as if it's the most delicious thing ever.

Maybe it is to him—this little taste. This tiny tease.

When he's done, he smirks. "Like I said, I'm very helpful."

I smile dopily, the aftereffects of the climax still rocking me. "You sure are."

He sets the brush on the counter, then tugs off my skort. I'm not sure what he's doing, but seconds later, he skims off my panties too, taking them. He drops them in his pocket, then he puts my skort back on.

When he finishes adjusting it, he smacks my ass. "That was just help. That was all."

"Of course. And it won't happen again. The help."

"It won't," he says, with a longing that tells me he wants it to happen again and again.

He takes the basting brush, my panties, and the kitchen towel with him when he heads out, saying over his shoulder, "We should really get a new basting brush. This one is mine."

24

DAYS LIKE THIS
CORBIN

The puck drops, and I'm off, skating hard down the ice at the start of the second period. Chicago has possession, but I'm closing in fast, stick ready to steal it away. Lake's calling for it, and all I have to do is snag it, then pass it to him.

Instead, my mind rewinds to this afternoon and Mabel standing in nothing but that too-small towel.

The Chicago player cuts left, and I follow—a half-second too late. An image of the towel falling flashes before me, and I lose my focus and the puck.

"Fuck," I mutter, skating hard to catch up. Chicago doesn't score, but that's not the point. That's not how I play the game, not who I am on the ice. I'm the goddamn playmaker. I ought to act like it.

I reset my mind and blot out anything but hockey.

It works.

Mostly.

Later in the third period, Lake passes to me, and I snag it clean, skating around the back of the net. For a second, everything clicks—the ice, the stick, my blades. Then I see the towel falling to the floor. Revealing her creamy flesh, her glorious tits, her pert nipples, and—

The puck slips off my stick.

Again.

By the end of the game, we've won 3-2, but when I look at that scoreboard, I don't see the W. I see three goals scored by my teammates with zero assists from me. Three opportunities where I should have been there, should have contributed, and instead I was thinking about the way Mabel's skin smelled like sweet peas, and fantasizing about how she might taste. Everywhere.

In the hallway after I've showered and changed, Theo catches up to me, slapping my shoulder like he didn't even notice how scattered I was when I played.

"Tomorrow. Be there. Don't forget," he says.

I laugh, because of course I'll be at Afternoon Delight. "What would I do without your reminder?" I deadpan.

He starts to walk away, then turns back with that grin that means trouble. "And don't forget to show up on the ice too."

I wince. Shit. He noticed. He fucking noticed.

But then he adds, "Just kidding. You're always here, buddy. I don't know how you do it."

My head feels like it has whiplash. Is he saying I played badly? Is he giving me a hard time? But then I remind myself that Theo's always given me a hard time. That's what we do. That's our friendship.

"Thanks, man," I say, then ask him how he's doing. He talks about the job a bit, since he works too hard, but then mentions he had a good date the other night.

"Nice," I say, offering a fist for bumping. "You're getting back out there?"

He knocks back but shrugs. "Maybe. We'll see."

He's skeptical, since like most people, he's been burned by love. When Ginny left, he was devastated, and I did my best to help him through it. Sometimes that meant golfing with him, which was no hardship. Other times, it meant just having him over for dinner with Charlotte, Mom, and Ray. "I'm rooting for you."

"I know. And I appreciate it," he says, then takes off, leaving me standing in the corridor with the uncomfortable realization that for the first time in my career, hockey wasn't the only thing on my mind during a game.

His incomparably sexy, incredibly flirty, and big-hearted sister was.

Yet even though I wasn't on top of my game, I just can't seem to shake these thoughts of her. They chase me home as I leave the arena. They follow me along the highway as I drive. They whisper in my ear as I park my car in the garage and head into my quiet home.

I should review the to-do list for tomorrow morning. Do some light yoga. Ice my shoulder since my shoulder's always sore.

But nope, as soon as I'm inside, I set the basting brush in my nightstand drawer. Put the towel next to it. Then, I take the panties out of my pocket and put them on top of the nightstand. I get ready for bed, and when I get under the covers, I grab the panties, bring them to my nose, and inhale them for a good long time.

Long enough that I replay her coming undone that afternoon.

That I rewind the sounds of her pleasure and picture the way she looks, blissed out and beautiful, as she comes.

I'm a grown-ass man spending the night with a pair of stolen underthings, hoping to catch the fading scent of a woman. This is beyond pathetic.

And yet, I don't stop till I imagine her spread out here on my bed, legs wrapped tight around my head, fingers gripping my hair, calling my name.

The fridge is humming, cooling drinks. The café tables are polished, inviting soon-to-arrive customers. The mismatched plates from Reprise are stacked and ready to hold cakes, bars, and cookies. The speakers are itching to pump playlists, which I've programmed. The shelves are stocked with merch. And they're apropos because we have our Fuck Mornings line of tees, mugs, and plates, with the swear word spelled with an asterisk. That's the point of Afternoon Delight, after all. A bakery for those who want a fresh treat in the afternoon or evening too.

And I'm yawning.

Maybe in retrospect we should have picked a date to open that wasn't after a night game, but there aren't that many days like this—Saturdays, when my whole day is free.

Which means I'm here at the crack of dawn hanging this cake chandelier. It arrived yesterday—a surprise thing Mabel ordered. She said she found it late one night on an online shopping bender. It's thrifted, pink, and painted like an old-fashioned, over-the-top frilly cake with chandelier teardrops hanging from the upside-down tiers.

"It's so kitschy and cute, I can't stand it," Mabel told me.

The problem is you have to turn off the power to the circuit breaker to install it, so I'm here fuck-all early, mounting a cake chandelier to the ceiling.

As I finish adjusting the chain so the chandelier will hang at just the right length, I think about Riggs's question on the plane about the pressure of being good enough to play, the ribbon Mabel's going to wear in her hair, and whether this chandelier chain is the right length. My head's a mess, thoughts yanking in too many different directions.

Fuck.

If I don't concentrate, this light monstrosity will turn into a smashed chandelier. I can't stand it for real, but Mabel loves it, and that's all that matters.

I climb down the ladder, grab the chandelier from the floor where it's resting, and haul it back up. It's not heavy, so that's good. I spend the next thirty minutes wiring it up, and it takes so much focus I can barely think of Mabel and how she looks under a kitchen towel.

Edible.

When I'm done, I install the bulbs, then restore power at the circuit breaker and pray hard when I flick the switch.

Let there be light!

I give a fist pump. Mabel will be happy, and that's good.

I picture her reaction, and I start to let go of some of this tension. If only I can keep it at bay during the next game.

But first, I go home and catch a few more hours of shut-eye. Well, there are benefits to our late morning store hours.

* * *

Around ten, I roll into the bakery with bouquets of irises, and I'm greeted by the warm, inviting scent of melting chocolate and mouth-watering sugary flour. My heart rate starts to settle. Tension begins to melt off.

It falls to the floor when Mabel strides out from the kitchen and into the bakery, her gaze landing on the flowers. "You really did it," she says, with something like wonder in her voice.

I cock my head, giving her a *really* look. "What do you take me for? A man who doesn't keep his promises?"

She wraps a hand around my biceps. "I love them. They're my favorite."

"I'm glad," I mumble, since I really, *really* need to be careful around Mabel.

"I'll get some vases. I picked some up at the thrift shop just for this," she says, and returns a minute later with three vases filled with water. We put the irises in them and set them on the pink tables. I watch her as she arranges them, positioning them just so, moving each one an inch farther away, an inch closer till they're perfect. She steps back and releases a satisfied breath, clearly pleased with her work. "I love it."

And I can't stop looking at her. The way she works, the way she smiles, the way she wants this to succeed.

Which means I really need to do something else. Like I told Riggs on the plane, I bake to relax, and I could use a little relaxation right now. So I join Mabel in the kitchen, but blink when I find she's not alone.

My daughter's there, wearing a bandana and an apron. "Hi! Travis dropped me off when I told them I wanted to help. Mom will pick me up later."

Mabel is mixing cake batter at the counter. "She's very helpful."

"I am," Charlotte says, and then I join them, rolling out my shoulders and trying, really trying, to let the baking relax me.

But it's harder when you're baking for business rather than pleasure.

Then, this business is a pleasure.

"By the way, the chandelier is perfection," Mabel says with a smile. And it looks like she wants to come over and hug me.

Or is that my own wishful thinking?

Who even knows? "Glad you like it. Your dress is nice," I say, nodding at her pink-and-white outfit under the apron. The compliment is the understatement of the century.

But her eyes say she knows she looks good, she knows I like it, and she knows I can't say more in front of my kid.

And her thank-you smile? That slays me.

I'm so fucked.

* * *

It's almost time to open. I run a rag down the fire pole, making sure it's shiny. I adjust a few trays in the display cases, arranging them just so, making sure the cards are out listing all the ingredients and which allergens are in them, and which ones aren't.

I roll my shoulders. There's always been something to juggle. Mom's illness, Charlotte's needs, the demands of the season. Helping to run a business is one more thing to balance, but that's what I've always done. And the reward at the end of our first day will be another letter waiting for us and pride too—pride that I've finally begun to realize Mom's dream. For now, though, I focus on the present.

I'm setting a heart-shaped card in front of the coconut cake, which says, *When you need to get away to someplace sweet and tropical,* when I hear little Converse sneakers slapping the concrete. Then Charlotte marches into the front of the bakery with a tray of cookies straight from the oven. Her tongue sticks out of the corner of her mouth; she's so intensely focused, making sure she doesn't drop them.

"Cookies coming through," she calls out, as if there are more workers to warn than the three of us.

A few seconds later, Mabel follows, the ribbon now twisted through her French braid. No idea when she did that. Maybe when I was up here, organizing recipe cards? Maybe she did it in front of the dressing room mirror? The thought grips me hard, and I can't let go of the image of her wearing the ribbon like I asked her to. It feels like a private message just for me.

I stare at her for far too long, itching to undo her braid, strand by strand, and let the ribbon fall to the floor. Roam a hand through her hair and tug on it hard, jerking her head back. Kiss my way down her throat. Her breasts. Her belly.

Why the fuck did I go into business with a woman I can't stop thinking of naked? A woman I can't stop touching?

I really need to stop touching her.

I pinch the bridge of my nose as if I can eradicate thoughts of her that way. But I put that to bed, too, when we switch the sign to say *Now Open* and turn the music to an upbeat rock song. Minutes later, a bell tinkles above the door, a pretty chime, and we invite in our first customer.

It's not one of my teammates. It's not one of Mabel's friends. It's not Sarah or Annabelle. Or Theo or Mabel's parents. It's better.

It's someone I don't know at all.

Evidently, Mabel doesn't know her, either, since she tells the woman, "Hello, and welcome to Afternoon Delight. Let us know what we can help you with."

The woman nods and says, "Excited to be here. I heard about this on socials."

Mabel shoots me a side-eye smile, and the excitement that someone we don't know is here bounces back and forth between us.

When I slice a piece of coconut cake for the customer and box it up as Mabel chats with her, I'm more thrilled than I ever expected to be at being a part of this.

The woman from the thrift shop where Charlotte likes to do her back-to-school shopping arrives next, snapping up a dozen mini cupcakes in a variety of flavors. "For my employees, but mostly for me," she says.

"As it should be," Mabel says, and they chat for a few minutes. Looks like Mabel's made a new friend in town. That warms my chest.

A few minutes later, Abe from The Cheesery pops in, giving a gruff hello and then picking up some shortbread for his husband.

There's a lull after that. Tension curls in me as I watch through the garage door windows, scanning for an influx of customers.

Soon enough, the bell rings, and Lake strides in, rubbing his palms. "Well, well, well. What have we here?"

Miller and Riggs follow him, and Miller points at Lake while speaking to me. "This is his happy place. It's his only happy place."

Lake shoots our goalie a stern stare. "It's not my *only* happy place. I've got a few others."

Riggs holds up a stop-sign hand. "Don't want to know about your happy places."

"Guys," I warn, nodding toward Charlotte, who's folding napkins.

Ivan strolls in right behind them, holds out his arms wide, and says, "I will take one of everything."

Mabel blows him a kiss. "And I love you most of all."

Riggs asks for a slice of the London Fog cake, and I steal a glance at Mabel, giving her an *I told you so* smile. I knew that it would be a good one for the menu.

Mabel slices it. "Thank you so much for helping set this up," she says, nodding to the furniture.

"Anything for the GM's sister," Riggs says with a wink.

They head to a table as a pack of Mabel's friends wander in. My buddy Ford is with them. He retired from the Sea Dogs recently, and he's here with his fiancée, Skylar, a friend of Mabel's, as well as the rest of her crew, including Remy. She organizes a ton of community events that the Foxes do.

"Amazing work," she says of the bakery when I give her a nod and say hi.

Lake snaps his gaze in her direction, lingering longer than I would have expected. It's like seeing her in this context throws him off.

After that, I can't clock everyone's reaction, because I've got cookies to serve.

Things slow down again after that, followed by another rush. I'm glad, so damn glad, this one isn't full of family or friends. There's Luis from some clothing shop on Main Street. Then the woman who runs the Green Pantry, along with her kids. Next comes the barista from Rise and Grind, saying our cookies are better than the ones in her shop.

After that, someone I don't know comes in, and then a whole lot of other strangers.

Soon enough, someone I know well strolls in.

Sarah and her towhead toddler son.

"Hey," I say to the woman with the blonde pixie cut and the tattoos snaking down the pale skin of her arms. Mabel arches a curious brow, but then Charlotte waves and says, "Hi, Mom. Hi, Benny."

Mabel waves too, and smiles, and my shoulders relax.

Huh.

Did I think she'd be jealous? Wonder if she was curious about my relationship with Sarah?

For fuck's sake, man, you're thinking about her far too much.

I clear my throat. "Mabel, I want you to meet Charlotte's mom. This is Sarah. And Sarah, this is Mabel."

Dammit, just saying her name makes my lips twist in a smile that might give me away. I school my expression. "She's the genius behind this entire place. She had the idea, the name, the concept, the colors, and the foundation for the menu. The marketing. I'm just lucky to be along for the ride."

Mabel blushes and waves a hand like she's done none of those things, but I can tell she's happy. It radiates from her. It's in the color that stains her cheeks beautifully, and it's in her hand that pushes my shoulder playfully.

"Don't let the humble act of his fool you," she says to Sarah. "He is a pretty damn good baker, and he keeps me organized and balanced and..." She stops to look at me. "He's my biggest cheerleader."

Sarah's quiet for a long beat, then she smiles and finally says, "Sounds like you two are a perfect match."

I flinch, wondering if Sarah's onto us. But Mabel simply laughs. Charlotte scurries out from around the counter to show Benny around the bakery.

"I need to fetch the batch of cookies I've been baking," Mabel says, and when she takes off into the kitchen, I watch her go, the pleated skirt of the dress I got her swishing against her thighs.

When I turn back to Sarah, she's giving me a smug smile. "You like her."

"Shut up," I mutter.

"So I was right. You do."

Why bother to deny it? She's figured it out already. "Yeah, but it's complicated."

"She's Theo's sister," Sarah says thoughtfully, but she doesn't sound like she's chiding me, more like she's just making a basic observation.

"I'm aware. And I'm not going to do anything about it."

Well, I'm not going to do anything about it again. Not after the basting brush. I'm really, truly stopping this time.

She sighs. "Corbin, that's not what I was going to say."

"What were you going to say?"

Sarah checks behind her, then glances toward the door to the kitchen. "That I know you'll do the right thing."

My gut churns. Pretty sure it's too late for that. I've been doing the forbidden thing too often and making excuses for my choices.

"Thanks for letting Charlotte spend the day here. Means a lot to me," I say, shifting gears.

"Of course. I want to see this succeed too. I know it will," she says, then nods to the display cases. "And I'll take some of the monkey bread and a half dozen cookies. An assortment."

"Thanks, Sarah," I say, grateful to focus on the food order rather than her spot-on assessment.

When the treats are packed, Charlotte folds her apron and tucks it away in a drawer, then reminds me of my schedule for tomorrow.

"Yes, I know I have morning skate, and then a game."

"See you on Monday after school," she says, then leaves.

My gut twists once again when Theo enters with his parents a little later. Mabel told me recently about how they aren't terribly supportive. All my protective instincts kick in. I stand a little taller, move a little closer to her, like I can shield her from something. Their disapproval? Their lack of support? Well, whatever it is, I'm going to look out for her.

And I'm going to do whatever I can to make this go smoothly.

"Welcome to Afternoon Delight. How can I help you?"

And as if I summoned it by wanting to help her, a crowd pours in. That's good. Since Mabel won't be able to spend too much time tending to two people who don't entirely support her with our shopfront full. And it's good too, because her parents can see how successful this bakery will be.

Her mom scans the display case with skepticism, but maybe some hope? I'm not quite sure.

As Mabel waits on them, her mom says, "Don't forget the food services option, just in case," and Mabel answers with only a smile. I wonder what that's about, but then Theo raps his knuckles on the counter, and I give him my full attention.

He looks around with approval. "Impressive." Then he nods toward his sister. "And look how happy she is. Fuck Dax. He was wrong."

Wait, was this all about proving someone wrong?

"Did you encourage me to do this because you were pissed at her ex?"

Theo shrugs in admission. "A little. But I knew you wanted to do it too, and she needed a partner, and it all worked out. And it worked out for me too, because I let the producers of the show know exactly what I thought of them and this store's success is proving me right. But mostly I want her to be happy, and I think she is."

Right. That's true.

I glance at Mabel, and even as she chats with her parents, she seems...enchanted with this place.

This—Afternoon Delight—is exactly why I need to stop messing around with basting brushes, and thieving underwear, and taking towels just to get a whiff of her.

Because this bakery is her happy place, and I don't want to mess it up by pouring out this overwhelming bucketful of feelings in my chest. This pride. This admiration. This fondness. This lust. This wanting. Better to stop it.

I will. I really will.

As closing time nears, there's a commotion outside the bakery, and I spot a head of frizzy hair. Pretty sure that's Joni. She stands shoulder to shoulder with a guy with a shiny bald head. Something about him looks terribly familiar.

It clicks.

Her *Did you hear...?* yesterday makes sense as I see her smiling and snapping a photo.

Did we hear that Ronnie Legend was coming to Cozy Valley? Because he's here.

And no way will I let him ruin Mabel's moment. I will do whatever it takes for her.

25

THE SMASH-CAKE QUEEN
MABEL

I'd have been more surprised if Jonas had shown up. Or even Dax.

But Ronnie? The man who wanted me to be *on my way* after ruining his event? He might have talked down to me then, but this is my turf, and I'm going to defend it.

Although it looks like Corbin already has that covered from the way he squares his shoulders and crosses his arms, lasering a dark stare Ronnie's way when the celebrity chef steps inside Afternoon Delight. "What can I do for you?"

It's a *don't fuck with my woman* voice.

It's hot as hell. Unfair.

The British celebrity chef is flanked by two women I judge to be in their early twenties. A pretty redhead with a pert nose and a pretty brunette with a freckled nose. Joni has already waved goodbye and left, and now it's just Corbin and me behind the counter with Ronnie and his entourage in front of it.

Ronnie strides toward us, a smug look on his face as he sizes me up. "Look what you've done. This is just really brilliant."

Is he mocking me?

"Thank you," I say, keeping my guard up.

He waves a hand from the redhead to the brunette.

"Tiffany and Brittany told me I simply had to make an appearance," he says, gesturing from one to the other with obvious affection for them.

Tiffany's the redhead, and she hugs Ronnie's right arm. Brittany clutches the other. They both lift phones and snap pictures of themselves with him.

Wow, okay, so that's what we're dealing with.

"And we were right, sweetie," Tiffany says.

"We had to make sure he came here," Brittany tells me.

Are they groupies? Girlfriends? It's hard to tell. But it doesn't really matter. He's the cake king, and I need to be polite even if he wasn't entirely polite to me.

"I'm so glad you stopped by," I say.

Tiffany gives a cutesy little wave to me. "We heard about it on the socials."

Brittany clutches Ronnie tighter and chimes in, "It was all over."

"*The* place to be," Tiffany adds.

"So that's why I'm here. I never want to let my *friends* down," Ronnie says with a wink as he looks at them. Okay, so they're his *friends*. Whatever that means.

"Then you should get a smash cake," Corbin says in the most deadpan voice in the history of the world.

Ronnie blinks, then his gaze swings to the display case and the tray full of smashed, extra pieces of all sorts of cake. "You were serious about that?" Ronnie asks me.

Well, I was ad-libbing at the time, but Corbin insisted we put it on the menu, and we've sold a couple smash cakes today —smashed up bits of various cakes, served in a cup.

Corbin steps closer to me. "Very serious. My partner and I

have been planning the smash cake for some time," he says, defending the fuck out of me once again. It's so sexy, I don't even know what to think.

Mostly, I feel a little hot and bothered as he doubles down on the smash-cake story.

Ronnie arches a brow, clearly not quite buying it. "Really?"

"It's been quite a popular offering. It's a wonderful expression of bakery and cake artistry," Corbin says, selling it to the judge, the jury...hell, to the bailiffs outside the courtroom.

Tiffany peers through the case while twirling a strand of red hair, bracelets jangling along the ivory skin of her arms, the same shade as her friend's. She drops Ronnie's arm and urges Brittany over.

"I want to try this, babes," Brittany says, pointing to one of the smashed numbers.

"It looks so good," Tiffany seconds, and I just watch the two of them talk like it's a tennis match.

But when I pull my gaze away, Ronnie's staring right at Corbin, eyes narrowed. "So you'd been planning it?"

"It's our centerpiece," he says, holding his ground. "We sold out. We had to make more."

That's not true, but it hardly matters. "Everyone loves it," I add.

"Mabel gave you the preview at the fair," Corbin says with a *you lost* sigh. "Bummer you weren't able to jump on it, man."

Ronnie blows out a breath. "Win some, lose some."

"But you can try one here. You can even get toppings, like crumbled cookies, sprinkles, or bits of brownie. It's sin in a cup," I say, joining the *egg Ronnie on* action.

"I suppose we really ought to try it," he says to the women he's with.

"Yay," they say in unison.

"We'll share it with you," the redhead adds.

"One smash cake, coming right up," Corbin says.

As he scoops some cake bits into a small compostable cup, excitement rushes through me.

This moment is a vindication. This is a glow-up. This is a redemption story.

I'm living in a rom-com, and today has been the it-all-works-out scene montage, culminating with me telling my one-time nemesis to eat my smash cake.

As Corbin chats with Ronnie, Tiffany and Brittany stare at me conspiratorially.

"Can we totally take your picture?" Tiffany asks.

And look at that. I'm a social media darling already.

"Sure," I say, then scurry out from behind the counter, dusting my hands on my apron.

They usher me between them. I flash back briefly to that moment with the woman at the gym, thinking how different this is. They want pictures with me—the smash-cake queen, not the loser woman from the meme. I say cheese as they hold out their phones and take pic after pic. Tiffany pets my arm, like I'm a doll. "We just love you so much. We're *Romance Beach* fans," she adds offhandedly.

I go cold. Shit. My smile evaporates. Of course, their adoration is connected to that...incident.

Brittany must sense the shift because she grabs my arm. "No, babes, it's totally okay. We love you. We're so on your side. We think Dax is such a dick. We were talking about it at pickleball, and we love both you and your pickleball outfit," she says, plucking at the sleeve of my dress, while Tiffany pets the skirt.

"I mean, look, you play pickleball, we play pickleball," Tiffany adds with a smile that seems real.

It's not like we just became best friends or anything, but I feel a little better. "That's great. We all love pickleball. Yay."

"We love pretty ribbons too," Tiffany puts in, twirling another strand of red hair. "You're basically, like, our queen. You were dumped, but look what you did."

I wince but try to hide it.

Brittany gives me a supportive smile. "Like, it sucked so much. But then look at you. You turned it around."

I die a little inside. Is that how they see the whole situation?

Obviously, it is.

Brittany gives me a side-hug, her shiny brown hair soft against my shoulder. "You opened a whole bakery to try to be less sad," she says. "That's amazing. Isn't it amazing, Ronnie?"

The Brit snaps his focus to the love fest, offering me a patronizing smile. "It's so wonderful to think about how you took that terrible, awful day at the romance fair and turned it into something better. You were dumped on TV, and then you opened a bakery thanks to my cake contest and unwavering support," he says, somehow taking credit.

But also...*what?* That doesn't add up. I couldn't have been dumped the day Dax talked about me on TV because the show was recorded in advance.

Before I can point out this flaw in the timeline, Corbin comes around the counter and wraps a strong, toned arm around my waist, beaming at me with something like adoration. "I don't know why she'd feel that way. We're very happily together, and we have been since before the fair so you must have your timeline wrong. We've been working on this bakery for a while. We were even talking about it in the trailer that day." He squeezes my shoulder harder, holding me like a boyfriend would, urging me to play along. "Weren't we, sweetheart?"

Sweetheart.

That day.

His eyes.

All the hearts and flutters.

This man is utterly convincing.

I'm so sold. "Yes, we were. You really saved the day, then. You've been doing that ever since," I say, flashing a *doe-eyed* grin at him.

"I'd do anything for you," he says, lifting a hand to dotingly stroke my jaw.

Impulsively, I inch closer.

A second later, maybe less, I gasp when Corbin drops his mouth to mine and kisses me in front of them. He's sweet and tender, gently cupping my jawline in front of my nemesis and his two young *friends.* Declaring me his with a kiss that makes my stomach flip and my pulse skitter.

When he lets go, I'm swimming in endorphins. Corbin has the most sheepish look on his face. "So hard to resist," he says to me, but maybe it's for them.

I'm still woozy from that knee-weakening kiss when he turns back to Ronnie. "I couldn't really stop from kissing her in your trailer too, Ronnie. I hope you don't mind. That's why it took us a little while to get back out there. But you understand, don't you? Man to man?"

Ronnie chuckles and says, "Right you are."

Well, two can play at this fake-dating one-upmanship. I grab the ties of Corbin's apron, and I tug him close to me again, taking another kiss.

A hot, prelude-type of kiss. One that has me wanting them all to go away so he can Dirty Dog me.

When we break it, Tiffany and Brittany clap and cheer, then spin to face each other.

"I totally know what we should do," Tiffany says to Brittany.

The brunette grabs the redhead's hands, and they nod as if they can read each other's minds. Maybe they can.

"Are you thinking what I'm thinking?" Brittany asks her friend.

"I'm totally thinking the same thing you're thinking," Tiffany confirms.

They turn to me, and Brittany declares brightly, "We should all do a pickleball date."

"We're both in a league, and we're the doubles champions," Tiffany adds. "It would be so fun to play with our queen."

Doubles champions? No fucking way.

I'm about to say *thanks, but no thanks*, when Corbin plants a kiss on my cheek. "My girlfriend and I would love to join you."

Are you kidding me? He just signed me up for a fake date with a couple of pickleball champions?

I'm so screwed.

* * *

Once they're gone and the door is locked, I advance toward Corbin. He stands proudly in front of the display case, looking pleased with his fake-dating pronouncement.

I'm more conflicted, half turned on and half annoyed. I point at him. "What were you thinking?"

He holds his hands out wide, his brow furrowed. "You're mad at me?"

"What gave it away?"

He drags his hands through his hair. "Why are you pissed? You went along with that fake-dating thing."

"Ronnie's kind of powerful," I fire back. "He's a celebrity

chef, and he came to our bakery. I want him to say nice things, if he says anything at all."

"Right. And my point is, you played along when I said you were my girlfriend. It didn't seem like you had a problem with that."

I blow out a harsh breath. "That's not what I'm mad at. I'll be thrilled if they talk about our bakery. Going along with it made sense." I poke the bib of his *ALL THIS AND I CAN BAKE* apron. "I'm pissed you signed me up to play pickleball with two pickleball champions. Why did you do that?"

He grits his teeth, blows out a breath. "Same reason I said we were together."

"And what's that reason?" Seriously, I'm dying to know.

He heaves a frustrated sigh. Huffs out through his nostrils. "When they started that whole ridiculous bit that you were sad, it set me off. I needed them to know that this bakery isn't about *Romance Beach*. This bakery isn't about the wildly inaccurate things your ex said on TV. This bakery isn't about you being upset. They're wrong, and they needed to know it, and I showed them the only way that I could at that moment."

Oh. I'm definitely more turned on than annoyed now. "What is this bakery about?"

He steps closer to me, inches away, so close I can catch the last remaining notes of his lake-and-campfire scent. "It's about your dream. It's about my dream. We started it," he says, like he's making a speech. No, a declaration. "And fuck anyone else who tries to tell our story."

The frustration I felt earlier? It's gone. The frustration over having to play pickleball champions? Who even cares?

"What's our story?" I ask, anger now stripped from my tone. Only curiosity is left.

He swallows roughly. "It's you challenging me to do something that I've wanted to do for years. Something I've been fucking afraid of doing. Something I've been putting off, thinking that I needed to wait. It's you making me realize that there's no time like the present." He pauses, takes a soldiering breath. "It's you finally getting to chase your dreams. And it's us taking a chance together. So when they said all that, I felt fucking protective of you, okay?"

This vibration in my chest. This fluttering in my heart. This storm swirling around me. I lick my lips. "Then you're going to have to teach me how to play a serious game of pickleball. One where we can win. Because that's what I want for the fake date with Ronnie and his girlfriends."

"With so much fucking pleasure," Corbin says with a flirty, dirty grin.

Heat shimmers between us. Vulnerability does too. It's crackling, pulsing in the air, though neither of us moves.

His eyes are fiery. His fists are clenched. His jaw is tight. He's a man restrained but breaking apart.

I've never been that good at resisting him. I've gotten quite adept at winding him up though. That's why I say the next thing. "Why do you feel protective of me, Corbin?"

He glances at the locked front door. He looks toward the back door that leads to the kitchen, away from the window, away from anyone walking by.

Then, in a low, ragged voice, he says, "Because sometimes I forget you're not mine."

I shudder everywhere. "I'm not," I say, "but sometimes I wish I were."

"Sometimes I don't know what to do about it. About the way I can't stop wanting you."

I grab his apron for the second time in an hour. "Show me. Show me how good you'd fuck me if I were yours."

26

JUST IN CASE
CORBIN

I scoop her up, toss her over my shoulder, and stalk through the doorway that leads to the back of our bakery.

"Corbin. I can walk."

"It's faster if I carry you."

"Is it really though?" she asks as I cross into the kitchen-slash-dressing room area.

"Woman, don't test me right now," I say.

She drums her hands against my back. "Why? Are you going to put me down and strip my apron off me?"

I smack her ass. "The sass from you."

I can't see it, but I can feel her smile.

Like I stood a chance at staying away from her. From the dress she wore today, to her hair, to the apron. The goddamn apron that drives me wild for some reason. I guess apron kink is a thing, and I have it. But mostly it's the way she's so goddamn bold and bright. She's like the sun shining as she chases what she wants. And that somehow, incredibly includes me.

I set her down on the concrete floor. The kitchen's on one side, with its gleaming appliances, mixing bowls, and trays.

The other side, with the makeup tables and exposed light-bulbs, is what this place might have been. For a moment, my thoughts linger on Sticks and Dicks, or whatever the strip club would have been called.

If that place had gotten off the ground, if those past owners hadn't had trouble with it, Mabel and I might not be working together.

Those last two words echo like a warning—*working together*.

We are definitely working very closely together, and this—kissing, touching, fucking—is a recipe for failure.

But when she looks at me like that, lips wet, eyes dark, I can't bring myself to care about consequences. Not when she's right here in my arms and I need her so damn badly.

I make quick work of the apron strings, undoing them at her neck as I crush her lips with mine.

Her mouth feels so good, soft and pliant. She moves with me, our tongues skating together. Our moans mingling.

"It feels like forever since I kissed you," I mutter as I briefly break the kiss, frantically tugging down the apron, exposing the collar of the dress that I bought her.

"A day is a long time," she teases.

"I didn't kiss you yesterday."

She seems to think about that for a few seconds. "You should keep making up for that."

"Oh, I will."

She glances at the staircase, nodding to it. "Want to go upstairs?"

The bunk. Of course. That makes perfect sense, but I shake my head. "Too far. Can't wait. Been wanting you for too long."

She laughs, a flirty kind. "All day? Or since the romance fair?"

I back her up to the makeup table. "Try since I met you, Mabel. Since I met you."

She blinks. "Really?"

"Yes," I say, relieved to get that off my chest.

She scoots up on the table, looping her arms around my neck, and now it's her turn to undo my apron strings. "That's a long time."

"You're telling me."

Her smile ignites. "You really have?"

I nod, breathe out hard. "When I didn't see you all the time, I just lived with it. It was there in the background. Now I see you, and it's like a life force." I shouldn't admit this. I know I shouldn't. But here she is, tossing my apron to the floor, tugging at my shirt, jerking it over my head, and then running her fingers down my abs to the scar where my appendix was.

"I love all your scars," she says in a reverent voice. My head swims with lust. And I'm tossing her apron to the floor with mine.

My fingers tease at the hem of her dress, ready to yank it off too. But she sets a hand on my chest. "What about protection?"

My lips quirk up. It's hard to say this without seeming like sex has been premeditated. "I have one."

I brace myself for...attitude. She might think that me carrying is presumptuous.

Her eyes sparkle though. "You have a condom because you planned to fuck me tonight?"

I squeeze my eyes closed for a moment, then admit the truth. "I wanted to be prepared. Just in case."

I open my eyes, and the wicked delight has not left her face.

"You have a lot of restraint," she says, grabbing at my jeans, unbuttoning them but not taking them off me yet.

"I don't know about that. Doesn't feel like I've been restrained at all around you."

"And you're not going to be restrained tonight," she says, and then she strips off her dress.

It feels like ages ago that I last saw her naked, even though it was just yesterday. But I gaze at her in her bra and panties like a ravenous man.

After seven years, I finally get to have her the way I've dreamed about. For seven years, she's drifted in and out of my life. Now she's all the way in it. Dangerously in the middle. If we're not careful, we could mess with a good thing—the bakery. Sex complicates everything.

It's already more than sex.

I tell that voice to shut the fuck up as Mabel bites the corner of her lips. "Well, what are you waiting for?"

I blink because, holy shit. I got a little lost in my thoughts, and here she is, taunting me.

"To do this," I say and rope my arms around her chest, unhooking her bra, letting the white cotton fall to the floor and those gorgeous globes swing free. Full, lush breasts greet me. Dusky nipples. Hard peaks. My cock aches, an insistent throb in my jeans.

I can't stop staring at her.

"Get it, Corbin," she urges.

I shake my head, amazed, impressed with this woman. I slide a hand up the back of her thigh, smooth, soft flesh, savoring the feel of her. I lift her thigh up, raising her leg slightly off the table. "Do me a favor. Will you?"

She juts up a shoulder. "Maybe," she teases.

I dip my face to dust a kiss across her delicious lips, making her whimper when I break the kiss far too soon. I take a step back, lower her thigh, glide my hands down her legs to her knees, then I meet her hot gaze. "Part these pretty legs and show me how much you want it."

With a shudder, she spreads her thighs, offering me the most fantastic view ever—the soaking wet panel of her white panties. A groan rips from the center of my chest, loud and carnal. A rasp that gives away exactly how much I want her.

I drop to the floor, kneeling, spreading her thighs. Dragging my nose along the panel, I inhale the scent of her pussy. My brain sizzles. My skin is on fire.

She spreads her thighs farther while roping her fingers through my hair. I plant a kiss on the fabric, then flick my tongue along it, tasting how hot and turned on she is even through her panties. She trembles. Grips me harder. Shudders.

I tap her ankle. "Ask me again," I murmur against all that wetness.

"What?" she asks, dreamily, rocking against my mouth already.

"Ask me what I'm waiting for."

In a breathy voice, she complies. "What are you waiting for?"

I meet her gaze. Her eyes are hooded. "I want to taste you all over my face."

She moans. Grips me harder. And I tease her more, kissing her undies, winding her up, homing in on her swollen clit. She clamps her thighs against my face and shudders. "Oh, god."

That sound. Those words. I grab her panties, yank them to the side, and clamp my mouth on her pulsing, needy clit. She cries out, a breathy gasp as she tries to fuck my mouth.

"Don't worry, Firecracker. I'll take care of you," I say, reveling in the hot, wet taste. In seconds, she's thrusting, jerking, and falling apart.

And holy fuck. That did not take long at all. I feel ten feet tall. Like a king. Like I won the Cup.

When she comes down, she blows out a breath, saying, "That was a surprise."

"You don't usually come that hard?"

"No," she says, sounding drunk off me. Pride radiates through my chest.

"Well, then let's test it again." I rise up and free my aching cock. She gasps, hitching in a breath as she stares at me.

Finally, she tears her eyes away. "Give me your cock."

"Oh, you're getting it, sweetheart. You're definitely getting it."

She arches a brow playfully, wraps a warm hand around my dick, and lets out an appreciative sigh.

I shudder. Groan. Grab her shoulder and hold on. It feels that good.

"Just like I imagined," she purrs.

"What did you picture, Firecracker?"

Her gaze strays down to my cock, pulsing in her hand. "Hard." She runs her hand down the length and back up. "Long. Pretty. And so fucking eager," she says, sliding a thumb along the crown, then swiping off a drop and bringing it to her lower lip.

I am a live wire as she rubs it into her lip, then licks it off, nice and slow. I nearly come right there. "Fuuuuck."

"What are you waiting for?" She stares at the space between us. A cue.

I grab the condom from my back pocket, rip open the wrapper, and roll it down. Then I notch the head of my dick against her sweet, slick pussy, and I push inside.

The first inch is unreal, warm and tight. She fits so fucking perfectly. I take a moment to savor the feel, then my gaze roams over every inch of her creamy flesh, her flushed chest, her darkened cheeks.

And those big eyes, flickering with heat, darkening with lust. It steals my breath for a sharp, hot moment that I don't want to end. Ever.

But I focus on business. "Put your feet up," I say, patting the edge of the table.

She complies, lifting her knees, resting on the balls of her feet, giving me even more room to slide deeper. And looking so unbearably sexy with her thighs spread wide and her wet pussy on full display.

A red-hot spike of pleasure shoots down my spine. Then I get it together so I can focus on her. I grab the back of her thigh, holding on tightly, gripping her there. I ease out, then back in, then out. Her breath catches.

I stay like that, teasing her for a few long seconds.

She whimpers. Whines. Stares at me with the most petulant look.

My lips quirk into a grin. "Wait for it," I say in a low rasp.

She lifts her chest, pushing out her pretty tits and making it impossible for me to wait any longer. I slam back into her.

"Oh, god," she shouts.

"Fuuuuuuck," I groan.

Her hands dart out, grabbing my biceps, nails digging into my skin, holding on for dear life.

I swivel my hips, thrust back in, letting her feel the absence, then letting her feel all of me. My muscles tighten. I curl my hand tighter around her thigh. Drive deeper. Rope my free hand through her hair and tug it. Another gasp.

My brain is scrambled. I can barely think.

I dip my face toward her neck, burying it in the crook of it as I layer kisses along her sweaty skin, murmuring until I reach her ear and whisper, "Knew you'd like that. Want to know how?"

"Tell me."

I pull back. "When I braided your hair that day?"

"I was pretty turned on," she says, with a smile that tells me she likes being known.

"Yeah, I knew you'd like this," I say, then I pull her hair again.

She lets out the sexiest cry. I drop my hand from her hair, my palm skating down the side of her neck to the hollow of her throat. She shudders, legs squeezing me tighter as I curl my hand around her neck, pressing lightly, squeezing her.

Hot breath gusts across my hand. I grip a little harder. Another sexy gasp that ends when she grabs my hand and shoves it between her thighs.

She's a woman who knows her mind. I'm so far gone for her.

But not so lost that I can't give her everything she needs.

I stroke her needy clit. Faster and faster still. Seconds later, she's shaking, chanting, alerting the whole town to her orgasm, then coming hard on the dressing room table in the back of our bakery in the little town of Cozy Valley.

Lust plows through my entire body as I thrust hard, groan, then spill into the condom. My brain blurs. My chest heaves. My soul quiets.

I want to just stay here and breathe her in. So I quickly ease out, dispose of the condom in a tissue and place it on a table, and pull up my jeans. Then I inhale the sweet vanilla scent of her hair. "Mabel?"

"Yeah?"

I raise my face, run a hand through her hair. "There's something I want to know."

Her eyes widen with curiosity. "What is it?"
"What color is your hair?"

27

NIGHT AND DAY
MABEL

I could say chestnut with honey blonde streaks. But that won't help.

I think back to the way he talked about the lavender frosting—like a pre-dawn sky. Then, to the mural, when I said the teal was the shade of a tropical lagoon.

My hair though? I'm not sure how to describe it, but I want to try. I twirl a strand of the brownish shade around my finger, considering. "It's chestnut, like a rich, warm wood. It's like... you drink coffee, right?"

His smile is clever—hopeful even. "You know I do."

"It looks the way that first sip of coffee tastes. Strong. Dark."

"Perfect," he says, then gently moves my hand aside and runs his fingers along the light streaks in my hair. "And these? Are they sunlight coming through the window, bright and warm on your skin?"

My heart jumps, and I nod vigorously. "Yes."

He dips his face into my hair, inhaling me. "Mmm."

I shiver in a whole new way, feeling adored. Savored.

When Corbin lifts his face, he says, "So your hair is like nighttime and morning all at once?"

My chest warms. My heart pounds. This man is making me feel things I have no right to feel. "I suppose it is."

The way he's looking at me now, like he's memorizing every detail, makes my breath catch. There's something different in his eyes, something deeper. But riskier too.

He doesn't say anything for a bit, just studies my face. "Your eyes are the same color as your hair."

"They are."

He looks down at my breasts. A bead of sweat slips between them. "And these are a perfect shade of pale."

"You did say you could see white. Your girl is very, very pale."

Then I blink. I just said "your girl." Fine, I said it the way we often talk to friends. Still, it doesn't go unnoticed.

His lips quirk up, saying he likes it. So do I, being his, but I should move on. I reach for his hair, a mess of brown waves. "Yours is lighter than mine. More like a latte."

"Enough about me. Let's talk about..." He stops talking and drags a finger down my chest to my right breast, tracing a circle around the nipple. It pebbles under his touch. "Dusky rose? Soft brown? Pale pink?" But before I can answer, he drops his face to it, sucking on it, and drawing out a needy gasp from me.

He smiles against my skin, murmuring, "Yes. That color. Mmm. The color of *mmm*."

I swat his hair. It's playful, then it turns urgent as I drag my fingers through the strands, tugging him closer. As he sucks on my nipple, tugging it between his teeth, I'm trembling all over again.

He cups my breast like he's weighing it as he sucks, and I drop my head back, basking in the sensation of his attention.

Soon, he lets go, then says wolfishly, "I could make you come again."

My god, is he insatiable?

"Corbin...?" There's a question implicit in the way I say his name. *What are we doing?*

He drags a hand down his face. "I know. We can't keep doing this."

It hurts to hear, but it's a relief too, because someone needed to say it. Even though he's now running a hand gently down my arm.

"We can't," I agree, also trying to hold firm. Ironic since I'm naked on a makeup table, having been fucked hard and good by my brother's best friend, who's also my business partner. "There's so much we have to do. We just opened today."

"I know." He gets it, even as he steals one last touch. Then, he lets go. "We need to focus on the business."

I scoot off the table, grab my clothes, and tug on my panties and bra. "This place deserves our full attention. So it can be the success we want it to be."

"Sex is a distraction," he says, hunting for his shirt and finding it on the floor behind us.

I grab my dress, pulling it on. "It will complicate everything. Remember when we painted the mural and you said you made a promise to yourself not to touch me again?"

"Yes," he bites out.

"I made a promise too. To put romance aside for a while. To focus on myself and on this business. To give it the attention it deserves."

He's quiet for several seconds, as if he's letting that register. "I get that. You don't want to lose sight of the goal."

That's so him, putting it in hockey terms. "Yes. I've wanted this for too long, and I don't want to get...distracted."

He nods. Vigorously. "Building something lasting takes focus."

I'm glad he sees it the same way I do. "And we can do that. Hell, we did it with this opening. We had a great day. We can keep having them."

"This has to be a one-time thing. It was inevitable, but it's done now. And we can go back to how we were before." It's like he's trying to convince himself, but I get it. My heart hurts, but it's truly for the best. "We need to..." Corbin snaps his fingers. "Code-switch."

A laugh bursts from me. "What do you mean?"

"It's when you switch from the way you talk at work to the way you talk with friends."

I roll my eyes. "I know what code-switching is. Remember, I'm younger than you."

"As if I could forget," he says. "Anyway, it's what my daughter says she does when she comes home from school. She code-switches. That's what we need to do. We need to code-switch from whatever *that* was to reading the letter as business partners, as friends."

I don't think he's wrong, even though part of me wants to ask him a million questions. *You've really wanted me for seven years? How often did you think about me? And did you feel the same way I did that time we met right here in this firehouse?* But the parallels are almost a little too much.

"Let me just clean up, and then we'll get the letter."

He grabs the tissue with the condom. "I'll do the same."

Nothing like tossing a used prophylactic into the trash to kill the mood.

After I pop into the restroom and freshen up, I smooth a hand over my dress, pick up my apron from the floor, and fold it. I set it on the makeup table—the scene of the crime of passion.

He folds his apron too. Puts it next to mine.

They're symbols of our new resolve, somehow.

We stand there for a beat, dressed again, hair smoothed over, trying to pretend the last hour didn't happen. That he doesn't think of me as his. That I didn't ask for *and* get everything I wanted in bed and more. So much more. My heart is still jittery from the way he talked to me, the things he told me, how he opened up. But it's time to ignore all that.

With a *moving-on* nod, I head to the kitchen cupboard where we keep the letters and ask, "Ready for another cookie?"

"Ravenous."

I grab the step stool, but before I can climb it, he sets a hand on my arm. "I can get it."

"Show off."

"Well, I'm presuming my ability to reach the top shelves is why you like me."

"Who said I like you?"

He shoots me a salacious look. "The way you come."

"Shut up. We said it was a one-time thing."

"True. But, Mabel, I have to acknowledge that you come so fucking beautifully." He turns around, reaches for the ceramic container, and leaves me with that dirty, delightful thought, which I know I'll hold onto for a while.

Once he has the strawberry jar, he hands it to me, and we head to the front of the bakery.

I pull the blinds down. I'm not sure I want any Cozy Valley-ites who happen to be walking by to see us in our closed shop, reading a love letter.

They're personal. And they're special, so once I put the jar down, I say, "Hey, want to have a cup of tea? Or a glass of champagne as we read?"

"We have champagne here? Young lady, do you have a liquor license?"

I laugh. "Nope. I got it for you as a little opening day gift."

"Really?" He sounds like he's not used to someone giving him things.

"Does no one give you gifts?"

"Does my daughter sneaking stickers onto my water bottle count?"

"Of course that counts," I say, then open the fridge up front that we use for drinks and grab a demi bottle of champagne.

"How did I miss that?"

"I hid it," I say.

"Sneak."

I grab some of the mismatched porcelain cups with delicately painted roses on them, pour two cups, and usher him over to a table by the window.

I lift one. "To Afternoon Delight."

"To evening delights." He clinks back, his words sending sparks down my spine.

I'm the evening delight, even though I can't be one again. Shame. But I shove that wish aside and focus on our partnership and the bakery.

I drink some champagne, and it tastes like winning must feel. It does feel as if we won today. Our receipts seem to agree.

I look around, resetting to friendship once again, then I take out the stack of letters, touching the delicate corners, feeling the soft edges of the old pages. He put the last one— the one we read in the flower and plant shop—back so they're in their proper order. That's so very him. Neat and organized.

I flash back to what Russ wrote to Harriet: *Save that part just for me.*

With that in mind, I unfold the letter the rest of the way and read.

. . .

Dear Russ,

You're right. (You like hearing those words, don't you?) Things at work are getting a little easier.

Not all the way. Not yet. But better. Thank you for encouraging me when I needed it, and I sure needed it.

Can you believe we saved a kitten from a tree today? It's the proverbial firefighter cliché. But it really happens, and I'm pretty sure that little silver tabby was grateful.

But what's not a cliché is this—when it was just us in the kitchen this evening making roast chicken and veggies for dinner, cooking together and talking about the kitten, and where we'd most want to travel, and what's the one thing that can make the day better, I nearly forgot we were co-workers.

I feel like we've connected on another level. A deeper level. And that makes me happy each day as I come into work.

Your friend,
Harriet

My heart thumps, but it aches too. "I want to know what his response was. I want to know what makes his day better, and if it's her," I say, both sad and happy as I meet Corbin's eyes and process this next chapter in a love story from the last century.

But what I see surprises me. There's a knowing smirk on his face. A smile that says he has a secret. He rolls his lips, lifts the cup of champagne, and swallows a sip.

Then he blows out a very satisfied breath.

Okay, I'll bite. I point at his lovely mouth. "What on earth is that smile for?"

He shrugs confidently. "I know what he said."

My eyes pop out. "Did you peek?"

"Nope."

"Then how do you know?" I'm genuinely confused.

He tips his forehead to the back of the letter, the side he's staring at. "He wrote a reply."

"What?" I whip the paper around, and I can see on the bottom that it's Russ's handwriting.

My body floods with sunlight. "Read it."

The reply is short, but full of a kind of longing that Corbin seems to capture perfectly as he reads.

I know I'm not supposed to say these things. I know it's risky. But I can't seem to stop. Seeing you is my favorite time of the day. Seeing you is what makes my day better. Spending time with you is what I enjoy most. And I shouldn't write that, but I can't let another day go by without letting you know.

I shudder out a heavy breath, full of admiration for these young lovers. "He was really vulnerable with her."

"And taken. He was very, very taken with her."

That's a fair assessment. "He was."

Corbin turns to the bakery, staring at the display case, like it's too much for him to look at me.

But that just means I can enjoy a long glance at him.

* * *

After we clean up—both from the champagne and from work—the day catches up with me. A yawn takes over as I head to the door, ready to drive back to San Francisco. Before I set a hand on the knob to open it and fall into my car, Corbin says, "Why don't you sleep here?"

That's not a bad idea. The thought of driving another forty minutes is too daunting, since it's way past nine.

"I have no jammies. I don't want to sleep in clothes. Or undies."

"I'll bring you something."

"Something of yours?"

"Considering I don't keep a spare set of women's jammies at home, yes. The clothes will be mine."

"Get them now," I say.

He smacks me on the ass. "Get upstairs. Get in bed. I'll be back with a comfy outfit."

"Yes, sir."

He leaves, and I head upstairs, yawning, then I strip down to my bra and undies, wash my face in the bathroom, and tumble onto the naked mattress.

Oh fuck.

No sheets. This was dumb. Why didn't I think of this bedding issue? I should go. Head to the city or see if I can crash at Theo's or maybe Clementine's. I should at the very least put my clothes back on, in the spirit of our "no more sex" pact.

But the day drifts behind my eyelids, a packed store, a pickleball challenge, a possessive man, the falling apart, and the hoping for more. And then the night floats before me as the day dissolves into just sensations and feelings.

The sound of footsteps climbing the stairs stirs me awake. I push up in bed, on the mattress, yawning, bleary-eyed.

Corbin's here with affection in his eyes. Fondness, even, as he stares down like he's been looking at me for a little while. "Hey, let me put the bed together for you."

I rub my eyes. "You brought sheets?"

"Of course I did." He offers me a hand and tugs my tired body off the mattress. My limbs feel heavy. My heart is both full and achy.

"I'll help you," I say.

He points to another bed in this bunk area and says, "Sit."

Before I go over there, he hands me a T-shirt and a pair of basketball shorts that are way too big for me. I bring them to my nose anyway, both of them, inhaling the clean, fresh laundry scent.

He shakes a sheet out over the mattress as I duck into the bathroom to change. He's seen me naked and fucked me senseless, but if we're sticking to the partnership plan, I don't want to make things harder for either one of us. When I return, swimming in his clothes, he's spreading a blanket on the bed, and my chest squeezes from the thoughtfulness. It's white with a sage green-striped pattern and flowers around the edges.

"Did you pick that out?"

"It's Charlotte's. She said it was pretty. It was just an extra blanket from the house, but it's fairly big."

"And she has good taste."

"She does." He fluffs the pillow and puts that down, then pats the bed.

I trudge over and sink onto the mattress again, this time reveling in the clean sheets and soft blanket. I rest my head on the pillow, sighing contentedly. "This was a good idea."

"You need some rest."

"So do you. Don't you have a game tomorrow?"

"I have hockey, and you have baking." He bends down and dusts the sweetest, most poignant kiss onto my forehead.

It's hardly the code switch we promised earlier, but I'm not going to protest. Especially since it feels bittersweet, like the kiss is saying it wishes it were more but knows it can't be.

"Good night, Mabel." When he pulls back, his brow is furrowed, as if something just occurred to him. "I meant to ask. What did your mom mean about the job in food services?"

Oh, right. That. A pang of sadness lances me as I remember what Mom said. The way my choices never seem like enough for her. "She said she could get me a job at the university in food services. She wants me to have benefits. It's her weird way of looking out for me."

"I take it you don't want to work in food services?"

I shake my head, a soft smile tugging at my lips. "I like it here."

"We're going to make this work," he says, and it's a new promise, one that settles into my bones as he leaves.

But even though he's gone, I can't help but think—or maybe hope—that I'm his favorite part of the day.

28

SEE ME IN MY OFFICE

CORBIN

Morning skate just hits different. Every shot feels loose and relaxed. Every sprint down the ice is powerful. Every pass lands.

I don't want to rest on the laurels of practice, though, since the devil is in the details, and the details are in the game.

As I finish my pre-game warm-up with a sweaty, intense session on the bike, where I log nine miles in twenty-two minutes, a text pings on my phone.

> Mabel: Alexa, send a note to Corbin letting him know I sold out of orange habanero cookies and his sweet and salties, the gluten-free kind. Alexa, set a reminder to place an order for more gluten-free pretzels for the sweet and salties. Everyone is asking for them! Alexa, tell Corbin I didn't think of his dick once today. Just kidding, Alexa, don't tell him that. Okay, customers coming. More later.

I crack up, but I can't resist replying in kind.

> Corbin: Alexa, tell Mabel I approve of the above message.

> Mabel: Are you kidding me, self???? OK, gotta go.

As I ride, I place an order for pretzels from the local grocery store in Cozy Valley, asking for a rush delivery. The app tells me they'll be there in twenty minutes. Perfect. Not sure if she'll be able to bake more today, but at least she'll have what she needs for tomorrow. I've been trying to help out with inventory and placing orders, since I'm good at that stuff, and it's easy enough to do on the go. I send a message letting her know to be on the lookout. Then, I hop off the bike, head to the locker room, and put on my uniform, hoping that easy feeling lasts through the game.

And it does.

I score in the first five minutes, flicking a wrist shot right through the Miami goalie's legs. He curses, and that makes the goal even better.

Miller gives a fist pump from all the way on the other side of the rink, while guarding our net.

Riggs claps me on the back.

Lake knocks the back of my helmet. "Fuck, yes."

When it's time for a line change a minute later, I jump over the boards, revved up and full of energy from the goal. I should be exhausted after working all day yesterday, but my head's clear. No distractions pulling me in different directions. Just hockey. Just this moment. It's so damn welcome.

It's tempting to ease up, thanks to the early goal. But nope. I watch every play from the bench when it's not my shift, tracking the Miami defenders and their tactics, trading my observations with teammates on the bench, then passing pucks to them on the ice.

When the game ends, we've put another W on the board. It's one game, but it's better than the last one I played, and in this business, I'll take that. Maybe code-switching is what I need in...everything. Keep work separate from personal, hockey separate from the bakery.

Yeah, that sounds like a good plan. One I'll have to use when I return to the bakery next week after a short road trip. And one I'll need when I teach Mabel how to ace pickleball.

* * *

The Foxes hit up Dallas, absolutely destroying the team there, and not gonna lie—it's satisfying to pummel them. Next up is Seattle, and we win there, too, thanks to an assist from me.

When I head into the visitors' locker room at the end of the game, I yank off my helmet with a newfound lightness in my limbs, a veritable fucking spring in my step.

Miller strides in next, clunking around triumphantly in his leg pads. "Dude, are you thinking what I'm thinking?" His eyes are bright, his smile is wide.

Lake follows, giving him a side-eye and scoffing, "Unless you're thinking about the badass owl that landed in my bird sanctuary last week and is making a nest, then no, you and I are not the same."

Miller ruffles Lake's messy hair. "Your brain is a funny place."

"Yours is," Lake says to him with a grunt.

But Miller is undeterred. "I'm thinking, we had kind of an

uneven November there. Then we won four in a fucking row in December. And what changed this month, boys? What fucking changed?"

He mimes a drumroll. Riggs grins slyly. Lake does too. Ivan laughs knowingly.

"We ate at Knighty Night's bakery," Riggs puts in.

Miller mimes slamming a buzzer. "Riggs is always right."

"Say that again. I need to record it for posterity," Riggs says as he unlaces his skates.

Miller clears his throat. "I vote that Knighty Night needs to bring us monkey chow or cowboy cookies before every game. That's what worked."

The names are so ridiculous, they're funny. "Monkey chow for you. Done," I say.

Ivan taps his stick on the floor over and over, chanting, "Streak, streak, streak."

We all get in on it, and when the repetition ends, Lake says, "But the logic adds up."

"You are such a superstitious motherfucker," I say. Even now, the winger is taking off his gear in the same order he does after every game. "Seriously, is there anything you guys won't do for a free meal?"

Lake seems to consider this, staring at the ceiling, then shaking his head. "Nope."

I'm feeling generous. Call it the code-switching effect. "Fine. Tomorrow night you can all come over for sandwiches and cornhole."

Miller pumps a fist. "Dude. Your sandwiches are legend."

I toss my shoulder pads into the stall. "I know."

"Cosign," Riggs says from his stall.

I point at him like a cocky fighter pilot in a slick film. "Thanks, Fanboy."

He flips me the bird, but I'm pretty sure he digs the new

name. So do my other teammates since the new chant becomes, "Fanboy, Fanboy, Fanboy."

That amuses me, and I'm pretty sure it delights Riggs too.

When it ends, Miller calls out from the other side of the locker room. "Wait. Is Lake coming too? To the—"

"The single dad club," Lake says. "And yes, you assholes, this cat dad'll be there. Since...well, food."

I shower and get dressed, the good mood following me. Tomorrow night, I can set up the garage for Charlotte and some friends to watch a movie while the guys hang out in the yard with the cornhole board and some grub. The first week at the bakery went well. We hired a part-time employee to help us out—Zakiya's little sister, Aisha, was looking for a job, and we needed the help. And...Mabel and I stuck to our no-touching plan. Fine, it was easy to do since I wasn't there. But I won't let details get me down.

We head to the team jet and make the quick trip back to San Francisco, where the bus takes us to the arena. After I grab a hoodie I left in my locker, I head toward my car, phone in hand, ready to go home and crash. Mabel just sent me a text —a pic of a cupcake with a candle on top. *Ode to the firehouse —our special for tomorrow*, the caption says, and I smile. She's good.

But as I'm walking down the corridor toward the players' lot, Theo swings around the corner, dark eyes lasered in on me. That's odd. But maybe he's stressed from all the late nights he's putting in. He didn't travel with us on this trip, though that's not unusual—he doesn't go to all the away games.

"You're working late," I say by way of greeting.

He doesn't offer a fist bump, a clap on the back, or a "good game." Instead, he points to the doors leading up to the second floor. "You. Me. Now."

"Your office?" I ask.

A crisp nod is his answer.

That's not good. I gulp but try not to show a shred of emotion. I follow my best friend up the stairs, and the click of his wingtips on the floor is ominous.

When we reach his office, he shuts the door with a decisive snap, and my gut twists. I tell myself to stay stoic. He has to have found out I've been messing around with his sister. Not once, not twice, not even three times.

My head swims with the realization that it's been four times. For fuck's sake, I'm addicted.

But more so, I'm a liar. I've been lying to my best friend about all these goddamn feelings for his sister. These emotions that claw at me. I haven't been forthright with him. But how can I be forthright when Mabel and I aren't a thing? Not really. What's done is done, and the guilt over the lies of omission is mine to live with, and mine alone.

"I heard something, Corbin," he says, jaw tight, tone sharp.

"What did you hear?" I ask, as nonchalantly as I can while dread swirls in me.

"I heard from my former first-grade teacher, who's in the knitting club, who heard it from Zoe at the gym, who heard it from the barista at Rise and Grind, that you hooked up with my sister in the middle of the bakery."

A laugh scrapes my throat because that is a serious game of small-town telephone. But still, the words *hooked up* hang heavily in the air.

I scramble for an excuse. Except, hold on. The mental gymnastics he just went through tell me he doesn't actually know what we did in the kitchen, so he doesn't know I've lied to him. Sure, he must know that I kissed his sister on opening night. But I did it in front of Ronnie, Tiffany, and Brittany.

I stay on the facts—just the facts.

"What did the barista see?" I ask, keeping my cool.

He huffs. "You guys were kissing. She saw it, and it was in front of that fucking flying asshat from Webflix."

Must have been Joni who started this somehow. She probably lingered outside out of view. She probably saw that kiss.

Think fast. Think really fast. But then it hits me—I have to do what I do on the ice. Pivot and go with a new play. And that play just happens to be...the truth.

Or *some* of the truth.

"Dude," I say in a conspiratorial tone. "Ronnie and his friends were coming at Mabel and saying stuff like, 'Oh, you're so sad about your ex talking shit about you on Webflix.' So I claimed we were together. I wanted to shut down the idea that she opened the bakery because she was sad over Dax. I wanted to mess with them, change the narrative, as they say."

Theo pauses, his eyes narrowed, but he's clearly considering my take. "You did it to fuck with Ronnie?"

I see the spark in his eye, and I know where this is going. "Yes, your enemy."

Sometimes I soothe him with monkey bread. Sometimes I soothe him by distracting him with his other enemies. "And Webflix, by extension, since Ronnie's show is with them," he adds, like he should be twirling a mustache in an old-timey movie.

I keep going, so he knows I'm on the good side. "I had to sell it, so I kissed her in front of them. They made it seem like she was desperate over Dax, and fuck that."

"Fuck Dax," Theo echoes. After a few seconds, he unleashes a huge sigh of relief. "You are a motherfucking genius. I knew it. You are the playmaker."

I feel a little oily taking that compliment from him, even though I know this lie of omission is better than the truth. Since there won't be a fifth time with Mabel.

"Exactly. And we want people to say good things about the

bakery, so if this little charade helps, so be it." Then, I tell him about the pickleball challenge, so he knows we'll need to fake date for that.

"You'd better make sure she destroys them. If you have to fake-date your way through that, you need to do it."

"I will," I say, wishing I weren't looking forward to spending time with Mabel on the court.

But I seriously am.

29

THE LAWN MEN
CORBIN

In my yard the next night, under Christmas lights that Charlotte and I hung twinkling from a maple tree, I toss a bag at the cornhole board, but miss badly, the bag skidding to the grass.

"Bummer. Can't win everything," Miller says, blowing on his nails and peacocking because he keeps winning game after game. He taps his chest. "I mean. I can. But you? Not so sure."

I hand Miller the striped bag of mine from the ground. "Would you like this for your trophy case? A memento of when you came to my backyard and won a lawn game?"

He takes it, holds it up, and considers it. "As a matter of fact, I think I would."

"You need something for your trophy case, Lockwood," Tyler says from his spot a few feet away. He's one of our friends from the Sea Dogs, our cross-town rivals, and he tries to hang out with us when he can. His kids are in the garage with Charlotte, watching a movie.

"This will be your first recognition of any kind, right?" Riggs asks. He's on the deck, stretched out in an Adirondack chair.

"Right," Miller deadpans. The dude has won multiple awards as a top goalie. "And I will display it proudly."

"All right, let's see who wins this round," Tyler says, then goads Ivan and Lake into joining in the next game.

I join Riggs on the deck, pouring myself an iced tea from the pitcher. Don't want to drink liquor since Charlotte is here with me tonight. I pick up the glass and then flop into the chair next to my teammate's, glancing at the few remains of the spread that had covered the table earlier. We plowed through all the sandwiches and left no crumbs.

"How are you doing, man?" Riggs asks.

"Good."

He scoffs. "Don't give me a rote answer. How are you really doing? You've got a ton to manage. The kid, the regular job, your side hustle."

I appreciate the thoughtful question. Most guys are afraid to ask how another dude is doing. We haven't been taught that in a lot of cases. But Riggs tries to practice the hard stuff.

And he's not wrong, so I give a better answer. "It feels doable. I feel good. Maybe because we're playing well, or maybe because the bakery's first week was a success. But then again, I'm not the one who's at the bakery all day long. Mabel is." A smile tugs at my lips as I think of her regular reports and how much I look forward to them. She sends me photos of empty trays with only crumbs left, pictures of the card reader displaying the sales at the end of the day, and mouth-watering images of what she's baking. Those pictures give me life. "She's doing a great job."

Riggs arches a brow, then shakes his head, like something amuses him.

"What's that for?"

He smirks. "Nothing."

"Bullshit."

He takes a drink of his seltzer water, then sets it on the railing. "I was partly wondering how it's going since it's always seemed like you were into her."

He said something similar back in Los Angeles when we kidnapped Lake. But that felt like a lucky guess. Not sure if this is the same.

"Yeah?" I ask nonchalantly as I try to figure out how to answer, if at all.

"Just something I pick up on now and then," he says, tone serious.

He leaves it at that—an offer to listen.

I was truthful earlier. I've been truthful whenever we've had tougher conversations. Might as well be now. It's clear his remark isn't in the vein of lucky guesses or giving a teammate a hard time.

I scratch my jaw. "I'd be lying if I said I wasn't into her, but I'll be one hundred percent honest and tell you it would be a bad idea if I were to do anything about it."

Any more *things about it.*

He blows out a breath. "I hear you. I think the same thing sometimes."

I arch a brow. "About Sapphire?"

He shakes his head. "No. Things are cool with her. It's going well." He pauses, like he's rewinding something in his mind. "I meant I have in the past. Some women are just off-limits."

Briefly, I wonder who's off-limits for him, because it doesn't sound like Sapphire is. But he'll tell me if and when he's ready. He fiddles with the label on the bottle of seltzer water, then looks back at me with a shrug. "What can you do though?"

That's the question, isn't it? I don't have any answers. I'm grateful when my attention snags on a silhouette near the sliding glass door leading to the deck.

Riggs turns to it too. "Speak of the devil."

Charlotte slides the door open, and Mabel's right behind her, carrying a grocery bag. My heart slams hard against my chest.

"Don't worry. We won't be out here long, interrupting your man time," Charlotte says, precocious and far too observant.

Mabel cracks up, then says to my kid, "Why do I feel like you've said that before?"

Charlotte shrugs. "I let them do their thing. And I can do my thing. Do you want to watch this cool documentary with me? It's all about the planet's diverse ecosystems and which animals thrive in them."

Riggs snaps his gaze to Charlotte. "That does sound interesting."

"It is. I'm learning a lot," she says. "You could learn more for your trivia nights."

Riggs looks tempted, but then he says, "I should keep your dad company."

"Good plan," she says.

I turn my gaze to Mabel, who's wearing one of our Afternoon Delight sweatshirts that says *F*ck Mornings* on it, and it just looks so damn good on her. Bet it'd look good off her too. Quickly, I strike that thought from my head since one, I shouldn't be thinking it, and two, my kid is right here.

"How's it going, Mabel?" I ask evenly, trying to strip all the longing and affection from my tone.

She lifts the canvas bag. "Charlotte asked me to bring some things over. She thought you guys might want a little extra food here. I made some of your famous seven-layer bars, even though I didn't taste them because they have nuts. And I made some grilled cheese sandwiches."

"Thank you," I say.

Riggs sits up straighter. "Did you say grilled cheese sandwiches? Because we just ran out of sandwiches."

Mabel smiles. "I did. I had some cheese from The Cheesery and some bread from the gourmet market, so I thought I would try it out. Here you go. They're still fresh and gooey, so you'd better eat them now."

Riggs beelines for the bag, then holds it up toward the lawn. "Behold, the grilled cheese, boys."

The games stop, and the guys descend on the bag like bears at a campground.

"Knew I liked coming up here for a reason," Tyler says, grabbing a sandwich.

"Because we're a better team and you want our awesomeness to rub off on you," Miller says.

Tyler scoffs. "I see you're still practicing for a career change as a comedian."

Mabel tips her head toward the sliding glass door. "I'm going to leave you to your lawn games."

Lake's ears must perk up from the yard, since he whips his gaze to us. "The Lawn Club. That's our new name."

"That's a terrible name," I say, cringing.

"It is," Lake says. "That's why we're going to use it. It's ironic."

"Not sure that's irony," Riggs says. "Irony is..."

I leave them to their discussion of irony as they devour cheesy sandwiches. Like there's an invisible force pulling me, I follow Mabel and Charlotte inside, stopping in the kitchen. "Thanks again," I say to Mabel as she leans a hip against the island. Damn, she looks good here in my home, all casual and comfortable.

"No problem."

"Especially for the sandwiches. That was really thoughtful," I add, leaning against the other side of the counter, maybe needing a barrier between us so I don't run a hand down her arm, absently touch her hair, or reach for her hand.

"It was Charlotte's idea, so credit where credit's due."

"I had a sandwich when she arrived," Charlotte says matter-of-factly, patting her belly. "They're really good." To Mabel, she adds, "I'm kind of a grilled cheese expert. My grandma made them. It was her specialty, and I learned it from her, but I think you did a really good job too."

Mabel smiles warmly. "High praise, and I will take it."

Something about the way they interact, like they're friends already, does funny things to my heart.

Charlotte beams, then turns to me, whip-fast, like she's just remembered something. "Dad, the rescue emailed about the volunteer options, and they listed a bunch of things that we could do."

Mabel tilts her head, looking right at Charlotte. "Does that include fostering?"

Charlotte taps her chin. "I think it did, actually."

From my vantage point, I watch them volleying, which seems kind of...rehearsed.

"I have a friend who does that," Mabel begins. "I was thinking about what your dad said about his schedule and your schedule, and I know it'd be hard for you guys to have a dog, but fostering is a great way to help animals in need. Even if you can just foster for a weekend here and there, or be a temporary foster. Rescues need that all the time."

Charlotte's eyes widen as she turns to me. "Dad, that actually sounds perfect, doesn't it?"

Mabel smothers a smile. And I've got a feeling. I've got a damn good feeling that they've plotted this. I wouldn't put it past either one of them. Also, I kind of love that they're in on something together.

"Works for me," I reply.

Charlotte rushes to me, wraps her arms around my chest. "You're the best, Dad."

I hold her close. "I have the world's best daughter."

When we break the hug, Charlotte high-fives Mabel. They both look pleased. And I like making that happen for them.

I walk them to the front door, with Charlotte heading to the garage and Mabel to her car. But I need to catch up with her on some bakery business.

"Got a sec? I wanted to touch base on some of the holiday delivery plans," I say. I arranged for Mariah's son, Carson, to deliver some cookies and other holiday items for us in the afternoon when he's home from school.

"Definitely," she says, and we chat about the details for a few minutes.

"And we need to make sure we have enough pretzels—both kinds—so we don't run out again," I add. "I'm going to do some ordering tonight."

I figure that helps take some things off her plate since she's been doing so much. But when she gives a not-quite-full smile, I've got the sense something has disappointed her.

"About that. The pretzels you sent last week weren't gluten-free."

"What?" That makes no sense. I ordered them. I grab my phone to double-check the invoice.

"They were fine, don't get me wrong. I was able to use them for the regular sweet and salties. But the grocery store in Cozy Valley didn't have any gluten-free ones that afternoon. I went out in the evening to get the gluten-free kind, so I was able to make some for the next day's batch."

Shit. That's a lot of work for her. And the app doesn't lie—I'm staring at the order, and I did hit the button for the wrong kind. "Why didn't you tell me last week?"

"You had a hockey game," she says. "And it was fine. Bakeries run out of items. Plus, I got them myself, so it was fine."

She's not wrong, but still. I feel like a fuck-up. "I'm sorry, Mabel. Let me make it up to you."

She laughs me off. "Corbin, it's not a big deal. We're all good."

But this mistake doesn't sit well with me. I want to do my part, even if I'm not at Afternoon Delight as much as she is. Or even ten percent as often. My brain lands on an idea. "Hey," I say, before she can head down the steps toward her car.

"Yes?"

"Last year, around Christmastime, I was helping my friend Rowan bake cookies for a sort of matchmaking-meets-speed-dating event. My agent took some pics of all of us baking at Rowan's house. Rowan, Tyler, and me. He joked that a pic of me and my *sports-ball buds* baking would help sell my future bakery." Even though I've opened a damn bakery with her, it still feels vulnerable as hell to admit how long I've wanted to do this.

"You'd better still have that."

I'm glad she knows where I am going with this. "I'll send it to you tonight. You want to post it?"

"Like, tomorrow. I will post it tomorrow. Got any other secret promo material you're hiding?"

I hum like I'm considering the question even though I'm mostly stalling. "I'll have to look."

"You do that."

"You know," I say, thinking out loud. "We could host dating events with cookies. Maybe it's a blind date with cookies. Or all sorts of baked goods. No one knows what they'll be getting, just like—"

"You never know what you'll get when you go out on a date!"

"Exactly."

"I can see it now. Cookies are better than apps," she says.

For a moment, my chest burns as I think about Mabel having used dating apps. I should leave the topic alone, but the words rush out of my mouth. "Have you been on the apps?"

Worse. Is she on them now? Shit. Why have we not discussed this?

Maybe because you keep saying it's a one-time thing every time you touch her.

But before I can spiral into a stew of my own stupidity, Mabel scoffs. Loudly and far too amused. Or is it annoyance in her voice? "Seriously? Are you really asking me that?"

"Yes. I am."

She folds her arms across her chest. "Are *you*?"

"On the apps?"

"Yes," she bites out.

Is Mabel jealous? "Nope. Haven't been in a long time."

"Same here," she says, with the stubborn air of someone digging in her heels.

My shoulders relax. "Thank fuck."

She shakes her head in annoyed disbelief. "You think I'd sleep with you if I were seeing other people?"

Sleep with you. Those words sound too good on her lips, even chased with her annoyance.

"I hadn't thought about it," I admit.

"Well, think about it. Because it's insulting."

Oh, shit. She's not just annoyed. She's offended. This is the Mabel who pulls no punches, and I've pissed her off.

"I didn't mean it like that," I say, dragging a hand through my hair, trying to get my thoughts together.

"How did you mean it then? Other than to ask if I'm sleeping around? Just last week, I literally told you I was on a romance break, to focus on myself and our business. And you think I'd be on the apps then, just to, what, fuck?"

This is bad. She must think I'm a crass asshole. "I really didn't mean that."

She breathes out hard. "Then, maybe don't ask questions like that. Questions that imply I'm sleeping around. Or, worse, lying."

Is that what I implied? I rewind the conversation, and damn, my words do sound insulting. "Mabel, I was just trying to figure out—"

If we were exclusive when we were one-time-only fuck buddies? For fuck's sake, this conversation is too hard to have.

But she blows out one breath, then another, then one more. "It's fine," she says, waving a hand dismissively. "It's no big deal."

Clearly, it is though. I hurt her because I was...jealous. Territorial.

"This is all new to me. This...thing," I admit. "With us. Even though I know there's no *us*."

We are business partners, though, and we promised to navigate problems like adults would.

"I get it. Same here," she says more calmly, maybe realizing that the conversation escalated far too quickly. "I just didn't like the assumption. But it's fine. I promise."

I'm not buying her half smile though. "Are you sure?" I ask with real concern.

"I swear," she says, holding up her hands in surrender.

I should apologize properly. But as I try to figure out what to say, her gaze sails to her car. "I should go," she says.

And maybe it's best if I let her. "I'm sorry. I'll see you on Tuesday for pickleball practice." I'm counting down to two days from now. The bakery's closed Tuesdays, so it's the best time to do it.

"Sounds good." She stops in her tracks. "Theo rented out the entire court for us."

I stand straighter, worry shooting through me. Is he going to babysit us now that he knows we've kissed? "Is he coming?"

"No. I wouldn't let him. He just didn't want any distractions, so I guess it's you and me and a pickleball game."

Ordinarily, that would sound tempting. But her pretty eyes don't flicker with secrets between the two of us. They're hard, like she needs to protect herself.

"I'll focus solely on pickleball," I say.

"Me too," she says with resignation, then whirls around, trots down the steps, heads to her car, and slides inside.

I watch her the whole time as she drives away, the arc of her headlights swooping down the street then turning the corner, out of sight.

I wish that had lasted longer. I wish she'd come back. I wish I knew what to say.

Heaving a sigh, I drag a hand through my hair and head back out to the deck. I slump down next to Riggs.

He shakes his head, muttering, "Good luck with that."

"Thanks, man."

I need it. Because I've got no clue what just went wrong. But I know this much—I have to fix it.

Once everyone's gone and Charlotte's in bed, I collapse onto the couch and tap out a text.

Corbin: I'm sorry. If you were here, I'd bring you flowers, or bake apology cookies, or give you a dress, or braid your hair. I should have asked that in a different way. Mostly, the thought of you being on the apps drove me a little insane. If I can't have you, I don't want anyone else to. Which is caveman of me. Sorry for being a caveman.

Mabel: You are the last thing from a caveman. Also, I don't want anyone else to have you either.

It's like a shot of adrenaline to the heart. Or the dick. Maybe both.

Corbin: No one else does.

Mabel: Good. But also, we promised to work through arguments like adults. How are we doing?

Corbin: I give us a ten out of ten. Like our bars, brownies, and blondies.

Mabel: Same. But you do not owe me an apology for anything.

She might be right, but I'll probably do something anyway.

30

PERSONAL DELIVERY

MABEL

The words from the last love letter still echo in my mind.

Thank you for encouraging me when I needed it, and I sure needed it.

They've played on repeat for more than a week. Along with Corbin's words to me the day I unveiled the name for the bakery, when I was feeling like the town thought I was a joke.

I believe in you.

Those four words burrowed into my heart, taking a spot right next to Grandma's lifetime of encouragement.

It's time to act on them, starting with the grumpy guys at the chess tables. They're more loyal to their grocery store pastries than a toddler is to the toy truck he doesn't want to share.

But the next morning, before Afternoon Delight opens, I head toward the town square, a pink box in one hand, and a thermos from Rise and Grind in the other.

I pass Whiskers and Kisses, decked out for Christmas with a red-and-green drawing of cats and dogs on the window and say hello to the woman who runs the sandwich shop, then to Mariah at Havenly as she's adjusting the wreath on the door.

Soon, the town square comes into view. I draw a steadying breath as I spot the pack of retired men—a Black man, a brown man, a white man—all hunched over their concrete table with the painted-on chess board.

There's no coffee yet. No Danishes. Like I suspected, since I have spies on the inside. Clementine at the bookstore told me they play an early morning game, then stop to grab coffee from the gas station and pastries from the grocery store before returning for another round.

Annabelle tipped me off about the flavors of Danishes they like.

And Abe—Abe, of all people, who also gets a caffeine fix from the gas station—told me how they like their coffee.

Here goes nothing.

They blew me off last time I showed up. But maybe the second time will be the charm. I cross the street, then march into the square, the Christmas tree looming in the center, with lights that'll flicker after dark.

As the man with the short Afro plunks down a rook on the board, I arrive.

They all turn to me with suspicion in their eyes.

I plow forward. "Hi, gentlemen," I say, then waggle the thermos with *F*ck Mornings* written on the side. "I brought you all coffee, fresh-brewed and strong, and black from Rise and Grind." I take the liberty of setting the thermos down, then don't waste another second. I flip open the bakery box, letting them sniff the freshly baked goodies.

Noses lift, inhaling the scent of blueberry Danish, raspberry Danish, and peach Danish. "I heard you guys like these flavors, so I made them for you this morning so you don't have to go to the grocery store."

The man with the pale weathered face and a few stray

nose hairs arches a dubious and bushy brow. "You're trying to trick us into coming to your hipster bakery every day."

He sounds just like Dottie at the yarn shop.

The man with the Afro scoffs at his friend. "Just eat it, you old fool. Of course she's trying to convince us," he says, then takes a bite of the peach one, and his eyes pop. After he chews, he turns to me. "Do you deliver to the town square?"

I laugh. "Maybe I can. Except on Tuesdays. My oven takes that day off."

"Perhaps we'll put in a standing order. Name's Jackson."

"I'll be on the lookout, Jackson."

The nose-hair guy harrumphs, but then takes a bite of the raspberry Danish. He doesn't say a word when he finishes chewing. The third man adjusts his San Francisco Cougars baseball cap, pours coffee into his own to-go cup, and drinks some. "Not bad," he says, then gives me a once-over. "You're the kid who ran over the mailbox, let the llamas run free, and then ran out of town, right?"

I wince as my past bites me again. But I own it. "Yes, that's me."

He nods. "Good on you for doing the hard thing. We'll place an order for Wednesday morning. Not sure about Arnie," he says, turning to the raspberry Danish guy, arching a brow in question.

"Fine," Arnie grumbles.

"But this time I'll pay," the Cougars fan adds, then tells me his name's Lorenzo.

I didn't come here thinking I'd gain them as customers, but I'll happily take it. I say goodbye, then head to Annabelle's shop to grab some flowers for my next mission.

* * *

This is long overdue. It's been weighing on me since I ran into Joni at the coffee shop when we first started working on the bakery. That encounter this morning with the chess guys only reinforced it. My palms feel clammy as I park my car, and grab a sampler box of brownies, cookies, and bars, along with a bouquet of orange marigolds, since I checked that Mrs. Henderson had that color and type of flower painted on her current mailbox, and open the car door.

I head up the cobblestoned path to her front porch. It's one of those cutesy homes with ladybug pots for plants, and sunflower wind chimes. When I reach the porch and lift my hand to knock, I freeze, hand mid-air.

Who answers the door anymore? This is dumb. I hate the doorbell. I avoid it. Most people look in the security camera and hide out of sight till whoever knocked goes away.

But I have to do it anyway, rapping on the wooden door.

I'm greeted by a yap.

Then another one.

A few seconds later, two aggrieved black-and-tan Chiweenies pop up on the couch in the window and give me hell through the windowpane.

"Sorry, cuties. Just wondering if your mom is here," I say to the pups.

Seconds later, the sound of boots squishing in the front lawn draws my attention. Then there's a voice. "Quiet there, you little monsters," a woman says.

But it's said with affection.

She turns to me, tilting her head, forehead wrinkled, mouth unsure. She's got a tall shovel in her hand, and she plants a booted foot on it. That shovel could bludgeon me. She's giving badass grandma vibes. "What can I do for you?"

"I was..." I trot down the steps. "I'm Mabel. I ran over your mailbox ten years ago, and I never said I was sorry. I know my parents replaced it but I didn't know what to say so I avoided it. And I just wanted to apologize in person."

She chuckles warmly. "Oh honey, that was years ago. Water under the bridge. But what made you think of it now?"

That's a reasonable question, and it has an easy answer. "I guess it just seemed overdue. And like something I *could* do."

She nods thoughtfully. "I get that. It's just a mailbox, but it takes character to face something that's been nagging at you, even something small."

My gaze drifts to the painted mailbox, and sure, it's no big deal. But I want to be part of this town, baking for these people, asking for their support day in and day out. It seemed the least I could do.

My throat tightens, but I thrust the flowers I've been holding at her, along with the treats. "For you. Thank you."

She takes both. "You didn't have to. You could have just called, but I appreciate the flowers and treats very much."

"Thank you. Also your dogs are adorable. I can bring them dog cookies if you'd like."

"They're fosters. Through Little Friends. They're a bonded pair, so they'll only be with me till they find a forever home."

Well, isn't this kismet. "You know, I have a friend who's going to do that too. Foster."

"You don't say. I need a temp foster for them for a couple days next week," she says, eyes twinkling. "And I bet they'd love dog cookies."

"Sold."

* * *

Thirty minutes later, I'm back at the bakery, setting up to open in an hour when I spot a familiar face at the door, waving to get my attention.

I scurry over to answer it. It's Clementine and she strides in, the picture of preppy in her argyle sweater vest over a white top and trendy jeans, with cute white sneakers. Her blonde hair cascades in waves. She holds up a small canvas bag. "Who's a goddess?"

"You are. And I am not worthy." I pretend to genuflect.

"Please, your adoration is not necessary, though it is much appreciated," she says, faux regally.

"It is necessary, since I'm seriously impressed you found it."

"I'm a knitter. And a finder. It's what I do."

I peek inside the bag and shimmy my shoulders at the skein of magenta chenille inside. "You're the best. Do you play pickleball?" I ask, hoping to enlist her in our friend group game.

She shudders. "I'm not a sports fan. But I love a game of poker if you ever want a round."

"I bet I'd like poker. Can we start with penny bets?"

She crinkles her nose, doubtful. "Maybe a dollar?"

"I'm in."

She leaves and soon after I leave too, repeating the words from Russ to Harriet when she was struggling to fit in—*Don't let them get you down.*

With that sentiment propelling me, I leave the bakery with cookies and something else. Something Dottie wanted badly —the specialty yarn Clementine tracked down.

I pull open the door to A Good Yarn, steeling myself. This might flop, but I have to try. I can't let the knitting club get me down.

They aren't here, but I didn't expect them to be. The owner is, with her head bent over a book, and her short, gray-streaked bob hitting her chin.

"Hello," I say.

Setting her book down, she gives me a friendly but quizzical look. "What can I help you with?"

"When I was here the other week, Dottie said she was looking for a type of yarn, and I think you said you didn't have it. Magenta chenille. But a friend of mine who's a knitter tracked some down. And I thought I would bring it to you in case you want to..."

She makes grabby hands. "Sell it to her?"

"Yes."

"Damn right I do," she says, "but what do I owe you?"

"Nothing. Just maybe tell Dottie I found it for her?"

Her smile is a deal signed. "Done," she says, eyeing the yarn again, then me. "You're industrious."

"I am."

I also want to prove the ladies at the knitting club wrong. They'll take more time than the guys in the town square, but I can show them I listened. "And here are some cookies for you."

The store owner tugs the box to her in a sort of *mine* gesture, then thanks me.

I leave, and I don't feel like such an outsider anymore.

Especially the next day when I head to the pickleball court for my lesson. After all, I have a fake date coming up soon. And I plan to win.

31

DOUBLE-USE SCRUNCHIE
MABEL

Corbin strides over to me along the side of the court, holding a paddle and a small pink gift bag. He's pleased, judging from the size of his grin. I let myself enjoy the view of him as he moves, loose and easy in basketball shorts and a gray T-shirt that hugs his pecs.

"Corbin," I half chide as he passes the net, then stops in front of me, offering me the bag. "You didn't."

"Oh, I did, Mabel. I definitely did."

My heart jumps as I reach for it. "I told you that you didn't have to."

"And I didn't listen." He's unrepentant in his gift-giving. "I told you I was going to get you an apology gift."

"You don't owe me an apology. It's fine. We cleared the air. Just like we said we would."

"We said we'd handle things like adults." He taps his chest. "This adult likes to apologize to you with gifts. Now just open it."

As I peer inside, it's my turn to smile. "It's my favorite color."

"Wear it," he says.

"So bossy."

"Damn right I am. Want to let me put it on you?"

So much.

I fish out the lilac scrunchie from the bag and give it right back to him. "Do your thing, you bossy man."

"I will."

I turn around as a charge of anticipation races down my body.

The clink of his paddle hitting the court registers as he moves behind me, combing his fingers through my hair, pulling it up. I lean into the tug as he arranges my strands into a high, neat ponytail.

He takes his time roping his fingers through my hair, adjusting it, tweaking it, then dropping my hair and doing it all again. "Sorry. Need a second try," he mutters, but he doesn't sound sorry.

I don't feel sorry either.

My stomach flips as he runs those fingers through my hair once more, then loops the scrunchie and steps back to admire his work. "Perfect. Now let's play ball."

Once I turn around, I give a flick of my hair just for fun. "You're so good at giving gifts that we just might have to fight again."

"I'm in," he says with a wicked smile that burns off quickly as he picks up the paddle and points at the net. "Time to teach you how to destroy your enemies."

I love competitive athletes. I just do.

* * *

The ball bounces and Corbin lunges for it, serving it back to me. Of course he hits it. He never doesn't hit it.

It's exhausting, playing with him.

"You're doing great," he calls out even though I miss the next ball.

"Ha. Hardly."

We've been playing for an hour and he's giving me tips on how to serve it more cleanly, and how to hunt out weak backhands and attack them, and it's all good stuff.

"But the reason I keep hitting it is because you need to vary your shots more," he says.

I shoot him a doubtful look. "You're a pro athlete."

"But not a pro pickleball player. I can help you."

"I can't believe I'm doing this on my day off," I say, rolling my eyes.

"Or you could let Tiffany and Brittany destroy us this Friday."

"I have you. You'd never let that happen."

"We're a team," he says, then comes around the net. "Let me show you how to vary your shots." When he reaches me, he runs a hand through his hair, pushing a few sweaty strands off his forehead.

Hello, sweat. What would it feel like, to run my hand up under his shirt, over the sweaty ridges of his abs right now? His chest? How easy would it be to slide my hand down into his shorts and—

Oh, great. Now I've learned I have a thing for his sweat. And I need to stop thinking dirty thoughts about him.

"Show me," I say.

The facility has four courts but we're the only ones here. The best part is these courts are screened by hedges that are easily ten feet tall. At first, I joked that they meant no one could see how badly I play. Now I'm thinking this privacy will be useful in other ways. He moves behind me, wrapping his arms around me, and...oh, yes.

That's nice.

It's been a while since he touched me. Fine, it was only an hour ago when he looped his hands through my hair. But before that? Ten days to be precise.

His arms slide along mine, his chest brushes against my back, and my insides do the hula.

He's just so warm and solid behind me, and that campfire-and-lake scent mingles deliciously with sweat as he reaches for my wrist. "If you want to do a two-handed backhand for power," he begins, and the rest is argle-bargle as his hand circles my wrists, holding me tight.

As his scent wafts past my nose, enticing me.

As his chest presses against my back, tempting me.

As my restraint—already frayed—breaks even more.

"Can you do that?" he asks.

"Sure," I say, then I bump my ass back against him, testing to see if he's affected too. And the answer is a warning growl.

"Mabel," he says in my ear, voice husky and warm.

Cock thick and hard.

"Corbin," I tease back, giving another pop of my ass against the hard ridge of him. There, right there. Against the thin fabric of my skirt.

"You're being a troublemaker," he says, holding still, keeping us in place like he doesn't want me to move.

"I'll stop," I say, and I should stop rubbing my ass against his hard-on, but maybe he should stop too.

And he's not. He's going. He's pressing back. Grinding against my butt, gripping my wrists harder.

"I shouldn't," he whispers.

"I know. We said," I murmur.

"It was a one-time thing," he continues, a soft plea against the skin on my neck to help him say no to this.

"I'll stop," I say, drawing a steadying breath. I can do this. I can stop. I will myself to inch away.

But once there's a sliver of space between us, he growls in protest. Ropes his arm around my waist. Yanks me close in a vise. "Don't stop."

I sway against him. He rocks back, then dusts his mouth to my neck. He's always been obsessed with my neck.

And here on the pickleball court on a mid-December afternoon, he leaves a trail of open-mouthed kisses from my ear down to my collarbone, each one a little harder, a little more desperate than the last, like he wants to mark me.

I flash back to what he said the night we fucked in the bakery. *Try since I met you, Mabel. Since I met you.*

He's been so vulnerable with me about all this longing. He was even vulnerable in a way when he asked me if I was on the apps. *If I can't have you, I don't want anyone else to.* The more he shares, the more it cracks something open in me. Makes me want to give him the same. "I wanted you too. The day I met you," I confess.

His breath comes out ragged, stuttered. "Yeah?"

"When you were helping me clean up after the llamas. I kept thinking *this guy is fine*," I say, remembering how handsome he was then.

"You have no idea what that does to me," he says with a groan as he tugs me tighter against him.

Well, I think I do know. It excites me.

He kisses me more urgently now, like my confession revved him up another level. Like he can't hold back anymore today. I've been terrible at holding back too. Restraint, evidently, is for other people. Corbin's still gripping my wrists and the paddle, and that seems wholly unimportant so I drop it to the court.

"I wanted to, Mabel. So badly. Then I learned you were—"

I know where that's going. He learned I'm his best friend's sister. I learned he was forbidden too, in lots of ways back then. "Same. You were off-limits to me too," I say, my eyes fluttering closed, my body melting like butter on a warm day.

"But now." His hand reaches for mine, and he threads our fingers together. "Now I just..." He sounds as lost to whatever this is as I am.

And I am utterly lost, so I wiggle free, spin around, cup his shoulders, and say, "My turn."

"For what?" he asks.

I glance around, making sure it's still just us, then I push him toward the edge of the court, near the hedges. A few strands have fallen out of my ponytail, so I undo it, then redo it, giving him a sly smile when it's fixed. "My turn to apologize. Good thing I have this scrunchie to hold my hair back."

His eyes widen. A thrill flickers in them. Then dirty, filthy hope as I drop down to my knees.

"Wait," he snaps.

I arch a brow in question, but he's already stripping off his T-shirt—of course—and setting it down on the court for me to kneel on.

"The filthy gentleman," I muse, as I settle in on the gray cotton.

"I am. And now I'll ask you the question like a gentleman. You going to apologize with that pretty mouth of yours?"

"I am. It'll be a very deep, full-throated apology."

He grabs the side of my face, stares hotly at me, then ropes his fingers through my hair once more. "Open wide, then."

I tug on the waistband of his basketball shorts. "Give me that big dick so I can."

With a groan that seems to rumble all the way up his chest, he pushes down his shorts, frees his cock, and wraps a fist around the base, offering his cock to me like a gift I ought to be grateful for.

I am. I'm so grateful my panties are wet.

Nope. Make that *wetter*. Just like his dick, with a drop of liquid arousal beading at the tip. Leaning in, I dart out the tip of my tongue, flick it across it, then moan, murmuring, "More."

Giving a small pump of his hips, he thrusts a little deeper, offering me another inch. Grabbing his hips, I wrap my lips around his shaft. I draw him in, sucking on the crown, then more, then as much as I can. Soon I'm lavishing attention up and down him with my tongue. I'm making a mess of his cock, licking him sloppily, wrapping my hand around him and drawing him deeper. So deep that I bat his hand away from the base. He's mine right now, and I want all of him.

"Fuck, baby. You look so fucking beautiful like this. So fucking perfect on your knees."

My pulse beats hot and fast between my thighs.

He grips my head harder. Ropes his fingers in my hair that's getting messier. "This scrunchie is so fucking helpful," he mutters.

With my fingers digging into his skin, I urge him to pump his hips. He obeys, and I relax my throat as best I can. Somehow, I drag him in deeper, caressing his cock with my mouth, letting him hit the back of my throat.

I gag. Coughing. Letting him drop from my mouth.

"You okay? Want me to stop?"

I grab his hips harder, digging my nails into his flesh. "You'd better apologize for saying that."

He runs a big hand over my hair. "Yeah? How do you want me to say sorry?"

"By filling my throat with your come," I tell him.

The sound that rips from his chest is animalistic. I draw his wet cock back into my mouth, inhaling him, it seems. He fills my mouth, so there's hardly room for me to breathe, but I don't care.

He's groaning, grunting, thrusting. And swearing so damn much.

So fucking beautiful.

Yes, fuck yes, do that.

I can't fucking take it.

But I can. I can take it all, and he gives it all in one deep thrust as he jerks, shudders, and comes down my throat. I swallow it all, savoring the taste of my business partner and pickleball coach out here on the court.

When he eases out, he's panting, and moaning still. But he must blink off the haze quickly, since he says, "What a mess I've made of your pretty hair. Let me fix it."

32

THE RIGHT AMOUNT OF YOU
CORBIN

"I messed up your hair," I say as I tug her up from the court, then grab my T-shirt from beneath her knees.

"I'm sensing a theme," she remarks, smoothing her skirt.

"And that is?" I tug my T-shirt back on.

"One: you like to strip in front of me. Two: you like to make a mess of me."

Damn, that's a little spot on. A little scary too, for a guy who's a neat freak. "I do."

"Or maybe you like it when I'm messy, so you can fix me," she counters.

Immediately, I shake my head. "You don't need fixing," I say, taking her hand and walking her to the bench at the edge of the court where we left our phones.

"I'm not sure about that," she says, shrugging in acceptance.

I tilt my head. "Is that how you see yourself? As somebody who needs fixing?"

"Maybe a little bit, but my track record *also* suggests that," she says, though it sounds like she's okay with who she is.

"Does it though?"

She gives me a look that says *c'mon*. "I've been trying for years to get my business off the ground. I do need a little fixing."

"I don't really see it that way. I see it like the way I see hockey. There are ups and downs, but you just have to keep on practicing every day. It's not always a straight line. There are a lot of different ways through a career."

She seems to contemplate that for a bit, then nods. "Maybe you're right."

"I am right. But also, I don't *need* to fix you. I do, however, *like* to do nice things for you. Like braid your hair. So sit down and give me that damn scrunchie," I order.

"So, *so* bossy."

"Yes. Yes, I am," I say and sit her on the bench, gently pushing her shoulders down.

"You have a thing for braiding my hair."

I move around to stand behind her. "Guilty as charged," I say, taking the offered scrunchie and setting it on top of the bench, then finger-combing her hair once again. I lean closer, whisper against her cheek, "Or maybe I just like your hair."

And you.

And touching you.

And being with you.

With a contented shiver, she leans her head back. "Play with it then."

Slowly, I drag my fingers through the strands. "Your coffee with cream hair," I murmur feeling a little vulnerable saying that since it both reinforces that I'll never really see what color it is but also that I pay attention to every damn thing she utters.

But when she tips her head back and smiles warmly at me, I don't have any regrets for opening up. "I like teaching you about color," she says.

My heart jumps. "Why's that?"

"It makes me think about color in different ways but I also like that you want to know."

"I do. I really do."

I want to know all the colors of her. I want to feel what she sees. I want to experience her world. And those aren't thoughts that usually come post-blow job.

I'm not really sure what the hell is happening in my brain or my chest, so I focus on the task at hand. Separating her hair into sections and contemplating where the two of us stand. The age-old question—*what's next?*

"Mabel?"

"Yes?"

I loop the first strand in. "You said you were taking a break from romance. That you wanted to just focus on the business. But is it also because of Dax?"

"Yes, but," she says, pausing as she seems to consider the question, "I was with him for a year. And in the end, I feel like I lost a lot of time, and a little bit of myself. He took up so much energy in the room. Also? I've been trying to open the bakery for years, it seems," she says, with some clear regret in her tone. "When I was with Dax, I got distracted. I didn't give it my all. Seems like being all in with this new business is how I need to approach it."

She's not wrong, even if that answer somehow stings the slightest bit.

"That's true of things you love," I say as I weave in another strand.

"I don't want to look back and ask, did I do enough?" She gazes up at me again, and I see something in her gaze. Reassurance? "You know what I mean?"

My heart winces. "I do. I felt that way about my mom, honestly. I never wanted to wonder if I did enough—if I helped out enough. If I was there for her. So much was hard for her in the last few years, even measuring a cup of flour without spilling it, but especially in the end. I wanted to do everything I could when I was home, and to make sure she had help when I wasn't."

"And you did all that," she says.

"Back then, I wondered a few times if I should have taken a year off, but I also knew that wasn't realistic. I'm so glad she didn't argue when I wanted her to move onto my property, so I could look out for her. I know I've said it was tough, everything she went through, but it was also a privilege, you know? To spend that time with her—to take care of her when she needed it. But also, just to see her. To have her nearby. For me, and for Charlotte, and for Mom."

Mabel's eyes shine. "A lot of people don't do what you did."

I nod, keeping the emotions at bay. "I think so too. It's a relief to feel that way," I say, weaving in a few more strands. "And I'm glad we started the bakery. She would have wanted that."

"She would have loved it, Corbin," Mabel says, still a little choked up.

My throat tightens as I finish her braid while thinking about the past until I wrap the scrunchie around the end of her hair. I'd rather focus on the present. "Beautiful," I murmur, then kiss the top of her head.

She sighs softly, and I want to capture that sound, listen to it again and again.

Instead, I let go of her, move around the bench, and sit next to her. "For what it's worth I do think you give your all to Afternoon Delight, and I seriously appreciate it."

"Thanks. Sometimes I feel like...like whatever I have to give isn't the right amount." She meets my gaze and something deeply vulnerable passes in those lovely brown eyes of hers.

"Like I never have quite the right amount of whatever it is that I need to succeed. Whether it's in business or romance. But with Afternoon Delight, I finally feel like *maybe* I have the right amount of me for the recipe of the store." She laughs self-deprecatingly. "It's ridiculous."

"It's not in the least ridiculous." I set a hand on her thigh, squeezing it. "It would sound really trite to say you're enough. But I mean it. You are entirely the right amount of you."

I want to add—*for me. You're the right amount of you for me.* But that's not what this moment is about.

"Thank you. But that's also why I decided to take a break from romance. I'm not sure I can do all that and be in a relationship at the same time," she says, with a wistful shrug, like she wishes it were different maybe.

A part of me wishes she wanted to date right now. That I could tell her how I'm feeling. That I could tell her brother too. That I could be the one to be good to her.

But I don't want to get in the way of her dreams since I feel the same about the bakery too.

"It's hard to balance it all," I say, thinking back on my own romantic past with its lackluster colors. "I dated this one woman on and off for a few years. It wasn't serious, but I don't know that I ever really gave all of myself to it either. Maybe because I was so focused on hockey or my mom or Charlotte."

"You have a lot of demands in your life. It's hard to know how much you can give to a romance, don't you think?"

"It is," I say, taking the easy way out of that question.

We're silent for a beat or two as a cool breeze drifts by, a reminder that it's December in California. "Was it hard to be in a relationship though because of your mom and your focus on her?"

Way to see right through me. My throat tightens but I swallow down some of my emotions so I can answer.

"Maybe it was. Parkinson's is, well, to state the obvious, it's rough. It wasn't fair." I scrub a hand across my neck, then blow out a breath as if letting something go. I meet Mabel's gaze. "I hope I'm contributing enough to the store."

"You are," she says, then she reaches for my hand and squeezes it. "And I'm pretty sure you gave enough to your mom as well."

I wasn't looking for some sort of validation of the past, but maybe I needed it. "Thanks. I think so too."

She looks around the courts, then back to me with an amused sigh. "We're not really doing the one-time-only thing very well, are we?"

I laugh. "Oh, we are definitely not doing the one-time-only thing well at all."

And maybe, just maybe, it's time to let that rule go. Or, really, to break it.

Before I can get a word out, she taps my thigh. "Hey! What if we stop pretending it's a one-time-only thing?"

Holy shit. Does that mean she wants more? My heart sprints. I hold my breath as she keeps talking.

"Maybe if we keep romance on the back burner, we can do *this*." Ah, it's clear *this* means sex, and I shouldn't complain. "We've been able to navigate all these *one-time-onlys* without ruining the store or our business."

There's a part of me that wants so much more than just these moments. But I'd be a fool to turn her down, especially since that's all we can have. "Mabel Llewelyn—are you asking to be my fuck buddy?"

She cracks up. "Business partners with benefits."

There's a lot riding on Afternoon Delight—so many moving parts and so many people who could be collateral damage if something went wrong. Even though I want more of

Mabel—more than I've been willing to admit before, but I'm realizing now—I'll take what I can get. "Sold."

I'm about to seal it with a kiss when she holds up a hand and presses it to my chest. "But I want you to know something."

Is this when she tells me this arrangement is all we could ever be? That business partners with benefits is the end of the line? I brace myself.

"I'm not asking my brother's permission."

I blink, jerk my head back. "For...what?"

She gestures from her to me. "For this. Whatever this arrangement is we just struck."

I bark out a laugh, but I'm not sure it's one of relief so much as surprise. We honestly haven't talked about her brother much in relation to, well, whatever this has been with us.

Possibly because we've played the one-time-only game for so long. But maybe also because the real issue isn't him. The real issue is *us*.

I school my expression. "I get it. I wouldn't expect you to tell him."

"It's not because it's secret," she says, in that same tone she used at my house the other night, when she thought I was asking if she was on the apps. That tough, take-no-prisoners attitude. And goddammit. That's another thing I like about her—her fortitude. The list is getting too long.

"It's because I'm a grown woman. I don't need his approval over who I—" She swallows whatever verb she was about to say, and I'm on the edge of my seat wishing it was *date*, especially when she sets a hand on my arm as she finishes saying, "Who I'm with."

With.

It's not quite a consolation prize, but I'll take *with* for now.

At least it's something, along with her hand on my arm. The whole mood feels daringly girlfriend-y.

But it's not.

I blow out a breath, and add, "I don't like lying to him by omission, but I also get what you're saying."

Her expression softens. "I'm sorry. I'm sure that's hard, and I don't want to come between your friendship or cause problems."

I shut her up with a kiss. A firm, quick kiss that makes my heart thunder more than it should. When I end it, I run my finger along her bottom lip. "You're not a problem, Mabel. Not ever. Not one bit."

Her smile warms my soul.

We've walked into one hell of a mess, but I can't stay away from my business partner—and I don't want to. I reach for her hand from my arm, take it, and thread my fingers through hers.

I sigh...happily.

Maybe giving myself away, but I'm not sure I care. My gaze drifts to our joined hands, and I picture walking through town like this someday, little touches, a swipe of food off the cheek, an adjustment of a shirt, a kiss on the nose.

My fantasies break apart when my phone buzzes.

For a worried second I think it's Theo. That I'll be explaining myself sooner than I'd expected—*Hey, man I have it bad for your sister, and it's just not going to stop.* I snag it from the bench and swipe it open.

"It's Lake," I say, laughing, relieved, since I don't want to have that uncomfortable conversation right now. I wag the screen at Mabel. "He changed the name of our group chat to *The Lawn Men.* It amuses him."

"And me," she says, as I scan the message that he's sent to the guys.

Would you look at this? Our very own baking hockey player got a fantastic review today. I couldn't be more proud of our teammate, and we must give him hell tomorrow at practice.

"Mabel," I say, whispering so I don't break a good news spell. "We got a great write-up in *California Eats.*"

Her lips part in a huge grin. "Really? Read it."

I square my shoulders and adopt a newsman voice. "Who wants a cookie the size of their head? Not me. Give me a cookie I can actually finish—and that's exactly what After-noon Delight delivers. These aren't oversized, novelty bakes that leave you with more sugar than satisfaction. They're the kind of cookies that feel homemade in the best way—fresh out of the oven, warm on the counter, just-right sized for an after-school snack or a stolen bite before dinner. Afternoon Delight's cookies hit that sweet spot: chewy centers, crisp edges, and flavors that taste both nostalgic and elevated. They remind you of childhood, but with the skill of a baker who knows their craft. In short? These are cookies as cookies should be. Three whisks up for Cozy Valley's llama-loving baker and the baking hockey player."

Mabel's speechless, staring slack-jawed at the screen. "Corbin. This is incredible."

Happiness spreads in my chest, and it's a damn good feeling. "This review is a reminder that we're going to make this work. When you put enough into it, and *you* are putting so much into it, it pays off," I say, since I fucking love encouraging this woman.

"*You* are too," she adds.

"It's mostly you. And I want it to stay that way." I also don't want to be a distraction for her. I don't want to be the wrong amount in a recipe. I need to keep my eyes on the prize—for me, and for her.

My cautionary thoughts are interrupted, though, by Mabel grabbing my biceps. "We can read another love letter."

That's right. We made a plan to read another one when we got a great review.

We leave so fast.

* * *

As we race over to the bakery, we pass A Good Yarn. Mabel flaps an arm toward the shop. "I dropped off some special yarn yesterday for Dottie. To win her over. I'm hoping it helps," she says. "Along with cookies for the owner."

"Look at you," I say, impressed, but not surprised. She's been impressing me from the start.

"And I visited the guys in the town square yesterday. Brought them Danishes and coffee. They placed an order for tomorrow morning. It might even turn into a standing order—and since it's before the bakery opens, I can deliver to them myself," she says.

I tilt my head, giving her a perplexed look. "Mabel, we can hire someone to do that. You don't like mornings."

"Carson's at school in the morning. He's only available in the afternoons. And it's easy," she says. "It keeps me in shape —the walk."

My gaze roams down her body, but I can't get distracted. I stop her with a hand on her arm. "Let me do this."

She sighs. "But it'll cost extra to hire someone else, and we don't have a ton of money coming in yet."

I don't want to throw my wallet around, but...I also don't want her adding more to her to-do list. "Let me do it for *you* then, okay?"

"Corbin."

"Mabel," I say more sternly.

"I really don't mind."

"You do so much already. I'm hardly around. Let me take one thing off your plate."

"Fine," she says, a little grumbly but maybe relieved too.

"You're cute when you pretend to be mad."

"Shut up," she says.

"I can think of plenty of things to do with my mouth." I wiggle a brow, and she rolls her eyes. But as much as I want to linger in this flirty space, there's something more important at play. "And listen, I think it's seriously incredible what you're doing to connect with Cozy Valley. The way you're making such an effort to be a part of the community. I admire it. And you."

"Oh, stop. Now you'll make me blush," she says, as we arrive at Afternoon Delight.

"You'll match our bakery then." And as she opens the door, I lean in close, and whisper in her ear, "It's my favorite color."

The hitch in her breath makes a good day even better.

* * *

The bakery is closed. The blinds are down. The porcelain cups are out. The next letter is unfolded in front of me. It's a ritual that Mabel seems to enjoy, and I want to give her everything she wants.

The full love letter ritual.

I hold the delicate sheet of paper from years ago, then read the words written in a blocky pen.

Dear Harriet,

As we played cards late into the night, the hush of the firehouse falling over us, I appreciated you sharing with me why you had wanted to be a firefighter. It means a lot to me, the way you opened up. I'm grateful to know that you feel the same as I do about the service—called to help.

This job, this world, this life means everything. It's what I've wanted to do since I was a young boy.

For you to have wanted it since you were a little girl too, feels extra special. I appreciate it's not easy for you as the only woman around here. I want you to know that your stories are safe with me. I will treat them with care. I feel lucky to work with you, to cook with you, to play cards with you. (Even though you beat me at rummy!)

If you ever need someone to talk to, to lean on, to just share your day with, I want to be that person for you. I might not always open up right away when we talk, but that's why I turn to these letters. For some reason, it's easier for me to share my thoughts after dark as I sit down to write.

I hope you'll keep these. I hope they mean

something to you. When I leave at the end of the shift, I find myself hoping the time passes quickly so I can see you again.

Until the next shift, I'll be counting the hours.

Yours,
Russ

Mabel covers her mouth with her hand. For several seconds neither one of us says anything. After a weighty pause, she says, "He fell in love with her through letters *right here.*"

I look around at the firehouse-turned-bakery, and marvel at all the stories these walls hold, the secrets this building has kept for decades. "It's kind of surreal."

Briefly, I picture a romance from years ago unfolding between two people who worked together, who became friends, who fought their attraction. For a moment, I wonder about...possibilities as I watch Mabel, her wide eyes, her pouty lips, her agile mind. Her big heart.

I want to reach across the table, to kiss her, to tell her that I feel the same as Russ, that I want the days to pass quickly when I'm playing hockey, when I'm out of town, when I'm heading to the arena.

I want them to pass so that I can spend more stolen moments with her.

But we made a deal, and I won't let romance get in the way. Even though it's getting harder to stick to that deal by the hour.

33

PICKLEBALL SLAYERS AND RSVPS
MABEL

Trevyn steps back and gives me an assessing once-over in the sleeping quarters of Afternoon Delight. AKA my new part-time residence. It's just easier to crash here most nights. I peer at the clock—the big pickleball game starts in forty-five minutes.

I'm ready to…well, to look fantastic as I play mediocrely.

"My work here is done. You look simply fabulous," Trevyn says with an approving nod.

"You're only saying that because you did her eyeshadow," Skylar points out, while giving belly rubs to Simon, her rescue pup, the world's sassiest Dachshund mix who's lounging on my bed, along with my girlfriends.

Trevyn whips his gaze to our redhead friend. "Like I'd leave it to Mabel to look fierce on the court."

"Hey. I can do my own makeup."

"Of course you *can*," Trevyn says.

"He's just better," Skylar says impishly.

"Eyeshadow is a serious commitment," Remy observes from her spot next to Skylar. "Eyeshadow says *I have more free time than you do.*"

"Eyeshadow says *I took makeup training classes at Goddess*," Clementine puts in, as she kicks one black Mary Jane shoe back and forth.

Trevyn rolls his eyes. "Do not start insulting makeup tutorials, classes, or the world's best store. That's where I met Jean-Paul Patrick the other week," he says with a curve of his lips.

"We know," I say in unison with Skylar, Remy, and Clementine, since Trevyn has been gushing about his new beau.

"And they've been having the most fabulous dates," Remy adds, a note of pride in her voice.

"She designed them for me," Trevyn explains.

"We know," I say, this time with Skylar and Clementine backing me up.

"They're just jealous," he says to Remy, like they're co-conspirators, and they are.

But Skylar clears her throat then waves a hand, her big diamond ring glinting in the morning sunshine. "I go on great dates too."

"We know," the rest of us say, then Trevyn walks in a circle around me, reviewing my ensemble one more time. I opted for a red dress with small white polka dots and a cute little pleated skirt.

"Perfy," he declares. "You look fabulous for the fake date."

I bristle a little, even though it *is* a fake date. "Good. Because I need to play the part for Ronnie Legend. For professional reasons, of course."

"Understandable," Remy says. "He's powerful in the baking world."

"Exactly. I want to look good, play well, and be believable even though it's fake."

But everything else between Corbin and me feels...weirdly real. Like the conversation we had the other day on the court.

Our conversations are easy and natural. Our arguments are too.

"I'm not so sure it's a fake date though," Skylar says, reading my thoughts.

"And since you took so long to tell us about The Filthy Gentleman rendition, I think you should 'fess up now with what you've been up to," Remy adds.

My chest flutters. *Maybe* my nipples tighten too. So annoying, being in a frequent state of almost arousal thanks to Corbin. But I'm also grateful for the chance to confess. I don't want to keep things from my friends.

I drop to the floor, sitting cross-legged in front of them. "This is a secret, so don't tell anybody but we've agreed to be... business partners with benefits."

Skylar laughs. "How sophisticated and mature."

"It is," I insist.

"How not risky at all," Clementine deadpans.

"How utterly adorable," Trevyn says, sitting next to me and patting my shoulder.

"Hey! It just makes sense."

"It's totally a thing," Remy confirms, straight-faced. "I've had a lot of couples submit their how-we-met stories for my show, and many started as business partners with benefits."

But I shouldn't even entertain the thought that we might become *more*. It's too risky for the bakery. "This is truly all it is. Just an arrangement. I honestly don't have time for romance," I say, and that's the full truth. Even if I wonder every now and then what it'd be like to date him, I know it'd be a bad idea for business. "I'm really trying to focus on work. It's important."

"So are daily *O*s from your hockey playing business partner who's crazy for you," Skylar says.

A zing rushes through me from her words, but it's best I deny it. "He's not crazy for me."

Remy scoff-laughs. Does she know something more?

"What's that for?" I ask.

"I've seen the way he looks at you."

"When?" I wish I didn't sound so excited.

"At games when you're there," she says matter-of-factly.

"Here at the bakery whenever I come in," Clementine adds.

My chest warms. Corbin did say he'd wanted to ask me out when he first met me.

Since I met you. When I didn't see you all the time, I just lived with it. It was there in the background. Now I see you, and it's like a life force.

"Maybe," I say, waving a hand in front of my face, trying to erase all these wild thoughts, but also the effect this conversation is having on me. I'm getting all...fluttery when I need to put my hot-girl game face on.

"Not maybe. Definitely," Skylar says.

"The man has always given off *into you* vibes," Trevyn confirms.

I set a hand on my cheek. It's so warm. I shouldn't like this so much. "Nothing is going to come of it," I say, breezily, like this intel just doesn't matter. Because it can't matter. "We're running a business together. One that's barely been open two weeks. I'm not going to get romantically involved with my business partner for real."

"Just for pretend," Trevyn says.

"And in bed," Skylar adds.

"Bet that's not fake," Remy puts in with a saucy smile.

I give her one right back. "Oh, there's nothing fake about that."

"I don't fake it with my toys either," Clementine says with a too innocent grin.

"Get it," Trevyn says, then high-fives Clementine, before

he gives me a kiss on the cheek and shoos me off. "Go! You have to pretend you're not madly in love with the man you're secretly banging, but pretending you're not banging, in front of your brother." He furrows his brow. "Now I'm confused."

I think we all are.

I blow them a kiss, including Simon. Clementine has to take off soon, but since Aisha can't start till noon today, Remy, Trevyn and Skylar are going to run the bakery while I play ball. "Love you. You guys are the best for running the store this morning."

"We know," they echo back.

* * *

Corbin lunges for a ball, but it's supercharged, flying past him.

Tiffany and Brittany slap palms, then get back in position, game faces on, bouncing on their toes. With nothing but focus, Tiffany serves and the ball heads my way.

After it bounces once, I return the serve with a grunt. We volley for a heart-pumping minute till Tiffany smashes the ball hard. I stick out my racket in desperation, but the ball has some serious topspin on it, and it whizzes past me in a blur.

They high-five again. The match goes on like this, and they've already won two games.

I'd like to win, but I also would like someone to put me out of my misery. This game is brutal, and my body is crying.

They play fast, sharp, and clean, and they take no prisoners. I thought I could hold my own thanks to the lesson from Corbin. But I also thought he'd be a secret weapon, being a pro athlete and all.

But nope. They're massacring us as Ronnie watches courtside, sipping a matcha and snapping photos.

"How are we doing, Ronnie?" Tiffany calls out after Corbin misses their next missile.

"Brilliant," he replies, then snaps another shot of the action.

If my silver eyeshadow is smeared I'm going to kill Trevyn.

But at the end of the match, I'm dead.

Just dead.

I'm breathing hard, my thighs are screaming, and my ego is bruised. But it has nothing on Corbin's ego. He seems dazed, like he can't believe the carnage on the court.

"Yay! We won," Brittany shouts, and she and her pickleball friend hug fiercely. But they don't gloat. They bounce over to the net and we join them.

"You two did so great," Tiffany says with a bright smile.

"You kept us on our toes," Brittany adds, sounding earnest.

"And you're the cutest," Tiffany says then turns to Corbin. "I just love the way you said *Good job* to Mabel every time."

Brittany smiles my way. "And you were like *We can do this* to him."

Huh. We said that? I barely realized. But that is pretty nice. I steal a glance at Corbin, and the shock in his eyes disappears, replaced with...affection when he looks at me. He steps closer, drapes an arm around me, and drops a quick kiss to my cheek. "Because I love doing things with you," he says, and it's for them.

I know it is.

But it feels like it's for me.

I lean into his side embrace, enjoying this part of the fake date so much. He drops his nose into my hair again. I swear he can't stop doing that. After a quick hit, he pulls back and breathes out, like he's inhaled relaxation and sunshine.

Brittany and Tiffany coo. "Aww, I just love this. Are you

going to his game tonight? You two are so encouraging," Brittany says.

"You're couple goals," Tiffany adds.

I wasn't planning to, but I kind of like the sound of it.

"I love it when she comes to my games," Corbin jumps in, giving a squeeze of my shoulder and leaving the invitation in my...court.

It feels like a real invitation, so I RSVP. "The bakery closes at six, so I'll be there."

"Wearing my jersey," he adds, in that possessive tone that sends sparks down my spine.

Tiffany waves to Ronnie. "Picture time."

We smile for the camera, and all of the smiles, from all four of us, feel strangely real.

It's weird. But weird good.

"I'll tag you and mention your smash cakes. You were such good sports," Brittany says after Ronnie tucks the phone away.

"That would be amazing," I say, since publicity is publicity.

"And we're so glad you aren't sad," Brittany adds, patting my arm.

"Ronnie, we can't stand Dax," Tiffany says. "Can you please tell *Romance Beach* he's such a tool?"

Ronnie laughs. "I have no say over that show, and you know it."

"But tell them we don't like him. We do love Mabel though," she adds.

"I'll pass it on." Ronnie offers me a hand and I shake. "You really are a good sport. And your smash cake is shockingly brilliant. I underestimated you."

That makes losing worthwhile. "Thank you. I appreciate that."

They leave, and once they're gone, I turn to Corbin, whispering in awe, "He just apologized."

"As he should," Corbin says, but I'm not sure I agree.

"I don't think you're wrong, and on the one hand, Ronnie was harsh that day," I say, then blow out a breath, and face the facts head-on. "But I was impulsive. I was also distracted. I think I'm doing a better job now managing...well, managing myself."

"Fair enough," he says.

I pause, noodle on that a few seconds more. "And I think it's because of you."

He shoots me a curious look. "How so?"

"You have a calming effect on me," I admit. But he's giving me more than that. His faith has been a boon to my self-confidence.

His lips quirk up in a smile but then it burns off. "I was hoping to have a horny effect on you."

"You have that too, but you also have a calming effect. It's a compliment. Accept it."

A hint of a smile returns. He tucks a strand of my hair over my ear. "I accept. And I'll see you tonight. In my jersey."

A real invitation indeed.

34

THE HAPPINESS EFFECT

CORBIN

It's funny how at the beginning of the season something felt slightly off on the ice. Like we'd lose a few more face-offs than normal. Like we'd be a millimeter late skating past the neutral zone.

Tonight, my blades are a step ahead. I slice through the ice, a spray shooting off them as I curve around the back of the net, evading a Sea Dogs defender—none other than my friend Tyler Falcon. Tonight, he's my enemy.

And man, it feels extra satisfying to fly past him and around to the front of the net where Lake's signaling he's open.

I slip the puck to our winger and he's ruthless, gunning right for the spot between the goalie's legs. But the goalie drops down to his knees and blocks it, sending it back to the ice with a flick of his wrist.

No big deal. We'll get another chance.

Tyler reaches for the rebound, jamming his stick into the middle of the action.

But nope. I'm feeling possessive tonight. That's mine. That's my chance. I want it now.

I strip it away from him since…fuck pickleball losses. This is the game that matters.

Ivan cuts off Tyler, slipping me the puck with ease. I spin around, scan the ice. The net's in my sight. Their goalie, Max Lambert, is a formidable beast though, shifting back and forth, guarding his property.

Now's not the time to mess up a chance. But Riggs is open so I feed him the puck, staying close.

When he skates to his right, Max darts a couple inches to his left, protecting the side of the net where Riggs is aiming. Riggs doesn't shoot though. A millisecond later he passes the puck to me. Ivan's looming nearby, menacing. I take my chance, sending that baby soaring past the posts. The puck lodges in the twine. The horn blares, and a goal pops up on the scoreboard.

Yes!

I clap Riggs on the back, then Ivan.

"That's the way we do it," Riggs shouts, buoyant.

"Let's get some more," Ivan seconds.

Lake races over. "You're on fire tonight," he says.

My gaze swings to center ice where Mabel's up on her feet, cheering, right next to her brother.

My heart sprints, but then stalls. All my worries slam right back into me. The game, my kid, the bakery, my friendship, and most of all…her.

What am I doing with all of this? How the hell am I managing all these things in my life? The questions I've been asking all season loom above my head like storm clouds. But one more look at her—cheering, exuberant, fearless—and the storm cloud vanishes.

I'm just doing it.

I'm managing it somehow.

I'm tempted to skate over to her, or give her some sort of

searing *you're mine* look, but this peaceful, easy feeling in my chest is enough for me right now.

Someday.

Somehow.

After I hop over the boards and sink down on the bench, I grab my water bottle covered in stickers that Charlotte's sneaked on. I down a thirsty gulp. When I set it on the floor, my brain feels calm.

Finally, I don't feel torn between hockey and my attraction to her. Maybe because I've accepted this attraction isn't disappearing anytime soon.

It's staying, because it's so much more than attraction. It's deep and real, no matter how forbidden my business partner might be.

* * *

We skate through the tunnel with a W. When I reach the corridor, Remy's there with her tablet, congratulating us. "Now don't forget, we have an upcoming teddy-bear toss before the holidays. Well, a fox toss, but you get the idea."

Lake grumbles as he rips off his helmet. "A fox toss? Don't those get old?"

She's undeterred, smiling his way, all bright and sunshine. "They never get old, Lake."

"Beg to differ," he mutters.

"Oh, hush. It'll be great."

"It will," someone else says.

I turn to see some dude in a vest and an undercut. Judging by the way he sets a hand on Remy's arm, he must be her boyfriend.

Lake scowls, and yup—that scowl's directed at Mister Too Hip.

But I push thoughts of them out of my head when my attention snags on someone else. Striding toward us is none other than my best friend and the woman in a lilac jersey that I bought for her.

Sure, I saw her in it the whole game, but now I can savor it since I'm off the ice—the way she looks like she was meant to wear my number, in a shirt that I bought her, with the V-neck and all, with her hair twisted up in a scrunchie that I've used on her. It's like everything has a double meaning for us and it's driving me a little wild.

That's a problem, though, since my whole damn team's surrounding us, along with Theo.

He holds his arms out wide, directing his attention to Lake. "The fans love the fox toss. We're doing a couple in the new year, so get ready. And let's all embrace the chance to give back like that since it's for charity. And for the record, that was an excellent game."

After the team nods their thanks and filters toward the locker room, Theo hangs behind in the corridor, tapping the back of Mabel's jersey. "We need to get you a custom one that says Afternoon Delight too. I swear you two need to market the llama-loving baker and the baking hockey player."

I roll my eyes, but he's got a point. "Fine, fine. We'll get on that stat."

"I'll order one tonight. Will that make you happy?" she says to him.

"Yes. I like it when people do what I say."

I laugh. "I know. Trust me, I know."

He nods my way. "Nice job out there."

"You were definitely the hockey-playing baker tonight," Mabel seconds.

Her praise makes my pulse jump. It's annoying feeling this way about her in front of him, but I'd better get used to it.

Because—dammit—she's having a happiness effect on me. I feel ridiculously good near her, even though I probably shouldn't, considering I'm lying to her brother. Someday I'll say those words to him—*I've got it bad for your sister*. But not today. Not till she's ready. *If* she's ever ready.

I've made my choice—to have this secret fling with her, no matter the cost.

But for now, I turn my attention to Theo. "Why are you so happy tonight? Is it just the win?"

His grin grows bigger. "It's my first as the official GM."

My jaw drops. "Holy shit, congratulations, man. That's fantastic. You got it." I clap him on the back in a side hug. "Let me take you out to celebrate. Both of you."

Mabel's eyebrows shoot up, but she nods a yes too. Another stolen moment, and I'll take it.

* * *

Thirty minutes later, the three of us are in a booth at a bar, toasting to my friend. Once we set our glasses down, he says offhand, "Oh, I heard something about the two of you."

Shit. Tension shoots down my spine. Mabel's eyes widen in worry. Is this going to be another one of Theo's ambushes? I didn't see it coming. Not sure how to handle it either.

The happiness effect vacates, and now I'm only feeling the *I'm a guilty liar* effect.

But he whips out his phone and shows us pictures that Tiffany and Brittany posted and tagged us in. It's Mabel and me wedged between the pickleball twins. The caption reads: *Cutest couple ever, but didn't stop us from destroying them like we destroyed their smash cakes! Yum!*

Okay, that's not bad, but I brace myself for whatever he heard. I stare at the screen, so I don't have to meet his eyes.

Looks like Ronnie reposted it on his social, tagging us and saying: *And she can bake a fierce cake.*

That's good, and yet, I can't quite relax. "What did you hear?" I ask the screen.

"Zakiya at the thrift shop texted. I guess the town thinks you're dating."

I snap my gaze up.

Mabel gulps. "Does this mean we're fake dating for the town now?"

My pulse spikes annoyingly. With hope. Seriously fucking irritating.

Theo scoffs. "Up to you. I said it was none of their business. You two are adults and you know what you're doing, and then I said, if you like each other that really is no one's business."

Wait. Is that his way of approving of something between us? Like giving some sort of blessing? Holy shit. The clouds part. The sun shines. This is too good.

But then I remind myself I'm not seeking his approval. Because I'm not telling him about these feelings. Mabel has already made it clear romance isn't on the table for her. That this thing between us is after dark. It's only an arrangement. And that's not the kind of thing you need to mention to some- one's brother, no matter how close you are with him.

When he gets up a minute later and heads to the restroom, I turn to her. I really shouldn't take this chance here, I really shouldn't. But she's irresistible. "You look so fucking sexy in my jersey."

She nibbles on the corner of her lips. "So good I bet you'll slip out in the middle of the night and come over to the firehouse."

And that would seriously help the happiness effect.

35

ANYTIME FLING

MABEL

I step out of the shower, half expecting Corbin to walk in on me again, and definitely wanting him to.

But I resist checking my phone for a text. We didn't make official plans for a midnight visit after all.

I simply offered a suggestion, then I left before they did. I have no idea if he'll come or not. I dry off, spend some time on my skin-care routine—since I toted all my essential lotions and potions and serums here—then head into the mostly bare sleeping quarters that I've turned into my temporary home away from home. Moonlight streams through a window, casting a soft silvery light across the floor. The walls are sad though, bereft of artwork, photos, or posters that would make it feel more like home.

I grab a sleep shirt from the suitcase next to the bed that I stuffed my clothes into. As I tug it on, I wonder if I should get rid of my place in San Francisco and properly decorate this place.

But then I'd be living in Cozy Valley, on top of this bakery, where I work.

That feels like too much, too soon. I should wait and see how things go with Afternoon Delight.

I sigh as I stare at the bed waiting for me, covered with the white and sage green blanket that Corbin brought over the night we opened.

I'm not tired though. My brain is racing from the hockey game, my brother's excitement over his job, the pickleball post Ronnie reshared. And the effect of it—I've already gotten some orders for Christmas cookies thanks to the socials exposure.

No way can I sleep now.

But I'm also...waiting for him. Wondering if Corbin is going to take me up on my offer to slip over in the middle of the night.

My fingers itch to check my phone. I give in, grabbing it from the bed.

My shoulders sink. There are zero new text messages. I fling it back on the mattress.

I pull on sleep shorts, grab the phone, and head down to the kitchen. Time to do some prep for tomorrow. I pull out ingredients from the pantry and the fridge.

It's okay if he doesn't show up.

We're not a thing.

We're also not a fake thing anymore either.

It's not like we need to fake date for the town, like Theo said. Even if people make assumptions from Tiffany and Brittany's post, there's nothing riding on us pretending to be together. Corbin and I aren't fake dating, and I feel a little empty about that.

Which is an annoying way to feel. I remind myself we're just business partners with benefits and that's fine. It was my damn idea. It's fine, too, if we don't have the benefits tonight.

I'll survive, even though my chest aches with the wish that he'd come over.

Fine, it's not *only* my chest aching.

I toggle over to my playlists and queue up some Christmas music as I prep the dough for the Christmas cookies I'll make tomorrow—red trucks, wreaths, trees, and snowmen and snowwomen.

When that's done, I wash my hands, my gaze straying to the cupboard with the letters. There's a tug in my chest, like an invisible rope is pulling me toward it.

I check my phone again.

Nothing. I *could* text him. But I don't want to be needy. I was already the neediest when I twisted his arm to open this bakery. I have no idea what the rules of the road are for navigating a one-time-only fling that morphs into an anytime fling. I don't want to text with a *Hey, are you coming?*

That feels like relationship territory. I need to put my mind on something else. Maybe I'll peek at the next letter myself.

I pull out the stepladder, climb it, grab the strawberry jar, and then freeze.

I'm the kid with her hand in the cookie jar.

Isn't this how I wound up leaving this town in the first place? I wasn't patient. I didn't put the sugar cookies away, and the llamas ate them, and the story of *Old McMabel and the Four Animals of the Firehouse Apocalypse* began.

Here. Right here in this firehouse. And I hightailed it out of town.

This time around, I need to slow down, be patient, be precise.

I made a deal with Corbin, so I put the jar back, climb down, and turn off the lights.

I go upstairs, and tumble into bed, slipping under the covers as a yawn comes over me at last. The full-body kind. I stretch and before I know it, the day floats before my eyelids and the night pulls me into its embrace.

* * *

A hand slides up my thigh. A voice, gravelly and familiar, drifts past my ears.

I reach for the strong hand, guiding it toward the ache between my legs. I wriggle closer. My hips arch. My legs fall open. I chase the sensation, needing more, but it's still not quite enough.

I part my lips to ask for more pressure, more contact, something, but—

I wake with a start, blinking, pushing up onto my elbows, eyes orienting to the dark.

"Hey." Corbin's standing by the bed wearing jeans and a T-shirt. His shoes are off. He's not sitting on the bed. He's not touching me either. Was I...dreaming?

"I just got here," he adds.

"You weren't—" I cut myself off from asking *Fucking me with your fingers?*

Shaking his head, he sinks down on the edge of the bed, clearly knowing what I was about to ask. "No. I wouldn't touch you like that while you were asleep."

Oh, right. "Of course."

He roams his hand over my thigh, covered by the blanket. "Were you dreaming?"

"I guess," I say, feeling a little embarrassed. I fiddle with the covers. Was I moaning out loud? Punching up my hips? I can only imagine how horny I must have looked if he saw that. "I was baking earlier. Well, prepping for tomorrow. I made the dough for sugar cookies. For Christmas." And now I'm rambling.

"I had a feeling," he says, nodding to the stairs that lead down to the kitchen. He must have seen some of the mixing bowls I left out as he walked through Afternoon Delight. Tilting his head, he studies me with a furrowed brow, eyes soft in the moonlight. His dark hair is a little messy, his stubble thicker than it's been lately. "You okay?"

It's asked with such concern.

I tug the blanket up, protecting myself as I say something vulnerable. No point hiding it. My weird mood is obvious. "I thought you weren't coming."

He slides his hand down my arm. "I thought when you said slip over in the middle of the night that's what you wanted. The middle of the night."

I wince. He took me literally. He waited to show up when I asked him to. And I worked myself up for no reason. "I did say that. I'm being silly," I say, waving a hand like I can dismiss my own desire for him to have arrived earlier.

His lips curve in amusement. "You were wanting me over sooner?"

I say nothing.

"You were wanting me," he says, too pleased.

"Shut up," I mutter.

His smile grows into a full-blown smirk. "I did what you wanted, but you were horny and wanting me, and also annoyed I didn't show up right away to eat your sweet, sweet pussy?"

Now he's just gloating. "I admitted I was being silly."

He brandishes his phone, miming typing. "You could have texted. *Corbin, get your mouth over here.*"

I huff. "I was honest and admitted I was sad when I thought you weren't coming, and now you're making fun of me."

He arches a brow, giving me the most satisfied look ever.

"You were sad that you weren't coming on my tongue." Setting the phone on a nightstand, he tugs down the blanket. "Spread those thighs, Mabel. I'm a man of my word."

"Jerk," I mutter, but I'm pushing the covers the rest of the way.

"Say that when you're fucking my tongue." His grin turns wicked. "Better yet. Why don't you just sit on my face? That'll remind you that you have the power to summon me." He leans closer, that campfire-and-lake scent seducing me. "You have all the power to text me and tell me to come over and fuck you with my tongue. And I will come running."

A hot spark shoots down my chest. "I felt foolish for wondering if you were coming," I admit.

Brushing his lips to mine in a soft kiss, he whispers, "You're not foolish for wanting me. I fucking love that you wanted me so much you spiraled."

I swat his arm.

He grins some more. "Yes, Firecracker. Put all that energy into sitting on my face. Now."

He tugs off my shorts, yanks off my panties, and shifts me over on the bed, making room. After he flops down, he positions me so I'm straddling his shoulders. "I want to taste how horny you are. I want to see how worked up you are. Give me that sweet pussy now."

I give in, sinking down onto his eager mouth. The sounds we both make should be illegal. His groan is craven. Mine is desperate.

I press my hands against the wall, and I don't waste time. I rock against his mouth, his tongue, his scruff. I seek just the right angle, the right friction.

He laps me up, his tongue licking a hungry line up and down, his lips clamping on my swollen clit, his mouth devouring me.

It's filthy, the noises he makes. It's wanton, the way his hands grip my hips.

Rocking back and forth, I ride his gorgeous face with an after-dark abandon, like I wanted to do in my dream. Like I've wanted to do since I mentioned him coming over in the middle of the night.

My thighs shake. My belly tightens. My hands scrabble at the wall.

He stops, pushes me a couple inches off his face. I whimper. "Jerk."

"Use your words, Mabel. Tell me how much you wanted me to come over. Fuck my face and tell me how desperately you needed my tongue." His eyes are fierce, his need evident in the set of his jaw, his face wet with me. He doesn't lower me yet.

"I wanted you so badly," I confess.

"How badly?" He keeps me hovering above him.

"So badly I'm aching."

His eyes swing to my center, then back to my face. "And so fucking wet."

"Do something about it."

"Oh, I will. I definitely will." He drags me back down to his mouth.

Apparently, I've earned the right to fuck his face again. But I don't want to lose it, so I narrate as I rock. "I wanted you to wake me up with your tongue."

A groan, chased by a hungry lick is my reward.

"I wanted you to devour me."

A suck on my clit. Then a growl.

"I wanted to come on your face," I pant out.

He smacks my ass with his hand.

I yelp, but it transforms into a moan as pleasure coils in me.

He smacks me again, this time on the other cheek. Sparks burst behind my eyes.

I'm this close.

One more smack, and I shudder, falling apart on his face, coming ridiculously hard. My cries bounce off the walls. The pleasure spreads to my every cell.

It takes me ages to come down from this orgasm. I'm so blissed out I barely register the sounds he's making. The unzip of his jeans. The rustle of fabric.

I ease off him, and he's jerking his cock. He's that turned on he's shuttling his fist up and down.

"Who's the horny one now?" I taunt.

"I'm so fucking turned on by you. I always am," he bites out, his fist flying.

He's not playing around. But neither am I.

"Finish in me. On me. Anywhere," I offer, desperate. "I have an IUD. And I'm negative."

"Negative too."

I take the wheel, climbing on him, sinking down on his cock. I'm so wet he fills me in less than a second, and I revel in the feel of him.

His arms snake around my back, pulling me close. "Mabel," he grunts.

"Yes?"

But he says nothing, just thrusts up again and again, holding me tight. After a few minutes, his breathing turns more ragged. "Fuck, baby. You're so wet. I fucking love how turned on you get."

"You do this to me."

"Want to keep doing it to you," he rasps out, like a raw admission.

Pleasure slides down my spine and so do his hands. As

they reach my ass, he squeezes my cheeks, bringing me down hard on his thick cock.

"I can't stand how good you feel," he says, like he's angry with himself for wanting me. "I want to feel you all the fucking time."

"Have me," I murmur as I ride him, finding just the right angle, hitting just the right pace till I break apart into thousands of pieces of pleasure.

And he falls with me, sounding like a man who's losing control, and he couldn't care less.

36

JUST LIKE A DOG
CORBIN

Fifteen minutes later, I'm yawning, and my limbs feel too heavy to move. "I should go. Sarah's dropping Charlotte off in the morning. I have her this weekend," I say, as I try to muster the energy to drag my ass out of bed.

"What time?" Mabel asks, sounding sleepy too. Well, I *did* wake her in the middle of the night.

"Nine. I could wake you up at eight-thirty."

And yes, dreams do come true.

The firehouse only had twin-size beds, but a few minutes later, we've pushed two together, and we're flopping back down. It's not perfect. I have only one set of sheets here—but we put a fitted sheet on one twin, and a flat on the other. There's a thin space, naturally, between the two mattresses. But it'll do for now especially since the blanket I brought the other week is pretty big.

I kiss the back of her neck. "Feel free to wake me up with your mouth at eight-thirty," I say, and even though I'm sinking toward that cleft in the bed, I drift off to sleep.

* * *

"I wanted to let you know the plan for the next week or so," Charlotte says, as we walk along Main Street, passing Reprise, where a window display of sweaters with animal illustrations on them draws my daughter's attention for a couple seconds. And mine too, since Mabel would like those. But I turn my focus back to my daughter as she resumes her pace and her calendar review. "Monday, you have a bakery event. Then we're picking up Mischief and Mayhem on Tuesday. You have a game on Wednesday night. So I can take care of them myself."

I arch a brow. "Are you sure?"

She gives me a look like she's offended I'd even ask. "Dad, I'm twelve. I can stay home alone. And if there are any problems, I can call..." She trails off and I expect her to say she'd call her mom, but Charlotte smiles impishly. "Mabel. She connected us with Mrs. Henderson. She'd be the one to help."

I can't argue with the logic there, but still, I need to poke fun at her too. "Are you saying you'd rather take care of the foster dogs than come to my hockey game?"

She pats my arm. "You're cute, Dad. And hockey's fine, but taking care of foster dogs will help me become a veterinarian. Did you know there's a shortage of vets?"

"I didn't know that," I say. "Why?"

"It costs a lot to get an education to become one, and it's a high-stress job. But that's why I'm learning everything I can about it now," she says. "So I'm ready when it's time."

I ruffle her hair. "Proud of you, kid."

I go quiet though. My daughter doesn't have to worry about the cost of education but others do. I mull on that disparity, and the high cost that could be a deterrent for others, until Charlotte breaks my thoughts as she says, "And then we leave for New York. You have a hockey game there, and that's where we'll spend Christmas."

Charlotte and I always have fun during the holidays, especially in New York since my cousins and my stepdad, Ray, who Charlotte adores, live there. So do Charlotte's cousins on Sarah's side.

But what will Mabel be doing? Will she miss me when I'm gone?

I know I'll miss her.

But since she likes gifts, I stop Charlotte with a hand on her arm. "Hey, can you help me pick a sweater?"

"Of course."

My kid spins around and marches right back to the store as if an invisible thread is leading her there. She stops at the window display that includes a llama sweater.

"I presume this is for Mabel," she says.

The straightforwardness of the statement throws me off for a second, but only a second. "Yes. How did you—"

But I don't finish the question. It's clear how she knows. I'm obvious.

"I saw the llama sweater too, and I filed it away as a gift for her," she says, tapping her temple. "But you should give it to her."

"You were going to give it to her?"

"Of course," she says. "She's a big part of our life."

I freeze. Is Charlotte getting attached to Mabel? If I pursue something with Mabel eventually and it doesn't work out, will Charlotte get hurt? I hadn't thought about that issue, but I really should. It's a whole new *what if.*

Except, fuck that.

It's ten steps down the road, and I've raised my daughter to handle life when shit goes wrong. Charlotte's a strong person. I'm not going to let my kid be an issue.

Besides, if I want Mabel to want more than an arrangement, I need to show her why I'm worth breaking the rules for.

Operation Win My Business Partner's Heart begins today.

"Let's give it to her together," I say.

"Works for me."

We go inside and find more sweaters with animal illustrations on them. "Which color do you think will look best on her?"

Charlotte picks one, then holds it up. "It's a very pretty sky blue that'll look great with her big brown eyes."

I smother a smile. But whether it's from the description of Mabel's eyes, or the fact my daughter's wanting to give her a gift, I don't know.

Either way, I like it.

When we head into Afternoon Delight, there's a beautiful sight. A long line at the counter. Aisha's here, helping out and taking orders, and damn, this is good to see. A busy bakery, with customers scooping up Christmas sweets, dog cookies, and other treats. I hate to say it, but *Thanks, Ronnie.*

"Want some help?" I ask as I head behind the counter, the gift in hand.

"Yes, grab the boxes of iced snowwomen in the kitchen, the trees, and the Christmas unicorn cookies," Mabel says, all business as she points like a gate agent directing traffic at the airport.

"Christmas unicorns? I want one," Charlotte says as she grabs her apron from a hook.

"She likes unicorns," I add as I head into the kitchen and set down the sweater for later.

"Dad, everyone likes unicorns," Charlotte calls out.

"I like unicorns," Aisha chimes in as I return with the boxes of cookies and my apron.

Mabel gives a nod as she rings up some smash cakes, then points to the counter and the customer who ordered the cookies. I hand over the goods.

"Everyone likes unicorns," Mabel says to the line of customers. "Am I right?"

And the answer is a resounding yes.

* * *

The day is long, longer than a day with travel and practice and a game it seems. After we close, Aisha helps clean, then she heads out, leaving the three of us to finish.

When we're done, Charlotte clears her throat, her gaze swinging pointedly to the kitchen. "Dad, is there something you wanted to give Mabel? From us?"

I stare right back at her. "Charlotte, is there something you wanted to give Mabel?"

She grins a little evilly. "Why, yes."

She scurries to the kitchen and grabs the gift box, then marches it right back to Mabel. "My dad and I saw this and thought it would be perfect for you. It's from both of us."

"You two are so sweet," Mabel says.

We settle down at a table in the front of the store, the holiday lights still twinkling outside the shop. Mabel unwraps the paper with anticipation in those big brown eyes, then takes out the sweater, her expression softening. "This is perfect. I love it so much," she says, then gives my daughter a hug.

Charlotte hugs her back, and that's a real good sight. So good my chest tightens with emotions. Dangerous things. But things I'm not as scared of as I was a couple months ago.

When Mabel lets go, Charlotte gets straight to business. "The fosters are coming over on Tuesday. Mischief and Mayhem. Do you want to help with them?"

"Obviously," Mabel says.

Like it's that easy, and maybe some things just are.

What's not easy?

Making it to the first blind-date cookie event on Monday night. I promised Mabel I'd be there early to help set up, but the team meeting started late. It's going overtime too.

"You've done a good job turning things around after last season's rough ending. We've got a few more games to play, but I just want to remind all of you that we don't have much time off during the holidays," Coach Ahmed says—stuff we should all know by now.

But I've learned over the years that some players go a little too hard over the short Christmas break and come back sluggish.

Translation: hungover as hell.

"So hydrate, men. Okay?"

Ivan chuckles. "Shouldn't you save this speech for New Year's?"

"And I will," Coach deadpans. "Because that's when you'll really need it. Keep up the workouts, keep up the conditioning. Let's finish the year strong and start the new one even stronger."

"Yes, sir," Miller says, like a good soldier.

"Suck-up," Lake mutters.

"Feel free to do extra push-ups, Axelrod," Coach fires back.

"I love push-ups," Lake says matter-of-factly.

"Of course you do." Coach shakes his head.

He turns it over to the assistant coach to review plays and strategy for our next few games, and I check my watch. Shit. No way I'm helping set up now.

"Got somewhere to be, Knight?" Coach asks.

Chastened, I look up. "Right here, sir."

"I thought so."

Twenty minutes later, the meeting finally ends. Soon I'm flying along the Embarcadero toward the Golden Gate Bridge, and I call Mabel on the car's speaker.

She answers after a few rings. "Hey, what's up?" She's friendly, but sounds busy.

"The meeting ran late. I'll be fifteen minutes behind. Maybe twenty."

She pauses. Plates clatter in the background. Shit. Did I piss her off?

"And here I thought you were never late," she teases. "Or was that just what you told Ronnie to get me into the trailer?"

The callback makes me laugh, tension loosening in my chest. "I'll make it up to you."

"It's all good. No worries," she says. "I've got Aisha here—we can handle it."

But that doesn't sit right with me. I want to handle things too.

After we hang up, I call Annabelle. "Got any mistletoe?"

"Of course I do, hun. I'm a plant dealer."

Her shop's along the way, so once I exit into Cozy Valley, I swing by, grab the sprigs, and race over to our bakery.

I walk into Afternoon Delight, waggling three bunches like contraband. "Look what I brought."

From behind the counter where she's straightening a display card, Mabel gasps. "Great idea. So glad you thought of it."

Yup. I've still got it. Even though, as I look around at the bakery—the tables with Christmas pine cones, the plates with snowflakes, the napkins decorated with reindeer—I wish I'd been here to set up.

That's why I insisted on being a hands-on investor in the first place.

But at least there's mistletoe.

* * *

Are we matchmakers? Not exactly, but the event goes well, and I get the sense that there might be a second date or two.

The potential lovebirds leave, and then after Aisha helps clean up, she heads out too, leaving Mabel and me to finish.

When everything is done, Mabel yawns, then turns toward the stairs. My chest aches with the desire to follow her.

But I can't. Charlotte's with me tonight, so I steal a kiss under the mistletoe instead.

And it does feel stolen.

Maybe someday it won't.

* * *

On Wednesday night, we destroy Montreal in our barn, and it feels damn good to crush them.

"It's a very fucking Merry Christmas indeed," Ivan says as we skate off the ice with the W, and he taps his stick on the gate.

Lake follows suit.

It's their ritual. They started doing it a few weeks ago when we went on a tear, and who am I to disagree. I tap too.

After I chat with the media, talking about tonight and then the game coming up in New York against the Ice Kings, I take off to the locker room.

Once I'm showered and dressed in my gray suit, I'm out of there, sliding into my car, texting Charlotte that I'm on my way, then cruising home as I listen to my post-game pump-me-up playlist, a mix of upbeat anthems and rock songs. When I reach Cozy Valley, its familiar sign with an illustrated squirrel curled up asleep in the V, I'm antsy to get home.

To see Charlotte. And those little dogs we picked up yesterday for a brief two-day stint here. I pull into the driveway, and my gaze swings to a familiar car at the curb.

Mabel's ride.

My heartbeat speeds up. So annoying, but annoying is becoming my new normal. I head inside, and the second the door closes, the scrabble of paws ricochets through the house. The sound of yaps echo too. Then two little critters race over.

They bark their little brains out, but they're excited to see me. I kneel to give them scratches.

"Hi, Mischief," I say to one of them.

Mabel cracks up as she sets her book on the living room table and walks over to me. "That's Mayhem."

"Well excuse me," I tease.

"Mayhem has the tan head—it's lighter in color. Mischief's more black," she explains simply.

And...that's helpful. But honestly, the issue wasn't that I couldn't differentiate the colors. It's that they seriously look alike. "Good to know," I say, then peer around my house. It's quiet. No pitter-patter of tween feet. "Is Charlotte asleep?"

As Mabel returns to the couch, she nods. "She crashed around ten."

It's nearly midnight now. "You stayed? You don't have to babysit." Shit, the last thing I want is for her to feel that way. "She convinced me she was old enough to stay home alone with the dogs."

Mabel gives a dismissive wave as she sinks down onto the couch, and two little Chiweenies jump up next to her. "It wasn't babysitting," she says, then strokes one dog's head, then the other's chin before she looks up at me. "Oh, sorry. Are they allowed on your couch?"

But she doesn't sound contrite, or like she cares what the answer is as she pets the pups. And yup. She didn't babysit at all. But the effect is the same. She stayed here at my house with my kid, and I appreciate that. "You were dog-sitting."

She gives me a smile that says I've nailed the answer.

"And yes, they're allowed on my couch. Not like I had a say."

"Not to throw your kid under the bus, but she totally let them on the couch," Mabel says.

"Why am I not surprised? Last year she made a Christmas ornament with Scrabble tiles and it spelled out D-O-G-G-Y."

Mabel's expression is thoughtful. "I know you travel a lot and you don't think it makes sense, but would you ever share a dog with, say, Sarah?"

"That's a fair question, but kids usually think they'll take care of the dog and they usually don't," I admit. "And if I adopted one myself, I wouldn't want to board a dog half the time during the season."

"True," she says with a sigh.

After I toe off my shoes, I set my phone on the table and join Mabel, petting the little dogs too. They're soft and playful and Mischief rolls onto her back, letting me pet her belly.

"What about you?" I ask.

"I wish I could have a bakery dog."

I laugh at the concept, but then stop laughing in a second. "Actually..."

"We should totally get a bakery dog?" There's so much hope in her voice.

"What if we host dog adoption events *outside* the bakery? Set up tables right on the sidewalk, work with the local rescue and so on?"

Her eyes sparkle. "I love that. And we could use the store's social media to highlight adoptable dogs."

"Yes. We could put their pictures on the top of the display case too. With QR codes, in case someone is interested in learning more."

She hums appreciatively, running her nails down my shirt. "I don't think you've ever been hotter than you are right now."

"Saving animals gets you going?"

"Absolutely," Mabel says, then scratches Mischief's belly some more. "Right, girl?"

Mischief waggles her rear end, and I pet her some more too. The little critter snuggles against me, rubbing her snout on my leg.

"She likes you," Mabel observes.

I raise my face, wiggling a brow, inviting Mabel to say that she does too.

"Oh my god, you're so shameless. Seeking praise just like a dog," she says.

And damn, she sees right through me. And yup, I'm just like a dog.

I cup her cheeks and kiss her on the couch, with two little foster dogs snuggling up against us, and my daughter sleeping soundly upstairs.

And everything feels right.

* * *

The next day as I'm packing, the little dog with the darker head nudges aside the socks I've dropped in my suitcase.

"You want to come to New York, little cutie?" I ask Mischief.

She's a determined beast, and she keeps nosing at the socks. Her friend trots into my bedroom, and Mayhem gets in on the action too, checking out my suitcase, tunneling through socks until...they find something white and shiny in my suitcase. It's got a silvery bow on it.

I pick it up, turn it over like it's a treasure.

Some dangerous hope builds in me. It's stupid and yet it has a hold of me. There's a small card on it. It's white with the words *Merry Christmas* in black letters.

Holy shit.

She custom-made this card. She must have. No one makes black-and-white Christmas cards. But Mabel did. For me. And she must have snuck this into my suitcase when Charlotte invited her over last night.

I should wait till Christmas morning to open the gift, and I will. I swear I will. But I sit on the edge of the bed, two small pups staring up at me, as I peek at the card for now.

Dear Corbin,

This is just a small token of my appreciation for all that you've done for me. From the day you came to my rescue at the romance fair, to the day after that when you said yes to a wild plan to start a bakery, to every day since then.

It's been quite a ride, hasn't it? From the knitting club bets against us (ha, take that!), to paintbrushes (not to mention basting brushes), to a strawberry cookie jar, then love letters from another century, and, unexpectedly, a pickleball challenge.

I wouldn't want to have done this with anyone

else. And I can't wait till we open another letter.
That's become the favorite part of my day.
Actually, it's the second.
My real favorite part? The way you believe
in me.

Thank you, and Merry Christmas!

Mabel

She's not quite saying I'm the favorite part of her day. But it's damn close.

37

DELIBERATE TEXTS
MABEL

My real Christmas is with my friends—Friendsmas, as Isla dubbed it a few years ago when she started it. This year we're at her place two nights before Christmas. Rowan, the man I'm sure will propose to her any second, is out with his daughter, so tonight it's just us—Isla, Skylar, Remy, Clementine, Trevyn, and me. We exchange silly gifts, blast Mariah Carey too loud, and drink spiked eggnog.

As the night winds down, Skylar taps my thigh. "What are you doing on Christmas Day?"

A little knot of tension rolls through me. "Seeing my parents and Theo, so I'm sure Mom will try to convince me to get a real job," I say, then try to shake that off. "But she did ask me to make something for dessert. So maybe that's a sign she sort of approves of my bakery?"

"I approve of your bakery," Clementine says, stretching her legs out and plopping her feet on my thighs.

"I double approve," Remy chimes in.

"Triple approve," Skylar adds.

And truthfully, it's not just them. Customers seem to approve too.

Still, something nags at me. A worry that I can't seem to chase. "Do you think it's only successful because I opened it with a hockey player?" I ask, my gut twisting.

Isla shakes her head, steady and certain. "Don't tell yourself you wouldn't be good enough without him. You have the talent, friend. You always have."

"Yep. You both bring plenty to the table," Trevyn says.

And you know what? I think they're right.

That's a comforting thought—one I'm maybe finally letting myself believe.

* * *

I wake on Christmas morning to a text message.

> Corbin: Alexa, text Mabel and tell her the gift is incredible. Let her know I look superhot in this tie. Cancel that, Alexa. Alexa, take a photo of me to show her how superhot I look.

> Mabel: SEND IT NOW!

> Corbin: Alexa, send Mabel the photo of me looking superhot.

I'm expecting a picture of him in one of the dress shirts he wears for travel, modeling the tie I got him, looking smoldering and stylish. A few seconds later, the image lands, and I click it so fast.

Oh. *Oh.*

He's not wearing a button-down shirt. He's not wearing a

shirt at all. Just the black-and-white tie I bought him for Christmas, with illustrations of foxes on it.

I'm staring at the silk resting against his bare chest, his strong pecs, the ladder of his abs, mesmerized by the hardness of his muscles and the softness of the fabric. It takes me a beat to realize the phone is ringing. I blink off the fog and answer it. "Hey."

"This tie is perfect," he says, and I can hear the appreciation in his voice over the color choice. It's a tie just for his eyes.

"It looks perfect on you."

"That's because you're hot for me," he says.

"You can't ever resist saying that."

"True."

"And I am," I say, stating the obvious.

"Good. Let's keep it that way," he says.

I snuggle deeper into bed as I take a chance with my answer. "I will."

It feels like the start of something.

* * *

My mom takes a bite of millionaire's shortbread and actually moans. "Mabel, this is delicious. But then again, it always has been."

"Thanks, Mom," I say, smoothing out my napkin, listening to the faint clatter of plates being cleared in the kitchen later that day. The tree lights glow from the living room, little bursts of red and gold spilling into the dining room.

I made it through the meal with minimal grilling. Okay, fine—some grilling. *How's it going?* Well. *Do you have health insurance?* Yes, I pay for it myself and have for years. *What about a retirement fund?* I'll set one up eventually. *Can this really work?* I hope so.

Theo takes a big bite of shortbread—caramel gooey, chocolate silky—and shakes his head in appreciation. "Mom, are you tasting this? Of course her bakery can work."

Dad exhales, long and doubtful. "Just because you can bake doesn't mean you can run a business."

The words land like a slap.

Theo jumps in, defending me the way he always has. "Dad, it actually does."

But this time I don't back down. Since...screw it. "Corbin and I have great recipes. And honestly, Mom, Dad—I'm a great baker. You're just going to have to accept that this is my career."

Holy shit. Where did that come from? Theo grins, more pleased than I've ever seen him, pride shining in his eyes.

And, apparently, I have more to say. "But I'm more than just a great baker. I've been running a pop-up bakery for years, and it's done well enough to support me. I've learned a ton, including how to market, and I put all that expertise into Afternoon Delight. And you know what's been an utter delight? Watching the numbers grow. We're already running within our budget, and we'll be turning a profit soon," I say. Sure, the fact that we don't pay rent helps, but Corbin invested a lot in the business, and I can see profitability not far off in the new year.

The table goes quiet.

Mom takes another slow bite, sets the rest of the bar down, and nods. "You are an excellent baker, dear. And I'm glad to hear the business is growing." High praise from her. She turns to my father, her voice firmer now. "She is. These bars are incredible and Cozy Valley is figuring it out."

Dad doesn't argue. Not this time.

Mom clicks her tongue and furrows her brow like she's thinking. She turns to me. "Sweetheart, would you like to bake some cakes for my faculty luncheon next month? There will be about forty of us, so we'll need a few."

Would I? My throat tightens. "I would love to."

* * *

I don't go home to the city that evening. Since the day after Christmas is a busy shopping day, the bakery will be open tomorrow, so I head to Afternoon Delight, which is weirdly becoming my home. But before I bake, I head upstairs to change out of my *look nice for my parents* clothes.

When I turn the corner at the top of the stairs, I stop in my tracks. "Are you kidding me?" I whisper to no one but myself.

I can't quite believe what I'm looking at.

A brand-new king-size bed with a huge silver bow wrapped around it. Like the kind you'd find around a shiny car in the driveway.

The bed is covered in a lilac duvet, with delicate iris illustrations along the edges. Several fluffy white pillows adorn the top of the bed and a few silvery ones too.

I cover my mouth with my hand, shocked, unable to move. My throat tightens. It's not just the bed. It's what it means.

That *this*—the bakery is working.

That he sees us pulling this off.

That he believes in me.

I let out a big breath, walk toward it, and run a finger over the shiny bow till I reach a white envelope.

I slide it open and a piece of paper falls out, folded in quarters. I unfold it, and I feel like sunshine as I read.

Dear Mabel,

*The biggest dreamer should have a proper place
to keep dreaming big.*
Also, I miss you.

Corbin

My heart catches in my throat, and I'm not even sure what to say. Or do. How to respond. It's such a huge gift, so thoughtful, and so perfect for me. And the letter is somehow even better.

I set the paper down on the bed, then run my hands across the cover.

Oh god. It's so soft. The bed is calling out to me. I turn around and fall back on it, sighing contentedly.

I'm going to sleep so good tonight. I open my phone and instead of an accidental text, I dictate a deliberate one.

> Mabel: Alexa, send Corbin a note telling him I miss him too.

* * *

"Enjoy the smash cake and the gingerbread," I call out to a middle-aged woman who came in for both treats for her kids.

"I will," she says, and as she leaves the bell above the door tinkles.

Business has been good on the day after Christmas, but now that it's evening, it's slowing down. As I straighten up and do some prep for tomorrow, the bell rings again, and in walks...a woman with gray hair and a knitting bag, and a stern expression.

I square my shoulders but hold my own as I head to the register. "Hi, Dottie. Let me know if I can help you with anything."

She marches right over to me. "I have a bone to pick with you."

Tension slams into me. "Over what?"

She points a wrinkled finger my way. "I'm going to lose the betting pool."

My brow knits. "Excuse me?"

"Don't play innocent with me."

I shake my head. "I really don't—" Wait. I think I know what this is.

"We had a bet about how long you were going to stay open. And here you are, proving me wrong, clearly. Little Miss Cozy Valley. Little Miss Sassy Baker. Little Miss Redemption." She shakes her head, tutting. "Making me look like a fool for betting against you."

Oh, okay. I see where this is going now, and I don't mind the direction at all. With a smile—somewhat smug—I say, "Sorry, not sorry."

"Neither am I. Arnie's been slipping me some of those seven-layer bars. And the pistachio chocolate chip cookies," she says, and that makes sense—his orders have expanded beyond the original Danishes.

"Has he now?"

"And now I'm going to have to eat my shoe."

The image pleases me to no end. "Or I could just give you a seven-layer bar on the house," I say, feeling a little like victory is mine.

She pffts. "You'll do no such thing. I'll buy it. In fact, I'll take a half dozen for the knitting club."

"Coming right up," I say, boxing up the bars and handing them to her.

She pays and harrumphs her way out.

* * *

* * *

Corbin returned home last night, and since Charlotte went to Sarah's house this morning, this is the first time I've seen him. We're at Happy Cow in Hayes Valley, and I'm eating a quinoa bowl as Corbin slices a piece of salmon, then says, "I'm having a good season."

It's a bit out of nowhere, but I go with it. "You are."

"I didn't think I could manage it all. Charlotte, hockey, the business. Everything."

I'm not sure where he's going and if it's someplace good or bad, so I just nod for him to keep talking.

"But I think when I stopped fighting my feelings, I was able to...relax on the ice. Have fun. Handle it all," he says.

"Yeah?" I ask, feeling a little glowy.

"And you—you're kicking ass at the bakery."

I think of Dottie. Of the chess guys. Of Abe and even of Joni, who's asked us about supplying cookies. And of my mother, and her request to cater the faculty event. "I am," I say, and it feels good to admit that. But he's played a huge part too, so I add, "Actually, we both are."

"It's mostly you making it happen, Mabel," he says.

I couldn't have done this without him though. His investment, yes. But also his faith in me. And his seriously delicious recipes. "You might be more behind the scenes, but we're doing this together."

"We're good partners." He sounds so certain, so unafraid.

And once again, he has a calming effect on me. He takes another bite of his salmon, then a drink of water, before he asks, "How's the bed?"

Something about the shift in topic amuses me. "Perfect," I say.

"How were your holidays?"

"Good."

"Will you go on a date with me? A real date."

I freeze, fork midair. "You just asked me on a date?"

"I did."

"We're not just business partners with benefits?"

"We're not." It's said decisively, brooking no argument. It's hardly a question. It's more like a decision. "This was a date today. You should date me again."

Clearly, he's not worried about balance. He just said as much. But still, I've got to know this one thing. "You're not worried about us running a business together?"

He sets down his fork. "First of all, see above. The answer is no. So what do you say?"

He's unrelenting in his pursuit of me.

I take a moment to catalogue my reaction—the rapid beat of my heart, the warmth in my skin, the smile on my face. "I say yes."

He exhales, like he's been waiting a while for this. "Good. We should finish this date with another letter. To mark the occasion."

"Which occasion?" I tease. "A month in business? Or you asking me on our first date?"

He leans closer, his eyes holding mine, a small smile shifting his lips. "Both, Mabel. Both."

38

I'LL TAKE A DARTBOARD, PLEASE

CORBIN

"There are only two left," she says, taking out the next letter as we settle at a table in the bakery, the streetlamps flickering beyond the garage-door windows. "I'm dying to know how they worked it all out."

So am I. Not gonna lie. I keep hoping there's a final piece of advice from a couple that worked together decades ago about how to make *this* work. I might know what I want, but I could also use a road map.

"We've been good though. We didn't gobble them all up at once," I say.

Mabel fidgets with the corner of the letter. "I wanted to. I was tempted to read one without you," she admits, a little guilt in her averted eyes.

I lift a brow. I can picture her about to dip her hand in the cookie jar, but resisting. "Over Christmas?"

"No. Before—the night I wanted you to come over."

For some reason, this admission excites me. Maybe it's because she wanted me so badly that night—and almost caved by reading a letter solo. "And you waited," I say.

"I'm used to edging," she says, her eyes flicking with mischief.

"You're very patient," I say, praising her.

"I never was before," she says as she glances toward the display case. Tomorrow it'll be filled with brownies, bars, and cookies. Then this shop will be teeming with customers. "Weird for a baker."

"You're full of contradictions," I say. *And I love all of them.*

"I am. But maybe that's why I've always liked baking. There's a recipe to follow, and I needed that when my life was a mess."

"You're not a mess, Mabel. Not even close," I reassure.

She draws a deep breath and nods, perhaps finally believing that. She opens the letter. "Oh, it's a short one." She unfolds it and passes it to me. "It's from Russ."

I smooth out the paper, clear my throat and read.

Dear Harriet,

I shouldn't do this. I truly shouldn't. But I can't hold back anymore.

I can't stand the nights without you. I think about you all the time. I want to be with you all the time. I know it's against the rules, but sometimes you have to break them. Will you go out with me?

I'm yours,
Russ

I set it down as Mabel gives me an *I caught you* look. "Admit it. You read it in advance. Before you asked me out."

A laugh bursts from me. "Nope."

"Really?"

I hold up my hands in surrender. "I swear." I glance around at the firehouse-turned-bakery. "Maybe it's this place. Maybe it's got some kind of magic. It worked on them."

She holds my gaze, her eyes warm, inviting. "Maybe that's why my grandmother gave this firehouse to me. Their story sort of mirrors ours."

"It does in a way," I say.

"It's almost like she knew. Hey, did you tell her you had a crush on me?" she jokes.

I laugh harder. *This woman.* She just makes me so happy. "I didn't even meet your grandmother."

Mabel shrugs. "Still feels like she wanted this to happen."

Does she have any idea what these words are doing to my heart? It's expanding by the minute. I take her hand and squeeze it, then tell her the thing I have to do next. "Before we go out, I want to tell your brother."

She tenses, but nods. "What are you going to say?"

That's the easiest part of all. "That I'm crazy about you."

Her smile falters—not in a bad way, more like surprise. "You are?"

"Mabel. Have I not made myself clear? I was taken with you the first time I met you. And I'm not missing my chance this time around. Even if we have to break the rules."

The don't date your business partner rule. The don't fall for your best friend's sister rule. The no-romance rules we both set. I'm smashing through all of them.

She brushes her thumb over my knuckles, a soft smile curling at the edges of her lips. "Then break them, business partner."

"I will."

* * *

Theo's been traveling, and I've been on the road for games, so I haven't had a shot at a face-to-face with him until several days into the new year.

It comes after Charlotte and I return Lola one morning—we had the sweet senior Beagle mix for one night when her regular foster needed to go out of town for twenty-four hours. I head to the city and drop off Charlotte at school, then cruise to the arena next, pulling into the players' lot at the same time as Miller.

He hops out of his car, giving me a chin nod. "Is today the day?"

I push my palm down in a *keep it quiet* gesture. "Yes, but it hasn't happened yet. So let's lower the volume."

No point hiding my feelings from him. Besides, he figured it out a long time ago.

"Oh gee, I'm so sorry. I didn't know Theo had spies in the parking lot."

I roll my eyes. "Everyone has spies everywhere."

"Paranoid much?"

"Nope," I say, then hedge. "But I do hope I leave his office in one piece."

"Dude. Me too," Miller says, shuddering as he yanks the door open. "The guy scares me. He's intense."

"Who's intense?"

Speak of the devil. I gulp. It's Theo, walking toward us.

I scramble, thinking fast. We're playing Seattle soon. That's it. "The Seattle goalie. He's like the abominable snowman."

"He's like a dragon guarding his gold," Miller adds, backing me up.

"He's the Loch Ness monster."

Theo gives us a look like we've lost it. "Are you two practicing metaphors now instead of drills?"

And that doesn't help either. "We were just planning to do some extra sprints, right?" I say, clapping Miller's shoulder.

"Excellent. More sprints. Less metaphors," Theo says, then grabs the stairwell door, but before heading up to his second-floor office, he ducks back and looks at me. "I got your text about wanting to meet. Perfect timing. I have something to discuss with you too."

The door swings shut, and he's gone.

Miller gawks at me. "What the...?"

I go cold everywhere. "Shit."

"I mean, this is it," Miller says, frowning. "He knows."

My gut twists. It's not like I've been Mister Secretive. I've taken Mabel out to lunch, kissed her in the bakery, fake-dated her. I've basically stopped hiding.

And yeah, it's not his business and all, but my stomach curls with the realization I should have had this talk sooner. A lot sooner. "He probably does."

Miller claps me on the back. "It was good knowing you," he says as we head to the locker room, the sound of sneakers echoing behind us.

In a second, Lake catches up to us. "Is Knighty Night retiring?"

"Yep. He's going to bow out because he's about to get traded," Miller deadpans.

Riggs is next, and he joins us. "Shit. Seriously?"

"No, I'm not getting traded. I have a no-trade clause. I just need to—" I stop and shed all these worries. She's worth it. That's the point of telling Theo. "I need to see Theo and tell him I'm going to date his sister."

Lake winces, a rare show of emotion. "Got a death wish?"

Riggs pats my shoulder. "It was fun while it lasted. Playing with you and all."

I flip them the bird, then turn around and hustle down the hall. I was going to do this after practice, but since Theo's free now, I guess it's now or never.

I bound up the steps, and rap on Theo's open door. He's at his desk, holding a cup of coffee.

"Come in—"

I barely let him finish the sentence. "We've been friends for more than a decade, right?"

His brow knits. "Yeah."

"And I'm guessing you don't think I'm a dick then."

"No," he says, then hesitates. "But should I?"

"Nope. Because I'm not. Was I there for you when Ginny left?"

"Yes. And what are you getting at?"

"Did I water your plants when you went out of town and your plant sitter flaked?"

He motions for me to spill. "'Fess up, Knight."

"Did I root for you when you wanted to be GM?"

He heaves a sigh. "Yes. What. Is. It?"

Undeterred by his impatience, I square my shoulders, blow out a breath, and come this close to saying, *I'm in love with your sister.*

Because I am. I've been falling for her for a long time. I'm also sure I *fell*. Pretty sure I've known it on some cellular level since the night she came to my game right before the holidays —when I felt relaxed on the ice, steady even, thanks to her. When I stopped fighting the way I felt. When I accepted that these feelings weren't going away. But I'm not going to tell him before I tell her. And I'm not going to tell her until the right moment.

For now, I meet Theo's steely eyes and say, "I'm crazy about your sister, and I wanted you to know we're going to start dating. For real."

He drops the mug of coffee he's holding.

The mug crashes to the wood floor, hot coffee splattering everywhere, along with the handle. Theo doesn't even flinch. His eyes are locked on me, wide, furious—or maybe just stunned. "You're *what*?"

Damn, that felt good to get off my chest. I roll my shoulders and practically strut to the chair opposite his desk. I stop though. The polite thing to do would be to help clean up.

I head to the men's room, grab some compostable paper towels, and return to wipe up the coffee on the hardwood.

He takes some too, and we clean together. He scrubs harder than anyone needs to, breathing out with each push of the towel.

"Did you just...did you seriously tell me you're dating my sister in the same tone you'd use to ask me for extra tickets to a game?"

"I did," I say, feeling a thousand times lighter.

He shakes his head. "Back this up. Try again. Tell me something that doesn't end with me wanting to aim darts at your picture."

"Want me to pick you up some new darts? Game store's right by the rink."

He exhales heavily. "And she's...into you?" He sounds like he can't quite believe it.

A small laugh escapes me. The floor's clean enough now so I rise, toss the towels in the compost bin, then nod. "She is. And I'm...just fucking besotted."

He blinks. "Fucking besotted? Are you a wordsmith today? From your metaphors to this?"

Maybe the love letters are rubbing off on me. "I guess I am."

"I..." he begins, but he can't seem to form words. He's never speechless.

So I take the reins. "Listen, I get that you don't like her exes. I don't either. I get that you're protective. I am too. I also understand that you don't want her to be hurt. I don't either. And you should know I'm going to treat her like a queen."

He doesn't need to know I've already been doing that.

"When did this start?" he asks.

And that's also something I won't answer entirely. But I can be honest when I say, "I've been interested in her since I met her. You might even say she's the one who got away."

He runs a hand through his hair, blows out a breath. "I'll need an addendum to your contract. A waiver signed by Mabel saying she won't sue when this ends badly."

"It won't end badly."

He stares hard at me. His voice is steely now. "If you break her heart, you're dead to me."

And that's fair. I nod. "I hear you."

He pins me with a hard-edged stare. "I mean it. I don't want to see her hurt. I don't want to see her cry. I don't want to see you talking shit about her ever."

I hold up a hand. "You have my word."

"It's not that you aren't a good man, but if by chance you do any of those things, we're done." Then he smirks. "And I will find a way to trade you, or bench you, or make sure you never get any ice time. I will call up a young guy and tell them to give him ice time right away."

I love this guy. He has to find a way to get the last word.

But I'm not worried. I know what I want. And it's not simply to date her. It's to win her heart. So all those threats— they don't mean a thing because I won't hurt her.

"Heard," I say, then extend a hand.

He huffs, but he shakes back.

I head to the door when I remember he had something to discuss. I turn back. "You wanted to talk about something?"

He still looks shell-shocked, but he clears that away, his expression all businesslike. "Right. I do. Remember *Romance Beach*?"

How could I forget? "Of course."

"I was in touch with them," he explains, and I have no clue where this is going. "And then Ronnie started posting about you two and mentioned you to them. They emailed me today asking for your contact info. They want the two of you to come on a reunion episode and serve some cake."

If I had a cup of coffee it'd spill right now.

39

WHEN YOU'RE VENGEFUL

MABEL

I'm not saying the universe still has it out for me. But I *am* definitely saying that having to bake a cake for a reality TV show one day and a few cakes for my mother's faculty luncheon the next is both an embarrassment of riches and immensely stressful.

But obviously, I'm not turning down either opportunity.

After we close Afternoon Delight in the early evening, I round up the crew for a review of the plans. Aisha's here, along with Corbin and Charlotte.

We settle in at a table and I go over the marching orders for tomorrow, mostly for Aisha, reviewing the schedule for the morning deliveries, then the items we need for a huge birthday cake order for next weekend. "Just double check that we have everything. I put the ingredients down in the task-management list."

"Buttercream frosting, fondant, raspberry filling. It's all there. I'm looking at it now," says the world's most self-sufficient middle schooler as she reviews everything on her phone.

Aisha smiles from the counter, tapping the top of her

laptop. "I see it all too. If you want to come by and help though, Charlotte, you're always welcome."

"I'm happy to work."

"She's offered a few times already," I say to Aisha. "Not surprised, knowing who her dad is."

Corbin points at his daughter, going all stern daddy. "You need to focus on school. And you'll be with your mom."

"I know, but I'm like you, Dad. I'm pretty good at doing it all."

I smile at how very much like him she is, then return to my tablet and the plans for tomorrow. That's when Corbin and I will head to the Webflix studios in the city. There we'll bake a gorgeous Valentine's Day heart-shaped cake for several *Romance Beach* alums, including Dax, who won his season. But the thought of seeing my ex doesn't bother me like it might have months ago. He's so far in the past, he's out of the rearview mirror visibility. I'm excited to prove him wrong, though, and show the world I have my act together.

That includes running this shop smoothly. We need to hire more help, and I've placed some ads, but won't be able to do any interviews until I get through the mountain of tasks over the next week.

I close my tablet and busy myself with organizing the merch better on the shelves. A few mugs are out of place. "We're about to get busier with the Valentine's season coming up, plus we have a dog adoption event next weekend."

"Orders are coming in left and right, and we've been asked to supply a couple other restaurants and cafés," Corbin puts in. "What can we do to speed up hiring help?"

Charlotte sticks her hand straight in the air. "I can assist."

"Girl, you have school and homework," Aisha says with a laugh, taking the words straight out of Corbin's mouth.

"Fine," Charlotte says with a huff. "What about Audrey? She worked at the Green Pantry during the summer and just returned to town. She's looking for work, but the Green Pantry doesn't have any openings at the moment."

"She's hired!" I shout.

Corbin hums doubtfully. "Maybe not that fast."

"But if Charlotte knows of someone and she's worked in food services before, why not?"

Aisha reaches across the table and squeezes Charlotte's shoulder. "If you don't become a vet, be an HR director. You've got VP written all over you."

"Thanks, but I prefer D-R."

"Of course you do," Aisha says. "And I think we should hire Audrey too. I have her info."

I'm glad Aisha feels the same way. "I say let's do it. Corbin?"

"I'm outvoted, but it doesn't matter. Hire her."

Aisha calls her right then and there, and after a quick call, Corbin's officially sold.

By the end of the night, we have everything ready for tomorrow's baking extravaganza, and a new employee hired right away, which means she can help with the faculty luncheon cakes since Aisha has a doctor's appointment that morning. "I love it when a plan comes together," I say.

* * *

The next morning, we pull into a lot in the Dogpatch District in the city, where the studio's located. "You don't mind that I can't help with the luncheon?" Corbin asks as he turns off his car.

Tomorrow he has morning skate and then a game.

I shoot him a look like he's nuts for asking. "Yes, Corbin, it bothers me immensely that your pro hockey schedule is getting in the way of our bakery."

"Seriously," he says, sounding far too concerned.

I set a hand on his rock-hard thigh, reassuring him. "I know who I got into business with. I will take what I can get of you at Afternoon Delight. It's all extra."

He frowns though, like he wants it to be more. "That wasn't my goal though."

"I don't mean that in a bad way," I add. "But you do have a full-time job, and I knew that when we went into business together."

"I just want to help as much as I can."

"And you are helping, like with this," I say, nodding to the looming brass doors at the entrance to the studio. "Let's go show my ex we bake better than he dates."

That seems to cheer him up. "We date better than he dates too," Corbin says, then reaches for my face, cups my chin, and kisses me fiercely.

He groans against my mouth, ruins my lipstick, and sends my heart fluttering all at once.

Gently, I place a hand on his chest and push him off. "I'll be a hot mess if you keep doing that."

His lips quirk in a lopsided grin. "Good."

"Ha. I'm trying to stop being a hot mess."

He slides his hands through my hair. "You can be a hot mess in bed."

A kiss on my neck. A hand on my waist. His scent drifting past my nose.

But I steel myself and push back. "Later. When we're *in bed*. Now, get your hockey stick and let's go show Dax that dating a hot hockey player is the best kind of revenge."

I mean, maybe I had ulterior motives in saying yes to today.

"You're even sexier when you're vengeful," he says, as he takes the stick from the trunk—*Romance Beach* wanted the whole baking hockey player schtick.

He grabs my bag too, with my apron, some specialty tools, and a few other items I'll need, while I carefully pick up a cake I've baked in advance. Just in case. Hot Mess Mabel is definitely *not* going to chance being in the house today.

I walk up the steps with the man who's good with his hands. I'm ready to show how sexy, vengeful, and together I can be.

* * *

"And as you can see, this is the vital moment—when our baker finishes decorating the delicate heart-shaped cake she'll serve to our lovebirds," Ronnie says, and it's déjà vu as I carefully set the fondant heart so it cascades around the cake.

"Well now, Ronnie," comes a pretty female voice. "We might actually have the hockey-playing baker serve it."

That's Sapphire, the *Romance Beach* hostess—sweet as sugar and one of the kindest people I've met. I can see why Riggs is dating her. And she and Ronnie have definitely been playing up the *hockey player* angle. The producers even had Corbin walk on set holding his stick, which he now keeps tucked under our table.

I shove all of that out of my mind as Corbin hands me the final fondant heart.

What a change—the last time I decorated a cake in front of Ronnie it was for a local contest and streamed on local TV. Now it's being recorded and my ex is sitting there with a backward baseball cap on, holding hands with a woman in a silver dress that looks like it was made of Spanx. More power to her. She's hot, and that's fine with me. I don't care about him. His presence doesn't stress me out. His words don't concern me. He's just...the past. If I moved past the way I ran out of Cozy Valley, I can move past him.

"You've got this," Corbin whispers encouragingly as Ronnie prowls the set, pacing in front of the open-faced kitchen that leads into the living room where the couples sit.

"You're right, Sapphire," Ronnie crows. "They'll both serve it. What a comeback—last time Mabel baked in public, it didn't go well, but she's holding her own now."

Tension spikes in my chest, but Corbin shoots me a look that says: *ignore them.*

Drama feeds reality TV. I'm not feeding it back.

Sapphire glides over to Dax on the couch, who's busy petting his girlfriend's leg. "So, Dax," the show hostess says sweetly, "how is it watching your ex become a popular baker? You didn't say very nice things about her."

Oh, they're baiting Dax.

But Corbin skates to the puck first. "You sure didn't," Corbin says, his voice smooth as ice.

It's protective and sexy. And I won't let Dax distract me either. I focus on smoothing the icing. No mistakes. Not this time.

Dax gives a lazy shrug. "Well, let's see if she messes it up again."

And—seriously?—he starts *walking over.*

Corbin's hand lands gently on my back. "We've got this," he murmurs.

"It's hard to turn your life around," Dax says, all faux sympathy.

What did I ever see in him? Oh, right—bad choices. Everyone makes them.

"It *is* hard to change, Dax. You're a case in point," I say sweetly. "But I changed because I owned up to my mistakes—like dating you."

Sapphire's gasp is delightfully dramatic.

Corbin grins, puffing out his chest. "She found someone better."

Dax snorts. "Yeah, well, let's see how this cake is," he says, taking another swaggering step.

That's when Corbin subtly stretches his leg under the table. The toe of his shoe nudges something long and narrow. The hockey stick slides forward and right into Dax's path.

Dax doesn't look down. He's fixated on me, swagger in his step, but his foot catches on the hockey stick. For a second he teeters, arms windmilling like a cartoon, then gravity wins.

He belly-flops into the heart-shaped cake, pink frosting and vanilla cake smearing across his chin and chest.

The sound guy snorts. A producer shouts, "Keep rolling." Someone else barks out, "Get a close-up."

Sapphire gasps. Ronnie's jaw drops.

But Corbin's the picture of calm. Giving Dax a chin nod, he says dryly, "Watch out, buddy. Those hockey sticks can trip you up."

Dax glares at him, but with his chin smeared in pink icing, it's hard to take him seriously.

"Enjoy the smash cake," I say sweetly. Maybe I'm a little petty. But also prepared.

I turn to Ronnie. "Good thing I baked a backup."

A little later, once Dax has been toweled off, Corbin brings out the second cake, and we serve perfect slices to all the couples.

As I set the last plate down, I flash a *fast on my feet* smile at the camera. "And you can all get your very own smash cake at Afternoon Delight."

Dax doesn't touch his, but I don't care. When this episode airs, *he'll* be the meme—and I'll be the woman who got her act together.

Thanks in no small part to the man who believed in me.

40

FUCK MORNINGS
CORBIN

I can barely keep my hands off her. The house is mine alone, so we go back to my place, and the second I shut the door, my fingers are in her hair.

"I want you to spend the night here. For the first time," I say. The first of many.

"Do you now?" she teases.

"I really do, Mabel. Everything's better when you're with me—falling asleep next to you, waking up next to you, seeing you as often as I can. Working with you. Playing with you. Talking to you." God, I sound like a sap. But I don't care.

She slides a hand up my chest and curls her fingers around my collar. "Same," she whispers, sounding more vulnerable than I've ever heard her.

Maybe soon I'll tell her how I feel.

But right now, she brings her mouth to mine and kisses me ravenously—harder than she ever has before, more desperate. She's all need and fire, and that trumps everything else.

We grab at each other's clothes, kick off shoes, and stumble toward the staircase in a flurry of hands, teeth, and heat. At the bottom of the steps, I hoist her up, toss her over my shoulder, and carry her upstairs.

"It's faster this way," I say.

"Is it, or do you just like being all...protective?"

"How is this protective?"

"I'm sorry—possessive," she corrects playfully as we reach the top.

I set her down, look her in the eyes. "Want me to show you how possessive I am while I fuck you?"

She trembles and nods.

Soon she's flat on her back on my bed, shiny hair spilling across my pillow, moonlight streaming over her pale skin, her head tipped back, her throat exposed as I thrust into her—her wrists pinned above her head.

She moans beautifully.

Writhes.

Arches.

"This is how possessive I am," I rasp.

"How?" she pants.

Letting go of her wrists, I lower myself closer, still moving inside her. "Mine. You're mine. You're all mine."

Her lips part. She shudders. She whispers, "Yours," before she comes.

And I follow her there.

Later, I'm yawning, and she is too. Exhaustion kicks in, but she tells me she needs to set her alarm. "I have to get up early and bake for my mom. I'll need to grab a Lyft then too. I don't have my car."

"I'll drive you," I say, sleep tugging at my eyelids.

"It's super early. I have to be up at six instead of seven-thirty."

"Anything for you, even mornings," I grumble as I drift off.

*** * ***

The sound of birds chirping before the sun even rises hurts my head. Their happiness over the dawn is awful. They've never been this loud before.

It's like there's a flock of them.

My eyes float open, and I realize the sound is coming from Mabel's side of the bed.

What the hell? Her phone is chirping. It sounds sick. My head is a fog. The room is pitch black. Mabel looks so peaceful, sleeping soundly, so I reach across her and hit the snooze button.

Except sometime later—I don't know how much later—she's bolt upright, hopping around the room yanking on panties, muttering, "Shit, shit, shit!"

I push up in bed, groggy. "What's wrong?"

"It's *nine!*" she shouts, one hand in her hair, the other grabbing her bra. "I was supposed to be up at six. So I could be at the bakery by seven. I have to get the cake in the oven right now or it'll never cool in time for the event."

Oh shit. My stomach craters. I didn't hit snooze on her alarm. I hit off. This is my fault. Come to think of it, "Nine?"

She's already running around, hunting for her shirt. "I set my alarm. I swear I did. I don't know why it didn't go off."

Oh, I know why. Because I turned it off.

I just stare at her, my heart pounding with guilt as she yanks on her sweater, then grabs her phone. I want to say *I'm sorry,* but she's already halfway down the stairs, calling someone, then saying, "Aisha, can you come in early?" A brief pause. "Shoot. That's right. What about Audrey?"

And it hits me that she's holding everything together, and I'm the one unraveling it.

Like when I ordered the wrong pretzels and she saved the

day. Like when I was late to the cookie swap but she set up everything without me.

She's the one who fixes things.

And here she is, running out of my house because I fucked up. And she's probably about to call a Lyft.

"Wait," I shout, then pull on shorts and a T-shirt in record time. I fly down the stairs, and drive her to the bakery, where she left her car yesterday before we went to the studio.

She's on the phone the whole time, then says the fastest of goodbyes, racing into the bakery.

As I drive back to my house all I can think is I'm...the hot mess.

And now I'm late for practice—for the first time in my career.

* * *

Don't speed. Don't speed. Don't fucking speed.

But even if I wanted to race through the city, traffic is making an ass of me. I grit my teeth, swallowing down ten thousand gallons of self-loathing as the clock on the dashboard warns me of my fate. I avoid the clogged Embarcadero and maneuver through the side streets to the arena.

So much for that strategy though. They aren't much faster.

Every muscle in my body is tight. I breathe out hard, barely relieved when the sign for the arena comes into view, along with the fox statue.

Never been so happy to see it—or so embarrassed.

And I'm showing up ten minutes after ten to the goddamn players' lot. It'll take me another five minutes to suit up.

I slam the car door, sprint to the players' entrance, and run hard down the hall to the empty locker room. The silence is shameful. I should have done better. I can't believe I was so...

so high on sex and love and romance that I skipped an alarm. For both of us.

I tug off my shirt and jeans in record time, then pull on my pads, shorts, jersey, and skates, lacing them faster than I ever have before.

It's just practice, but it's more than that—it's a rule. Coach's rule. You can't be late for practice.

I practically jog through the corridor, then fly through the tunnel and out onto the ice...right in the middle of shooting drills.

I swallow roughly.

The whole team is here. Of course. Because it's a game day, and morning skate on game day is mandatory for the Foxes.

I skate past Coach, giving him a quick chin nod. He barely acknowledges me, but that's fine. I want to blend in, and I do my best, lining up to take shots on goal, with Lake and Riggs both giving me arched eyebrows.

I say nothing. I speak better with my skates and stick. I'm fast and aggressive, putting the puck past Miller in the goal. Then we run through the rest of our drills.

My lungs are on fire at the end, but at least I made it without much ado, after all. That's a relief.

I catch up with Riggs as he's heading toward the gate.

"How was yesterday? Or is it a secret?" he asks.

"Guess you'll have to ask your girlfriend," I say, grateful to talk about something besides my tardiness.

"She tells me nothing about the show."

"Smart woman. And that means I'll tell you nothing," I say.

I survived. And I'll have to apologize to Mabel next. *Again.* I'm starting to feel like a fuckup.

When I step into the tunnel, a deep, commanding voice calls out from the ice, "Knight. A word."

Riggs gives me an *oh shit* look, then skates off unscathed.

As my stomach drops, I turn around and skate toward Coach, putting Mabel out of my mind as best I can so I can focus on my job. Coach stands by the boards, reviewing something on his tablet.

He tucks it under his arm when I arrive. "Knight, everything okay?"

I furrow my brow. "Um, yes."

"Good. I wanted to make sure. Since I know you've been through some tough stuff, and you've never been late before."

He noticed. He tracked it. My stomach churns. "Sorry, sir."

"That's why I wanted to make sure everything's good with the family, your daughter, and all?"

"It's all good," I reassure him.

"Excellent. Then I'll be fining you."

I blink. "What?"

"I expect more of you. We have rookies and veterans alike who look up to you. Don't be late again."

He turns around and skates off to join his assistant coaches, and I don't move.

It's not about the money—it's the embarrassment. This isn't me. I don't even know who I've become.

41
____

AT LEAST I PUT ON DEODORANT
MABEL

If I had been at the firehouse last night, I'd have slid down the pole to save time getting to the kitchen. Instead, I jumped out of Corbin's car, slammed the door and vaulted through the front entrance of Afternoon Delight.

Aisha has a doctor's appointment and Audrey is, unfortunately, sick on her first day, and couldn't start. Which means it's been me flying through the bakery for the last two hours.

Solo.

But I called for backup and Clementine has joined me and Remy too, since she's not working for the Foxes till this evening.

I grab the last cake from the oven, set it down on the counter to cool, and whip off my oven mitts. I swing my gaze quickly to the clock. "I've got an hour to get to the university," I say, rushing over to the freezer, where I grab one of the two cakes that have been cooling for twenty minutes.

"This is the best cake hack I've ever heard of," Remy says, as she hands me the container with icing.

"It is," I say quickly, as I unwrap the plastic wrap from the cake. When you're in a time crunch, the Saran wrap helps prevent freezer burn and moisture loss as the cake cools enough to ice it.

Quickly but carefully, I apply the frosting, then sculpt some flowers as decoration. Once the cake on the counter is ready for its chill session, I Saran wrap it and slot it into the freezer. Then I race against time and ice another, then the final one.

"You're Wonder Woman," Clementine says when we finish.

"If Wonder Woman is a hot, sweaty mess, who smells like —" I stop to sniff my armpit. "Don't answer that."

"Sex?" Remy asks, wiggling her brows.

But I can't even laugh or gloat. I just feel gross. I haven't had time to change since I sprinted out of Corbin's bed.

"Speaking of," I say, then nod to the stairs.

There's barely enough time for me to run upstairs and put on fresh panties and jeans, then slick on some deodorant. I fly downstairs and then mix some cookie dough that Aisha will need, stat, and put the cakes in boxes.

At eleven-thirty, Aisha walks in, and I say hello, give her the batter, then say goodbye to my friends.

I set the cakes down in the back seat of my car and peel away from the bakery, taking a back road to the highway, then tapping the gas. I'm cruising along at five miles above the speed limit. That's safe. Everyone knows you can go five miles faster than allowed.

I get off at the next exit and I'll maybe, possibly make it to the university on time when sirens blare. There must be an accident up ahead or behind me. But when I peer into the rearview mirror, I groan. A highway patrol officer is pulling me over.

* * *

Fifteen minutes later, with a speeding ticket in hand, I resume driving to the university. I call my mother along the way, but she doesn't answer. I dictate a text at the light. Soon enough, I arrive but the parking lot is full since the universe hates me all over again. I pull into an overflow lot and somehow I'm able to balance two boxes of cakes as I rush through the lot and up the steps, and then yank open the door to the brick building.

It smells like old books and ideas, and I hustle down the cavernous hall, past portraits of thoughtful-looking men and women to the faculty dining room. When I reach the stately oak door, my mother's standing outside pacing, arms crossed. The second she sets eyes on me, she breathes a sigh of relief.

"Mabel," she says, but her voice is sharp. "What happened?"

All I can say is, "I'm sorry. I tried to text you. I called too."

"My phone is on silent right now. I didn't want to be disturbed during the luncheon. Are you okay?"

That's a loaded question. I'd thought I was. I'd thought I was handling everything well. But I'm not sure I'm okay at all. "I'm just running a little late," I say, not wanting to admit the truth.

She sighs. "Well, you're here now."

She gives me a once-over and even in my fresh jeans and slicked on deodorant, I must still look like somebody who rolled out of bed and went straight to the bakery.

BECAUSE I DID.

She gives me a nod. "I'll take it from here."

"I have one more cake to get."

She nods down the hall. "Please go do that."

Shame coursing through me, I rush back out, jog across the parking lot, and snag the last cake from the car. I find my mom once more in the hall and hand it over.

"Dear," she says in her *this is going to be a lesson* tone of voice. "I get that this is new for you and there's a lot to balance, but running a business is a lot of work. Like we talked about at dinner."

When I bragged about how well I was doing. Revenue, budget, marketing. But what about the most important skill of all—*managing the business*?

Today, I failed at that big time. "I know."

"And I'm just saying, you seem a little *off* right now," she says, her tone gentle, caring even, and somehow that makes me feel worse. Frazzled.

"I'm fine," I say, but I'm clearly not fine, and that's obvious.

"I just don't want you to get distracted." She sets a hand on my arm in a reassuring, motherly way. "What if this had happened to another client? Someone who's not your mother?"

My stomach drops.

The implication is clear—at least I didn't mess up in front of someone else. I hate that she's right. "I appreciate you giving me this chance," I say.

She squeezes my shoulder. "Let me know if I can help you with anything."

But right now, I feel like I need help with everything, and that's the problem. I've never felt more childish, foolish, or unlucky. Except it's not luck at play.

It's just me.

42

THE ANTI-CONTRIBUTOR
CORBIN

This is the worst game of my professional life.

I've spent more time in the sin bin tonight than I have in the last month. It's penalty after penalty, and that's unlike me. I move the plays along. I don't fuck shit up.

But tonight I've done plenty of the latter.

I grind my teeth, ready to bolt when the seconds tick off.

At the end of my jail time, I fly out of the box and race across the ice, hell-bent on making something happen. Riggs feeds me the puck, and I'm fast and aggressive, slapping it toward the opponent's net.

And missing.

Of course.

The rest of the game goes just like that. When it's mercifully over, we've lost and I've contributed nothing.

No. That's not true. I anti-contributed.

I stomp into the locker room, slam my stick down on the floor, and head straight for the showers. I avoid everyone. Coach, the publicists, even my teammates as best as I possibly can. Once I'm dressed, I leave, stalking to my car. On the way home, I blast loud rock music that drowns out all the thoughts of everything that went wrong today.

I've got to apologize properly to Mabel. But when I reach Cozy Valley, surprise, surprise, the flower shop is closed. Hell, the grocery store is even closed.

Great, I'll show up empty-handed. Isn't that perfect?

I park outside the bakery, turn off my car, and head inside, where I find Mabel spraying down the display case. Her eyes are empty. Her expression, grim. My heart hurts so much. I did this to the woman I adore. The woman I love.

"Hey," she says, her tone flat.

"Hey." I walk toward her. She looks like she's had a worse day than me. "I'm sorry," I add, but it feels hollow. Not because I don't mean it, but because I keep doing this—apologizing. Which means I keep messing up. "Just like I was sorry for the pretzels, and I was sorry for not getting here to help for the cookie swap, and I'm really fucking sorry about this morning."

"It's fine. It's not your fault," she says with a shrug. But she sounds wooden. No, it's not that. She sounds depressed.

"It is my fault," I say, pinching the bridge of my nose.

Just admit it, man. Just tell her what you did.

But those aren't the words that come out of my mouth. Instead of admitting my failure this morning, I try to put a positive spin on it all. "I'm sure you saved the day though, like you did the other times."

And that's not telling her the truth either, dickhead.

"Actually..." She breathes out hard, sets down the cleaner, and comes around the counter. "I was twenty minutes late to the luncheon. I got a speeding ticket along the way. Earlier, I had to cool down the cakes in the freezer with Saran wrap. I had to call for reinforcements from Clementine and Remy because Aisha had that doctor's appointment, and Audrey wasn't feeling well. When I returned here after the event, we didn't have enough cookies and bars since I simply didn't have time to make enough of everything. A few people left the store without buying anything because we didn't have our usual stock."

My soul sinks to the center of the earth. This is all on me. "Oh shit. That's bad." I drag a hand through my hair, needing to man up and tell her what I did.

She moves and straightens up the bakery chairs, tucking them in. The vases are empty on the tables. Another reminder.

"I didn't get you flowers for today either," I say.

She waves a hand dismissively. "It's no big deal. Like I said, I should have done a better job at everything. Including paying attention to my alarm."

"Mabel," I say, heavily, regret and guilt swirling into a cocktail in my gut. "I turned off the alarm."

She stops cleaning, peers at me like that doesn't compute. "What do you mean?"

"I heard your alarm go off this morning, and I was tired, and I thought I just snoozed it but I must have turned it off. I wasn't thinking. It was my fault."

She shrugs listlessly. "It really doesn't matter though, Corbin. These things happen, and I need to handle them. I even got tagged in a meme today about me not getting my act together. It was posted by somebody who came in here and couldn't get what they wanted. I should have had a second alarm set."

I hate that she's taking this all on. "It's not your fault."

"It is though. Ultimately," she says, returning to the display cases and arranging the cards in front of the empty trays. "I've been trying to get attention for this bakery, and I should have been more diligent."

"It's my fault," I say, stabbing my chest, wishing she'd let me take the blame. "That's what I'm trying to say, and I'm so sorry it came down on you. That's not fair."

"Some days are just not in your favor," she says, and she sounds broken.

It hits me like a piano falling from the top of a building—*this* is exactly what I worried about when I signed up for the bakery.

This is why I wanted to wait until retirement. Because all this—this fledgling, wonderful new business—is too much to handle. I have a demanding job. I have responsibilities. I added another job on top of that, and on top of being a dad, and then tried to add a romance too. Look what happened.

I kept sliding down the slippery slope of mistakes.

It's not fair to this ambitious, bighearted, funny, kind, incredible woman who I absolutely adore. Who I love madly. "Mabel," I say heavily.

She looks at me, her gaze wary. "Yes?"

I don't want to do this, but I can't keep hurting her. "I can't take a chance of this happening again to you. I almost ruined your business. I *did* hurt your reputation with your mom. You got a speeding ticket. You had more online harassment. And I pushed you into this romance and into everything when you wanted to take a break." I'm shaking my head, disgusted with my actions. "This is so unfair, what I did to you."

"What did you do to me?" she asks, taking a step back.

I blow out a breath, scrubbing a hand across my chin. "Even though you'd told me you wanted to take a break from romance, even though you told me you made a promise to yourself to not date, I still decided I was going to convince you that I was the best boyfriend possible. I didn't listen to you. I decided to give you the full-court press and get you to fall for me even when you wanted to take a break from romance."

"You think you manipulated me into...what? Liking you?" she scoffs.

For fuck's sake, now I sound like a douche. What the hell has happened to me? I shovel my hands through my hair. "Point is, I didn't listen to you. You wanted a break, and I should have honored that." It breaks my fucking heart to say the next thing, but I have to. "I should have listened to you. I should have given you...space."

"Oh." That one syllable is loaded with hurt, but also self-protection. "I understand."

"I just don't want to mess things up for you. This is a huge chance here, and it's going so well. And I feel like—"

"It's fine," she says, agreeing almost too soon. "I understand. It's too much to deal with all of this. It makes perfect sense. We should cool it."

My chest feels like it's being torn in half. "It's for the best, don't you think?" I say, since this has to be what she needs. I can't keep trying to win her over when she's made her feelings clear.

"Case in point—today." Her tone is crisp, but then she lets out the biggest yawn I've ever seen. Possibly, it looks forced, but she's dealt with a lot today. "I need to go home, sleep in my own bed. Can you lock up?"

A second later, she's already at the door.

I didn't see that coming. But it's my turn to help her out, rather than stand in her way. "Of course," I say, racing over to open the door. At least I can hold it for her, but she beats me to it.

She leaves, gets in her car, and drives off.

I watch till the lights vanish in the distance. She's not sleeping in the bed I got her for Christmas. It's like a punch to the gut, but I deserve it.

43

FIVE-ALARM FIRE
MABEL

The banging of a jackhammer rips through my apartment.

I sit bolt upright.

Blink. Check the time. Stare longingly at my pillow.

But nope. I drag my exhausted self out of the bed at the ungodly hour of six.

I had to wake up even earlier than usual since I stormed off to make my point of sleeping in the city.

Like I wanted to sleep in the bed he got me.

I set five alarms. No more chirping. No more pleasant sounds. I'm going to be a morning person if it kills me.

I march out of bed straight to the shower. After cranking the water as hot as I can, I step under a scalding stream. That new leaf means I'm going to be all about Afternoon Delight, Afternoon Delight, Afternoon Delight.

Not this hole in my heart.

This sting in my eyes.

This tightness in my throat.

No one notices your tears when you cry in the shower.

But it was inevitable—the breakup. It never works out when you try to strike up a romance with your business partner. It just doesn't. You can only break the rules for so long. Eventually, you have to choose. I'd do well to remember that.

I get out of the shower, and I think of recipes. I get dressed and imagine names to call new treats. I get on the road and plan the day ahead. I am focused. I am a new Mabel. I am all business.

I arrive at Afternoon Delight earlier than I've ever been there before, and I'm in the zone, prepping for the day. Before anyone else can even show up to help me, I take off. The Danishes are ready, so I drop them to the guys in the town square. The cookies are all set for Joni, so I take those to her.

Then, I do the hard thing. I head to the university, going the speed limit the entire way. I find my mother in her office, towering shelves of books along the wall and papers all over her desk.

She blinks and looks at me. "Mabel?"

"I was late yesterday, and that was rude," I say, cutting to the chase. I thrust out the flowers I picked up for her as well as a small box of baked goods. This is getting to be my life. Apologies and gifts. Gifts and apologies.

"You really didn't have to do that," she says, taking both and setting them down.

"I did though," I say, keeping my chin up and staying strong. "Because you were right. I was distracted yesterday. I should have been more focused. I should have been early. I should have dressed better. I didn't even run a brush through my hair, and I'm sorry I showed up like that for you. That was wrong."

She takes a beat, giving me a soft smile. "All of us have bad days."

But it's not that simple. "You were right about everything. I was distracted by a guy. But he broke it off. Well, we broke it off last night. But it's fine. I'm not going to worry about that.

I'm going to focus on the bakery like I should." I'm resolute and give a nod.

She frowns sympathetically. "Did you like him?"

My chest aches. My heart hurts. I liked him so much it was, well, more than like. I was in love with him. "I did," I say, swallowing past the hurt. "It's Corbin. Theo's friend."

Recognition dawns in her eyes. "He's always seemed like such a generous, thoughtful guy."

I wince but then tell myself to stay strong. "He is. But it was clear it wasn't going to work out since we're business partners and all. I need to focus on business. That's what you've been telling me, and it just makes sense."

She tilts her head. "But is that what you really want?"

What I want is to wake up next to Corbin. To feel his arms around me. To hear him whispering words of support in my ear. To experience his kisses on my neck. To know that we could do this together. But clearly that's not going to happen.

"I know myself. I wasn't giving enough to anything. You know me—I'm always too much or never enough," I say, trying to make light of the truth of my life.

She stands, strides over to me, sets her hands on my shoulders. "Mabel, that's not true."

But the aching in my chest tells me that it is true. It's too true. My eyes sting. "It's okay, Mom. I need to just make the best of this bakery. You said it yourself. I was distracted."

"Dear, I just don't want life to be hard for you. I want you to have opportunities. That's what I've always wanted. But love isn't always a distraction."

In my case it was. I look at the clock. "I'm going to be late if I don't go."

She squeezes my hand. "Thank you for coming by. Everyone loved the cake."

"Thanks," I say, then tears streak down my face as I walk

out, shoes echoing in the wide hallway. I don't know why her colleagues liking the cake is doing a number on me, but it sure is. It's shot all my emotions sky-high.

On the drive back, I swipe at my cheeks. When I arrive at the bakery, Corbin's bike is locked up by a lamppost out front.

Seriously?

I steel myself.

Don't let him see you cry. Don't let him know you're hurt. Don't let him know you missed him.

I march inside, and apparently I don't listen to myself. All of my hurt blasts out in an accusatory: "Why are you here?"

I didn't mean it for it to come out like that.

But he takes it in his stride. "I wanted to help."

"Dude," I say, and I want to shout, *You dumped me.* But he's my business partner, and I can't lash out at him like I would at Dax. We agreed to be adults. We agreed to be civilized. At the very least I can do that.

"I thought you had hockey and stuff," I say, moving behind the counter but keeping my distance.

Oh, do I sound annoyed? I think I do. I think I don't care.

"I have the day off. And I try to help out here when I have the day off. I always planned to be here today."

Well la-dee-dah.

If I had looked at the bakery schedule this morning like I should have, I would've seen that. It *is* his day to be here. "Of course," I say brightly, cheerily, as happy as I could possibly be. Because I'm not letting on that he's hurt me.

"We've got a lot going on, so it's good that you're here," I say. "And Aisha should be arriving any minute. Audrey too. She's feeling better."

Even though I want to say *I wish you didn't come in. It would be a lot easier for me to nurse my irritation and to cry occasionally if you weren't around.* But somehow I have to white-knuckle my way through the day because seconds later Aisha strolls out from the kitchen with a tray of orange habanero cookies. "The gang's all back together," she sings, "and today is going to be a great day."

Doubtful, but I keep that to myself.

I'm all business until he leaves in the afternoon to pick up his daughter.

I've never been more grateful to see him go because it's just too hard to work next to the man I was falling madly in love with.

44

THE SPARE-PARTS MUTT
CORBIN

At least the dog isn't fining me for feeding him after I drink my morning coffee.

Taco, a spare-parts mutt—since he looks like he was put together from a Lab, a Collie, and somehow, a Chihuahua—waits at the kitchen entrance for a second walk while I down my second cup and place bakery orders on my tablet.

Least I can do—try to help a little more.

The whole time Taco's wagging his tail and staring at me, and it almost looks like he's smiling.

Trick of the light, probably. Sunlight filters through the kitchen window.

"Almost ready, buddy," I tell the dog.

Charlotte and I picked him up last night, since his regular foster had an overnight in Darling Springs, an hour away. He'll be going back to her this afternoon before I take off for a quick road trip.

I finish the order, double-checking it. No gluten-full products that should be gluten-free and vice versa. Next, I pay the delivery service, the specialty chocolate supplier, and the distributor for flour and sugar, and then I check on the merch inventory. We're a little low on T-shirts, so I place an order for more.

There. I've done something useful for Mabel. It's all I can do. I send her a message, letting her know. I can't fix my own damn heart, but I can fix the bakery order.

I set down the tablet, then put the mug—it says *She's the Boss, Just Ask My Daughter*—in the sink.

I pat the pup's head. "You're a patient boy."

He happy-whimpers, then follows me as I head to the mudroom to grab a dog bag and the leash. When I grab it, he spins in a circle, bopping my thigh with his soft head.

I kneel and pet him some more. He rubs his head against me, then nudges me. He must need to go. "All right, that's something I won't fuck up," I say, then put the leash on him.

Once we're outside, I walk down the sidewalk, but he doesn't do his business. He turns to me, tilts his head, then nudges my thigh again.

I bend down and pet him a second time. He bumps his head against my leg a third time.

"What do you want, Taco?" I ask curiously, then pet him some more.

He keeps rubbing his head against me, so I wrap my arms around him. He lets out a sigh, and it sounds happy. I pat him some more, and a few seconds later he's finally ready for a walk.

He just wanted a hug. I get it.

"That all you wanted?" I ask.

He doesn't answer, but the answer seems to come in his gait—fast and proud. He's focused on his walk now, sniffing the occasional bush or tree, but mostly full-speed ahead. He's a cutie, with white and brown markings—Charlotte did a color show and tell—including spectacular ears. Charlotte adores him, and Mabel would love him too. A pang shoots through my chest at the thought of how much she'd have loved him. How she'd have shown it. She would have kissed his head, pet his belly, and thrown him a frisbee.

My heart craters. Like it's been punched by the annoyingly fantastic image my dickhead brain just supplied of Mabel playing with the dog. Something she won't get to do. Because she's not here hanging out with foster dogs with me. Spending the night with me. Waking up next to me so I can make her breakfast, shower with her, go to work with her—together.

Because I ended things. I had to, of course. I was too much. I was messing up her dreams. No other choice but to cool things off.

Hell, it already seems like Afternoon Delight is running smoother since we took a step back two days ago.

Soon, we near Annabelle's house, and my attention snags on a fluffy orange cat sniffing grass in the front yard.

"Seven, did you sneak out again?" I ask, but my gaze lands on a harness on the big boy. It's attached to a long leash, and what do you know—Annabelle's holding it on the porch, letting the cat roam while keeping him safe.

When Taco spots him, he jerks his head toward the cat, then ignores him.

Another point for this perfect dog.

"Someone has a leash now," I say, nodding to the cat.

"Every now and then people can change," she says. "I had to change to keep him safe."

"Smart move."

"And look at you, being a dog dad now," she says, standing and coming down the steps to join me, leash in hand.

"Just a foster-dog dad," I clarify.

She gives me a look. "You say that like fostering isn't important."

"Well, it's just—it's all I can manage right now," I say, then sigh. That's something I'm learning a lot about unfortunately. What I can actually handle, and what I can't.

Annabelle shoots me a worried look. "What's going on? Your energy is..." She narrows her eyes, studying me, and here we go again.

"I'm sure my energy's fine. I just had coffee," I say, trying to make light of things.

"No. It's...dark. Inward," she says, tilting her head. "Painful. Like a thorn."

No shit.

But wait. Hold on. Last time she read my energy, I was dismissive. Turned out she was right. Maybe this time, I should let her. What if she can help me manage...life without Mabel?

"Yeah, that's true," I admit, more vulnerable than I want to be, but maybe I have to be.

She motions to her porch, and I join her, the dog gamely trotting by my side. "What's going on? I sensed you were happy. Falling in love. Learning the colors at my shop for a woman. Buying flowers every day for a woman. Bringing me cake...for a woman. Now you're walking around like... honestly, I haven't seen you like this since your mom was diagnosed."

I bristle. "It's not the same. How could I compare the two? This is just a breakup."

She pauses, as if she's giving that some thought. "Why did you break up with her?"

"How do you know I did it?"

"You did, Corbin."

I drag my hand through my hair. "I didn't think I could manage it all. And I was messing things up for her—a luncheon for her mom, some of the orders, the scheduling. She wanted to focus on the bakery, but I kept trying to convince her she could manage a romance too. Turned out I couldn't manage things, and I was late to practice. It was all a mess. It was all too much. So it's not the same as my mom."

Annabelle hums, doubtful. "When your mom was first diagnosed, you felt helpless. Out of control. Like there was nothing you could do."

"That's true," I admit.

"And then you moved her in. You and Ray found some help. You learned about Parkinson's. You walked with her when you could. You baked with her to keep her moving."

I nod, remembering those days all too well.

"And now you feel like you can't manage a relationship. Or that Mabel can't." She stops, furrowing her brow. "Corbin, you don't like it when you're not in control. When you think you could fail."

I pull back, feeling a little too seen, a little too raw. "I... don't...but..."

"You hate it when you're not the one holding things together. When you're the one being helped instead of helping."

"I don't need help," I insist. I don't. How could I? I'm a grown-ass man. A dad. A hockey player.

She smiles, squeezes my hand, then nods. "That's a lie."

Ouch.

I swallow, not answering her. I don't want to answer her. *You don't want to face the truth.*

"Do you love her?" Annabelle asks pointedly.

My chest constricts. "Why does that matter?"

"Oh, my sweet summer child. It's the only thing that matters."

Is it though? Or is that just hope talking? Hope doesn't win games, hope doesn't run bakeries, and hope doesn't raise children. "I'm not sure I agree."

"I'm not surprised you don't," she says, sitting down, "but maybe think about the thorn. Maybe see if you can remove it. For your own sake, at the very least."

Seven pads back up the steps and jumps into her lap. She pets his head, then meets my gaze once more.

She looks serene, like the cat is transferring his laid-back energy to her.

I swing my gaze to Taco, wishing I could pick up his vibes by osmosis.

But I don't know how to remove the thorn. When I leave, I pet his head some more. I swear he smiles again. Warm and simple and sure.

I'm jealous.

Of a dog.

45

THE START OF MAYBE
MABEL

"It's a royal pair! That's totally a thing."

I give Remy a sharp stare. "A king and a queen are not a pair," I say.

"But a king and a king are," Trevyn says, wiggling his brows. "So there."

"Fine, fine." Remy pouts.

We're at Afternoon Delight for our brand-new "friends night out" activity—since apparently we can't survive on pickleball alone. And yes, I decided I needed a new poker-night wardrobe: jeans, black boots, and a black top.

It suits my mood.

Clementine sets down her cards with a catlike grin. "But a trio of threes beats you all," she says, scooping up the chips.

Skylar sighs. "And here I thought I'd be great at this."

"Because you're great at everything," Trevyn teases.

"Well, yeah," she says.

"Keep playing," he tells her.

It's my turn to deal—another distraction.

"Hold on," Skylar says, eyeing me. "You've been awfully peppy tonight."

"And?"

"And what's up? How are you really handling things?"

Ugh. The question I'd hoped to avoid. They all know about the breakup. And tonight is clearly *Let's Make Mabel Feel Better Night*, which I genuinely appreciate. But I just want to move on.

I've had enough heartache for one year—losing my grandma, the Dax breakup, the loan rejections, the high of the firehouse, the thrill of the partnership, the wonder of falling. Then, another blow to the heart.

"I'm fine," I say, shuffling the cards. "Honestly, it feels like a permission slip to focus on the bakery and just the bakery. I don't need any distractions."

The more I say it, the sooner I'll believe it.

Trevyn coughs under his breath. "Liar."

"What? It's true."

Skylar gives me a knowing look. "Mabel, I get that. But sometimes we tell ourselves what we want to be true."

That hits harder than I expect. "Look, he made it clear he thought this was for the best," I say, then recount the breakup one more time. "The whole *'made you fall for me'* speech? Come on."

"It's kind of sweet," Remy says. "He basically admitted he did everything he could to make you fall for him."

Clementine nods. "Totally a thing. When a guy falls hard, he goes all out."

"I mean, the man did buy you a bed," Skylar points out.

And a sweater, a hair tie, a dress, and, oh yeah, an investment in a business he wasn't ready to tackle yet.

"Fine, he did," I admit. "It's a very lovely bed."

"So...did you tell him you fell for him too?" Skylar asks.

I hesitate, focusing on the cards—shuffle, shuffle, shuffle

—until that's the only sound in the bakery. Sheepishly, I mumble, "I said it made sense. That we should cool it."

The collective groan is deafening.

"Seriously?" Trevyn asks, thumping my shoulder.

"He was dumping me!"

"Yes, but *not really*," Skylar says.

"Um, it was clear," I fire back.

"I think he was being what's known as a *male idiot*," she says, "and making a bad choice. But sometimes they do it because they don't know how you feel."

"It was still a bad choice," I grumble.

Remy lifts a finger. "So you admit this whole *woman against the world* thing isn't what you actually want? You miss him."

"I do," I say quietly. "But it's too hard to deal with everything else." I flap a hand at the bakery.

Skylar shakes her head. "Hard disagree. We can have it all —if we let ourselves."

I blow out a breath, turning that over.

Is she right? Could we? But that would mean telling him how I feel, and there didn't seem to be any daylight for that.

"Maybe," I say at last.

"Maybe is a start," she says.

46

YOU'RE A DUMBASS
CORBIN

On the plane home from Toronto, Theo drops down in the seat next to mine the second we reach cruising altitude.

I flinch. "What's up?" I ask.

His eyes bore a hole through my skull. "Do you think I'm stupid?"

"What do you mean?"

"Do you think I don't notice things?"

"No," I say, wary.

"And you think I can't figure out what's going on?"

And I think I know where he's going. He's using my approach from when I told him about Mabel and me. "Probably."

"Good. Because maybe you can tell me why you'd be the kind of man who'd come to me and tell me—not ask, but tell —you were in love with my sister, but then also break her heart."

I hate that I hurt her. "I'm sorry, man."

He shakes his head, sighs the most aggrieved sigh in the universe, then mutters something that sounds like *asshole*. Hard to hear over the hum of the jet hurtling through the night sky. He turns to me again. "My mom told me. For fuck's sake, Corbin. You made a show of how you were a good guy, and then you freaked out when you had one bad day."

"That's not true," I point out, eager to clear my name. "She had a bad day too."

He sneers at me. "Grow up. People have bad days. They don't do *this.*"

This. It's said so derisively.

"I thought..." I stop, rewind what he said. "I never told you I was in love with her."

"You didn't have to. It was obvious. Am I wrong?"

I swallow roughly. "You're not."

He shakes his head. "I thought you were better than this. The kind of man who storms into my office and throws down for a woman, who says, *I don't need your blessing, but I love her*—that's the kind of man who stays."

He gets up and walks the other way, leaving me with something that feels worse than a fine.

* * *

When I land, there's a new text on my phone.

> World's Best Daughter: Are you doing any better, Dad? You seemed so sad when we talked on the phone earlier. Maybe we need another foster dog, and we can bake him dog cookies. Also, if you want to talk about why you've been so sad, I'm a pretty good listener.

My throat tightens. She's the best listener. Truly, she is. But I can't go to my daughter with my romance problems.

Corbin: Love you so much, kiddo. And I think another temp foster is a fantastic idea.

As I exit the plane, I re-read her note, wondering what the hell I'm going to do about the part I didn't answer.

47

CAUGHT IN THE COOKIE JAR

MABEL

The next morning, I'm up with the birds. New leaf and all, and I don't mind it. I'm starting to like the quiet time before the rest of the world wakes. I start my baking prep, listen to some music, and enjoy the solitude.

I work through the morning like that. But after I slide a tray of cookies into the oven, my gaze strays to the cupboard with the strawberry ceramic jar. Something tugs at my chest—that same pull I've felt before. We never finished the letters.

What does the last one say?

After I set the timer, I check the door. Aisha and Audrey aren't here yet. Impulsively, I grab the stepladder and pull it over to the counter, climb the steps, and open the cupboard.

Guilt pricks at me, but I tell it to screw off. I can open these on my own. They're mine. I climb down with the jar, check the door again. Seeing the coast is clear, I return to the counter and dip a hand in the proverbial cookie jar.

Quickly, I flip through the stack, finding the one unopened letter—looks like it's two pages. My heart is beating so fast, with worry, with excitement, with fear.

But I've come this far.

One more glance. Coast is clear. I unfold the delicate pages, my pulse kicking fast. I read the first one.

Dear Harriet,

It's too hard like this. Every day at work, I feel the weight of the secret. Every night, I feel the pull toward you. I can't stand hiding. I'm ready to be done sneaking around. I'm through with breaking the rules. I want to take a chance. I need to be with you. You're worth it.

Let's tell the captain. If he says we need to get another job, we'll both leave. If one of us has to quit, I'll be the one to do it. I can't be without you. That's the only thing I know for sure.

With all my love,
Russ

My heart cracks. It shears, breaking in two, calving like a glacier into the frozen waters. A tear rolls down one cheek, then another.

He loved her so much he wouldn't let go. I close my eyes, try to collect my thoughts, working hard to calm my pulse. When I open my eyes, footsteps echo in the firehouse.

Shoot.

Aisha must be here already. I scramble, shoving the letters

with the stack, back inside the jar, then rushing out to the front to say hello. Better to greet her there than here as I tuck away a strawberry jar.

But when I enter the bakery proper, I come face-to-face with Corbin, carrying a box.

"Hi," he says, and he looks...awful.

Eyes dark. Bags under them. Sadness in his irises. "Are you okay?" I ask.

He gives a sad smile, then, like he's at war with himself, he says, "Sometimes."

My chest aches. I swallow uncomfortably, nodding in understanding. If I speak, I might cry. But I collect myself and say, "Are you working today? I didn't see you on the schedule."

"No. I have a game this evening. And morning skate in an hour."

"Don't be late," I say, earnestly.

"I won't," he says, then offers me the box. It's been opened, but the cardboard edges are tucked back in together. "The T-shirts arrived at my house. I wanted to bring them by."

"Of course. Thank you."

He takes them out, sets them up on the merch stand, then folds the box up to recycle. He doesn't leave though. He looks like he wants to say something. "Mostly I just wanted to see how you were doing."

My chest warms, and that small gesture touches me deeply. "I'm fine," I say, right as the timer goes off.

Shit. Cookies.

I race back into the kitchen, grab an oven mitt, and pull them out before they burn. I set them down on the counter, spin around, and see Corbin staring at the cookie jar. He's no longer holding the cardboard. Is he hurt I read one alone? Does he feel left out? Disappointed?

But when he looks up, there's only longing in those sparkling green eyes. Maybe even hope.

I shrug. "I read it. Well, one page."

His smile is soft, forgiving. "I'd probably have done the same."

He sounds so...kind and sad all at once. But maybe there's wistfulness in his tone too? And want. Yes, definitely want. "Did you want to read it?"

It feels weird to offer, but worse not to.

He seems to consider that as I grab a spatula and slide the cookies off the tray and onto a rack. "I do, but also...I probably shouldn't be late."

"I hear you," I say. "Don't want to be fined."

"I don't," he says, but he makes no move to go. "Was it...a hopeful letter?"

I smile, both sad and optimistic. "It was. They have a happy ending. I mean, they did wind up together."

"True," he says, wryly, a hint of his humor coming through. "But how they got there is what matters."

"It is."

He nods to the door. "I should go."

This time he turns to leave, but he stops once more in the doorway. "How hopeful?"

I laugh, for the first time in ages. "Very."

He repeats that word as he takes the cardboard and leaves, the morning sun making a silhouette of him as he strides down the path, and I feel a little bit lighter than I did last night.

48

OPERATION RESUMED

CORBIN

The whole drive down to the arena, voices repeat in my head.

Annabelle from the other day: *Do you love her?*

Theo from last night: *Grow up. People have bad days.*

Annabelle again: *You don't like it when you're not in control. When you think you could fail.*

Theo: *You should be the kind of man who stays.*

All through morning skate, they grow louder. I wonder, too, what the last letter said. But I also don't know if it matters. Not right now at least.

After, as I grab some lunch with the guys, I hear another voice.

Mabel's. Saying: *Very.*

That one sticks with me when I go to my friend Ford's place. He's out of town and said I could use it. I don't want to go back to Cozy Valley for only an hour, so I lie on the couch and close my eyes to rest before the game—because yes, I should rest. It's part of the job.

I don't sleep though.

I think about failure. How much I fear it.

I think about bodies breaking down. How terrified I am of that.

I think about losing the things, and the skills, and—most of all—the people I love.

And I think about the way I've handled the hard stuff in the past. And lately.

I take a short nap.

When I wake, I change into the suit I brought with me, swing by Charlotte's school to pick her up, and say, "Want to help me with something, Miss Helpful?"

Always circumspect, she quirks a brow and asks, "What is it exactly?"

As she buckles up, I tell her.

In the rearview mirror, I can see her eyes widen. "That's a good idea. I'd been meaning to have a chat with you, Dad."

"I know, sweetheart. And I appreciate that."

"I hope this cheers you up."

"Me too, kiddo. Me too."

We run a few quick errands on the way, then arrive at the arena. She heads straight to the kids' lounge. Since we're playing our cross-town rivals again, some of her friends are here as well. Tyler's daughter is camped out in a big comfy chair, watching something on her laptop, his son is doing a puzzle and Rowan's daughter is reading a book.

"Bye, Dad," Charlotte says, practically pushing me out the door.

I'm glad she's happy. It's such a relief to know your kid is doing more than okay.

Now it's time for me to fix my own shit. In the locker room, I march up to Lake, Riggs, and Miller, and say the hard thing. "I need help."

"You take off your pants one leg at a time. Try it," Miller says, nodding to me. "Go ahead."

I roll my eyes. "No, seriously. I need to tell Mabel I love her. I need to tell her she's the one. And I need to tell her something else too."

It pains me to admit this, but I tell the guys how I'm feeling about it. "I have this plan. And I can't do it alone. I think I need Remy's help."

Lake raises his hand so fast. "I'll find her."

I leave, march upstairs, and knock on Theo's door. I haven't spoken to him since the flight.

His jaw is clenched. He barely looks up from his computer screen. He's pissed at me. Of course he is.

I square my shoulders. Speak clearly. "You were right. About everything."

That piques his interest. He raises his face. "I know. What are you going to do about it?"

"Will you help me?" I ask, feeling horribly vulnerable.

"Depends."

I tell him the plan.

He nods. "And you love her?"

"So much."

"You'll do right by her?"

"If she'll have me."

He blows out a breath. Leans back in his chair, sets his wingtip shoes on the desk. Parks his hands behind his head. "Guess you did need my blessing after all."

For fuck's sake. This guy. But I smile. "Fine. I did."

He sits upright and picks up his phone, grinning.

* * *

An hour later, I'm in my uniform, skating off the ice after warmups. Theo's waiting for me in the tunnel. He's all business now as he claps me on the shoulder. "She's on her way. I told her there was a VIP suite here with top sponsors I wanted to serve her cookies to, and to bring whatever she had."

"Brilliant," I say.

"I know."

"Was she...annoyed?"

"Not with me. Will she be annoyed with you? Guess we'll find out."

"Dickhead," I mutter.

He cups his ear. "Did you say 'world's most amazing friend'?"

"Actually, I did."

"I thought so. And she was excited, so you'd better make this more attractive to her than serving cookies to my top sponsors."

"I appreciate you."

"I know," he says, then walks off.

As I return to the locker room, Remy intercepts me in the hall, a can-do smile on her face, and a tablet tucked under her arm. "Lake told me the plan," she says, nodding behind me, and I guess Lake just came off the ice. "I'm all set."

Lake arrives next to me, saying to her, "Let me know if you need any help."

"I'm good, but thanks." She meets my gaze again, waggling her tablet. "Mabel messaged me a few seconds ago. She should be here in twenty minutes."

I breathe out a sigh of relief.

I pulled that off—getting Mabel here. Time to finish Operation Win Her Heart.

49

LOUDER IN THE BACK
MABEL

Theo's waiting for me at one of the side doors to the arena, and I'm so grateful I don't have to go through security.

"It's good to know the boss," I joke as I slide past my brother, nodding to the long lines outside the arena, queuing up for the game. I'm glad Aisha and Audrey were at the bakery today so they can close up in an hour.

"It's good to be the boss," he says, then reaches for the pink boxes I'm carrying. "Can I help?"

"You better," I say, unloading a couple dozen samplers of lemon shortbread, seven-layer bars, sweet and salties, and all flavors of my cookies. "I even included some smash cakes."

"Your signature dish," he says, then guides me through the concourse, past the expansive wall covered in all kinds of foliage, then to the bougie section of food vendors peddling artisan pizza, honey-roasted pretzels, and gourmet popcorn, among other treats.

"Hey, you should carry Afternoon Delight treats here," I say, feeling a little *Why the hell not*.

He gives me an approving nod. "We should."

When we reach the suite level, he looks down at his phone in his free hand, then says, "Want to come with me?"

But before I can answer, the sound of someone running up behind me intensifies. I spin around and jerk back in surprise. It's not that it's strange to see Remy here, but I wasn't expecting her to be racing toward me in jeans, knee-high black boots, and a soft cowl-neck sweater. Her brown hair is loose tonight, waves curling over her shoulders.

"Mabel! Theo mentioned you were coming tonight, and I need you right now."

"Okay," I ask, curious. "Why?"

She gives me a look. "Is that any way to greet a friend? Especially someone who helped you bake a Saran wrap cake?"

"Saran wrap cake?" Theo asks. "Gross."

"It's not Saran wrap cake," I say, then wave a hand. "Never mind."

"I have an idea for a proposal. A romantic one," she says. "Do you have a sec?"

"Sure," I say, turning to Theo. "Do you mind?"

"All good," he says. "I should handle the sponsors myself anyway."

"Okay. My business cards are in the boxes," I say, as he heads down the hallway toward the suites, and Remy grabs my elbow and ushers me back through the food concourse, nodding to her boyfriend, who works the taps at a local craft beer brewery here at the arena.

"So I have a potential client for my Romance By Design business," she says.

"Oh! That's great."

Remy's been hoping to use her podcast as a springboard to launch a business as a romance designer extraordinaire— from the meet-cute to the proposal, she's your go-to girl for picture-perfect moments to remember.

We weave past vendors and security guards before the concourse opens to the arena bowl. "Wait. Are we watching the game?" I ask.

"Do you have to go back?" she asks, concerned. "I thought the bakery was closing soon."

"It is. In thirty minutes, so this is fine. I just wasn't expecting to watch a game tonight."

"Well, you're with me. Special treatment," she says, and holy shit. Special treatment indeed. She ushers me down, down, down all the way to a row right behind the players' bench.

My heart squeezes, and a pang of longing digs deep into my chest.

Corbin will be here tonight. It'll be hard to see him. But I'm getting used to the challenge—like I had to get used to it at work earlier today. It'll be fine. I swear it'll be fine.

I steal a glance toward the tunnel. He'll be coming through there in a few more minutes. My chest flutters, and I will my body to settle down.

But my brain has other ideas. It flashes back on last night with my friends—the things they said.

Did you tell him you fell for him too?

When a guy falls hard, he goes all out.

We can have it all—if we let ourselves.

Maybe they're right. Maybe I should insist on sharing the last letter with him after all. And the last page I didn't read after all. I didn't feel right continuing to read it without him.

But for now, I join Remy and listen to her talk about her plans till the game starts. The lights dim. The music swells. And the fox mascot skates onto the ice as an announcer booms, "And now, your Golden State Foxes."

Excitement pings through me as the crowd roars.

The players fly through the tunnel as the announcer calls their names.

"Miller Lockwood."

The goalie skates onto the ice as the sea of fans erupts.

"Lake Axelrod."

More cheers.

And then my heart goes crazy when the announcer warbles *Corbin Knight*.

Number Fifteen flies across the ice, heading to the players' bench, but scanning...the stands.

Looking for...me?

He is looking for me. His gaze lands on my face, and his smile is bright and confident, a man who knows what he wants.

My pulse soars to the moon as he jumps over the boards to the bench. He shuffles to the end of it, determination in his every move. When he nears the end of it, he reaches under his shirt, grabbing something. Corbin stretches his right arm toward one of the slim openings between the glass, sliding an envelope through and handing it to me.

I'm still staring at the envelope in my hands as the National Anthem finishes.

Some people in the crowd are checking me out—the woman who just got a letter from a hockey star. With my name in a neat script on the front.

But all I see is my name on this paper. Every single molecule in my body is comprised of hope. Intoxicating, beloved hope that floods my cells.

I hope it's a love letter.

I hope it's a new beginning.

Remy nudges me. "Open it," she whispers.

Like that isn't all I've been thinking of.

"I will," I say, breathily, running my finger along the lilac envelope.

As the teams line up for the puck drop, with Corbin naturally on center ice, I slide a finger at last under the seal of the pretty envelope. I take out the sheet of paper.

Unfold it.

And as he battles for the puck, I read the first love letter delivered to me at a hockey game.

Well, my first love letter ever.

Dear Mabel,

I should have said this a while ago. I should have said this the other night. But I'm saying it now—please give me a second chance.

Because I love you.

I love you so much, it feels like my damn heart is beating for you every second of every day.

I love your hatred for nuts. I love your devotion to your friends. I love your obsession with colors, and pickleball outfits, and purple flowers, and baking excellence.

I love the way you stand up to me when I'm being ridiculous. I love the way you became friends with my daughter—like it was the easiest thing in the world. I love how you roped us into fostering dogs. That was brilliant and sneaky, and now I'm hooked.

I love how brave you are. Yes, you're brave, Firecracker, and you don't always realize it. But it was gutsy to come back to town and try again. To deal with the chess guys and the knitting ladies, not to mention Ronnie. I love the way you were determined to win the hearts (and stomachs) of Cozy Valley.

I love how you listen. How you understand. How you connect with people where they are, and most of all, with me.

Even when I'm being a stubborn, annoying perfectionist who's afraid of fucking up.

Especially then.

I love that you wear your heart on your sleeve and you can't hide when something excites you, like finding a jar full of love letters your grandma left behind.

I love seeing you in the morning, and seeing you in the afternoon, and seeing you at night. I love that you're the best part of any and every day, and my favorite part of the middle of the night.

The other day, I messed up big time. I was the biggest idiot I've ever been. A stubborn fool who thought he was doing the right thing.

I was wrong.

I was scared. Of losing you. Of feeling too much. Of not being everything you might want.

Because you, Mabel, are everything to me. Will you give us another chance?

Love,

Corbin

When I'm done, my heart is beating outside my body. My eyes are welling with tears. My world has turned upside down. Still, I do my best to reconnect to reality, to the game, to the man I love scoring a goal. I stand so fast, cheering loud and hard as tears rain down my face, and reality recalibrates to *this.*

To a love confession so big, so bold, so complete.

And to a man who flies over to the bench, locking eyes with me, his full of questions.

Did you read it? Do you feel the same? Do you want to give me another chance?

"Yes!"

He tips his chin toward me. "Louder for the back."

This man. "Yes, yes, yes!" I say, my heart bursting from my chest, this love spreading through the whole arena, this man mouthing "*I love you*" again and again.

Like he can't stop saying it.

Well, I can't stop feeling it.

And I can't believe I have to sit through three periods and two intermissions till they win the game. The guys pump their gloves, and head off the ice, but Corbin motions to me, then to the gate toward the tunnel. Remy nudges me. "Go!"

I'm so there. I hustle across the row, saying, "Excuse me."

When I reach the opening near the tunnel, he's peeled off

his gloves and sets his hands on the boards. I'm on the other side of the boards. His eyes are earnest, hopeful, and desperate all at once. "Take me back, Mabel Llewelyn. You're all the colors in my life."

My heart squeezes, then bounds over to him, safe in his hands. "I never left, and I can't believe you made me wait the whole game."

"I'm the king of edging." He smirks, and my heart feels like it might explode. "So what'll it be?"

He waits, as the whole crowd hoots and hollers.

"You're a yes, Number Fifteen. You're my yes. You're my enough."

He kisses me in front of everyone, thanks to a love letter.

What can I say? Some words just work.

50

PROVE IT

CORBIN

"You beat me to it," Mabel says when I find her waiting for me in the corridor after I'm showered and dressed again in my suit.

With the fox tie she gave me for Christmas.

I pretend like I'm hunting for something on her, tugging at her jeans pocket, her neckline. "Where's my love letter, Firecracker?"

She grabs the tie and yanks me close. "I meant—I was going to tell you I love you too."

"Feel free to say that again," I say, on top of the world. The woman I love loves me back. She fucking loves me. Life is good.

"Corbin," she teases.

"No, really. Say it again," I urge, unabashed in my need to hear it.

She runs her fingers down my tie while looking up at me with so much love in those big brown eyes. "I should have said it the other night too. And I didn't. I didn't want to get hurt again. But I should have been stronger. I should have told you how I felt. Because you know what?" She gives a bob of her shoulder. "You can have it all. I don't have to pick between romance and success."

I cup her cheeks, feeling stupidly happy. "You never do. Not with me. And I'm sorry I ever made you think that."

"You didn't. That was on me. I had to learn that my heart is big enough for all of it."

"It's the biggest heart," I say, then run a finger along a strand of her hair. "And you also don't have to pick between love and orgasms. Since I intend to give you many as soon as possible. Come spend the night with me."

"What about...?" She tips her head down the hall toward the kids' lounge. "Charlotte?"

"Miss Handles Her Own Schedule? She decided, since it's a Friday night, that she'd book herself a sleepover with Mia and Luna—Tyler's daughter—over at Rowan's house."

"Smart girl," Mabel says, her arms looping around my neck where she plays with the back of my hair.

"That means you're coming home with me."

She arches a brow. "Is that so?"

Before I can answer, shoes click. A voice groans. "Get a room."

I turn to Theo, glad I've got the last laugh this time. "Don't worry. We will."

"Gross," he mutters.

"You're gross," Mabel says to him.

"So are you," he says back.

She tilts her head. "What happened with the goodies and everything for the sponsors?"

Theo stops a few feet away, strokes his chin. "That was just to get you down here."

Her jaw drops. "Seriously?"

"Blame him," Theo says, pointing to me.

I shoot him a *c'mon* look. "Dude, I asked you to get her down here. Not play a trick on her."

He holds his arms out wide. "What do you take me for? I still had VIP guests. I gave them the treats. They loved them. We'll place a regular order for our VIP suites."

Mabel's eyes sparkle. "You're not gross."

"I know," he says, then walks past us toward the stairwell.

As his footsteps fade, I turn back to her. "All is well. Also, I was right."

"About what?"

I drop a kiss to her neck. "You're hot for me."

Laughing, she pushes me away. "You're hot for me."

"No shit."

"I'm all for getting out of here, stat. But we don't have to go back to Cozy Valley. I do have a place in the city."

"About that," I say, taking her hand as we leave and head to the lot.

"What about it?"

"I think you should get rid of it and move in with me."

She gives me a curious sideways glance. "Seriously?"

I laugh. "Mabel, did you think I wasn't serious about you when I gave you a love letter in front of our entire arena?"

She's quiet for a beat as we near the exit. "I didn't think you meant move in."

"Move into the firehouse officially then, so we can be in the same town until you're ready to officially move in with me," I say, then stop, making her stop too. I guess I wasn't clear enough before about my intentions. I will be crystal clear now. "I plan to win your heart and your hand. I want you to move in with me. So I'm just going to romance the hell out of you till you say yes."

She smiles as she shakes her head, but it's not a no she's giving me. It's more like she can't quite believe this is happening. When we reach my car, I open the passenger door. "You drove? I can drive you to your car."

"I did," she says, then tells me which lot.

We take off and once we reach her car, I open that door for her too, then lean against it. "Don't speed, no matter how much you want me to fuck you up against the wall the second we arrive."

She scoffs. "Please. You want to fuck me up against the wall, and you have since that day in the trailer."

I bend lower, grab her chin. "Wrong. Since the day I met you, and just for that, I'll show you."

"You better."

* * *

Forty-five minutes and zero speeding tickets later, my woman is up against the door, half-naked, losing her mind, and calling my name.

It's as close to perfect as I've ever felt. Mabel, falling apart in my arms, as we come together in a hot, frenzied reunion.

Her hands grab at my hair, her lips part, and she moans beautifully.

Seconds later, pleasure barrels through me and my eyes squeeze shut, colors bursting behind them, all the brilliant reds, rich blues, bright yellows, blazing oranges, and everything else in between.

At least it feels that way.

A minute later, after we straighten up and fall onto the couch in a heap of limbs and half-undressed bodies, I run a hand through her hair. "Guess what?"

"You're getting me a llama as a gift?"

"You want a pet llama?"

She shakes her head. "No, but a llama sanctuary would be nice. Not for me to run though. I have too much going on. Anyway, what am I guessing at?"

I wiggle a brow playfully. "Evidently, I can sometimes see colors when I come hard with you."

She laughs, but it dies quickly. "Seriously?"

"The world *felt* pretty red and orange and blue and brilliant a few minutes ago."

She plays with my shirt, unbuttoning it the rest of the way. "You should come often then."

I laugh. "I won't object." But as tempted as I am to hold her close, there's something else I need to say. "Mabel, sweetheart."

"Uh-oh," she says, sitting upright.

"It's not bad. But I want to be honest with you in a way I wasn't before."

Her easy expression vanishes. "What do you mean?"

"I thought I could do it. Hockey and Charlotte and the bakery and you."

"You don't want to be part of the bakery anymore?" She sounds terrified.

I reach for her hand and kiss it. "I would never back out on our partnership. Know that. You know that, right?"

She nods. "I do."

This is what I discussed with my friends. They helped me to see the solution was right before my eyes. "I don't think I should work there during the season. I bit off more than I could chew. I can still place orders, and help with dog adoption events. But in terms of working there? I need to step back. Are you okay with that?"

Her smile is like the morning sun. "I'm great with it."

"You've been wanting to kick me out?" I joke.

She shakes her head. "No. I was worried it was a little too much for you too. And I think it's good when we realize what we can do and what we can't. Work-life balance is a thing, and you should have it too." She relaxes again in my arms.

I stroke her hair, then ask, "What about you? Is there anything you need to make that happen? Do we need to hire more help?"

She's quiet for a beat. "Well, we're almost profitable, so I want to operate within our means."

"Business owners can make hires before they're in the black."

"I know. But sometimes I worry I can only do it because I'm partnered with a rich hockey star."

I kiss her hair. "Well, you are. So use me, baby. Fucking use me. But also, you could do it even if we weren't partners."

She looks up at me with a soft smile. "I think another part-time employee would be great."

I kiss her forehead. "Let's do it."

"There's something else I need though."

"Name it."

She sits up, spins around, and tugs at my open shirt. "Get dressed, and let's go to the bakery."

* * *

The lights are low. Music plays. A pair of teacups sits on the table in front of us—the same ones we've used all the other times.

In the middle of the white table is a stack of love letters, including the one I spotted this morning from Russ to Harriet, many years ago.

"Read it now," she says, urging me once again.

Earlier I wanted to, but I hadn't earned the right to. Now I read it out loud, catching glimpses of the emotion crossing her eyes as the words about taking a chance, being worth it, and love being the only thing for sure fill the air between us.

I set it down, then nod to the last one.

She picks it up, exhales, then reads.

Dear Russ,

Sneaking around was fun, but what's even better is coming home to you. It's lovely like this, working together out in the open. But even though the captain said yes—so funny to think of someone needing to approve our love, but such as it is in the workplace—we should still keep sending each other letters, don't you think? And maybe some-day, this place will tell the story of two people who fell in love between these walls.

Yours always,
Harriet

Mabel looks up at me, eyes shining, as she sets the letter down. "The stories this place could tell."

My heart swells. "The best stories."

"Like ours," she says, then leans across the table and kisses me. And I make a vow right then.

To write her love letters for the rest of our days.

* * *

The next day she wakes up to one on her pillow.

Dear Mabel,

You're my too much and my enough.

Love,
Corbin

EPILOGUE: ANYTIME DELIGHTS
MABEL

I swing open the door to Afternoon Delight one summer day, the bell tinkling as the blue-tiled antique mirror catches my eye—along with the postcard tucked in the corner.

And the words on it: *Life is short. Eat the cake.*

Words to live by. And that mirror looks fantastic here in the bakery. Well, I had to find a new home for it. I moved out of my apartment in the city in the winter—officially into this firehouse but really into Corbin's home.

I guess that makes me sort of stepmom-ish. But Charlotte and I talked about my role in her life and agreed I'm more of the cool aunt.

Works for her, works for me, and it works for her dad.

Who's behind the counter, looking hot as hell in his *ALL THIS AND I CAN BAKE* apron.

It's summertime, and he's working here more—as planned. As he serves Dottie some of her favorite brownies and chats with her about a chenille sweater she's knitting for the fall, I take a moment to just admire him.

The way his shoulders are relaxed.

His easy smile.

His way with people.

He figured out how to do this—how to realize his dream and his mother's dream without breaking himself.

I'm so seriously proud of him, and I tell him as much every day.

When Dottie leaves, I slide behind the counter and pinch his butt.

"Best part of working for you," he says.

"We work together," I correct.

He hums doubtfully. "That's cute. Keep telling yourself that, boss."

I roll my eyes, but he's not wrong. We restructured a little. Yes, we own Afternoon Delight together, but I'm the sole manager and make all the decisions.

He likes it that way, and so do I.

Turns out, surprise, surprise, I have a lot of opinions. Like what to bring for dessert to my mom's faculty luncheons, since she hired us as her caterer for the monthly events. And what goodies to deliver to the VIP suite at the Foxes. But also, what goodies to bake for *Romance Beach*, since this woman nabbed a regular gig providing cake at wrap parties. Mrs. Henderson also swings by a couple times a month for goodies for her gardening club. And I supply, free of charge, treats for dog adoption events.

Corbin mostly just likes baking and serving customers—and, of course, sharing his mom's recipes. That's always been why he wanted to do this, and it makes my heart happy to see him fulfilling their dream.

I sweep into the back, and say hi to Aisha and Audrey as they pack orders and slide cookies off trays, then to Arnie, who decided retirement bored him and he needed a part-time job.

He works in the front serving customers, so he grabs a fresh tray and heads out to join Corbin. Once my apron is on, I help serve a cake with fresh strawberries and whipped cream in honor of my grandma, who made this bakery happen.

And here, in Cozy Valley, with the man I love and the people who eventually welcomed me back, I feel like I belong.

A few mornings later, when we're both off, Corbin finds me in the kitchen, pouring a cup of coffee and feeding our newest foster dog. We don't have to temp foster anymore—I'm around enough that we can take on dogs for a week here or there.

Like this cutie, Isabelle. A shy little white-and-tan, wiggly Border Collie–Sheltie mix. She's been coming out of her shell more and more though.

As she scarfs down her nuggets, he comes up behind me and kisses me. I sigh happily, then offer him some coffee too.

"Fuck mornings," he mutters—but it's said with a smile.

We've had to become morning people occasionally, and that's okay. People can change if they try hard enough.

"I have a plan for today," he says, taking a sip of coffee.

"Will I like it?"

"Let's find out."

A little later, with Izzy in her dog seat, he pulls onto a block of Hayes Valley in the city, then parks his car.

Maybe he's taking us to lunch here?

We hop out and he takes my hand, walks me past a record store and a cute boutique, then stops outside a brick building with the most charming empty storefront.

When I look up, I do a double take.

My jaw comes unhinged. I turn to him in slow motion. "Corbin," I whisper, pointing to the sign for Afternoon Delight. "What did you do?"

"You always wanted to have a bakery in the city. I bought

one for you. It's in your name. You own it. You don't have to do it now, but it's here for you when you're ready—if you want it."

I'm shaking with excitement and joy. "Seriously?"

"Seriously," he says.

I don't have to think. "I want it. I really want it. This is wild. Thank you."

"No, thank *you* for making me so happy. When I saw this, I thought—if not now, when?"

And those are indeed our words to live by.

I kiss him on the streets of San Francisco with our expanding little bakery behind us, our foster dog at our feet, and our future unfurling ahead of us. Full of afternoon, evening, and anytime delights.

Remy's and Lake's romance comes next in Just Playing for Keeps! While you wait, binge the Love and Hockey series starting with The Boyfriend Goal, a roommates-to-lovers, he-falls-first, teammate's little sister romance FREE in KU! You'll also love Ford and Skylar's neighbor-to-lovers romance The Flirting Game, FREE in KU!

For more Corbin and Mabel click here for an extended epilogue or scan the QR code!

Turn the Page!!

EXCERPT: JUST PLAYING FOR KEEPS

Remy

Twenty-four hours' notice and I have everything ready. I can't leave a night like this to chance. Not after spotting a certain little jewelry box hidden among the sweatshirts in my boyfriend's closet.

Inside the arena, a peaceful warmth floods me, the bliss of thorough preparation for whatever the night brings.

Jameson gestures to the aisle in the arena, letting me go first. I move in front of him, walking down the steps toward our seats as anthemic rock music pipes through the hockey rink, pump-me-up tunes perfect for the players as they warm up on the ice.

Just look at Jameson. He's all dressed up, wearing his signature vest, of course, and a forest green checked shirt I picked out for him when he asked me to take him clothes shopping a few weeks ago. He's rocking an undercut, and his jaw is clean-shaven. When we reach the second row, he pats the cushy black faux leather aisle seat. "Isn't this great, Remy?"

His voice pitches with nerves. My chest tingles from that sign too.

"These seats are amazing," I reassure him, since he sometimes needs that.

When my boyfriend of eleven and three-quarter months surprised me last week with center-ice tickets to the one thousandth game the Golden State Foxes have played at this arena —seats I can't even get as the team's part-time community relations manager—I figured it was an early anniversary gift.

But then last night, I grabbed a hoodie to borrow, and a little gray jewelry box marked "Made by Fable" fell out of the front pocket.

I popped it back in its hiding place, borrowed a different sweatshirt, and shifted into planning mode, stat. A day later, here we are, at a place meaningful to both of us. And Jameson and I *did* meet by his craft beer brewery on the concourse, so it makes perfect sense he'd pick the arena for the occasion.

Once he settles into the seat, he waves a slightly shaky hand toward the boards. "I know how much you love these games."

I press my lips together so I don't burst into confetti. "I do."

Not the only time I'll be saying that in the near future.

I smooth a hand over my jeans as Lake Axelrod, the team's top right winger, glides past the glass, his gaze touring the stands like he's checking out who's here. I shed my jacket quickly, revealing my off-the-shoulder soft cream sweater.

Jameson's gaze strays briefly to my exposed shoulder, then he looks away, toward the ice. Eye contact must be tough when he's trying to keep a secret.

The game begins, and I focus on the action during the first period while mentally ticking off the arrangements I'd managed in one mere day. Like that slim videographer in the plaid beret weaving his way through the fans during the game breaks, asking them to share favorite memories of games in this arena, which are broadcast on the Jumbotron for all twenty thousand attendees to see.

I told Odin I'd help plan a special date for him and his wife if he'd stick near me during the upcoming fox toss when I think Jameson is most likely to ask the question.

And there's the curly-haired usher, Selena. I set up a hotspot on her phone once upon a time, and she told me she owes me (she doesn't), so she was happy to help. She'll have a bottle of Veuve Clicquot chilled to the perfect temperature and ready for her to bring over at my signal—a double tuck of my hair.

Then a row away is Savannah, the backup photographer I hired in case Jameson didn't think of it. What if he doesn't know I've always wanted a fun, frothy *you know what*, or that I'd want pics of every moment?

I stop myself from scanning the seats for photographers Jameson might have hired. It's best I focus on what I *can* control.

And I've prepared for everything.

I settle in for the rest of the game, trying to contain my excitement as the clock winds down to the second intermission. Finally, the loudspeaker warbles in the arena. "And now..." the announcer booms from the rink, "your Golden State Foxes are coming back to the ice a little early. Get ready to toss your stuffed foxes onto the ice as your home team collects them to donate to the local children's hospital."

The hockey stars fly through the tunnel in their purple and white jerseys, sticks in hand. The fans go wild, popping up in their seats to chuck their tawny stuffies over the glass and onto the rink.

The guys skate around, scooping them up with their gloves or sticks. I glance at the clock. The fox toss spans the final two minutes of the intermission—I planned the event. There are ninety seconds left. Plenty of time for Jameson to ask me to be his.

He rubs his palms along the denim on his thighs.

C'mon. You can do it, sweetie.

He reaches into his pocket.

My throat catches.

There's that tiny jewelry box-shaped bulge, right there.

Yes!

It's happening. And all I have to do is give the sign to kick off my embellishments. I tuck my chestnut strands over both ears as the music grows louder, the crowd turns wilder, and foxes fly over my head and onto the ice.

I glimpse Selena's curls as she carries a bucket of the best bubbly, then Odin in his beret, slinking down the row with his camera and mic, and Savannah, ready for the backup stills.

"So, Remy," Jameson begins, as he drags that box from his pocket. He curls his palm around it, and I can barely stand how fast my pulse is beating.

"Yes?" I ask, all my attention fixed on him. My cells are buzzing.

He reaches for my hand with his free one. "I wanted to let you know that I think you're really *great*," he says.

"So are you."

"And since you love this place so much, I want to ask you a question while we're here."

His words echo throughout the arena. Odin must have alerted the control room to switch to his camera feed and mic. We're live on the Jumbotron, like I'd planned.

"Ask me anything," I say to Jameson, but for the entire arena to see. I bet he'll be thrilled I engineered this. It'll be so good for his brewery, and he loves his little business like it's his pet.

Glancing at the screen where we're twenty feet tall, he swallows roughly, then speaks again. "Will you still be friends with me?"

Wait. What? I choke back my half-formed answer to the question he *hadn't* asked. "Friends?"

"Yes. Will you consciously uncouple with me?"

He opens the Made by Fable box. But inside is not a diamond ring, like the designer makes. There's only a friendship bracelet, cheap and plastic, and it says *Friends Forever* on it.

My throat tightens. On the massive screen above the ice, twenty-thousand Foxes fans watch me struggle to breathe.

This is not a proposal. This is a Jumbotron dump.

Lake

I rarely pay attention to the Jumbotron. But as I'm skating casually across the ice, scooping up another stuffed fox, something on the screen snags my interest.

I'm sure I've seen the guy around the arena. Right now, though, he's triple the size he should be and annoyingly earnest as he says to a girl not-quite on screen, "I can see it. You and me, hanging out, talking about our future partners."

What the fuck? Is some douchenozzle let's-be-friends-ing his girlfriend for everyone to see?

I drop a couple of foxes into a big laundry cart on the ice, then stop because...I know him. He's that jackass who works at the bar here and has somehow managed to date Remy, even though he doesn't deserve to lick her boots. And—fuck— that's her sharing the screen.

Remy, the chestnut-haired beauty with the upbeat smile and the snappy comebacks whenever I grouse about some event she asks us to do. Remy, my little sister's good friend. Remy, with the lone tear slipping down her shocked face.

Is the director in the control room ever going to cut to one of the other cameras for the Jumbotron? And why doesn't this guy on screen have the common sense to shut the fuck up?

"You could help me set up my Date Night profile," the fuckface continues with a too-sincere smile.

I bellow toward the control room, "Cut that off."

But the horror flick keeps playing as my new mortal enemy says, in all his pixelated gigantic assholery, "And I could help you set up yours."

Remy's lips part, and devastation rains down her pretty cheeks, just as a curly-haired woman arrives at her row with a bottle of champagne.

"Thanks, Selena, but—" Remy starts, and my god, she's thanking the usher while her heart's being broken.

This guy never deserved her.

There has to be another way to get the control room's attention off her.

I drop a stuffed fox onto the ice in front of me, swing my stick back, and launch that baby high into the stands. A few people in the crowd cheer as I make a game of this, and one of the camera guys on the ice to capture video for the Jumbotron feed swings his lens my way. Launching another fox, then another, I do what I despise—make myself the center of attention for anything other than the game itself.

"Here's your feel-good news clip moment," I growl.

Apparently, whacking a fox like it's a puck does the job because the impromptu demonstration of my stick skills replaces the douchebag's debacle on the overhead screen.

I send one more stuffed fox sailing into the stands for good measure.

Crisis averted, but only for now. The stuffed foxes are

carted off the rink, and while we line up for the face-off, I steal a glance at the second row.

She's gone.

There are two empty chairs, and not a bottle of champagne in sight.

I wish there were something I could do for her. For now, I dig in and channel my rage toward the opposing team. The instant the puck is free, I snag it, chasing it down the ice.

A D-man slams into me, or tries to, but I shove him away. Nothing is going to stop me now.

This puck is mine, and when I spot an opening, I sneak it past the goalie and score my second goal of the night. Another point to pad the total.

But even though we win, I'm not happy.

I can't stop thinking about what happened to Remy. There's nothing worse than people assuming they know you from what they've seen of you in public.

Read on...

AUTHOR'S NOTE AND ACKNOWLEDGMENTS

There are many types of colorblindness and Corbin's is not the only variety. I have attempted to portray his type of red-green colorblindness authentically, based on input from people with colorblindness as well as extensive research.

Corbin's mother's experience with Parkinson's is based on my experience caring for a family member with Parkinson's. Parkinson's manifests differently in different people and his mother's experience is unique to her.

Immense thank you to Shanna! You were everything I needed to help understand and represent Corbin's colorblindness. I could not have written this without you!

Thank you to Kim, KP, Lo, Sharon, Sandra, Kara, Virginia, Editor Lauren, Rosemary, Karen, Claudia and the whole team. You're all invaluable!

Love and hugs to my author friends who I rely on daily — Corinne, Laura, AL, Natasha, Lili, Laurelin, CD, K, Helena, and Nadia, among others.

Thank you to my family.

And thank you to you — the readers. I love hearing from you and knowing my stories touch your hearts.

BE A LOVELY

Want to be the first to know of sales, new releases, special deals and giveaways? Sign up for my newsletter today!

Want to be part of a fun, feel-good place to talk about books and romance, and get sneak peeks of covers and advance copies of my books? Be a Lovely!

I've written more than 100 books! **All of these titles below are FREE in Kindle Unlimited!**

The Love and Hockey Series

<u>The Boyfriend Goal</u>

A roommates-to-lovers, teammate's little sister hockey romance!

<u>The Romance Line</u>

An enemies-to-lovers, player and the publicist, forbidden romance!

<u>The Proposal Play</u>

A brother's best friend/marriage of convenience romance!

The Girlfriend Zone

A coach's daughter romance!

The Overtime Kiss!

A single dad/nanny romance!

The Flirting Game!

A neighbors to lovers, fake dating romance!

Hockey Ever After

Just Breaking the Rules!

A brother's best friend/workplace/one who got away romance!

Just Playing for Keeps!

A grumpy sunshine, fake dating romance!

Darling Springs

It Seemed Like a Good Idea!

An only one-bed-in-the-room, forbidden, small town bodyguard romance!

I've Got a Crush On You!

A grumpy sunshine, workplace romance where the boss has a secret identity!

Holiday Romances

Merry Little Kissmas

Fake dating my brother's best friend at Christmas!

<u>My Favorite Holidate</u>

Fake dating the billionaire boss at Christmas!

The My Hockey Romance Series

Hockey, spice, shenanigans and cute dogs in this series of standalones! Because when you get screwed over, make it a double or even a triple!

Karma is two hockey boyfriends and sometimes three!

Double Pucked

A sexy, outrageous MFM hockey romantic comedy!

Puck Yes

A fake marriage, spicy MFM hockey rom com!

Thoroughly Pucked!

A brother's best friends +runaway bride, spicy MFM hockey rom com!

Well and Truly Pucked

A friends-to-lovers forced proximity why-choose hockey rom com!

The Virgin Society Series

Meet the Virgin Society – great friends who'd do anything for each other. Indulge in these forbidden, emotionally-charged, and wildly sexy age-gap romances!

The RSVP

The Tryst

The Tease

The Dating Games Series

A fun, sexy romantic comedy series about friends in the city and their dating mishaps!

The Virgin Next Door

Two A Day

The Good Guy Challenge

How To Date Series

Friends who are like family. Chances to learn how to date again. Standalone romantic comedies full of love, sex and meet-cute shenanigans.

My So-Called Love Life

Plays Well With Others

The Almost Romantic

The Accidental Dating Experiment

A romantic comedy adventure standalone

A Real Good Bad Thing

Boyfriend Material

Four fabulous heroines. Four outrageous proposals. Four chances at love in this sexy rom-com series!

Asking For a Friend

Sex and Other Shiny Objects

One Night Stand-In

Overnight Service

Big Rock Series

My #1 New York Times Bestselling sexy as sin, irreverent, male-POV romantic comedy!

Big Rock

Mister O

Well Hung

Full Package

Joy Ride

Hard Wood

Happy Endings Series

Romance starts with a bang in this series of standalones following a group of friends seeking and avoiding love!

Come Again

Shut Up and Kiss Me

Kismet

My Single-Versary

Ballers And Babes

Sexy sports romance standalones guaranteed to make you hot!

Most Valuable Playboy

Most Likely to Score

A Wild Card Kiss

Rules of Love Series

Athlete, virgins and weddings!

The Virgin Rule Book

The Virgin Game Plan

The Virgin Replay

The Virgin Scorecard

The Extravagant Series

Bodyguards, billionaires and hoteliers in this sexy, high-stakes series
of standalones!

One Night Only

One Exquisite Touch

My One-Week Husband

The Guys Who Got Away Series

Friends in New York City and California fall in love in this fun and
hot rom-com series!

Birthday Suit

Dear Sexy Ex-Boyfriend

The What If Guy

Thanks for Last Night

The Dream Guy Next Door

Always Satisfied Series

A group of friends in New York City find love and laughter in this
series of sexy standalones!

Satisfaction Guaranteed

Never Have I Ever

Instant Gratification

PS It's Always Been You

The Gift Series

An after dark series of standalones! Explore your fantasies!

The Engagement Gift

The Virgin Gift

The Decadent Gift

The Heartbreakers Series

Three brothers. Three rockers. Three standalone sexy romantic comedies.

Once Upon a Real Good Time

Once Upon a Sure Thing

Once Upon a Wild Fling

Sinful Men

A high-stakes, high-octane, sexy-as-sin romantic suspense series!

My Sinful Nights

My Sinful Desire

My Sinful Longing

My Sinful Love

My Sinful Temptation

From Paris With Love

Swoony, sweeping romances set in Paris!

Wanderlust

Part-Time Lover

One Love Series

A group of friends in New York falls in love one by one in this sexy rom-com series!

The Sexy One

The Hot One

The Knocked Up Plan

Come As You Are

Lucky In Love Series

A small town romance full of heat and blue collar heroes and sexy heroines!

Best Laid Plans

The Feel Good Factor

Nobody Does It Better

Unzipped

No Regrets

An angsty, sexy, emotional, new adult trilogy about one young couple fighting to break free of their pasts!

The Start of Us

The Thrill of It

Every Second With You

The Caught Up in Love Series

A group of friends finds love!

The Pretending Plot

The Dating Proposal

The Second Chance Plan

The Private Rehearsal

Seductive Nights Series

A high heat series full of danger and spice!

Night After Night

After This Night

One More Night

A Wildly Seductive Night

Joy Delivered Duet

A high-heat, wickedly sexy series of standalones that will set your
sheets on fire!

Nights With Him

Forbidden Nights

Unbreak My Heart

A standalone second chance emotional roller coaster of a romance

The Muse

A magical realism romance set in Paris

Good Love Series of sexy rom-coms co-written with Lili Valente!

I also write MM romance under the name L. Blakely!

Hopelessly Bromantic Duet (MM)

Roomies to lovers to enemies to fake boyfriends

Hopelessly Bromantic

Here Comes My Man

Men of Summer Series (MM)

Two baseball players on the same team fall in love in a forbidden
romance spanning five epic years

Scoring With Him

Winning With Him

All In With Him

MM Standalone Novels

A Guy Walks Into My Bar

The Bromance Zone

One Time Only

The Best Men (Co-written with Sarina Bowen)

Winner Takes All Series (MM)

A series of emotionally-charged and irresistibly sexy standalone MM
sports romances!

The Boyfriend Comeback

Turn Me On

A Very Filthy Game

Limited Edition Husband

Manhandled

If you want a personalized recommendation, email me at
laurenblakelybooks@gmail.com!

CONTACT

I love hearing from readers! You can find me on TikTok at LaurenBlakelyBooks, Instagram at LaurenBlakelyBooks, Facebook at LaurenBlakelyBooks, or online at LaurenBlakely.com. You can also email me at laurenblakelybooks@gmail.com